for K...
with fond thank...
your interest, faith,"
affection.

Catharine

October, 2010

Parts of the Whole

Catharine E. Roth

authorHOUSE®

AuthorHouse™
1663 Liberty Drive
Bloomington, IN 47403
www.authorhouse.com
Phone: 1-800-839-8640

First published by AuthorHouse 9/7/2010

ISBN: 978-1-4520-7308-8 (hc)
ISBN: 978-1-4520-7309-5 (sc)
ISBN: 978-1-4520-7310-1 (e)

Library of Congress Control Number: 2010912430

Printed in the United States of America

This book is printed on acid-free paper.

To the memory of

Anne Rollins
1882-1974

My thanks to Dorland Mountain Arts Colony
for time, space, quiet and support.

Part One

CHAPTER 1.

Mattie

The tavern was crowded, for a Thursday: it had been a wet week, and men were restless. Snow melted to slush in the afternoons, ice formed overnight, with more snow. In the old man's youth the whole of the large stone building had been an inn, but by now, in 1915, the business had dwindled to the one long room, with tables, benches and some chairs, and big fireplace at the end. Cal kept the hearth warm, and there was still food to be had, soups and fresh bread and pies, he made sure his granddaughter Mattie saw to that. But the occasional traveler seeking a bed was sent on to Mrs. Geigley's, where he would wake in the mornings to strong coffee and temperance pamphlets.

"Fish, I tell you! Even the fish!" The old man, seated in a Windsor chair near the fire, pounded his stout hickory cane on the broad planks of the floor. "Every last – hell I mean from whales bigger'n this house to the littlest damn minnie. He got every last one in mind and you think you can sneak around past Him, outa his sight? There ain't nothin' dumber 'n a fish and He can use any one He wants any time He wants,

3

and if He can make a fish swaller Jonah what makes you think He couldn't open up the earth and swaller you?"

Laughter from the round table nearest Cal rose over the general hum of voices.

"Amen, Cal! Tell it, brother!"

"Every time Cal drowns in his cup he starts hollerin' 'bout fishes." Tucker Schultz belched gently and raised his glass mug. "Two more, Mattie."

The cane pounded again, and Cal was on his feet. "I said, gal, you think yer invisible? You think He don't see? Go on ahead, act like you don't hear me, someday too late you'll remember every word, too late though, I say –"

"Here now!" Tucker's brother Warren leaned back his chair and shouted right at Cal's dusty black coat. "Unhand her, Cal. I ain't fixin to fetch my own ale, now."

The girl twisted out of Cal's reach, collected the two tall glasses and moved on, pausing at another table to nod at an order for soup.

"You best go easy, Cal," Tucker said. "That young'un's the only thing between you and ruin."

"Ruin?" the old man stormed. "Ruin? She's ruin, she is. I'll keep her to the path, I will, long as I can raise an arm. But it's a heavy cross for an old man, I tell you."

Warren guffawed. "Not as heavy as buyin' your help, I'll wager."

"Damnation, you think she don't cost me? Who's raised her then, these fifteen years?"

Though her expression didn't change as she set down the drinks and took Tucker's four bits, Mattie was grateful for the men's interference. Both Tucker and Warren had come between her and Cal before, not so her grandfather noticed, but she did. Younger, she used to pretend that Tucker was her father; for all his reputation of fiery temper, he was always gentle toward her. Warren, who was leaner and quieter, actually resembled more her own dark scrawniness, and was in most ways a more appealing parent, but somehow she rather leaned toward Tucker. She knew all the while she was being as dumb as her grandfather said she was, to look in that corner. There was no father, and that was that. And her mother, who'd died ten years ago, was growing dim and soon would not be, either, in spite of Mattie's desperate morning ritual to call up her face.

Warren stood, stretched, and left, standing aside at the door to let three younger men in. They shook a little, dripping, glancing gladly at the fire, their bodies expanding almost visibly in the heat: the Kane brothers, and David Brown, the new fellow, who looked around the room to find Mattie, to smile at her. Mattie scowled down at the empty bowls she was clearing, but knew her grandfather would have seen the blush she could not stop.

The first thunderstorm was early in June, and sudden. Tucker Schultz came into the tavern to wait it out, which wasn't unusual; he was a carpenter and seemed always to be coming into Potter's Corner for something or other. But Forrest Miller came in right behind him, which was unusual. He farmed on a ridge way west of the village, further out than Mattie had ever been. He'd be one day, folks said, the biggest farmer in the county if he didn't lose too much putting everything in fruit trees.

"Got coffee, Mattie?" Tucker called to her, and she nodded and went into the kitchen. When she came out with the mugs, she realized they were talking about David.

"He ain't been here long enough to know it all, I guess," Tucker was saying.

Forrest laughed, a nice sort of rolling laugh. He had six young'uns already, Mattie thought wistfully, and she'd heard his wife Hazel was carrying again, and all those children knew their daddy, and could hear him laugh like that, maybe every day or so. "Maybe he's smart enough not to pay too much attention," he said, and Mattie's thoughts went back to David.

"You don't think that hill's hainted? How come you ain't bought the farm your own self, then? It's practically next door to you."

"The farm I got is making an old man of me, what I want with another?"

Tucker shook his head, his ruddy face looking mournful. "My daddy used to say that was a good farm, once."

"Well then, why shouldn't Brown have it?"

"Say what you want, that mountain's full of some strange goings on. I'm a Christian, and I ain't saying I believe it all. But I ain't saying I know everything, neither."

"There's no sign of ghosts on my place."

"Well sir, that's your place and not that other. The shadow of that mountain don't fall your way."

Mattie had to leave to take bread out of the oven. The kitchen was steamy with heat, and she propped the back door open, stood watching the slanting rain. It was Saturday, and the loaves and biscuits, along with the two kettles of soup, would be crumbs and dirty bowls by midnight. All week she had made strawberry and rhubarb pies. Whole families would stop, sometimes, on their way home from shopping, and Mattie was both eager for the evening and already weary. To make for my own, she thought, and her stomach twisted with yearning just as the heavy cane thumped against her upper arm. She gasped but didn't cry out, a habit learned early to protect her privacy.

"Git on in there!" Cal's whisper was a snarl. "You know I can't carry them mugs no more, didn't you hear me callin'?"

What if David was just fooling – she blinked back the sudden tears and ran past her grandfather into the big room, hurried to the group of men settled along the long table under the windows, then down the stairs to draw two big pitchers from the barrels in the cool cellar. He said he was serious, he had said it twice, he would get that farm and take her away if she wanted. Oh yes, she wanted. But what did he want with her, when he could go anywhere, see anyone? Oh, David. Mattie's knees buckled on the steps but she caught herself in time, her arms aching from the heavy beer, the blow, and the need to reach out to the thick curly black hair and merry, loving eyes.

She hid in the cellar until Cal left, cussing, for church, and then paced in an agony of terror. Perhaps he would turn back, or maybe David would not come. But she waited in the grape arbor only a quarter hour, and he was there, his fiddle riding under the seat of the borrowed buggy, a pretty bay mare in harness. She clambered up quickly, before he could get down to help, and they trotted away from the old inn, to the crossroads and west, to the hills. She had packed a lunch of bread and cheeses and cold beef.

For three miles the road was broad, well traveled, through open farmland or gentle rises and dips; for the next hour, the way was more wooded, steeper, with rutted and rocky stretches. She knew the area only by a kind of osmosis of talk: New Hope Church was up here somewhere, and the Miller farm, and Mertz Hollow, where the bottles of clear liquor came from, and of course Pine Mountain. David turned off the main track, finally, into a lane, and let the mare pick her way carefully, as rocks exposed by years of untended spring wash-outs stood sharp and uneven. The way was cooler, through deep woods on both sides, until a right angle turn opened a view, and she saw the house and caught her breath, clutching unconsciously at David's leg.

He tied the mare to a big shade maple while she leaped out and stood between two tall pines, looking at the front door with its little stoop. He came up behind her and she turned to meet his grin; they ran like children to look in through windows at the bare rooms with falling ceiling and peeling wallpaper. The kitchen was small, with an old wood range still in it; the other main room downstairs was a little larger, with a pretty stone fireplace at the end. They turned away and walked on to the barn.

"It's sound, I been all through it," David said. "Even the roof, save for the one end." They led the mare down to the springhouse, a stone replica of the farmhouse, and let her drink from the overflow while Mattie stood entranced in the doorway, excited by the images of bustle and routine that the place suggested, though no buckets or milk cans or butter churns had survived the long abandonment.

The rails of the narrow pasture between the barn and springhouse would not have kept in a determined beast, but the grass was thick and they decided to trust the hunger of the mare, and left her, and strolled slowly up through the berry-choked yard back to the house. It was tiny, for a stone house, without the additional wings most of the old houses had been given in the past century. David pushed on the front door and swung it open, and when his hand touched hers she took hold, and they went in.

She could easily avoid Cal's temper in the daylight. He would wait till she slept, she knew, and she propped a chair against the door of her bare little room. She was surprised to wake to its rattling, sure she would never sleep after such a day. She sat up, ready to run past him, knowing the chair was light and wouldn't hold, her heart thudding not from fear of Cal but from the rush of memory, the slight, sweet ache in her hips, the feel of David's hand here, and here.

Cal didn't persist, and she slid back down under the light blanket, and woke in the dawn to the door barred from the outside. She backed away from it, mystified, with no knowing of keys. She laughed a little at her grandfather's senile retribution, relieved her body's needs in the old chamberpot, and took the chair by a window to wait. The tavern was closed Mondays, but he'd want her eventually to clean or fetch something. Her window looked away from the village the inn was on the edge of, and there was little to watch. She looked around the room, pretending to decide what to take with her when David got the loan, but there were no decisions to make. Her clothes, even with the heavy wool sweater and winter shawl, would be easy to carry rolled in a blanket. It was beyond possibility, nowhere even in her pretending, that her grandfather would send with her any of the dishes or even one of the chairs. Perhaps the high stool from the kitchen, if she could lay her hands on it.

She came, like David, with no past to pack around. She had made no secret of that, since it was common knowledge, and he had laughed and said it proved they were meant to start one, together. She had nothing even of her mother. When she died one winter, still not naming her child's father, Cal in his rage and grief had burned all her things, telling the six year old Mattie that to forget her mother was her only chance of staying free of her wickedness.

By afternoon hunger and thirst had make Mattie anxious, but there was no use to pound or call. She dozed, sweat. One window didn't open at all, and the other, though she could get it open a foot, opened to hot westerly breezes bringing little relief into the stuffy room. She tried the door as dark came, but the lock was secure, beyond her strength. She contemplated the drop to the ground, briefly. She knelt by the window and called silently for David, knowing it wouldn't work, feeling it couldn't because she couldn't picture him alone, she didn't even know where he slept, how could her thoughts get to him? He slept sometimes in the lumber mill where he worked, doubling as a kind of night watchman, he had told her that but she had no image of it.

No sounds came to her from the house below. She slept only in snatches that night, and by mid-morning, as the room was heating up again, the panic struck her down.

"Pap! Grandpap!" She screamed to him, her throat sore, her head spinning, slapping hard, then feebly, at the door, sobbing.

He waited another hour. When he flung the door open wide, she was crumpled on the floor, and the strap was in his hand.

For two weeks Cal kept her locked in at night, practically tied to his side during the day. On Sunday he literally tied a short rope to her wrist and led her to church, where Mattie burned with a shame and rage new to her. There were sympathetic, disapproving glances, but no one intervened, and she interpreted the disapproval as knowledge, since Cal had wrenched the confession of mortal sin from her. She was afraid of him now, as she had never been all the years when his temper had been merely a part of the texture of her life. And now she knew she must get free of him, knew that he stood between her and life.

"Out!" Cal shuffled with surprising speed to the door, barring entry with his cane. Only Warren Schultz was in the room; he turned in time to see David Brown grin and tip his hat at the old man, and vanish. Cal thumped his cane and limped, muttering, back to his chair by the fireplace, which he stared at as if there were fire there to watch. Mattie stood frozen where she'd been wiping a table until feeling Warren's gaze she found him watching her with the slightest smile on his face. He cut his eyes toward the kitchen, then turned to Cal.

"Cal, you think if the womens get the vote they'll turn you out of business?" he said, and Mattie stood just a minute longer in confusion, then walked with careful slowness to the kitchen.

"Monday," David said, whispering it against her hair as he gathered her in close to his chest, just outside the back door.

"I'll come right this minute."

"No, Monday evening, before dark. This is Friday, give me the weekend, I'm getting a wagon and team and we can move in, proper. The bank's giving me the papers Monday morning."

She pulled her head back to look at him, to make it real, and he kissed her lips, then again harder, with a little moan in the back of his throat.

"Teddy he's been scroungin' for us," he said when he released her. "Found all manner of useful things."

"Don't come til then," she managed to say, though it hurt her throat to do it. "He'll watch me close all Saturday-Sunday, he'll be sloppy about it come Monday."

She rolled some things in the blanket, Monday afternoon, and brought it to the kitchen, where it sat only half-hidden. She glanced at it so often, her body so tense with dread and happiness, she could scarcely believe Cal didn't notice. He dozed in his chair on the broad wooden porch, while she went in and out the back, finishing the washing, the last she would do here. Did David remember to get wash tubs, she wondered, and nearly laughed out loud. She'd wash in the little creek by the spring, if she had to, and feel lucky.

Coming in for his supper of fried meat and potatoes, Cal noticed the blanket.

"I'm just fixin' to air it," Mattie said, "soon's I get the lines empty." She poured him coffee, and picked up the blanket and went out, right under his gaze. Not able to think of any pretext for picking up the stool, she left it behind.

David grabbed the blanket roll and tossed it to land where it would among the clutter of chests and pails and pots in the wagon bed, and lifted Mattie clean off her feet, swinging her around once before steadying her on the wagon step. He sprang up beside her and the team moved almost before he'd gathered the reins.

"Hey then, are you sad?" He leaned forward and peered into her face.

She laughed, shaking her head, wiping at the tears. "Nothin' like sad," she assured him, "nothing like that at all. Just can't hardly believe it, is all."

"It's true, my love, it's true." And he kissed her, right on the open road, in the twilight.

He told her of the bank president, leaning toward him from behind the shining big desk. "'You're a very big risk, young man,' he says. Hellfire, they're the risky part, they're the ones can make it all disappear, not me. They've got my hundred dollars. Here, want to drive? Just hold 'em across your palm, like that, there's nothing to it really, mules won't leave a road if they can help it."

Carl was born in early March. David had come home from working lumber with the Kanes and found her already on the bed, water warm for washing on the stove. He insisted on fetching Mrs. Simpson, the accepted midwife on the ridge, though Mattie pleaded for someone, anyone, else.

"She don't like us, David, you know that, and I can't stand her pryin' eyes and her lips all pursed up tight."

"She knows about birthin' though, and this a birthin', by god!" David's eyes shone with fear and pride.

"Fetch Mabel, she's had three boys already, she'd come."

"I'll stand here arguing and won't have time to fetch nobody." He gave her a quick kiss and was gone.

"Get me some light in here, man."

Mattie choked back a yell of pain when she heard the voice: she wouldn't scream in front of Mrs. Simpson, who would only say it was her due and quote the Bible about woman's travail, with heavy hint that some women deserved it more than others.

"And now get on out, this is no place for a man."

Mattie clung to his hand, and he looked miserable, but neither of them dared cross the older woman, so he went and paced helplessly downstairs. She could hear him, right under her in the kitchen, stoking the stove, wandering a circle into the other room. They had no chairs in there yet, but through the winter they'd sometimes piled blankets and lay watching the fire. There was no fire there now, it being an early warm spell, and Mattie was thinking of how she should have laid one just for comfort, when "Push, girl!" Mrs. Simpson cried, and there was a mighty wrenching, a cracking as if in her very bones.

"One more like that, child, and you'll be through it."

Mattie had shrunk so from the unfriendly gaze, kept her mind firmly from dwelling on the woman's intrusion, that the encouraging tone caught her by surprise. She turned her sweaty head to look at the midwife as if she'd just got there, and saw a face glowing in the lamplight with what had to be love, no matter what she thought of the mother. Mattie was startled into a joy and relief that swept her into the last contraction as if on angel's wings. Mrs. Simpson's hand was firm and precise against her burning skin, just at her hip.

"Come on now," she was saying, crooning softly. "hit's time you was born, time to get on out here, you've kep' us waiting long enough, hit's time . . . ."

Mattie heard no more, if there was more; she had barely caught her breath before a thin broken cry filled her consciousness and she without thinking raised trembling arms.

"Wait now, I'm just fixin' his belly-band." Again, the inexplicably gentle voice made Mattie want to weep, as if it reached in behind where she was hard into a place she had known nothing about. Then the baby was there, on her stomach.

"Let him feel yer heart," Mrs. Simpson said. "He been hearin' it all this time, needs to know it's still around."

There was the afterbirth, and warm cloths padded between her legs, and blanket tucked around her body, a body more weary than she'd ever known possible, more weary and more triumphant, and then David, his eyes full of tears, obediently and fearfully holding the bundled baby.

David kept working lumber, for cash to make the payments, but evenings and Sundays plowing the old patches for summer crops of potatoes and beans and onions and corn. Mattie's chickens thrived even with letting several hens go broody, and she was by summer trading eggs for flour and sugar and coffee from Guy Deardorff's grocery wagon when he came up the mountain every other Tuesday. She got squash and pumpkin seeds from him, too, and her closest neighbor Mabel Mertz gave her starts for a kitchen garden, lettuce and tomatoes and cucumbers, and little packets of zinnia and marigold seeds for a border.

Mattie sometimes stood in the June sunshine with a heart full to bursting, Carl cooing in her arms, waving fists and kicking as though swimming through the air. Never had she known the earth to be so full of goodness and bounty. Nor was it, she thought, anywhere but here. The pines between the house and barn did sigh at night, and the slopes of Pine Mountain did sometimes answer and call from beyond the springhouse and cast long shadows, but David would roll over in his sleep and throw an arm across her, and it was just tree limbs playing in the wind.

Ted and Harry Kane came most Saturday nights, with Ted's girl April. David's fiddle, Harry's banjo, April's clear high singing filled the night. Dorsey Mertz came sometimes, sharing his liquor for free, but always with an extra quart or two along for sale. David took a half-glass, making it last all night, never buying any jar of it, determined to squander no dollar. Mattie was glad when Mabel came along with Dorsey, their boys in tow, for she liked her neighbor woman more than April, who was gay and pretty and fun but hard to talk to. Bob and Billy danced wild to the music, the toddler Petey reached for David's fiddle and cried when he couldn't have it, until April swung him up on her hip and danced. Carl kicked and bounced on Mattie's lap.

"Hear about some fellow buying up Pine Mountain yonder?" Dorsey said one evening.

Heads turned as if the mountain started right there off the porch, right there in the yard beneath the big pines.

"What – all of it?" David laughed at the preposterous thought.

"Just about, what I heard."

"Back side," Ted corrected. "April here heard about it, too."

"From Mrs. Thompson, in at the courthouse," April said. "Mama sews for her."

"He paid more'n two cents an acre," David said, "he got taken."

April nodded. "That's about what he paid, the price of the ink."

"What's he want with it?" Dorsey demanded. "What's he doin' with it?"

"Settin' on it." April took up the fussing Carl in her arms, dancing with him to the first pine and back, so that he chuckled and was still.

They laughed, shaking heads at such craziness.

"A hermit, is he?" David tossed back his last swallow of moonshine. "I bet he don't last long, it's pretty damn weird up there."

"Maybe he's too damn weird for down here," Dorsey said, and they laughed again.

Word of the gatherings spread, and Mattie began seeing people she'd known in the village, in that other life. She shrank from that at first, but none seemed to care anything about her elopement. Tucker Schultz was as kind as ever, and Warren came with a fetching little sweater for the baby, from Amelia. Evvie Sites, who had used to walk with her along the tracks to the school, and look with her sometimes for mushrooms, came with Morris Sharrah in a little buggy.

Evvie was full of the village talk of the ladies from Baltimore getting off the train, looking for a country house to buy.

"And they went with Mickley in the mail buggy and what do you think! They've bought that old log house there below Morris's folks."

"The old Thomas place," Tucker said, affirming.

"Been empty for years." Mabel Mertz scooped up Carl from the porch edge, blew on his belly to make him laugh. "You figure they're crazy or rich or what?"

"Don't seem to be either one," Morris said, with some authority in spite of his youth, as closest neighbor.

"They got husbands at home?" April wanted to know.

But nobody knew that, for sure, though the consensus was they couldn't, and be leaving them for a month every summer.

"A summer place." April was impressed. "Whoever heard of such a thing?"

The next week, Evvie went with Mattie a little way off from the circles of men; they spread a blanket for Carl, surrounding him with rattles and rag toys. Evvie was quiet for so long Mattie finally asked. "What's the matter, Evvie?"

"Morris he wants to enlist."

"It ain't our war."

Evvie shrugged. "Men ain't so smart about things like that." The girl suddenly tossed a pine cone into the shadows and began to cry.

"Evvie. I'm sorry. Evvie don't cry. Maybe they won't take him."

"Ain't nothing wrong with him, and he turned nineteen this summer. Oh Mattie! You're such a lucky one, look at all you got!"

"It ain't paid for," Mattie reminded her, but more to ward off the evil eye than with any distress.

Then Ted and Harry Kane both signed up for the war.

"You don't got to go, David," Mattie said. "You got a baby, and this place and all."

But he was restless to go, and in September Mattie drove the team back from the train in Potter's Corner, without a glance at the tavern, holding back her tears until she got Carl to bed. "It won't be long,"

David had said. "Now that we're in it, we'll get it straightened out over there. I'll send every penny home, don't forget the payments."

Only a year ago, she wouldn't have dreamed that such loneliness as this was possible. She wasn't afraid, and was busy enough with the garden harvest and the baby that the month passed, she hardly knew how. In October she was surprised one afternoon by Hazel Miller, riding astride on a pretty bay mare. Mattie stood on the porch stoop, tongue tied and staring, as the handsome woman swung down and smiled at her. Auburn hair strayed from its bun, her face was tanned: she wore no hat and clearly never did, as free from such constraints as Mattie herself. And freer – she wore overalls, a thing that had never crossed Mattie's mind. And this woman had seven children, by all accounts.

"Hello. Mattie, isn't it? I heard your – that Mr. Brown took off to fight the Kaiser."

"Yes'm, that's so. I mean, he's gone for a soldier." Mattie had heard he was in France now, and she wasn't sure where the Kaiser was, or what he was.

"Yes." Hazel stood a moment, looking out under the pines, across the spent garden patches toward the little spring house, and back to Mattie. "Can I tie her here?"

"Of course." Mattie flushed with embarrassment at her own backwardness, but still could not make out what she was supposed to do. It had never occurred to her that she and Hazel Miller would ever visit or even meet. "Come and set down." She moved a little toward the two bent-hickory chairs Harry Kane had made last summer.

Hazel came up on the little porch. She had nice boots, the smooth leather tops disappearing under the pants leg. When she sank into one of the chairs as easily as if she visited every week, Mattie sat in the other, as if it were made of egg shells.

"I come begging favors," Hazel said. "No now, don't shake your head before you hear me out."

Mattie gave a small flick of a wrist in apology. "Lands no, I never meant . . . ." She stopped in confusion, and waited.

"With so many men gone. . . . Well, Forrest and I were wondering if you'd be able to bring over your team and wagon and help us get the field corn in? It's getting late. We can pay, a little, and maybe some in kind – milk, and fodder for the team –?"

Mattie was nodding eagerly, then realized with another blush she should speak. "I'd be real happy for the work, Mrs. Miller."

"You sure? I know you must be hard put too, to get everything done here, I hate to ask it." Hazel suddenly let out a small laugh. "And you're so *little*."

Mattie was taken aback again, then smiled with another flick of her wrist. "I'm a pretty good hand at work, though. 'Course, I never did pick corn before."

"That's no matter. You can handle the team?"

"Yes'm, that I can do. Oh, but –"

"What?"

"There's my baby."

"Bring him over, of course. One more in my house won't add any care. I'll watch him or Hannah will." Hazel gathered the reins of the placid mare, but stood a moment almost as if reluctant to leave. "It's right peaceful back in here. You don't mind it?"

Mattie shook her head. "I figure David and them will all be home soon, anyhow."

Hazel nodded, not smiling, and Mattie remembered with sharp sadness rumors of her brother missing Over There. "Well, then, Monday, if it's not raining. Thanks, Mattie, we sure can use some help."

Mattie did not quit going over to the Miller farm when the corn was all in the cribs, the apples all picked. Unless it was too wet to take Carl out, she drove over every day with him wrapped warm and safe in her lap, and that winter and spring learned the details of running a large farmstead. Forrest and the three oldest – Hannah and the twins Mary and Wendell – milked the four cows until the new year, when they were allowed to rest until they freshened. Hazel and Mattie did the butter and the cheeses. Mattie learned the ironing and to fold the shirts just so, and to smooth the clean sheets over the mattress corners, the blankets hanging pretty as a picture. The house was nearly as large as the inn in the village, but none of its rooms and wings was closed off or empty: Mattie cleaned and dusted and shook out rugs and polished the chests and dressers, running her cloth with a kind of reverence over the tables and chairs in the dining room and parlor. She got quick at simple mending, but was fearful of any cutting and sewing, and that was all right, as the daughter Mary was especially fond of managing the family's wardrobe. Sometimes Mattie spent mornings baking, lining up the breads and pies with a deep pleasure she'd never felt in the tavern kitchen.

"Where'd you learn all these pies?" Hazel asked.

Mattie had to stop and think. "It was a woman used to do for my grandpap, lands, I've near forgot her. Mrs. Robinson. She's gone this long time, that was 'fore I got out of school."

Hazel gave her soft laugh. "And how old were you then? Seven? Eight?"

"No now, I went – oh five years it was. Pap figured that was enough, and I guess it was, I made out."

In the spring she plowed the garden plots herself, and hacked at the clods with a hoe. She wanted it all neat for David, but had to give up before the soil was smooth, and plant the seeds as best she could in the rough ground.

"They'll just have to grow that way," she said to Carl, who was walking now, digging beside her. He nodded solemnly, folding chubby arms across his chest, so comically like an old man she scooped him up laughing in spite of her aching arms.

And then it was fall again. She heard of terrible sickness in the army camps, and fell prey to the terror she'd kept at bay for a year. As a kind of religious gesture, she hoarded even more carefully the weekly dollar, and anything left over from the army pay after the monthly payments at the bank in the county seat, where Forrest took her the first Saturday of every month. The influenza spread to the countryside. Old Mrs. Wilkes died, at the end of Mertz Hollow, and the older of the two Simpson boys. Grant Simpson was the preacher at the church on the ridge, and preached at his son's funeral.

"I don't see how he done it, Mattie," Hazel said, her voice low. Her face, bent over the toddler Esther she was dressing, was drawn with fear and weariness. "You'd think some gentleness might be called for, but he's turning harder than ever. Pestilence, hell and brimstone – it shrivels my soul, Mattie, it does." Hazel released the child and stood, arching her back, pressing her hands against it. Mattie was startled, her hands frozen around the potato she was peeling.

Hazel turned, saw where Mattie was looking, and smiled a rueful smile, smoothing the front of her dress. "Another one coming, sure enough. Well, Esther there's nearly three."

Mattie's grandfather died. The death barely registered with Mattie, except as another of the strange flu's toll. There had been no contact between them since she'd left that Monday evening; his revenge for her defection was to will all his property to the church in the village. Warren Schultz bought the old inn at auction, announcing his plans to renovate the wing of rooms for boarders, and to serve breakfast, lunch, and dinner. Forrest Miller showed her the cane Amelia had found in the kitchen.

"You can take that right back," Mattie said, refusing to touch it.

And suddenly, the war was over. Mattie stood in early December with a crowd at the little depot to welcome the soldiers home, holding Carl's hand tight, forbidding him to run as he wanted. She was straining to see around a family clustered in front of her, between her and the huffing train, when someone pulled gently on her arm, so gently she barely felt it through her coat. She turned wondering, a little impatient, and found herself looking right up into David's face. With a cry she collapsed into him; the little boy, instead of running off, clutched her coat with both hands and when his mother finally remembered him and picked him up to meet his father, wouldn't look, but buried his face to hide from the tears on the strange man's face.

He was not as pleased as she expected with her cleverness at making over old clothes for herself and Carl, or at the way she had stretched the money and added no frills to the spare little house. He frowned over the bankbook she so proudly handed him, and then suddenly grinned, tucking it firmly into his shirt pocket, buttoning it fast.

"All right then, let's go."

And he took her on a shopping spree that took her breath away, to show her, he said, what she had ought to have done with his pay. She accepted it all, after her initial fright, the new clothes, new pots and wash tub, the soft arm chair and new mattress for the bed, some kitchen chairs, a beautiful long chest for the kitchen for sweaters and gloves and scarves, a wooden train with four boxcars that Carl wanted – it all settled into the house as if into its rightful place.

He was not so happy, either, with her working, and she without much thought gave it up. That too seemed natural, to be home now that they were a family again. He went back to his old job for the winter, cutting timber for the lumber mill with Ted Kane. Not Harry, whose left sleeve was pinned up empty now, who carried a slim flask in his pocket, though no one ever saw him drunk. And with David gone from first light to last, the days sometimes seemed long to Mattie and sometimes, before she could stop the thought, she'd miss the big farmhouse and Hazel's low laugh.

There were the wonderful Saturday nights again, though, the

musicians rolling up sleeves, shedding layers in the hot kitchen. Ted played guitar now to David's fiddle, Harry blowing a bright harmonica; as long as no one played banjo, Harry contained the bitterness of his lost arm somehow behind his eyes, which showed nothing. April came too. Whatever the truth of the rumors about her the past year, she was Ted's girl again, and wore a ring.

Young Morris Sharrah came home safe, and took some ribbing about having more active duty on his last home leave than in the service. He and Evvie married and with the new baby moved in with his folks on the pretty homestead tucked in a little hollow down the hill from David and Mattie's lane.

"I ain't farmin' though," the young man declared. "There's a factory going up in Potter's Corner, me and Amos Lynn figure to get in on that. Let you'uns grow the fruit, we'll put it in cans."

"You work with Lynn," Ted said, "next thing you know you'll be passin' out tracts."

"Nah, Amos is all right. Just don't like earthly pleasures much."

"He ain't converted you yet?"

Morris waved off the bait, refusing to be drawn into that subject. One of the few Catholic families in the area, the Sharrahs attended Mass when they could, over the ridge in Stevens Valley.

Mattie and April were on the floor in the other room, watching Carl play with his train. "I hear Hazel Miller's havin' trouble with her baby she's carryin'."

It was the first Mattie had heard it, and felt the alarm hot in her chest. "She's near due, has she got anyone in to help?"

April shrugged. "Anna Jean Clemens, I heard."

Mattie sat up with a flare of jealousy. "That fat girl? What's she know 'bout keeping house?"

April giggled. "Not much, I don't reckon. Especially since what she's really after is Muley. He's finally home too, and working over there."

Mattie nodded, miserably not caring about Anna Jean or Muley

Wilkes, already thinking about her visit, she'd go tomorrow, she'd scarcely seen Hazel all winter.

"Really, that woman, though," April was saying. "Someone ought to take her aside."

"Hazel? What do you mean?"

"I mean there's ways not to have babies, you know." When Mattie merely stared at her, April giggled again. "No, you probably don't know."

Mattie wondered suddenly if the rumors had been true after all.

David went with her to the Miller farm that Sunday, wanting to talk to Forrest. He was determined to quit his job and begin reclaiming the farmland, fix a fence for a spring crop of lambs to raise, for cash in the fall, maybe put in a peach orchard. Mattie was mortified to find Hazel bedridden, suffering, and the older children on the edge of tears from the frustration of almost but not quite managing the housework. And Carl's delight at seeing little Esther and Philip again made her ashamed.

"David," she said on the way home, "I want to go back and help out Hazel. That Anna Jean's worthless and anyway she ain't much older than Hannah, really. I ought to go back."

"What about our house, then?"

"I'll manage, it ain't so much to do at our house, we ain't got seven young'uns and a barnful of cows to milk and all."

He agreed then, in too good a mood about his own plans to argue. "Forrest thinks havin' the sheep as a way to start makes sense, says maybe I ought to winter over some ewes. By god, I'm gettin' posts in the ground!"

So Mattie was with Hazel when the baby was born, too soon, and when he died two days later, in spite of all Mrs. Simpson's efforts.

"I tell you, Mabel," Mattie said to her friend one afternoon in early March, stopping at the Mertz's on her walk home. "There's some think

23

Hazel's got enough young'uns, but she's mournin' this one like it was the only child on earth."

Mabel nodded. "And so he was, to her right now. She'll come out of it, the living ones need her, she'll do right by 'em."

"And Mabel, guess what, I think I'm – you know . . . ?"

Mabel slapped her palm on the table with a quick, hearty laugh. "Well, I can't say as anybody'll be much surprised, the way you two look at each other."

"Mabel!" Mattie blushed and had to grin, but then sighed. "But I mean, I ain't going to be any good to Hazel if I –"

"You watch, that's one scrappy woman, she'll be up and doing for *you*, most likely."

During the hot weather at the end of June, Mattie and Carl would walk back to the hillside where David and Ted were clearing space for the peach orchard. The site was hidden from the house by distance and the curve of the mountain as it rose behind the springhouse, and the big poplars and oaks and hickory were dragged out by the big horses to the Jack Road on the far side of the farm, so it was easy for Mattie to put aside the uneasiness she had at first about disturbing the spirits. Silly thoughts anyway. Carl would want to stop and inspect ten things for every two steps, and some afternoons Mattie would be glad to go slow, other days would scold him for a slow poke and hurry him along the track around the base of the hill. And when they'd finally get there, back to the swath being cleared, the mess of trunks and brush and mud and rocks seemed such a tiny disturbance beside the stretches of untouched wooded hillside, and its purpose so good, that surely the spirits, if they noticed at all, approved.

David would drink half the bottle of water she brought, at a gulp, usually in good spirits in spite of the slow work. The timber was bringing a good price, they'd make the rest of the year's payments with plenty to spare, and not sell the sheep until the following summer, when with luck there'd by twice as many.

"I aim to take my time," he said, his gaze sweeping over the tangle of brush. "And do it right, prob'ly not plant till next spring. Plenty of firewood here to sell all winter."

She nodded, as happy as he. She wasn't working at Hazel's now, busy with her own gardens and tiring easily with the second baby coming. By the end of the summer, when she was big, her energy came back, and she put up tomatoes and beans, corn and limas, stashed away the winter squash and potatoes and carrots and onions as if her strength came from limitless source deep inside. But when the baby came in November, another boy, she was glad David was no longer working timber but close by. She took a long rest, grateful for his eagerness to help. They named the baby Jeremiah, which Carl pronounced Jem; by Christmas the given name was all but forgotten.

It was Dorsey who got David playing for square dances, mostly to the south, over into Maryland. Mattie was as glad for the extra cash as he was, but mourned the loss of the Saturday nights of music in the little stone house, and could never fall asleep until he got home, sometimes very near dawn. Even with those nights out, however, and even with the grueling days of hauling firewood in the cold, David was restless that winter, not so much cross with her as turned away. Carl could sometimes call him out of himself, begging for a song or a tussle, but sometimes David would walk away absentminded even from the boy.

They had to add to the loan, to buy the peach trees and two dozen Winesap, but David seemed more himself once the fragile looking sticks were planted in curving rows, the peaches on the far hillside, the apples just beyond the barn, edging the sheep pasture.

April and Ted came by on a Sunday afternoon, bouncing back the rough lane high on the seats of an open Ford. When April untied her long silky scarf, Ted laughed at Mattie's face.

"Ain't she a sight?"

For April had cut her wonderful hair and it was wonderful still. Mattie touched her own skimpy braids, wound and pinned across the top of her head.

"We're movin' out," Ted said. "This time I mean to do it, we been talkin' long enough about it."

Mattie listened in dismay to the plan, which now did for sure sound certain, with even the name of a lumber company hiring, in Colorado. David was skeptical.

"Take you a week to get there, how you know they're still needing you?"

"If they don't, I'll get me a pick and a pan and go prospectin' for gold. Hell, man, we're going West, I'll find something to do."

"Harry going with you?" Mattie asked, and thought David looked at her sharply, as if she'd said something wrong.

"We've asked him to," April said. "But he won't."

"He's clerkin' some at the store now, says he's set to stay put. He'll make out, I guess."

That night, David tried to pick a fight. "What do you care where Harry Kane goes?"

Mattie stopped unpinning her hair, astonished. "Don't you?"

"Well sure, but – no, not like that, like you're losin' your best friend."

"I only asked, just to know. And I am sad, about anybody goin' away. What if we never see Ted and April again, ever?"

"And don't you go cuttin' your hair, neither." He flung back the quilt, and hurled himself onto the bed, his every gesture so full of anger that Mattie lay stiff and careful, keeping her distance.

David was not home yet from the dance of the night before, when Mattie's water broke. She waited another hour, then called Carl in from his playing in the woodlot beside the house, and put a clean shirt on

Jem, now almost two. "Wisht you had a wagon, this is a mighty long way for such wee legs. No, I can't carry you, Jem, just hang onto my hand, you got to walk. Carl, come help him some." Cajoling, pausing, in a terror that she'd waited too long, she coaxed the youngster out the long lane. They rested there, she hiding the pain of a contraction; Carl carried Jem a short way, and she managed to prop him on a hip another short way.

"Where we going?"

"Over to Mabel's. You want to run on ahead? We're almost there, you can tell Mabel we're on our way."

So Mabel came out on the road to meet her, seizing Jem in one strong arm and propping Mattie with the other. She was sweaty and panting now in the close July heat. When they got to the porch, Petey and Carl, who'd been ordered to stay and watch the three-year-old Samuel, tore off together toward the barn.

"I've already sent Bob and Billy off to fetch Mrs. Simpson, told 'em to get her right out of church. I didn't guess you was out walkin' for the fun of it. Come on, set down, I'll fix up a palette here in the spare room, handy to the kitchen. Still got some fire from breakfast, I'll get more warm water goin. Dorsey he's not home yet neither, must've been quite a crowd, plumb wore 'em out, I guess."

"Don't you fret any about the law catchin' Dorsey?"

"Corn brings a bit more in a jar than in a basket," Mabel answered. "He'll brew the stuff whether hit's legal or not and whether I fret or not."

She kept up a steady chatter, and Mattie gratefully let herself relax into it, moving in meekly to the narrow mattress in the little room off a curtained doorway.

"Here, you two, stop that!" Mabel separated the squabbling Samuel and Jem. "There's plenty of blocks for you both. Well then, Jem honey you go on in and give yer Mama a kiss, then come on out on the porch, I'll do the dancin' doll for you a little bit. Where are those boys? Ever take notice, Mattie, how the men disappear when you need 'em most, no matter the age?"

The two older boys came in at a run. "She ain't there, Mama!" Bob said, and Billy took up the tale. "Muley come out when he seen us, and told us Miz Simpson's went over to the Millers, Hazel's taken sick, too!"

Mabel hung fire a second, then burst out laughing. "Well, go on out of here then, 'less maybe it's something catching. No wait now, listen, you two got to watch Sam and Jem."

"Aww. Can't Petey do it?"

"He's run off someplace with Carl. I mean you got to, no sass. I got my hands full. Take 'em to the crick if you want, but anybody gets hurt, you're in more trouble than you want. Hear?"

A bit after noon, Mattie's third son gasped and protested lustily. Both women laughed, crying with relief and exhaustion. Mabel washed him and wrapped him, and laid him in the crook of Mattie's arm, and found her tongue again while she cleaned the bed, rocking Mattie gently from side to side.

"Wonder where all the girl children have got to, we're havin' nothing but males on this mountain. Look at him though, Mattie, he's the prettiest babe ever I seen. Little mite, ain't he? But Lord he's like a picture and hardly an hour old. You got a name? I'm sendin' Bob and Billy over for word of Hazel, if ever they show their faces again today. I guess they'll all be expecting their dinner like so many young princes, bless 'em, they got no idea – Carl!"

Mabel flicked the blanket in place.

"Here, hon, she's all right now, come on in and see what yer mama's got."

Mattie dozed, after Carl ran out again, and woke to the baby's soft cries. Mabel propped her, and they smiled at the infant's guzzling two swallows and falling asleep again.

"He's a quick one, he is," Mabel declared. "Look here, a grip like a ten-pound hammer man."

And then finally, suddenly, David was there, looking panicked, contrite. He gathered Jem into his lap, with one arm encircling Carl, the other hand tight in Mattie's, staring at the new baby as if to keep his family forever in one tight small ring.

"He looks like you already." Mattie smiled at him, her voice hoarse with weariness and love for them all. "What do you figure his right name is?"

They started with A's, and settled on a D, Duane. Mabel wanted Mattie to stay the night, but Mattie agreed with David and let him pack her onto the straw in the wagon. Just as he climbed onto the wagon seat with Carl, settling Jem with her in the back, Bob and Billy came back with the news from the Miller farm. To Mabel's great satisfaction, Hazel had a new baby girl.

David is hers again, doting on the new baby. Carl is clever with numbers, and Jem is remarkably good with his hands, but Duane is purely perfect. He followed all the miracles – the first teeth, the first steps, the first words – as if no baby had ever done them before; he made up a Cutting Teeth Blues on his fiddle, with a spark of his old gaiety. But it was a hard winter; the lambs which were to have paid off the debt of the peach orchard came puny, refusing to suckle, the ewes sickened and over half of them died. The summer was too hot and dry, with sudden fierce downpours in early August that washed live and dead peach trees alike down long gullies.

Mattie walked out the lane with the boys one afternoon, to wait for David, who had gone earlier into Potter's Corner with the team. They dawdled, in no hurry, savoring the cool of the woods.

"He's already here!" Carl called from up ahead, and then they hurried a bit, but something went dead and still in Mattie's spine at the sight of the wagon. The mules were tied to the sycamore tree. The friendlier one, Cappy, raised his head and brayed a greeting to her, moving restlessly. She knew with bewildered certainty they'd been there all day.

She didn't hear his step on the porch; she felt rather than heard his form fill the doorway, and knew him immediately, through her terror and in spite of never seeing him before.

"Mattie Brown? I've brought you these, for your husband is dead."

He didn't approach her, she stood like clay or stone in the kitchen while he laid the armful of dark red climbers and pink wild roses on the table, their stems wrapped in a flannel cloth.

Mattie waited unmoving until she was sure she heard no trace or echo of his walking away, then firmly latched the door. She walked past the roses and went upstairs, checking on the sleeping boys sprawled together on the mattress in one room before lying down in the other. She lay very still, tense, listening to the shrill insect sounds outside the open window and staring at the thick dark hair and full beard and piercing black eyes. How does he know? What does he know? It has been three years since she led the mules home, two years since she sold them to Forrest. In all that time no rumor of David has reached her.

She got up and went back downstairs, finding her way by the natural dark and lighter places. Avoiding the roses, clear enough in the dimness, she knelt by the long trunk in the kitchen, felt under the tangle of sweaters and scarves to make sure of what she knew: the fiddle lay there under a winter comforter, in its case tied with a thin rope. "I'll farm Pine Mountain," David had said, "whether hit's haunted or whether hit's not!" But the mountain had driven him out. The fiddle would draw him back, she'd thought, more powerful than the mountain, stronger than the sickened sheep and failed peach orchard, louder than the debts. Mattie could no longer remember the cutting teeth tune, but she touched the hard case, assuring herself the tune existed.

By morning the wild roses had dropped their pale petals and the edges of the climbers had darkened. She meant to throw the whole bunch out but Jem saw them first and put up a fuss, so she let him pick out the nicest and set the six he chose in a jar of water.

"They come from Aunt Hazel?" Carl asked. "I didn't see 'em last night."

She could think of no evasion. "The old hermit man brought 'em, what do you think of that?"

"Why? He never visits people."

"He said. . . He said he was passing by. He didn't visit. Duane! Stop chasing that poor old hen and get in here, drink yer milk, it's time we got going."

"Can I have some coffee?" Jem asked.

"Coffee! You ain't growed enough by half, yet."

They set off together, not out the lane but around the big bank barn and across the hillside of new apple trees that Forrest had put in last year after buying the farm, when the bank foreclosed. He let her stay on in the house, taking nothing off her wages for it. The path wound through a woods and broke out at the top of Dorsey Mertz's long corn field, following the snake rail fence down its edge to the road. Petey and Sam ran out from a big garden to greet them.

"Let them stay," Mabel said from the porch. "They can make a nickel each if they help pick beans."

"Now Mabel – "

"Why not?"

The boys pleaded to stay, so Mattie gave in. "But you come on over to Hazel's for your dinner, noon sharp." She kept Duane with her, his protests stilled by the reminder that Louisa would be waiting for him.

"You know that old man they call the hermit?"

Hazel Miller glanced up from the beans on her lap. "Brustein? What about him?"

"Nobody's knowed any harm from him, have they?"

Hazel gave a soft laugh. "None except he don't seem to need us much. There's a dozen people like to tell him he can't live up there in that piney rocky hill, but he don't ask for their opinion, and he's been doing it now for ten years."

"Don't he ever talk to anyone at all?"

"Well yes, sure he must. He's got a box at the post office, so Harley told me once. Folks see him walking the road, every once in a while. And he gets stuff from Guy's wagon occasionally. Guy says it's hardly worth stopping the horses, which I take to mean Guy don't find out anything to gossip about. Why?"

Mattie looked up with a shrug. "He paid me a call last night."

Hazel's calm eyes showed her surprise, but she was silent for a moment, watching Duane and Louisa playing with sticks a little distance from the long side porch where she and Mattie sat snapping the summer's first beans. "What did he want?"

"To bring me roses, seemed like."

Hazel's hands went still now as she looked at Mattie in frank astonishment. "Mattie Brown, what on earth are you talking about?"

"He ain't as old as I thought, there ain't but a little gray in his beard."

"So he just hands you roses and turns around and walks away?"

"Yep. Or no, not quite."

"Mattie. He didn't, I mean. . . . You're awful alone back there. Did he frighten you?"

"Nothin' he done. But he says – Hazel, he says David's dead."

Hazel caught her breath in a short cry of dismay. "How would he come to know a thing like that?"

"That's all he says. 'Here,' he says, and lays them flowers on the table. 'Your husband is dead.' And he's gone."

"Oh, Mattie."

"I ain't believin' it," Mattie said.

"Oh, Mattie," Hazel said again. "Maybe – wouldn't it be best if you did believe it? Forgive me, Mattie, but I think he is dead. To you he's dead."

"I ain't believin' it."

Hazel sighed, and scooped more beans into her lap from the basket. Neither spoke for several minutes, until Hazel gave a low chuckle. "You mean to tell me he's settin' up there growing roses? Roses!"

Jem, playing with Duane on the springhouse roof, saw the car first and jumped to the ground running. Duane called to him to wait, but knowing he'd be ignored, crept down the back side of the roof, which touched the ground, and ran after him through the garden patches to the house, where Mattie and Carl were splitting wood.

"A car? Comin' here?" Mattie stood as if connected to the ax she had just whacked into the chopping stump.

"It's got a funny something on the top, like a bubble."

And at that moment the car pulled around the house to float to a stop in front of the two tall pines, clearly in view of them. Carl held an armful of wood, but made no move either to carry it in or put it down.

"Morning." He was a young man, looking uncomfortable in his stiff, pressed trousers and shirt and seeming slightly out of breath, as if he'd trotted in. "That lane could use some work."

Mattie stared at the hat strap on his chin, which seemed to her ineffectual.

"Mrs. Brown?"

Mattie nodded briefly, her hand tight on the ax, the words of the hermit loud in her head after two months of silence. And there was no proof that she was anyone at all, connected to anyone at all. Was there a law against that? A law to take away her boys?

"Could we go in the house, ma'am? In private?"

"The boys can go in." Mattie finally moved away from the woodblock,

33

touched Jem's shoulder to turn him toward the porch. "Go on, Carl, take that wood on in, and butter some biscuits for them."

They were reluctant, Carl more than curious, his face pale, his light brown eyes flashing anger at being dismissed like a child. Mattie prayed they would not cross her now, for all she knew giving the policeman cause, making his case. Her own shapeless cotton dress and untidy braid and broken shoes were bad enough, but he must not see the children unruly, must not look at the sparse roughness of the two rooms. She breathed again when Carl went up the two steps and Jem and Duane followed him inside.

"Mrs. Brown, do you – Is there a David Brown here?"

"What's he done?" Her voice was raspy, unfamiliar to her ears.

He shook his head. "We have no reason to suspect any wrongdoing. When did you see him last?"

Matter merely stared at the chin strap, and he sighed, rubbing the back of his neck. "Look. There's nothing to be afraid of. We've got a missing person report. I mean, we have to investigate this sort of thing. Do you know where your husband is, ma'am?"

It sounded like a crime to her, not knowing, and she straightened, forced herself to look at his eyes. "Who done that report?"

The policeman gave an impatient jerk of his head, looked behind him at his car with obvious longing to be gone. "Is he missing, Mrs. Brown?"

And Mattie said, "No, he ain't."

"He's here?"

"He ain't here now."

"But you know where he is."

"He ain't 'missing,' or whatever that report says."

"So you would withdraw the file?"

She had no image of what such an action would be, no way to be sure of a safe response, and stood silent.

"There must have been some mistake, then, perhaps," he suggested.

"Yessir." Mattie picked up the cue. "It must've been some kind of mistake." The words made her feel braver. "Who would make such a mistake, I wonder."

He seemed also to relax, his duty done. "Your pastor, I believe it was. I could look it up."

"No, it ain't important." She wanted no more of his attention bent on her or David. He touched his hat, bent his body into the car, turned it around in a smooth series of backward and forward turns and drove away around the house.

The boys backed away from the door and stood around the table, where each had an untouched biscuit. Mattie dipped herself a cup of water, and drank.

"Mama," Carl said.

She drained the cup. "I got to go over and see Reverend Simpson. You two mind Carl."

"I'm going with you," Jem said.

"No, I don't want –" Mattie looked at them, so quietly watching her, and shrugged. "Well, you can walk along if you want. Just don't bother us while we're talking."

"Me too!" Duane shouted, and dashed out to do a little dance on the porch.

"What'd he want?" Carl asked.

"You was listening," she answered. She took a man's shirt off the row of wooden pegs, slipped it on over her dress.

"You think Reverend Simpson done it, really?" Carl asked. "How come?"

"That's just what I aim to find out."

"Mama, you maybe Shouldn't 've lied."

She whirled to face him. "You maybe wasn't listenin' good enough. I never told him no lies, not one, you hear me?"

The boy backed against the table, but persisted. "You said Daddy wasn't —"

"I said he wasn't missing." Mattie hissed the word. "I never said he was here, I never said I knowed where he's at. He ain't missin', like a button off a shirt."

She saw then that Carl's eyes were bright with tears, his mouth clamped against trembling, and turned away from him quickly to hide her own anger and guilt. She can't produce his father, and it must be her fault. It most certainly wasn't Carl's, in any case. "You comin' too?" she said, more gently.

He shook his head, and she set out without looking back, Jem and Duane scampering ahead of her like puppies.

The day was suffused with the reds and goldens of autumn shining from all sides of her in the dry clear sunshine and it was hard to keep hold of her anger. Once they passed the Y in the road and took the right side, up the steep hill on Two Springs Road instead of the familiar turn into Mertz Hollow, the boys fell into step beside her, feeling shy.

The boy Paul was whitewashing the gate of the picket fence along the front of the impressive brick house. "He's currying the team," he replied to Mattie's question, and she turned to the opposite side of the road. Duane bumped against her hip.

"You stay here along the road, I'll just be a minute."

The horses were in the first of the six stalls along the bottom of the barn, a deep stall with room for four. Mattie stopped at the half-door, addressed the dimness. "The police come by today."

Grant Simpson turned to her from between his two large cream-colored work horses. He was not apparently surprised by the unexpected voice or the words. "I pray they'll find him for you soon."

"I told them he ain't lost."

"Mattie!" Simpson moved from the horses, laid the brush on a shelf and came out into the light, fastening the door behind him. Mattie backed up a step but kept her gaze level. He was a stocky man, with everything always in place. His gray hair even now looked newly combed and parted, the white shirt under his overalls washed and pressed. "Whatever made you tell such a lie, and to the law yet?"

"I reckon it's the truth, near enough. What made you sic 'em on me like that?"

"Don't you want him back? Mind what you say, girl."

So she clamped her teeth on the retort, unnamed terror thudding against her rage.

"Those boys need a father, Mattie. He has responsibilities. You better let us help you."

"You ain't tryin' to help me."

"Of course we are. It's not too late for you to straighten out."

"What? Straighten out what?"

"Make a decent, godly home for them."

"There's nothin' the matter with my boys' home."

"Who's going to teach them right from wrong?"

"Who's teachin' 'em wrong?" she cried.

"Carl's been fighting again, what I heard."

"Petey Mertz started that, they made it up. A schoolyard scrap, that ain't no crime."

"And liquor's no crime?"

Mattie was too bewildered to answer right away, thrown by the sudden attack in his voice.

"And where there's the poison liquor sold," Simpson went on, "there's any number of even worse things likely. That the kind of right-from-wrong you want your boys to learn?"

Mattie tried desperately to trace the preacher's thoughts. Harry Kane came by sometimes, but he only wanted to talk, and he brought his liquor with him. "I don't sell liquor," she said finally, her voice sounding so uncertain she clamped her teeth.

"No? What would visitors be wanting back there at night, I wonder."

37

He might as well have slapped her, for the shock she felt.

"How long you figure to hide such goings-on from those boys, Mattie? They see more'n you may think. You bring yourself and them with you into the church, girl. All of us gladly help you raise them up righteous, see to their earthly and heavenly needs."

"What goings-on? I never –" Mattie fell silent again, the image of Brustein suddenly before her, her own confession to Hazel. No, not Hazel, she'd never –

"It ain't only wages for housework going through your hands, Mattie Brown, don't think you can lie to me. I got a boy in the same schoolyard as yours, remember."

"I got nothin' to hide!"

"You go tell Dorsey Mertz to keep his customers to himself."

"Dorsey Mertz don't need the likes of me, and I got nothin' to sell to anybody."

He stepped toward her, his eyes under the bushy eyebrows flashing with righteousness. "I won't speak it, lest the wind carry it. A woman alone is an unnatural thing, and not what God intends. Take care, Mattie, take care!"

Mattie backed away, pulling the old shirt tight across her chest.

"Now tell me, mister, how come you just up and say a thing like that to me last summer."

Brustein got up from the stump, an ear of dry corn in one hand. He towered even out in the open, and Mattie edged back toward the woods even though she was thirty feet from him. It had taken her over an hour to find the place; her legs were trembly, there was an ache across her shoulders.

"I don't know why. It wasn't meant to torment you, forgive me." The dark eyes seemed milder, here, not mocking, not crazy. His voice was low, halting. He seemed almost more afraid of her than she of him, and she took courage.

"Where's he at? Where'd you hear it from?"

"I don't know."

"What do you mean, you don't know."

He looked down at the corn in his hand, tossed it to the ground with a small group of others, and ran his hands through his thick hair. She was mistaken, she realized: there was gray in his beard. But he shrugged, and didn't answer. She looked past him and saw the rambling rose on the side of the squat little cabin, with half a dozen late dark blooms. He had made a long, rough clearing, stumps still in the ground, tall weeds and brambles bordering several small plots where dry bean plants and corn stalks still showed. Mattie was for a moment distracted, wondering what the cabin was like, then pulled her scorn over her disappointment.

"So you don't know nothing about David, really."

"Was that his name?"

Was, he said. Her stomach churned at the simple authority in his voice, at the sudden pain and weariness in his slumping shoulders that leaped across to hers.

"Would you have some tea?"

"What? No. No, I got to get back." Duane was at Hazel's, the others would be out of school by now.

"You won't get lost?"

"No." She had had no idea how she would find this place, or why she had known she would, and now no idea why she had wanted to. On a hunch from the preacher's words, she had asked Carl again about the tussle with his friend, and he had admitted it was to shut him up about the hermit's visit. And how'd he come to hear of it, she'd asked. Jem blabbed it. Jem, too young to feel any danger, and Carl, too young to understand it, striking out blindly, and Paul Simpson standing by. Listen, it's of no account, she'd told Carl, trying to laugh as Hazel had at the strangeness of it all. She turned, feeling bereft and numb, away from the clearing, back toward a little creek she remembered and could follow down off the ridge.

Wendell Miller went off to university in Virginia, and his twin, Mary, argued against Forrest's resistance to her taking a job in the new shirt factory in the county seat. She got his Aunt Millie on her side, offering a room to board with her in town.

"What's he expect?" Mary exploded one afternoon. Rather plain but lively, Mary missed the socializing of high school days, when she and Hannah and Corie had ridden with Wendell on the train to the school in town. "Life to come find us way up here?"

"He would prefer, yes," Hazel answered in her usual mild way, "that Lloyd court you up here."

"He would prefer," Mary corrected her sourly, "that Lloyd not court at all."

"Mary, hush," Hannah pleaded, her voice low, suffering.

"Lloyd just seems unready to settle yet to any one thing, Mary. Your father's only –"

"Maybe I don't want to, neither!" Mary leaped up, slamming her pan of apple peelings onto the table. "Maybe there's more to life than this drudging from dawn to dark!" She rushed from the kitchen. Hannah waited for a nod from Hazel, then quickly set aside her own work and followed her sister. Corie, looking close to tears, ducked her face away from her mother's frown, though Mattie was sure none of the frown was meant for her, the sunniest, happiest, sweetest one of the whole bunch.

"'Maybe I don't want to, neither,'" Hazel muttered. "She's got about as much sense of what she's talking about as that pan there."

Forrest relented. And in November, had to assent to a hurried wedding. In a rush to get to Denver before Christmas to take a hotel manager job, Lloyd didn't want even a week's delay to plan a proper wedding, and Mary would have nothing to do with Hazel's advice to let him go get settled, join him in the spring. So Mary and Lloyd stood up together in his preacher's house, with all the Millers filling the parlor. Even Wendell came home, and even Charlie, who hated town and gatherings of any sort, shook his new brother-in-law's hand and kissed his sister's cheek. Aunt Millie gave everyone a wedding supper, alternately beaming at Mary's good fortune and weeping at the loss of a niece.

Mattie was surprised, then, when Forrest put up no battle when Corie and Hannah asked to go live with Aunt Millie, and join the ranks of working girls in the little shop. "I guess time can't be stopped," was all he said. "You'll all grow up with or without my liking it."

The first serious snow was not until the new year, beginning with thick lazy flakes midmorning. Duane and Louisa were uncontainable, tracking wet into the big kitchen to announce their delight every five minutes. Mattie tried to object but Hazel was lenient.

"They'll be gone from underfoot soon enough," she said, and Mattie glanced at her, marveling, but it was true. So little time ago, the house was bursting with children, from kitchen to tiniest top room, and now only Louisa was small enough to be counted a child. Philip and Esther were twelve and fourteen. Between them and Louisa, had been the two small graves added to the churchyard.

"Looks to be a deep one," Forrest said at the noon meal. "You better go on home, Mattie."

"I'll get the buggy out," Charlie said. "The younguns 'll get soaked."

No one smiled at the condescension; if at seventeen Charlie was little more than a youngster himself, he had for several years already thrown in his lot with his father and his father's work. Even strangers would not mistake him for a schoolboy. But Mattie waved off the offer.

"Never knowed a child yet minded a walk in the snow." She helped

41

clear the dishes, accepted an extra scarf to wrap around Duane's head. The teacher Ed Lakin dismissed the scholars at the little school when Mattie walked by, and Sam, Petey, Carl, and Jem all walked on with her, in high spirits at the unexpected half-holiday. Mabel made a big pot of hot chocolate, insisting they all pause and warm up. She showed Mattie a letter from her two oldest sons.

"Now why you figure they'd be layin' off coal miners and it the middle of winter?" she said. "My boys is fools, to stay out there."

"But they just got taken on, I thought."

"Been at it two months, and now settin' on their butts. They could be home cutting firewood, at least."

Mattie shuddered. "Anyway, if they ain't workin' they ain't down under the ground."

Mabel leaned closer, and lowered her voice, with a glance at the boys clustered on the deacon's bench, chattering over Dorsey's arrowhead collection in a cigar box. "They're talkin' about joining the Union, Mattie. I'm that scared about 'em I can't hardly sleep nights."

At supper, Jem didn't finish his potatoes.

"You sick?"

"Not hungry, is all."

"Drink your milk, then."

"But look, Duane's is all, he wants it."

"He can have all he wants in the morning. I'll get some more from Aunt Hazel until Bessie freshens again. That's your share, now drink it."

That night, going to their room to cover Duane, who always kicked off the blankets, she sensed that Jem was awake. "Why can't you sleep?"

"Mama? Mama, do we have enough of everything. For winter?"

"You been worrying about us?" Mattie drew a long breath."We got plenty."

"Potatoes? Have we still got –"

"Potatoes. Apples." She whispered the list like a lullaby. "Jars of soup put up. Hams and bacon. Beans, corn, onions. And pickles, why we even got pickles!"

He sighed, and she leaned over to give him a quick, rare kiss, and went tense with alarm. His face was burning.

"My neck feels funny," he admitted.

Mattie warmed a bit of honey in a cup, with a few drops of vinegar, and got him to swallow two teaspoons. She wrapped a strip of soft wool flannel around his throat and tucked the covers well. The other boys felt normal to her touch, but she paced the kitchen unhappily, opening cupboards in a vain search for some remedy or can of balm. She checked again on the boys, feeling now a definite swelling below Jem's ears, and remembered one of the Miller girls saying there'd been mumps in the town since Christmas. There was an instant relief in the knowing, but her alarm gripped like nausea. The litany of foods she had recited to her sick little boy would not protect him from this.

Jem finally asleep, Mattie pulled her heavy shawl off the chair by the stove and went out into the night. She took long gulps of air, licking the snow from her lips. Suddenly she was sobbing with terror and longing, the yearning to reach for a hand, hear a voice, to rest in the knowing that someone shared her vigilance through the nights, would smell the smoke, feel with wind, hear the cry.

The barn was nearly empty these days; only the brown cow, cumbersome with calf, shifted at her approach. Mattie leaned on Bessie's solid warmth and cried until her legs wouldn't hold her up. She crawled a little space away and sat, hugging her knees.

How long had Jem been worried and scared, she wondered. How long could she wait for David? This place – Oh David, I sold the place, it ain't even yours anymore. I sold the mules too. But I stayed here, didn't I? The house is just like it was ours, you wouldn't see any difference. And the fiddle is laying here, waiting for – Oh David. David.

43

The knock at the door startled her and Jem. She nodded to him, and he pulled on the latch, stepping quickly away. Mattie stared across the table, her hands unmoving on the lump of bread dough.

"I just . . . brought a little . . . ."

"Come in." Mattie remembered the simple rules of hospitality, though her voice was reluctant. And her determination not to be friendly to craziness kept her face stern.

Brustein obediently stepped inside, only far enough to swing the door closed, and thrust his hands into the big pockets of his coat. "Here, I have some whittling nonsense, just trifling things. Heard the boys were sick, maybe these will be amusing for a little while. But one of you is up, I see."

Jem ducked away from the gaze on him. "This is Jem," Mattie said. "He started it all, but he's about normal now."

"Ah. Well here, this one's for you, I think." The tall man separated out one of the objects into his right hand. Mattie nudged Jem away from her hip with her elbow.

"Go on, see what 'tis."

Jem edged around the table, but when he could take his eyes off the unaccustomed sight of the full beard his shyness changed to interest in the toy. At the change, the visitor too seemed to relax and stepped forward to offer it. Jem looked back at Mattie, who nodded. "Mind yer manners."

"Thank you," he whispered, and took the piece reverently, almost fearfully as if it might bite. Four interlocking wooden circles hung in a chain, whittled from a single block.

"Look, Mama. How can this be, now?"

Mattie rubbed the dough off her fingers, into a smooth ball, sprinkled flour on the table and on the rolling pin. "I wouldn't know, for a fact. Never seen nothing like that." She pressed the dough out from the center, glancing up at the hermit with a smile, in spite of herself. "Guess it takes some patience."

44

It was not quite a smile he gave her back, but his eyes were glad. "The others are sleeping?"

She nodded, and he set two carved figures on the corner of the table. Jem's eyes got even larger. "You make them, too?"

The whittler gave a half nod, half shrug, and pulled his coat tighter. "Well. I hope you're all well soon."

"Wait, no need to rush off." Mattie heard herself say it, as if she watched from another room, or the ceiling. "These biscuits only take a couple minutes, there's plenty of gravy."

"No, I won't – thank you, but I'll go on back, before dark. You need anything?"

"What?"

"You have enough wood? Water?"

"Yes," was all she said.

She walked out with Jem around the middle of the next morning to wait for Guy Deardorff's grocery truck. The sun was weak in a gray sky, but the day was not bitter cold. The tracks of vehicles and horses had worn the snow unevenly on the road, and they looked doubtfully toward where it disappeared around the slight bend, where there was a steep grade.

"Don't know if a truck can pull that hill, with the snow," she said.

"Can we get chocolate? You think there'll be oranges, like that time before Christmas?"

Mattie murmured noncommittal responses, which were enough for the boy, full of wonder at the world beyond the house walls. She cautioned him not to run and get sweaty, but still he ranged out from her and bounced back. He found a pheasant feather, a small gray feather, a woodpecker's sharply divided black and white feather; he brought her a quartz stone with pink marbling. He called to her to come see a track in the snow.

"Coon, maybe?" she guessed. "Or a groundhog out already? Lands, boy, I ain't knowing much about that sort of thing."

"You reckon he does? I bet so, living back in the mountain like he does."

Jem turned to look back toward the house but above it, his mind not on the farmland or any one spot but on the gray and purple winter woods and slopes that formed the word, mountain. "Yonder," he added, like an amen. He went so still that Mattie glanced where he was looking but there was nothing but a field of last year's corn stalks, a line of woods – not even, from here, a clear sense that Pine Mountain defined the world, edging as it did their home and Mertz Hollow and the Miller farm as well.

"Where *does* he live at?" Jem asked, his voice sudden and impatient after the quiet. He turned his thin face toward her now, frowning.

His intensity took her by surprise, not for the first time. He was in general the easy one, without Carl's impetuous temper or Duane's restless energy, but he was also the one with these sudden, passionate, unexplainable concerns.

"Somewhere back in where the pines is thick, they say." She kept to herself the image of the place.

"He ain't got a road to it."

"No."

"You only need a road if you got a car or a wagon to go on it, I guess."

"Or if you want other people to come see you."

"He don't, I guess." Jem's voice was mystified. "How come?"

"I ain't a mind reader."

"He come to us, though!" Jem suddenly brightened, triumphant. "And made us toys. Duane he slept with his horse the whole night through. That dog for Carl it looks just like Petey's hound, a-settin' back to watch you come in the gate like he does. But my circles is the best, ain't it?"

Mattie listened, astonished, to his accounting. He usually let his brothers do the talking.

"Mama –"

But the motor's growl below them cut off his thoughts. They waited, listening to a higher whine, a revving, then nothing.

"That's only the wind, now," Mattie said. "He couldn't get up the hill, sounds like."

Her disappointment was acute, her sense of isolation nearly intolerable since the hermit's visit, but Jem's slump of sorrow was so evident Mattie squared her shoulders and became brisk. "Never mind, he'll try again next week." And, remembering his feverish questions earlier, added. "We got plenty to eat."

"No chocolate, though."

"No chocolate, though," she agreed.

He looked back at the road every few steps until he could not have seen the square black covered truck even if it were there. They turned the sharp bend in the lane and the house was suddenly inviting again, their hands and feet cold, shoulders and knees tired. Thin smoke coiled nearly invisible from the kitchen stovepipe and from the brick chimney of the fireplace. Jem pushed on the heavy front door, and they hurried into the kitchen warmth, as grateful now to return as they had been to step out of it earlier. Duane dashed in from the other room, ran hard against her, sobbing.

"What –?" Mattie struggled to get free of her shawl and the empty basket, while Carl, feeding the wood range, would not meet her gaze or question. She tugged Duane with her toward the fireplace, where she had earlier made him a warm bed on the sofa. "You should be in bed, these floors is too cold for your poor feet. Carl, bring a piece for the fire in here."

She pulled Duane close by her on the now untidy couch, rubbing his bare feet, tucking the heavy comforter around him. He was still weeping, with shudders, and she fished for a handkerchief in the pocket of her skirt. "Now what's the trouble here?" She wiped at his face, reaching with her free hand to free something lumpy under her thigh. It was the wooden horse. Duane reached for it with a cry.

"Well, here, did you think it was lost? Oh." Holding it out for him, she could see a leg was broken, the foot missing.

"He throwed it," Carl said. Sparks flew as the log fell among the embers. "Ain't no fault of mine."

"He broken it, broken it," Duane wailed. "*Kicked* it."

"Oh, Carl, couldn't you –"

"I didn't mean to break it. And you did so throw it, crybaby."

"Hush Duane, hush now, yer as hot as a kettle, you can't get well if you drive your fever up, hush, you still got your horse." He settled against her, quieter, too weak and miserable to protest his case further. "How come did he throw it? Carl, answer me. Was you teasin' him?"

"Nah. He wanted to go outside after you and Jem and got mad when I wouldn't let him."

Duane hid his face, and Mattie stroked the sweaty curls back from the temple, where the fragile blood vessel pulsed.

"And he threwed it and I kicked it back, is all."

"He said –" Duane lifted his face – "he said he'd ought to burn it, he said we'd ought to burn 'em all!"

Jem's shock from the doorway was an audible gasp. "*Why?*"

"He's a crazy man!" Carl stood straight now, feeling the authority of his superior age and understanding. "Everybody knows that. What's he comin' around here for, anyhow? This ain't the first time," he added darkly.

Mattie looked away from his frown, with strange fear and guilt, and then averted her eyes too from Jem's dismay, and looked into the fire burning brightly around the locust log. Jem abruptly ran across the room to the little room off the side. Gone only a second, he came back with the little wooden chain clutched fiercely.

"I ain't burnin' this!"

"No," Mattie agreed quickly. "You keep that, there ain't no harm in it I can see." She tried to make her voice firm, and Carl stalked off, his question unanswered.

The next day the sun was warmer, and the temperature rose above freezing, a common February trick. On the second day of the thaw, Mabel walked through the mud and rivulets of disappearing snow, and thumped her heavy men's brogans merrily against the edge of the porch boards.

"Never mind the mud," Mattie said. "The floor 'll sweep. Lands, it's good to see a different face!"

"Look here." Mabel held out to her a small basket, and Mattie opened the cloth.

"Where'd you get eggs? My hens are doing nothing 'tall."

Mabel laughed. "Well, take notice there ain't but one apiece for you all."

"You can't spare them," Mattie objected, "with all your own to feed."

"Now it ain't nothin' to do with feeding either yours or mine." Mabel pushed the basket back and they came together into the kitchen. "I just had to get out from inside those walls once."

"You don't need to bring along excuse to come here. But I'm clean out of coffee. We'll have some mint." She dropped some light sticks into the stove, to work the fire up again.

Mabel settled at the table, caught Duane and gave him a quick hug before he could squirm away laughing. "You 'bout well, are you?"

"I can't keep 'em in anymore. Monday we're all clearing out of here. Is the school open yet?"

"I sent Petey back yesterday, that tired I was of bumping into him every other minute. But have you heard about Charlie?"

"Charlie?"

"He taken the mumps, they went bad on him. Poor Hazel, with all that —"

49

"She should've sent for me!" Mattie cried. "I could've been over."

"Don't take it hard, you had your own to tend. He's better now, but still in bed, I guess. And everybody else there is pretty well over 'em."

"I should've *been* there." Mattie shook her head sorrowfully. She poured the boiling water from the kettle into a saucepan with the dried mint, and set it covered on the table.

"Another letter from Bob and Billy," Mabel said. "They're back at work, and haven't got theirselves shot yet."

"Maybe they'll get a union without going to war over it." It was Mattie's turn to reassure. She poured them tea, and another cup for Duane, who came back in to show Mabel the horse, which could still stand on the table in spite of the missing hoof.

"Somebody's right smart with a knife," Mabel said. "How'd you come by that, now?"

Mattie saw now, too late, that Carl was right: better into the fire.

"That old man brought 'em," Duane said. "Only I was sick in bed, I never seen him."

"What old man? Muley's old dad?"

Duane looked at Mattie, confused. "It wasn't Pap Wilkes, was it?"

Mattie shook her head, forced a wry smile at Mabel. "That one they call the hermit."

"What?" But Mabel wasn't scandalized. "Now ain't you something, young man. He never come packing my boys any toy. He come here, Mattie, really?"

Mattie gave the barest of nods, a shrug.

"Well, guess we know one thing he does up there, now."

"And roses," Mattie said, then caught herself. "I heard he likes to grow roses."

"Not likely. In the middle of a pine woods? Where'd you hear that at?"

Mattie shrugged again, letting the subject die.

"Did he give you the time of day, or just throw the toy and hightail it?"

"Toys!" Duane corrected her gleefully. "He give us each one, a different one."

"My goodness. Come on, Mattie, do tell: what's he like?"

Mattie went blank, and had to laugh. "I can't hardly say."

Carl and Jem banged in the door, their arms full of wood, which they dropped with grunts of relief into the deep box.

"There!" Mabel burst out laughing. "There must be something in the brains, bred in, to all men-children, makes 'em drop the kindling every which way. Ain't a one of my four can stack worth a tinker's dam." She finished her tea, buttoned her sweater and got up, swinging the fringed plaid shawl around her broad shoulders. "I better be gettin' on back, Dorsey he wants an early supper, there's a dance down Thurmont way –"

She caught her thought at the very end, her good-natured grumbling cut off with a glance of apology and sympathy. Mattie turned from her quickly, reaching for the eggs. The image of David, cap set jaunty, fiddle under his arm, sliced across her consciousness like a knife across her chest, but her hand was steady.

"Here. I'll set these out, you can take your basket. We sure do thank you for the eggs."

Duane's first day of school was a fine September day, and Mattie scarcely knew whether she was happy or sad to see her youngest step out so proud. For three years he had begged to go, and could barely believe the promised time had come. She walked out with the boys, planning as usual to go on to Hazel's but first got sidetracked by Mabel.

"Go on now, the lot of you," Mabel told the boys. "I guess you all know where the schoolhouse is at, by this time, it ain't moved that I know of."

She set a heavy white mug of coffee on the table beside her own. "Have some coffee, there's nothing at Hazel's can't wait. Lord, you look like you seen a ghost, what's the matter?"

"No, now, don't talk to me about ghosts."

"Ain't seen any yet? Weeping mothers? Murdered boys? Indians with tomahawks, Rebel camps? Where'd they all go, I wonder?"

"April and Ted used to tell about how the mountain could shift itself, make paths disappear."

"Straight from a bottle, most of it. But who's to say what's what, for sure. But listen, what had you by the back of the neck, when you come in?"

"Nothin'. Only . . . . Did you feel queer-like when your Sammy walked off to school the first time?"

Mabel smiled, but did not laugh at her. "Some. Yeah, some, I remember."

"It *was* almost like seein' a ghost, just for a minute. Like I was walkin' in here six years ago, that Sunday morning lookin' for David."

Mabel did laugh then. "Scared! I was that scared the room spun."

Mattie was astonished. "You sure never let on."

With a sudden heavy sigh, Mabel poured them the last of the coffee. "And you know what, Mattie? I'm still scared, Petey's beggin' now to go off to the mines, not go in to high school. Who can blame him, really, but I don't like it."

Mattie walked on toward the Miller farm, the dust warm against her bare feet. She decided several times to hurry, and each time found herself dawdling again, and finally stopped. The big farmhouse was in sight, ahead; she stepped off the road to her left, toward the creek she remembered following down off Pine Mountain.

Up here the air was cool the earth still holding the chill of the night. She walked on with a suddenly light heart under trees so big the underbrush was gone, the sky nearly hidden, all sounds muted by a hundred layers of pine needles and oak leaves. She was unmindful now of the haunts and craziness tucked away in the ridges and folds and dark pine stands, she was merely walking. Walking unerringly to the clearing, so quickly reached she stopped short at the edge, surprised.

"Go on away now, I have nothing for you."

He stepped into her sight from behind the cabin, suspenders dark against a deep red shirt. He didn't look in her direction, but she stood burning with shame. What had she been thinking? But just before she turned to slip away she saw the true object of his words, a doe following him, head slightly lowered and stretched toward his pockets. The animal raised its head and looked toward Mattie, searching the breezes; the hermit's gaze followed.

"Hello." He stood up, and the deer vanished.

It was such a simple, unguarded greeting, with only a hint of surprise in it, that she walked into the clearing and nearly up to him. "My baby's went to school today." She blurted it like a schoolgirl, and she felt like one, and with an impatient little gasp at her own foolishness, turned to get away.

"No wait," he said. "Come sit down, the sun's nice on the porch."

She hesitated, then without really deciding to, found herself joining him as he sat on the edge of the rough wooden porch. His feet were bare too, firmly planted on the ground, while hers swung, toes just brushing the earth.

"What are your boys' names, again?"

She told him. "Jem he's still got those circles," she added, and then was sorry for fear he'd ask after the other figures, long since broken and forgotten. But he merely nodded and smiled.

"How do you know when it's Tuesday?" she asked.

He looked at her, puzzled.

"For Guy's truck, I mean."

"Oh. I do keep track of time, it's a hard habit to break."

She had so little notion of what he meant that she couldn't frame another question, and let the silence settle. She was beginning to rehearse a way to leave when he invited her inside for water and a taste of his skillet corn bread. Again without a conscious decision, she followed him into the tiny cabin, not much larger than her springhouse. She looked around as he cut a piece of the bread from the iron skillet on the rough table.

"How'd you cook it?"

He gestured to the fireplace, where she could see stones arranged around the dying embers. Mattie was taken aback. Poor as she was, she'd always had a stove. He didn't have a bed, either: blankets lay folded in a corner near the hearth. A few heavy plates and cups sat on crude shelves, some shirts and trousers hung on pegs. A large chest, and a small camel-back, and a rocking chair were the only furniture.

The bread was dry but good; hungrier and thirstier than she'd thought, she drank a full cup of water. "What will you do today?" Horrified, she felt red heat spread over her face and neck. "It ain't none of my affair."

He didn't seem to notice her embarrassment. "I should go down into Potter's Corner, while the weather's nice."

"And I better get on to Hazel's, I ain't usually this late."

"If you wait till I get –"

"Oh no, that's all right," she said quickly, alarmed. "Thanks for the bread, but I can get back all right."

She left abruptly, aware of the rudeness but unable to bear the thought of being seen at the road with him. She turned without stopping at the edge of the woods, and seeing him watching her, waved. His arm lifted in reply. Mattie went on, laughing softly, thinking suddenly how funny the whole visit was. As she walked she found herself wishing that he were with her after all, that she could go tell Hazel, hear her laugh and say the right, sensible thing. But what if Hazel didn't laugh? The Millers went to the same church as the Simpsons, and for all she knew had similar thoughts about certain things.

Or talk to Evvie, that would be just the thing. But they met rarely now, and only by accident. Evvie had her hands full, with a new baby about every year. No. To become linked with Brustein, to have gone to him, no she better keep still about that. No one need ever know any more than they did already.

On Sunday, Carl came to breakfast with his hair combed and carefully parted and slicked with water. He had on the clean jeans and shirt reserved for Monday school. Mattie raised a surprised eyebrow, then smiled at him. "You going to church?"

"Thought I might." He frowned out the window. "Nice enough day."

He was twelve, going on twenty. "Well, fine." She smiled again at his obvious relief not to have to fight for it.

"Me too, Mama!" Duane yelled. "Can't we all go?"

"Ask Carl, he'll have to look out for you."

"Sure, Duane, you can come, why not? I can't carry you though, and you'll have to set still."

In the end Jem, though less keen on it, decided to change his shirt and go, too. Mattie found herself standing alone in the kitchen. She poured herself another cup of the coffee she allowed herself on Sundays, took it to the porch, sat in the old hard rocking chair to drink it. I better get started on them tomatoes, like I planned – but she didn't get up. I ain't been alone since the day I hid, waiting for David to get me.

Mattie waved a hand in disbelief, as if the thought were attached to a fly.

I been alone a lot, I been alone since –

Not without a child somewhere, you ain't. Not without Charlie or Forrest in the next field or row, not without Hazel or Hannah upstairs or out hanging wash.

It wasn't possible to can tomatoes with such a thought in her head.

Asters and ironweed filled the meadow below the pond, all shades of purple, and she meant only to go pick some. When she got to the pond she meant only to follow the track around the base of the hill back to the clearing, that Forrest was thinking about re-clearing and planting again. The road was washed out and overgrown but still supplied the idea of a path to her feet, and before she was aware she'd gone that far, she stood gazing at the wrecked hillside.

She walked up along the steep edge, along the woods. David's work was barely distinguishable as orchard, but still there seemed a path here, and she could even see, here and there out over the slope, a few tropical looking peach trees among berry brambles and locust seedlings and root sprouts. She headed toward one, to see if some peaches might be hanging still, but got so quickly scratched by the brambles she turned back again to the woods. Before really deciding to do so she found she was following a path. She stopped: was this one of those paths folks said could shift and turn, and disappear?

She waved a hand as she had on the porch. She knew where she was, this wasn't like the wilderness Wendell Miller talked about, not his beloved Yosemite he'd discovered on his trip to visit Mary. She had only to cut down across the front of this hill, and she'd run smack into the springhouse, path or no path.

But she didn't turn off the path, which wandered on up across the hill. On a rocky stretch it did sure enough disappear but that was the way with deer trails. She paused on the edge of the rock outbreak to catch her breath, and saw five doe moving below her, browsing, unaware of her. She watched until they were out of sight, then crept carefully down the rocks so as not to turn an ankle, and began walking more quickly. She wasn't sure she could find him from this direction, and whether she did or not she'd have to hurry to get clear over this hill and into the far ridge and back before church was over and the boys were home.

Cora Miller's wedding the next spring was a legendary festivity almost before the vows were spoken. There was no discord in the house over this one; the perfections of Ed Lakin were so agreed upon Hazel had to joke quietly with Mattie about it to keep him human. As fine a teacher as the school had ever had, he was handsome; rather stern but not heavy browed. Careful about his person, he wasn't fussy or vain; he was unfailingly polite to everyone, even to Grant Simpson who at first demanded to pass approval on every bit of reading used in every lesson. He had coached Hannah so well at her chess game that she now could sometimes beat Wendell when he came home. Ed lived during the week in the cottage next to the school, and was neither helpless at keeping house nor above appreciating meals offered at his pupils' homes. Weekends and holidays he traveled several hours to bury himself in a library, but it had been no secret for the past year that he'd arranged his trips to cross paths with Corie either in town where she was working or at the Millers when she came home. He was not known to drink, or smoke, or gamble.

"And I finally caught the look in his eye I been waiting for," Hazel told Mattie after the engagement was announced.

"Ain't he always looked kindly at Corie?"

"Oh kindly, yes. With approval, well, how could you not?"

Mattie glanced up from the shirt she was ironing, with a mischievous smile. "Mrs. Simpson says she'd ought to tame her hair, what I heard."

Hazel laughed. "All right then, I guess it's possible to find fault with even beauty and cheerfulness."

"What look, then?"

"A little lust, Mattie. A little fear." Hazel shook a towel from the basket for folding. "A little passion, for God's sake!"

Mattie covered her startled blush by turning to put the iron behind her to heat on the stove, and concentrated on folding the shirt. By the time she had unrolled another damp blouse ready for her iron, she had banished Benjamin's face from her mind. – My name is Benjamin, he had said on her second visit, and on her third had offered yes a little lust, a little passion; on her fourth or was it fifth, she had walked knowingly into it, a patient, gentle loving so different from David's joyful coupling as to be a different act altogether.

"Are Mary and Lloyd comin'?"

"I'm still hoping for it. Our first two grandchildren, and we've still to meet them."

Corie happily browsed through catalogues and shops, taking her time with details, accommodating every suggestion, laboring hours over the dresses, sharing the event with anyone. And nearly everyone wanted some part in it, for Corie was a beloved girl turning woman with grace and enthusiasm.

And so they had to open the church doors and windows, and praise God for the sunny day, as a good third of the guests stood outside and leaned around each other's shoulders to get a glimpse as Corie was lifted down from the buggy by her father and walked with perfect blend of happy solemnity into the church and up to the crowded front. Her brothers Wendell, Charlie, and Philip stood with Ed at the railing, while her sisters Hannah and Esther processed in front of the bride, and Louisa carried a basket of flowers beside Duane with the rings on a cushion. Mary could not come.

Mattie sat with Carl and Jem pulled in as tight as they would allow on either side of her, in the pew right behind Hazel and Aunt Millie. She hadn't meant to come, since there was still so much to do at the house, but Corie had made her a dress. With buttons in the front, and just a hint of puff in the sleeves, the blue dress was a dream of comfort. Mattie felt dressed just right, and her pride at the sight of Duane walking up the center with a frown of concentration, and of Louisa, for once sedate beside him, turned her completely unmindful of her self so unaccountably sitting in a church, in a crowd.

Charlie drove a wagon full of folks back to the farm. "I *didn't* drop the rings, did I?" Duane whispered in Mattie's ear. "Indeed, you did not. You went walkin' up that aisle as smooth as water."

On a Sunday, Mattie was coming across the field from the springhouse when a car pulled around the house into sight. Panic hit her with several images at once: the policeman's car; one of her boys mangled or stricken; her own tired and unwashed feet.

She recognized the car as Grant Simpson's and hurried in spite of the increased dread. To her relief, all three boys tumbled out, Duane as usual rushing to meet her, with no air about him of bad news.

The preacher nodded greeting, waiting between the two pines. "Mattie."

"Reverend." She gave back the barest nod. "Thanks for packin' the young'uns home. I hope they ain't been any bother."

"No, indeed. It was me asked to bring them, I've been meaning to get back here, this long time."

Combing fingers absently through Duane's curly dark hair, Mattie waited uneasily.

"Can we go in?" he prompted her.

She moved toward the porch in assent, and he followed her into the kitchen. She hadn't done the breakfast dishes, but at least they were stacked in the round pan, so the table was cleared.

"Go on and change," she dismissed the boys, and gestured Rev. Simpson to a chair. He sat, and lay a Bible on the table.

"It's been a great joy to me, the sight of your boys coming into the church. A great joy to me. To us all." He cleared his throat. She knew it was her turn to say something.

"I hope they been behavin' themselves."

"No trouble 'tall. But Mattie, isn't it time you let them bring you along?"

Her relief made her smile at Duane and Jem, already back downstairs.

She motioned Duane to her, to rebutton his shirt, fastened crooked. "I'll think on it."

"Oh, that's good, Mattie!" Clearly, he'd expected some more troublesome response. "Here, I've brought you this." He touched the Bible. "If you truly have an open heart, it'll guide your thinking."

She reached up and took a sugar bowl from the top shelf of the cabinet. "How much would that be, then?"

"No, you don't need to buy this."

"I can't let you loan it," she said firmly. "What with three boys spillin' milk and trackin' mud, I couldn't promise –"

"But it's yours, I mean."

She laid the lid of the pottery jar aside on the table. "Well. I don't mind it being ours, if you got it to spare, and let us buy it."

"I certainly will not let you buy it." He stood up, pushing the soft-covered book closer to her. "It's for you, and the boys."

Mattie had a powerful urge to throw it at him, but was stopped by the eager look in Duane's eyes. "Well, then. This one he does dearly love to read," she conceded. "So here, you just take this for the plate, then." She separated a dollar bill from the coins and laid it on the Bible.

"All right, I'll do it. The widow's mite is dear to the Lord, we know that truly from the Book itself."

Mattie's mouth dropped open a little at that. A *mite?* She'd meant to overpay, to humble his righteous generosity, and watched with new anger and regret the bill disappear into his trouser pocket. And then nearly laughed: Benjamin would tell her it served her right.

"I ain't goin' to church," Jem said one Sunday in July. "I'm too tired."

Carl laughed. "There ain't nothin' wrong with restin' in church, Uncle Forrest does it all the time."

"You feeling sick?" Mattie focused on Jem, pushing aside the thought: not alone. "We been workin' pretty hard in the cherries."

Jem shook his head, and Carl leaned forward. "That ain't right, Jem, you don't just go to church when you feel like it."

"Stop tellin' me what to do!"

"I'm just tellin' you what's right."

"Here now." Mattie intervened. "What's this new thing with you two quarreling all the time? Don't seem right to fight about goin' to church."

Carl pushed impatiently at his plate. "How would you know? You won't make him go, you don't even –"

Jem leaped around the corner of the table and was on him, toppling the chair under them both. Almost as quickly Mattie was beside them, and pulled Jem up, shaking him a little as she pushed him back toward the table.

"Now you set down."

"I'm going."

"No you ain't."

He winced at her tone, and righted the chair, and sat.

"You two fight like that behind my back?"

"Just tell him to leave me alone," Jem said, holding back tears.

"I ain't tellin' him," she answered. "Not 'til you tell me how come you flew at him like that."

When the brothers glanced at each other, Mattie recognized the loyalty under the anger and nearly staggered with the sense of her exclusion, and guilt. Where has her mind been, this last half year and more, while they've been raising themselves?

She sat down beside Carl, across from Jem. "You better tell me, one of you."

Carl avoided Jem's eyes. "Ma, you believe in God?"

"What?" The question, in those terms, had never occurred to her. Benjamin liked to talk about what he called the nature of god, the divine, but he never put it in terms of belief.

"It's just that – some people – I mean –" Carl gave up and simply asked it again. "You believe in God?"

"Well, of course I do. I mean, God just is, ain't He?"

Duane pounded a fist triumphantly on the table. "I told you so!"

Mattie looked from one face to another. "I don't understand what this is about."

"It's Paul Simpson," Duane said. "He's been tryin to say you don't and that's how come –"

"Duane, hush yer mouth."

Carl's low snarl was sufficient. Duane sank back in his chair, pale with mortification.

"Well, I never. You mean to tell me you're fightin' over me?" Mattie wanted to laugh, but something hurt in her chest. "You'd be doing me a kindness now, boys, to tell me what you're talking about."

"It's only Paul's meanness, it don't mean nothin'."

"I don't believe in God, and that's how come what?" She was determined to hear it out, and looked so steadily at Jem he finally bit his lip, but spoke.

"Just how come you walk alone in the woods, instead of comin' to church, is all. He said in olden times you'd be, you know. . . ."

"What?"

"A witch. That's just what he said, Mama, just makin' it up."

"Do you walk in the woods, Mama?" Duane asked.

"Who says so? If I'm alone, who can say so? And what harm is it if I do?"

Duane shrugged.

"Well then. If that's the sort of thing you hear out there, maybe you better all just stay here and rest today, after all." Carl looked uncomfortable, but she made her face stern, her mind made up. "The preacher he'll understand, it being cherry season and all. Go put your everyday shirts on. Help me pick some beans, and you can do whatever you want."

Several times in the following week Forrest hinted that Mattie was
working harder than she needed to, and finally chided her directly.
"You're pushing the boys too hard at the picking, Mattie. There's no
such hurry as you seem to be in."

Mattie looked up at Carl and Jem on their ladders, in surprise. "I
never said a thing to 'em."

"They're trying to match you, woman, and you look all beat. It's
thunderin' hot. You don't have to pick all the trees, single-handed."

"Carl," she called into the tree. "You two ready to quit for the
day?"

She was taken aback by their instant descent. "Really?" Jem said.
"We could go over to Sam's, they've dammed up a swimmin' hole."

"Well then, git. I'll just finish this tree, so we can start fresh in the
morning."

The work did not help entirely, since her mind was free to wander,
but it was better than not being in motion at all, when her yearning
fairly took her breath away, made her feel crazy. She had once sent the
boys indoors, away from prying eyes, and now she must send herself
inside. If her walking was a block in the path that must stay open for
them, she would walk no more. But here, sticky with sweat and cherry
juice, aching from the bucket strapped across her shoulder, her hands
never ceasing, she could let images of the cabin in the pine woods flow
through her head and pretend they were merely pleasant memories,
not painful loss. She even called up snatches of Benjamin's talk, could
hear the rhythms of his voice as he read to her. The last was a man
named Emerson. Or that other fellow, Henry David somebody, planting
his beans and pitying his young friends who inherit farms and tools.
"Farms, houses, barns, cattle, and farming tools, for these are more
easily acquired than got rid of."

Well, she had laughed at that, declaring she knew for a fact it was
as easy as walking down the road, to get rid of the lot. But Benjamin
had shaken his head, and pulled her tight against him. "No, Mattie, it

cost a terrible price for him to get rid of the farm, a terrible price. He couldn't have wanted to leave you, Mattie, it's not possible."

Mattie held tight until she was sure the ladder wasn't moving; she opened her eyes and glanced guiltily around her, glad the boys had gone off. She had better not think even of the books, then, better forget that she'd ever heard any of it, seen the thin pages with tiny words or the thick volume of plays by the man with the dog's name.

"How much do you know of Shakespeare, Mattie?" And he had laughed, that time, when she'd said he was a black collie at the Millers, but she hadn't minded, because she'd been teasing, of course she knew who Shakespeare was. But she couldn't have said where or when he lived, and had never known he or anyone had written such speeches as rolled off Benjamin's tongue. He had read to her just last month the words of the money-lender: "Hath not a Jew hands . . . ? Fed with the same food. . . . warmed and cooled by the same winter and summer as a Christian is? If you prick us, do we not bleed?"

He had told her, that morning, that he was Jewish. It was, to her, only another proof of his difference from everything she'd known, and of no particular interest beyond that. She was more taken with the story. She thought now she would have to ask him why, if the Christians in the play were so against interest on loans, then why –

When she remembered she could never ask him, her hand jerked so that the bucket, propped on the ladder, tipped. In grabbing for it she tilted the ladder up on one leg. Swinging full on the strap, the bucket pulled her further off balance, making her feet slip from the rung. With a cry, she clutched at a limb, and crashed with it to the ground.

Charlie reached her first, as she rolled to a sitting position and tugged the strap from around her neck. "I'm all right," she assured him, hurrying to straighten her dress around her knees. "Hit the bucket, though, just look at it."

"Never mind the bucket, what about your ribs?"

Hannah helped her stand. Mattie winced but laughed off the pain. "That ground's hard."

"Where you hurt?" Forrest demanded. "Don't walk if you're hurt."

She waved him away. "Just a little sore here in the side, from the bucket. And shaken up a bit."

"You lay off now."

"Yes, all right. Thank you Hannah, I'll be all right."

She had to walk more slowly than she wanted, anxious to be out of sight before the awful lump in her throat became tears. By the time she'd come down the hill and around the barn, she had stopped crying, and hoped the sweat and grime of her face would disguise the tears; if not, the fall would be excuse enough.

"Duane went with Carl and Jem," Hazel said, and then gave her a second look, dropping her knife among the potatoes in the pan. "Mattie! You look terrible, what's happened?"

"Taken a fall. Not a bad one," she added quickly. "Had a careless moment. Dropped a whole bucket of cherries, too." She rubbed at the dirt and cherry stains on her dress. "I do look a mess."

"I didn't mean the dress. You don't look well."

"It's the heat. Come to think of it, I did feel a little sick to my stomach this morning." Mattie pressed her hands against the ache in her lower back.

"You should be home. Didn't Charlie or Forrest offer to drive you?"

"All that bouncin' around be a sight worse than walking, I think."

She set off, after a long drink of cool water, her step brisk enough as long as she felt the house at her back, but soon she slowed. The way had never seemed so far. She turned into Mertz Hollow, passed the empty school, wondering rather by habit than interest what the new teacher would be like; passed Muley's place, with no one in sight, Muley and Anna Jean and his old dad all up in Forrest's cherry orchard.

The cramp nearly felled her. Pressing both hands against her sides, she stopped, breathing in gasps. Lord, it's my monthly, already? With a shiver she realized: not already. Finally. And remembered, too, as wave after wave of pain washed through her back and groin and legs: not just this morning, but for a week now, queasy at the smell of breakfast.

Though the longing to stop at Mabel's was powerful, she knew it was impossible. She feared nothing from Mabel herself, but there was no way something like this would stay contained there. Rather than go by the house, Mattie turned up along Dorsey's corn field, and forced herself over the crumbling stone wall at the top and into the woods, where she could walk the ridge without being seen from the road. Her dress was drenched in sweat, her slip sticking uncomfortably to her shoulders and breasts, and the cool of the shade seemed one moment a heavensent relief, the next an icy torment. Her womb cramped again. She leaned with an arm around a shaggy-bark hickory until the trembling stopped, afraid to go down even to her knees, holding in her head the one thought, to get home before the boys.

Just as she saw the edge of the old sheep pasture with a cry of relief, her body opened. She went down, without choice now, and dug into the soft woods earth with clutching fingers, pressed against it with her hips as the constriction in her chest gave way to steady low sobs and the hot pain jabbed and spread and receded, and flowed out of her, away from her beyond her recall.

The absence of pain was all she felt. Neither relief nor grief could force through the simple sweetness of lying there, no telling for how long, until she heard her own voice say her lover's name. Simultaneously, another cramp wracked her loins and she was aware that she must move, bury the slip and underwear and move, and grief pinned her to the spot.

Luckily the swimming hole exerted a mighty pull on the boys, and Mattie was washed and changed into a skirt and cotton shirt, the dress soaking in a tub of water outside, when they came home. She had managed that much, and tied the soft clean rag against further bleeding, but could not manage to get up from the little couch.

"Mama!" Duane stood shocked in the doorway, Jem bumping into him.

"Have a good swim?" She tried to make her voice normal, but could see his eyes widen further with alarm. "Jem honey, run upstairs, will you, and fetch down my pillow."

Jem raced to the stairs. She heard Carl come in the kitchen and dump an armload of wood in the box by the cookstove, and then he too was in the room, seeing the obvious if not the truth. There was no way, she told herself firmly, that the truth would ever be seen. Not this one, ever.

"Hi, Ma. You sick?"

"Guess so. Thanks, Jem." Something of the sweet comfort of the collapse in the woods came back over her as he wedged the pillow between her head and the arm of the couch, and she smiled at them all, ranged awkwardly along her side. You'll be all right, she told them, or thought she told them. It's buried and gone back to the earth without even so much as a shadow to throw on your path, there's no pagan man or witch woman here, in your way.

On the table the roses didn't look like much, but when Hazel put them in water in a mason jar on the window sill facing south, by Mattie's couch, the dark reds sprang to life. Mattie woke in confusion.

"Hazel? Oh Hazel, I just dropped off for a bit, just a rest, I'll be –"

Hazel stopped her with a touch. "You dropped off for a bit yesterday afternoon, full twenty-four hours ago. Lay still. I brought some aspirin, Carl said he thought you had some fever. They're supposed to help, don't ask me how. You just swallow them." She handed Mattie a cup of water and two round white pills; they were bitter in her throat but she got them down and drank the water gratefully, and sank back.

"I'll be right up. You shouldn't 've cut your roses."

"I *should've* cut my roses, just look at the difference they make in this room. I'm shamed to admit it, I never thought of it."

Hazel gently straightened the light quilt covering Mattie, and Mattie remembered then that there had been an evening and a night, that someone had covered her, that there had been voices around her, but so far away they hadn't heard her answers.

"Forrest tried to warn you," Hazel scolded. "You've got yourself wore out now, with a touch of grippe, or something."

"But who –?" Even as she asked, Mattie knew.

"Your boys say it was the hermit. Again." Hazel cocked an eyebrow and smiled. "I hope he didn't come bearing messages of doom, this time."

The line of destruction bearing down on her crashed forward like one tree toppling another. The dirt from the shallow grave was still in her fingernails.

"Where are the boys?"

"I sent 'em out," Hazel said. "Carl's gone over to Mabel's to fetch some boneset or whatever she sends, she knows more about that than I do."

"But I ain't sick, I'll be all right." To prove it, Mattie tried to sit up, but managed only to hitch her shoulders a little higher.

"A cup of something won't hurt you. And if it tastes horrible, maybe you'll remember to take it easy in the heat, from now on."

Jem and Duane had been pulled back inside by the murmur of their voices, and Duane's relief at the sight of her open eyes made him manic. He did a little circle of stomping dance in the middle of the room. Hazel got up to start heating water for whatever tea Mabel sent, and the boys came close.

"Lookit the roses, Mama," Duane said.

"Yes, I see 'em."

"Mr. Brustein brought 'em," Jem said, his voice solemn.

"Man! but he's tall," Duane said. "He near give his head a crack comin' through the door."

"Mama? How'd he know you was sick?"

How indeed. "Maybe he just happened by. Remember when you had the mumps? I don't know how he knows, Jem, it just happens."

(How come you always hear me comin'? I never can surprise you, seems like, you always know.

Do I? It's just you come out of the woods there when I start to feel something glad open in me.

I'll fool you someday, and just pretend to come. Would you think of me then, and keep comin' off the porch?)

"Mama?" Jem said again. Startled, she opened her eyes. He leaned toward her, as if playing secrets. "I don't care what anybody says about him, he's nice."

She patted his hand. Foolish, weak tears sprang hot in her eyes, so she crooked an arm across her face. "Yes. You two go outside for a bit now, will you? I'll be up soon."

CHAPTER 2.

Sarah

My very first step in Potter's Corner, in 1930, sprained my left ankle so badly it was puffing up already by the time Ethan could set down our suitcase and reach down to help me off my knees. The train huffed at our backs; I felt we must be under scrutiny from scores of eyes, had even a vague notion of bodies scattering just out of sight. In the depot I collapsed gasping on the rough bench. I saw no evidence of bodies or eyes but couldn't shake the impression. Ethan propped my leg up on the suitcase, which didn't seem to help a whole lot but I recognized it as the proper gesture and let it there, adding impropriety to pain and lack of grace. I'm not a beautiful woman, and like to think I make it up to Ethan by being at least unremarkable in negative ways, so falling in public, tearing a stocking and propping the hole up for viewing, was not the sort of thing I thrived on.

We were the only travelers. The conductor had already informed us the only people he'd ever known to get off at Potter's Corner were a couple students who traveled the ten miles into high school in the next bigger town, the county seat. Yeah, courthouse and all, he informed us, but said nothing more about the village, our destination. In spite of my feeling watched, only one official lurked in the depot. He said there was a grocery store might have ice, or maybe Warren would.

"Warren?" Ethan's voice had a touch of irritation in it. He wasn't used to not knowing his way around a place.

"The Inn. Warren's."

I perked up. "There's an Inn? They take guests?"

"Oh yes, ma'am, they got a couple rooms. Food too."

"Is it far?"

"Quarter mile. Well, maybe a little more, out past the last house."

"Last house." Ethan stared at the agent with growing dislike, but it seemed to me the old fellow, heavy jowled and neatly pressed, had to be forgiven. He'd no doubt worked here forty years without ever giving directions to strangers. "Which direction would this last house be in?"

The situation seemed finally to dawn on the agent, who gave a jerk of his head in invitation. Ethan followed him out onto the street side; the tracks ran parallel to the road along which the village was strung. The place was so quiet I could hear his voice.

"Past Guy's store, that way. Couple more houses, you'll see it, big old stone place."

It was late August, with a buzzing heat that reminded me of home, in Chicago, and that I hadn't expected to encounter here. Pennsylvania, even southern Pennsylvania, I had imagined to be fresh and cool, fooled by calendar pictures of rippling streams and dark forests. I leaned forward awkwardly and loosened the laces of my shoe, and sighed. It had seemed a perfect lark, to come find the cabin I'd inherited and spend a week in it before Ethan's semester began. According to the solicitor's letter, there was furniture, and a kitchen, whatever that might mean out here. But I hadn't stopped to consider how to get to it.

At least it wasn't raining.

Ethan was gone an inordinately long time. I was beginning to entertain worries of burglary and horrible wounds when he reappeared, his gray eyes amused. "I'm sure they all thought I was a revenue agent," he whispered to me. "Which means spirits are available, somewhere."

"Not if they think we're government."

"Government doesn't travel with wives," he pointed out. "Can you make it out to the street? I've hired a wheelbarrow to get you to the Inn."

"Ethan!"

Grinning, he leaned down to tie my laces and help me up. Ethan didn't often grin, he smiled more with his eyes, and I wasn't absolutely sure he was joking. Standing up made me grunt with pain, and it was clear I wasn't going to walk any quarter mile. To my astonishment he slipped an arm around my back, the other under my knees, and hefted me up. I hugged his neck and was borne like some damsel out of the depot to the uneven brick sidewalk. While I was nearly as thin as he, I was also nearly as tall, and to suppose he could carry me all that way was out of the question.

"Ethan?"

He let me down in the shade of a huge maple. "Here, lean on mother nature while I collect our things."

"Oh Ethan, I am sorry, what a stupid mess."

He gave me a light peck on the cheek. "We'll manage. I've booked a room at the – at Warren's."

"You do pick up the local lingo quickly."

He made two trips with our luggage. To my relief, I saw no wheelbarrow approaching, and was about to ask him what he had hired when a clackety model-T Ford came toward us, did a U-turn and stopped by our tree. A white-haired man with a face mournful as a basset hound's got out and came around the back to greet us.

"Mr. Schultz," Ethan said, "my wife Sarah."

He nodded at me with a dignity that really needed a top hat to tip. I didn't offer my hand, afraid I'd topple if I let go the tree. "It's Warren," he said. "I'm sorry about your fall."

"Thank you. A bad job of disembarking, I'm afraid."

He looked down at my foot and grimaced. "You got some swelling, that's for sure."

Loading our suitcases, briefcase, our jackets and bedroll into the trunk, Ethan helped me into the back seat, climbed in the front, and the local limousine service brought us at a sedate, respectful speed to Warren's Inn.

It was an impressive stone building with two additions, also stone, which made it seem labyrinthine. It looked to be doing a brisk business, though it was just past five. A pair of drowsing mules hitched to a farm wagon switched and shuddered and stamped at flies; there was a battered truck with a flat bed, and two cars besides Warren's. He parked close to the steps at the end of a long, high porch.

With the hand rail on one side and Ethan on the other, I navigated the steps. Warren, hefting both suitcases, led us past the first door which stood open into the restaurant, and pulled open the one at the far end of the porch. More stairs.

"These rooms are quietest, here in the wing," Warren explained, as if we were preferred customers among many.

Drenched with sweat and faintly nauseous, I sank with gratitude close to tears into a beautiful wing chair, my throbbing foot on the convenient, softly upholstered footrest. Warren was explaining that the bath and toilet were a door down the hall, that his son's wife would be up with some chipped ice. "We can bring dinner up, if you want."

"Can we wait on that?" Ethan said. "But some water. I'll come down with you."

Glad to be alone, I found the room pleasing. The wallpaper, an unremarkable design of lines and small roses, was not new, and the woodwork needed a coat of paint, but all the furniture was crafted from an earlier era, solid and unpretentious. The walnut bed, with a plain gracefully curved headboard, was flanked on either side by matching pine lamp stands; a tall wardrobe stood against the wall, ample enough for a permanent stay. The prominent shades of red and blue in the braided rug were picked up by the print curtains and echoed in the handmade quilt, a basket pattern. Everything was clean, the hardwood floor shining, as if we'd been expected.

A pretty, very blonde and very pregnant young woman came with ice and towels, a pitcher of cool water and a glass, which I filled and drank off. With only a partial view out the window, with a throbbing ankle, with no conceivable way of getting to the cabin and the sinking feeling it would be uninhabitable if we did, with Ethan off god-knew-where tracking down bootleg, with no one to blame for any of this but myself, I felt wretched. I concentrated on that flash of Ethan's grin, the unusual jauntiness and sense of adventure that seemed to have surfaced in him; and reminded myself that it was he, after all, who had dissuaded me from selling the place unseen. Arguing that with capital becoming less secure and real estate values so deflated, it made more sense to pay the taxes and keep the little parcel of woods, he had taken me completely by surprise.

"It's a log cabin," I had repeated carefully, "not some romantic country estate. No electricity, no running water, and for all I know, no neighbors, no road even."

"Your aunt apparently got there every summer, was she some sort of Amazon?"

"She was a Baltimore City librarian." But I had to admit, guiltily, that I knew little more than that. I had seen my mother's sister only occasionally while I was growing up, and had done nothing as an adult to keep in touch. The legacy was inexplicable. The middle of seven siblings, I had never known I occupied any special place in Aunt Anna's affection. Raised in Indianapolis, escaping to Chicago, I hadn't even known about the cabin.

Our friends Agatha and Timothy Barnes had sided with Ethan, which made me marvel at them. "What's this sudden enthusiasm for roughing it?"

"It's not called real for nothing," Timothy, an economist, reminded me. Agatha, a journalist for a union newspaper, pleaded with me not to play into the hands of some unscrupulous land grabber.

We were not in dire need. Our bank, with our modest savings and the mortgage to our narrow little house, had not joined the thousand already sunken by that summer; Ethan had survived the first round of the university's faculty cuts; and the already over-crowded school where I taught second grade had so far not laid anyone off since we'd all agreed to a decrease in salary. So I did nothing about the cabin and twenty acres of woods, and gradually curiosity overcame my better sense, and here we were.

When Ethan returned, with his jacket carefully folded in the crook of his arm, it was nearly six.

"What an interesting way to carry a jacket. I'm surprised every cop in town wasn't all over you."

"I really don't think there are any."

I was about to lift out the quart jar when there was a tap at the door. It was Ruth Jean again, with a little square tin of aspirin. "Mother says a couple these 'll maybe help you get through the night, pain's always the worst at night."

"How very thoughtful." Ethan fished in his pocket but she backed away.

"Oh no, that's all right. Would you like supper brought up now?"

"I'll come down for it," Ethan offered. "Twenty minutes?"

"Did you already order?" I asked when she left.

"You don't order, you take whatever Mother cooked."

I admired the shot of liquor in my glass. "Clear as the wind itself."

"Warren swears by it. He doesn't touch it himself, mind, but he promises this is made right, no shortcuts, no impurities."

"He's taking a pretty big chance, selling it here."

"He doesn't, that's what took me so long. Had to go find the grocer, who, by the way, remembers your aunt, or I'm sure he wouldn't have known anything about any whiskey anywhere. Here's to Aunt Anna."

I took a cautious swallow. The liquor burned a hot spot at the base of my throat, spread smooth over my chest. Ethan threw back the whole gulp of his, growled appreciatively. He frowned at the glass. "You know, George and his troops must have marched right through here, or close."

"George." I clicked gates in my brain until I found the right one. "Washington, 1794. Or thereabouts."

Ethan poured himself another half-inch, raised another toast. "Over this."

"Which side are you saluting?"

"The whiskey makers of course, do you want me to choke?"

"The Federation did have to make its point, I suppose."

"Possibly. Otherwise this nation indivisible et cetera might never have got off the ground."

"As it were." Keeping his metaphors in line was one of my jobs, as first reader of his essays.

"What? Oh." He gave me his crooked smile. "The clock strikes behind Caesar again." He raised his glass again, this time to me, and for a moment my pain disappeared, he did still have that effect on me. "On the other hand," he went on, "if the whiskey makers had gained *their* point, one wonders what would have evolved."

He went down for our meal, and our thoughts focused on more tangible goods: chunks of pot roast, potatoes with dark gravy, fresh green beans, light biscuits tasting of lard, with enough butter for a family of six. We ate every scrap on the heaping plates, and groaned in unison. Ethan helped me over to the bed to stretch out, then went out to stroll the town, taking the dishes with him downstairs. I envied him the walk, longing to be out of the close heat of the room, curious about the village. But the aspirin and the ice had eased my throbbing pain, the liquor and feast lulled my body into languor, there was just a hint of breeze from the window, and I fell asleep.

I dreamed of berry brambles I'm sure I'd never seen, great walls of twisted briars higher than my head. Ethan appeared deep inside the green, brandishing the jar of moonshine, calling my name, and just as George Washington, resplendent in his red coat, rode toward us at stately pace on the heavy white horse nothing would stop, I ducked and found passage, but caught my foot painfully in a vine. I woke, and real pain banished the dream.

Ethan returned, bearing two enormous wedges of blackberry pie. "We're entitled to dessert, it seems."

I laughed, the image of the brambles flashing back. "Maybe that's why I've been fighting my way through briars to get to you, you had the pie."

"Bad dream?"

"Never mind. Odd as it seems, I'll take my pie." I raised myself up against the headboard, suddenly light-hearted, loving the very sight of him, his skinniness, the high forehead and hollow cheeks, the rumpled white shirt, the sweat showing at his temples and throat, the wrinkles at his eyes and the commas at his mouth, all of him. It's a weakness, this still being in love at fifty, unrealistic, sappy, dangerous. I knew Ethan's feelings had long since shifted to something more complacent, manageable.

The wooden porch across the front of the cabin was bare save for two bent-hickory chairs, priceless items in Chicago but apparently common enough here to be let alone. "I feel like I fit right in," I said, leaning on Ethan and making a flourish with my cane. Mother Schultz had produced it for me in the morning, explaining it had been found ten years before in the inn's kitchen, when they bought the place.

"Everybody knowed it, it was the old man's."

"You suppose he made it himself?"

"Likely enough. We tried to give it to Mattie, that's his granddaughter, but she wanted no part of it." Mrs. Schultz, a large woman with a bit of a limp herself from a stiff hip, leaned a little toward me and lowered her voice though there wasn't a soul around to hear. "I guess she'd felt its bite a couple times too often to have much fondness for it."

I'd looked at the cane with sudden distaste, then reflected the abuse wasn't the cane's fault, and it really did help. We agreed to return it at the end of the week.

It was not the amiable innkeeper, however, but Guy Deardorff the grocer who brought us up the mountain. The man was a natural gossip, or historian, depending on one's relation to the material, and no doubt couldn't let this rare opportunity for new material and audience to pass him by. With sturdy round front, he struck me as a copy of a storekeeper in a Tom Mix movie, complete with armbands to shorten his sleeves, broad checked suspenders, long sideburns and bushy mustache, and thick curly hair worn longer than the norm, so that it tumbled just slightly over the edge of his starched collar. He had a 1925 Star Phaeton, with room for the three of us, our things and a box of groceries besides.

At first the countryside was gently rolling, with a scattering of tidy farmsteads and bungalows, but we soon turned off the highway and the fields of corn and pastures got narrower, steeper, the gravel of the road sparser. My teeth felt coated with dust. All this while Guy kept up a steady commentary, pointing out new barns and shamefully neglected fences, homes with sickness, good fortune and bad, fields suffering from the unusual drought. A lot of it I couldn't catch over the noises of wind and motor, but he was careful to cock his head toward me in the back seat when he opened the subject of my aunt.

"1919 it was, she come up here. I'll never forget it, if I live to a hundred."

"Forget what?"

"Why, her walking in the store that first time. She got off the train, same as you folks, only a different train, of course, up from Baltimore."

He pronounced it "Bauld'mer," which I mouthed softly to myself a couple times, marveling.

"Sort of old-fashioned, yet somehow stylish at the same time. Carried a parasol, rolled up, like a walking stick. Long dress neat as a pin, tight at the waist, high boots with buttons. She was a looker, I tell you."

He paused, whether for breath or to savor the memory I couldn't tell; or perhaps to concentrate on the driving. I began again to feel faint-hearted. The scenery was beautiful, but I hadn't thought there'd be quite so much of it. We went through longer stretches of woods, with now some orchards cut into the hillsides, the road steeper and deeply rutted. We stopped at a roadside stand, and bought a few tomatoes, peaches, beans, potatoes, cucumbers, fresh bread and elderberry jelly. The corn, the girl there told us apologetically, had dried up, scarcely fit for the cow. Guy picked up his narrative without prompting.

"So there she stood, first stranger in Potter's Corner since I think the Civil War, and says, Young man – I was younger then, you know – Young man, I need a room for the night and a house for the summer. Never beat around the bush, she didn't."

"Why did she pick Potter's Corner?"

Guy slapped his thigh in delight. "Said she picked the name off a map of the railway stops."

"She stay at the Inn too?" Ethan asked.

Guy shook his head. "Back then it was Mrs. Geigley had a boarding house for the occasional salesman traveling through. Warren and Amelia didn't have the Inn yet, it was just a tavern. Still legal, you know. Old Cal died soon after the Prohibition, some say it was the shock."

He shifted to a lower gear.

"Steep," Ethan commented.

"This ain't the worst one. I bring the grocery van up here, and I swear I minded it less with the horses, that poor truck works up a real sweat."

The woods crowded close on both sides, the air perceptibly cooler. Guy pulled off without warning onto a cleared flat space barely wider than the car. The woods dropped off precipitously a few feet from my door. Neither Ethan nor I could disguise our startled searching glances, and Guy laughed softly, gesturing across the road.

"The house is up there, about buried in trumpet vine, under them walnut and locust."

Hefting the box of food against his ample front, Guy led us up the road twenty yards or so, where six broad stone steps suddenly appeared cut into the bank, and the house visible above them. I fished in my bag for the long ornate key, handing it to Ethan who went ahead of my slow progress up the steps and the stone path to the front door. The house sat facing not the road but back down the hill, a square two-storey structure, green mossy patterns showing on the shingle roof. The corner of the porch nearest the road was at eye level, the path climbing gently along the front and up some steps to be level with the heavy front door.

It was a dark little house, and damp, with low ceilings, heavy beams and uneven wood floors. Dominated by a wood range along the side wall, the kitchen had only one small window instead of a back door, with stairs twisting out of sight. A metal sink, small icebox, rough counter and a little hand pump lined the interior wall. The handle screeched when Guy worked the pump, and for a long minute looked to be out of prime, but suddenly the water gurgled and appeared, rusty at first then pouring clear.

"They say this spring's never gone dry, and I guess it if don't this summer, it never will."

I hobbled into the other room, which was indeed furnished. I noticed the armchair and round foot rest, the dark red loveseat, with appreciation, but was irresistibly drawn to the far wall, where I turned the key in a glass-fronted bookcase crammed with dark volumes, a complete set of Dickens.

At the front end of the room, Ethan was leaning over a table, working open the latch of the window looking out onto the porch.

"Miss Armstrong had those windows cut in," Guy told us. "There wasn't but one in the whole place, can you imagine?"

One on each outside wall of the room, all three windows were of the sort that swung out like shutters; Ethan's opened of its own accord when he'd worked the bolt back. The sills were a foot deep, the width of the logs, which were white-washed on the inside, a weathered gray outside.

"However did she find this place?" I asked.

"She rode with the mailman, went along in his buggy. The Thomases they'd moved off this place a couple years before."

"Why was that?"

He shrugged. "Wanted closer to their son, over in York. Liza never liked it here. But your aunt got along just fine here, every summer. Her and her friend."

"Friend?"

But Guy was already back in the kitchen, talking to Ethan about bringing ice on his grocery run. "You be all right 'til then, couple days?"

"With all this fresh food?" Ethan waved at the little kitchen table, laden with produce. "I'm sure we'll make do."

So we set about making do. We would at least have plenty to eat, and Ethan had thought to buy candles and extra matches. I managed the stairs, found a chest of bed linen and blankets, gave Ethan the sheets to take outside to air. Two lamps still had oil. We both bumped our heads on the lintel coming down, laughing at our inability to see the obvious. Ethan took a battered broom from beside the stove and we headed out to explore the facilities, following the path around the out-kitchen to a neatly tar-papered outhouse.

By twilight we'd managed to shake or pound or wipe or wash the worst of the dust of the past two years from the surfaces of the cabin's floors and furniture, and settled in the porch chairs, pleased with ourselves. Not a single wagon or vehicle passed. The road, though so near, was out of sight and might as well not have existed. A narrow stretch of yard sloping gently away from the porch was being reclaimed by berries and saplings and tall summer weeds. There was little evidence here of drought.

We had cigarettes, a bit of the local whiskey. "I do wonder what my aunt was after, to even imagine a place like this."

"Possibly just this," Ethan said. "This quiet."

Near dark, we were startled by a hoarse barking cough from the yard. It sounded again, then a shape moved from behind the summer kitchen, out into the brambles not thirty yards from where we sat: a buck, tautly sifting the scents of the air. We sat mesmerized, but he placed the dangerous foreign smell of us, turned his handsome rack our way, barked again, stamped a front foot twice, and ran. Down the bank and across the road, he was out of sight into the woods in three bounds.

"I never knew they barked," I said, when I could breathe again.

"This is his space, apparently."

"I feel like . . . ."

"What?"

I laughed softly, embarrassed at my words. "Like I've just been given a gift of some sort."

But Ethan, instead of mocking, reached over and laid his hand on mine. "Yes," was all he said.

I twined my fingers lightly in his. We went by candlelight up the narrow stairs. Ready for bed, I was suddenly bothered, however irrationally, by the curtainless window. There wasn't a curtain, in fact, anywhere in the house.

"Come here," Ethan took my hand, helped me to the window,

pushing it open, like the ones downstairs. Hundreds – thousands, billions for all I knew – of stridulatory insects greeted us shrilly, on a pulse of warm and softly humid air. "Look."

You could see right out into the night, the light from a half-moon casting shadows of trees across the roadway. Like a queen in a castle, I could look down into the woods. Ethan's fingers brushed through my thick bobbed hair and I turned to him, my hands locking behind his head.

"So who needs a curtain?" I whispered.

"Hang on," he said, and raised my light gown. I have never before or since made love on one foot, in front of an open window, nor climaxed as quickly or as long.

Ten seconds after settling with a novel, his feet propped on the porch railing, Ethan looked up with a laugh. "Listen: 'Between the former site of old Fort Dearborn and the present site of our newest Board of Trade there lies a restricted yet tumultuous territory through which, during the course of the last fifty years, the rushing streams of commerce have worn many a deep and rugged chasm.'"

I followed his gaze out over the tangled yard, and saw the discordance which amused him, between the mind's eye and the real one. "Never mind. Keep your eyes on the book, your mind on Chicago. If you can."

With water warmed on the handsome old range, I washed up our few dishes and wandered upstairs. The room over the kitchen, with a window facing south and a small one to the east over the porch roof, was the lightest room in the house, and was furnished with a small desk and chair, two caned rockers sharing a round lamp table, a large braided rug, faded and frayed. Half a dozen framed watercolors of various sizes hung on the whitewashed log walls. I'd already noticed the signature, a gracefully looping L S, not the double A's I'd been hoping for.

I had brought along a folder of my friend Agatha's articles, which she wanted my help in selecting and editing for a collection, and I sat at the desk, meaning to work. But I couldn't concentrate, pulled instead to thoughts of my aunt. I opened the three desk drawers, hoping for clues, found none. There was nothing left behind but a brown folder with a dozen well-executed pen drawings of flowers, which I supposed to be more of her friend's work.

My ankle was throbbing again, so I moved to one of the rockers, pulling the chair over for a footrest. When had I actually seen my aunt last?

Fifteen years ago. She'd come all the way to Chicago for my wedding, telegraphing ahead so I could meet her at the station, but not writing ahead in time for me to tell her we'd changed the date and already done the deed, because of an immigration symposium Ethan wanted to attend. She'd had a wonderful laugh about it in the streetcar.

"Well, that's a relief," she'd said. Her voice was throaty and rich, giving me the same surprise I'd had as a child when she visited. The accent was similar to my mother's, what I thought of then as Eastern but now knew to be more of culture than of region, as they'd both gone through the same academy and Anna on to a women's college besides. "Those ceremonies are so – oh well. Did you promise to obey him and all that?"

I had laughed too. "What were my choices?"

"My dear, there are always choices."

Why had none of this struck me as extraordinary at the time? I had to stop and think why I'd written her about Ethan in the first place. Merely showing off. I had not expected to marry, had embraced my own profession and freedom, yet here I was, choosing and being chosen by one of academia's rising stars. We'd celebrated Ethan's first book and our engagement at the same party. My mother was dead, my father implacably estranged from me, my only close sibling off in Alaska. There was only Aunt Anna to announce my changed circumstances to, and so, rationalizing it as the courteous thing to do, I had written her.

She had stayed three days. Ethan was busy with the conference, and scarcely more than met her, Agatha was in Colorado interviewing coal miners, so I showed her Chicago myself. At sixty, she was an indefatigable walker, impervious to the wind and heat, as long as she kept fortified with strong tea. She had heard about Towertown, and though there was nothing there specific to mark the area as a literary and artistic center, wanted to say she'd walked by the water tower. We walked virtually all of Michigan Avenue, from Lincoln Park to Grant, we did the Art Institute, the public library. She went with me to a suffrage rally, less troubled than I by Emma Goldman's arguments against trying to win favors from the male establishment.

"The vote and a women's rights amendment," she declared firmly. "We need them both."

"But why must we first grant the men the right to give them?"

"We're entitled. I grant you there's a contradiction there, but it's not really a matter of compromise but of redefining what's normal. Someday it will be incomprehensible to young women that they should ever have been barred from voting or public office. But for now we must get it declared possible."

"Goldman's point is, though, that we won't just by voting rock the boat."

"Rubbish, of course we will."

She no more than I had been prepared for Prohibition, the first legislation passed with the help of women's votes.

And she, no more than I, had broached the subject of my father, which seemed strange to me now but at the time must have seemed too obvious to discuss and a relief to avoid. Anyone even questioning the status of women, much less working to change it, would have fallen out with my father, and I did not pry for the details, assuming that with my mother's death, there had been little reason for her to keep contact with the family.

I could, in fact, dredge up memory of only a few visits from Aunt Anna. The February Beatrice was born, and Mother had trouble regaining her strength, Anna came for a month. I remembered a splendid birthday cake early in March for Celia, the oldest of us, which must have been Anna's doing, as I could remember none other.

There were rounds to the shops, which I must have done with Mother or Celia too, but the images were sharper with Aunt Anna. She did things differently. She pointed with her parasol in the butcher's shop, exchanging quips that made him laugh. She must have come in the summer at least once, for I remembered her juggling three pears at a street vendor's wagon, and we ate the one that dropped, sharing bites right there on the sidewalk. She would rub a horse's ears in passing, mindless of the dust on her glove. She bought flowers for the house.

She came for Celia's wedding, when I was nine. I detested the tensions and fussiness of the whole affair, disliked Bertrand for taking Celia away, and for his bushy side whiskers and starched collars and stiff ways. He was always tugging at his jacket, flicking at lint, smoothing his severely parted hair. He was not friendly with any of us younger children, only Horace, as stuffy as he. Perhaps because of this mood, I confessed to my aunt a degree of envy for the poor children who seemed free to run about the streets unrestricted by manners or tight clothing. She hadn't been shocked, hadn't scolded or reminded me to feel sorry for them. "Everything has its price," was all she said, and seemed a little sad.

The clearest memory was a visit when she and Mother organized a family excursion to a wooded park and lake outside Indianapolis. Beyond the trolley, we had to travel a few miles on the train, then pile into three buggies, laden with hampers of food, blankets and bathing costumes. The idea of this excursion did not fill me with glee. I had just turned twelve, had hit a growth spurt; I was awkward and self-conscious, and my younger brothers Noah and Amos seemed to know always how to deepen my misery. I had no intention of changing into my ugly swim costume.

My mother was animated, unusually bright-eyed and chatty, which was poignant to think about now, realizing how seldom she got out of the crowded, overfurnished parsonage. She and Aunt Anna, now that the work of preparing was over, relaxed in the train with each other almost as if on a separate journey. Celia and Bertrand and their baby came, too, and Horace and his wife. Six-year-old Beatrice, a beautiful and charming child, was drawn into their circle, entertaining the baby.

Which left my brother Harold and me. The one bright spot was that he didn't mind sitting with me. A good natured sort, Harold never minded me, nor I him; we also weren't anything alike. He, for example, was completely unmindful of his own growth and awkwardness and ill fitting clothes, or the public spectacle I thought we were all making. He didn't like sitting confined in a crowd any more than I but wouldn't have thought it worth pouting about. He could put his mind somewhere else, like he did every Sunday in church. And this was better than church, because we were heading out of the city, a direction Harold was without ceasing pining for, and because Father's attention was so thoroughly engaged with Horace and Bertrand.

The boys climbed a rocky hill, the men did lawn bowling, Harold disappeared, no one but me apparently noticing. Mother offered to watch her grandson while the rest of us took a gentle stroll along the scenic side of the lake. I walked glumly behind Celia and Floss, our sister-in-law, feeling less appreciative of nature's charms than uncomfortable in my sweaty petticoats. A shoe was pinching.

"Cheer up, Sarah." I had thought Aunt Anna was ahead with Bea. I straightened and forced a smile, embarrassed to be caught slouching. "It will be better after lunch, in the lake."

I went even hotter with new embarrassment. "Oh, I don't think I'll go in."

"No?" She looked surprised, which in turn surprised me, unaware that swimming was any very important part of the day. We walked a few moments in silence, as if she had to think about this astonishing news. "It isn't anything like the ocean, of course," she said. "But even in a pond, I find lying on the water a very special sensation. We all did first have life in a womb full of water, after all."

"Water?"

There was another pause. "Hasn't Olivia talked to you yet?"

I looked up at her with no comprehension whatever. My mother talked to me daily. But clearly she meant a conversation about something, and I couldn't imagine that. Then I remembered: not a conversation, more like an announcement.

"Oh," I said weakly. "Not . . . water."

"Blood," she said. "That's because there isn't any baby."

"Mother didn't say about babies," I blurted out.

"How on earth did she explain it, then?"

I couldn't remember any explanation.

Our pace had slowed behind the others, and she made no effort to speed up. She said nothing until we stopped on a little knoll that gave view of the lake. Then she explained my body to me.

She did not use metaphors and euphemisms, but names, and was so easy with the terms herself that soon my interest had wholly overwhelmed my consternation. She might have been explaining how plants grew, or why they didn't. When we heard the others coming back toward us, I was disappointed, knowing the lesson was over. I forgot most of what she told me, and had to relearn it as I lived, but for that day and long after, I felt a new kind of self-consciousness, not so negative, as if I had a pact with a remarkable living machine.

All through lunch under the pavilion, I worked up my determination to join in the swimming, after all. I tried to imagine, rehearsing it in my head so that I might pull it off gracefully, the change, the stride across the sand, the embrace of the gently lapping waters. There could be nothing wrong with it, or I wouldn't own a costume in the first place.

During the mandatory hour's pause after eating, however, three carloads of college men swarmed onto the beach. From the safe shelter, I watched them begin some sort of chaotic game with a rubber ball, running with knees prancing high into the lake and come out slowly, shaking water from hair and bare limbs like unleashed puppies. Watched with fascination and sinking heart.

Amos and Noah were released with a nod after Father consulted his vest pocket watch, and were off at a run. Harold, who had strolled off again after lunch, reappeared and with some help from Mother found his suit and a towel.

"Take the gray blanket," Mother said, and Father added the admonition to keep an eye on the younger boys. My heart sank further: the adults were not swimming. Not even Floss or Celia made any move away from the benches, while their husbands walked off for more bowling.

"Well, come along, Olivia." Anna seemed to rouse herself from the general languor. "There's certainly no danger of catching a chill, as Leona did last spring in the Chesapeake. Sarah, you coming?"

My heart did a little flip, but Mother gave a soft laugh before I could answer. "Oh Anna, you can't be serious."

Anna's gaze turned from the lake in genuine surprise. "You don't think it's hot? It's positively broiling."

My mother was a beautiful woman, whose face tended to register only mild, acceptable emotion, perhaps from long practice as a minister's wife. From my own years of practice, however, I had learned to read it. The least line of irritation could subdue whatever real or imagined improper impulse had surfaced in me, bring an elbow off the table, silence my voice, calm my step, straighten my back. It was not irritation that sprang into the smile that day. It was fright.

"And even hotter down there, I should imagine," she said. "No, Anna, I haven't swum in years. The lake's for younger people."

Father cleared his throat. "As might be obvious at a glance."

That it was a rebuke was clear, but my aunt appeared not to notice. "Well, for heaven's sake, did I miss the sign, somewhere?"

"Must you have it written, to know seemly conduct?"

There passed between them such a look of hatred as stopped my breath. My mother reached for a drawstring cloth bag at her feet, drew out a small embroidery ring. "I'm comfortable in the shade."

"Sarah."

"The lake is too crowded for Sarah."

My mind's leap toward my aunt was squelched by my father's words. I felt, indeed, grateful for the reminder, as I glanced again at the men at the water's edge.

"I'm sure there's a more secluded area, beyond the changing booths." Anna waited, but when I gave her no sign, not even a look, she picked up her little fabric case and strode off.

"Sarah is not to be left alone with that woman."

"Only a few days," Mother murmured, her face bent over the thread she was untangling.

"Not alone, is that understood?"

She did glance up then, but only nodded, before looking down again.

Father rose from his bench, stood by me a moment. "You did very well, Sarah, not to go bathing. You're not a child any longer."

Just as if the decision had been mine, I warmed to his rare praise. The cramp in my chest was gone. I watched him step up out of the pavilion and stroll off, once more the revered figure who provided for us all, kept us safe and wholesome, who created around him an aura of culture and erudition and grace.

"Did you want to go, Sarah?"

"Me? No, I hadn't meant to."

I adored my mother, saw her as content and wise, her life as perfect. I closed the door firmly against the light of truth threatening to shine on parts of the picture I wasn't ready to see. If I longed to tell her of my talk with Aunt Anna, my sudden yearning to lie on water and feel the tug of tides, my love kept me silent.

Guy stopped as promised Tuesday morning with his covered black grocery truck. He didn't carry any meat, but offered to order us a chicken from our neighbors up the hill. In midafternoon, a stocky boy of about fourteen appeared with a freshly plucked fowl wrapped in brown paper. With relief at not having a live chicken delivered, Ethan gave him a half dollar.

"What's your name, son?"

"Rusty sir. Sharrah." It sounded like Share; we didn't learn the spelling for years.

"Where is your place?" I asked. "Did you walk far?"

"No ma'am it ain't but a little piece. Aunt Bess said to ask do you want a pie tomorrow, the peaches is ripe, she's fixin' to bake. Two bits apiece."

"Tell her yes, sounds wonderful," I said, and Ethan gave him another quarter, and an extra nickel for his trouble.

"Thank you, sir." His gaze traveled over the yard. He seemed about to say something more, but left.

We set about cutting up the chicken, heating the stove and preparing a feast of the freshest foods ever to come our way.

When Rusty came with the pie the next afternoon, we found out he was the oldest of six children, and that his dad would be glad to take us down to the train station Friday morning. "He leaves early, though."

"Works at the cannery?" Ethan asked.

"They start at seven."

"We'll be ready at six."

"Six-thirty be all right."

Thursday evening I was surprised by Ethan suggesting we come next summer.

"It's a long trip for a week."

"I was thinking for the summer."

"Oh no," I said quickly, "we couldn't be away for that long. What on earth would you do?"

"Come, I'll show you."

I limped after him to the summer kitchen. He lifted the wooden bar latch and opened the heavy door. The whole far end of the little room was a walk-in fireplace, still equipped with several iron hooks for heating pots; a rough handmade ladder near the door led to a shallow loft under the steeply slanted roof. A fraying, threadbare rug and worn ugly sofa, a couple dented buckets and a wooden box of discarded dishes, another stacked with flower pots, gave the place a cluttered, abandoned look.

"A den," I said.

"I should have the research done by next summer, I could finish up those essays on the Midwest you're sick of hearing about."

And what would I do? With sudden sharp homesickness, I felt a longing for sidewalks, libraries and museums, public lectures, the press of bodies in bargain basements, concerts, long lunches with Agatha.

"Well," I said. "Next summer's a long way off."

Afraid of oversleeping, I slept fitfully, but was of course deep in slumber when Ethan roused me. Just as we settled to wait on the porch, an OOgah! sounded from the road, and we could see the top of a Ford stop by the steps. Our neighbor, Morris Sharrah, in clean, pressed overalls, shirtsleeves rolled up, left the car chugging and came up to meet us with a friendly smile, no wasted words. He took the suitcases, and had them tied to the back by the time Ethan helped me down the uneven steps. Ethan stashed the box of leftover food in the back with me, for him to take home as payment.

All the way down to the village, I thought of all manner of things to say. How do you get a wife and six children in here? What do you do at the factory? Who's Bess? She makes a wonderful pie, thank you, and thanks for the chicken. I watched the woods give way to orchards, to dry fields of corn, bits of pasture. The road flattened, widened, we were at the Inn, where Ethan ran in with the cane. We were at the depot, where Morris helped with the bags. With another handshake and friendly smile, he was gone, and I hadn't said a word.

We packed our Nash car the following summer with carefully chosen books and supplies, and took four days to make the journey. We were greeted like old friends by Guy's stout wife.

"They say once you drink the water you'll be back!" she shouted.

We went by the Inn. Warren also placed us immediately, his mournful face lightening into a smile. "How's the ankle, Missus?" One clumsy move was script for a lifetime, in this territory.

Heading out on our own, we guessed at some of the turns in the road, but we kept recognizing familiar landmarks, including the roadside stand, where we bought some strawberries and peas, and finally parked on the little flat space opposite the stone steps, around four o'clock.

I had agreed to a two-month stay at the cabin because I was worried about Ethan's health. I wanted him away from the crushing schedule of classes, meetings, speeches and panels and interviews, away from Congressional hearings and labor conferences, away from the political and historical conferences where scholars and diplomats made public optimistic statements and privately discussed what form the impending disaster would take. Proud as I was of his role, I knew him to be spreading himself too thin, becoming too driven. If I couldn't imagine what I'd do with sixty days in the woods, I wanted to see him there, away from phones, newspapers, and deadlines.

We woke the first morning to the most astonishing chorus of birdsong.

"Tell whatever that is we didn't order any." Ethan pulled a pillow over his ears, but I hurried into a dress and went outside.

I was disappointed that none of the singers lined up on branches for me, the song remaining disembodied, a part of the very air. But I caught glimpses among the trees and stepped through the ferns growing in a wide circle on the hillside beside the house, and into the woods. The songs quieted, so I stood without moving and waited. The noise started up again, and I began to see, first formless motion, then birds. I recognized by name only a cardinal who posed obligingly on a dark hemlock bough; nonetheless I was elated by the simple fact that I began to see birds, in the underbrush, at eye level, crossing among the high branches. I was filled with an urge to praise some cosmic force and for a moment I understood the Psalms.

I turned back to the house with an energy that dispelled my misgivings about coming here. I set about building a fire in the range, as the house felt damp and chill from the night. By the time Ethan came down, the coffee had percolated and bacon was curling in the hot skillet. He bumped his head on the stair doorway.

"Nequiquam!" He pointed a stern finger at the beam. "Ignibus aetheriis flagrabis!"

We worked all that day clearing the clutter from the out-kitchen, which we were already calling the study-hut. Taking a break for tea on the porch, we were startled by the sudden appearance of a boy on the stone steps. A small cloth sack slung over his shoulder, he came close enough to address us over the railing.

"My mother says do you want a chicken again?"

"Rusty!" Ethan came up with the name first. "You've grown up, I hardly recognized you."

I wasn't sure I would have recognized the boy at all. "Why yes," I said, "that would be nice. Are you sure she can spare it?" It might not be a sudden growth, I thought, that has turned you so thin.

He gave the merest hint of a smile. "For six bits, we can spare it."

"And pies?" I asked. "Your aunt still making those delicious pies?"

He shook his head. "Aunt Bess passed on last winter." He ventured a smile, showing crooked front teeth. "Baking for the saints, my dad says." He handed Ethan the chicken from the sack, wrapped as before in brown paper. "I was just wondering, um, I mean, could you'uns use some help, with the yard, maybe?"

Ethan regarded him a moment, then nodded. "Rusty, if that still looks like a yard to you, you got yourself a job."

And so each afternoon he came and turned a willing hand to whatever tasks we were struggling with, mowing with a scythe, scraping the peeling whitewash, digging thistles, pruning brambles, clearing sod and weeds from the paths.

Guy, stopping on his grocery route, praised our efforts. "Place looks lived in again."

"We need a carpenter," Ethan said.

"Morris he'd be happy to give you a hand. He's the closest."

"He has a job, I thought."

"You in a rush? He'll work evenings, I should think. He does a good bit of carpentry at the plant, from what I hear."

"I'll say something to Rusty."

"Come on down to the truck, I might have some whitewash stuck in the back somewhere, you can finish that room."

Ethan came back with a can of whitewash and a small sack of flour.

"We have flour," I said.

"Not this kind." He loosened the string and took out a jar of the local brew.

Rusty said his dad would be glad to work for us, and so we met our neighbor again. And once again I seemed strangely tongue-tied in his presence, as if my discourse had become over the years so rigidly codified I couldn't converse with anyone outside the known slots. I spoke easily enough with tradesmen in the city; they and their less fortunate brethren, the unemployed, had been after all my first passion and were now the parents of my children, my children the very breath of life to me. But out here suddenly I had nothing to say to our closest neighbor that sounded natural and appropriate. Ethan spoke his plans, made decisions, and I stayed out of the way. Morris brought along Rusty and his second son, Ellis, and by the end of June, Ethan had his study, with windows on either side, new flooring and wall board.

We went to auctions and second-hand stores, found a rug, and a long couch, and a table. With his heavy black Smith Corona, the clutter of journals and books and papers, the rickety desk chair, a kerosene lamp, a fire on rainy mornings, the room looked like it had never served any other purpose.

On the first of those rainy mornings – the drought had moved West – we discovered a leak in the roof over the bedroom. Rusty, who was still coming some afternoons to work on the yard and wood supply, told us there was a man up the hill made shingles, said his dad would see to it for us.

When Morris came with the shingles, curiosity supplied me, finally, with a voice. "I didn't know folks still made their own shingles."

"Zeke Wilkes does, makes 'em by the right sign of the moon."

"What sign is that?"

"I don't know, but you can't have 'em curling up the wrong way." He smiled, so that I wasn't sure if he was amused at Zeke's ways or at my ignorance. Then, as Ethan turned a shingle over in his hand, Morris's smile deepened, his usually unreadable face turning boyish, with a dimple in the rough cheek and crow's feet at his blue eyes. "He's up yonder, in that same holler your flour comes from."

After a startled second, Ethan nodded. "But not . . . ?"

"No, not Zeke." Morris turned away toward his ladder, still smiling but finished now with chatter, and not about to name places or names.

As Ethan burrowed in deeper that summer, I turned increasingly to the outdoors for my distractions, an altogether new thing for me. A timid walker, I nonetheless found plenty to investigate within the range of my courage. In a used bookstore in a larger town about fifteen miles from Potter's Corner, I picked up a book on wild flowers. The drawings were not always helpful, and the text was intimidating, but while I despaired of ever mastering the terms this author thought were essential, I was able to put names to a dozen or more plants and flowers over the summer. I could find no book on birds, but my pleasure in them stayed with me as I got better at seeing them and separating the chorus into separate singers. I began jotting descriptions in a notebook.

Two white stripes on the wings. Perky little crest, grey lighter on the breast. Flash of rust-red, some white, a black hood like a hangman; likes making considerable noise in the underbrush. Comes right down the trunk head first, dressed like a tiny penguin. Sounds like a water flute, the last to stop in the evenings, first with the cardinal in the mornings.

I began to feel pride in the pages, as if I were the first person here. But eventually a frustration crept in. "What the world needs," I complained to Ethan, "is a guide to all this. Not like that damned flower book, but real pictures, descriptions of songs, distinguishing marks."

"There are Audubon clubs, aren't there?"

"There are probably also local wizards, but I don't know how to avail myself of either one."

"Try Rusty."

I stared at my husband in amazement. "Well, of course."

The boy knew the wood thrush, the catbird and jenny wren, and three kinds of woodpeckers, and suggested his mother would know the others we spotted. "You could come ask her about it."

"I'd like that."

"Right now?"

"No, I know she's awful busy, maybe you should ask her first. Some times might be better than others."

"There's more birds sing in the mornings," he said.

He appeared the next morning while I was still savoring my coffee.

"She says the place is a mess, she always says that."

"Meaning she's expecting me."

"Yes'm, if you like."

It was my first excursion up the hill, which was steeper than I'd thought. Rusty let me take a breather where their lane split off from the main road. The lane was exquisite. Curving through heavy woods, it crossed a creek, with a heavy plank bridge.

"Wait a minute." In my surprise, I laid a hand on Rusty's arm. "There's a painting of this bridge, in the house."

"Oh, yes." Rusty looked delighted. "Miss Leona painted a lot of pictures, I showed her all around."

"You did?"

"I was just a kid," he apologized. "But big enough to help carry stuff for her."

"What was she like, this Miss Leona?"

He fell silent, as we slowly crossed the bridge and started up another ascending curve. Hesitantly, he tried to answer me, apologizing again for being so young. "It was a good while ago."

His voice and slight frown were so serious I kept my smile to myself.

"They didn't come, you know, at the end, I mean even before Miss Annie died. Or before Miss Leona died, she died first, I think. I was sorry, I missed 'em."

"You saw a lot of them?"

He shrugged. "No, not a lot. But Miss Annie was fun, she laughed a lot. Miss Leona, that's the one painted, she hardly ever laughed, but she was nice. I don't know why, used to wonder if you get happier when you get old."

"Do you mean Miss Leona wasn't old?"

He shrugged again. "Not old like Miss Annie, no I don't think so."

The lane leveled off at the top of a knob, with the house suddenly in view. The pasture fence along our left was a flurry of goats, ten or more, several with heavy bags. Rusty ignored them, hurrying me now to the side porch, to the kitchen door. Four black and tan puppies tumbled off the porch into our path, the mother thumping her tail but not moving. Rusty paused, scooping up one of the pups, which wriggled in a frenzy of delight, licking at his face and neck.

"Wouldn't you'uns like a pup? We can't keep 'em all."

"He wouldn't much like Chicago."

"Oh. No, I guess not. Mama!"

The door promptly filled with a broad form. "Lands, no need to wake the dead."

She pushed open the door, came to meet me outside on the packed dirt yard, a large woman, and largely pregnant, with a weathered, stern face, the type I imagined staring unflinching into the dangers of the prairie from a wagon seat. A small barefoot girl clung close to her knee, in a dress so clean it must have been put on her only minutes before, and regarded me solemnly from under wispy blond bangs.

"I'm so pleased to meet you," I said. "I'm Sarah, just down the road."

"Evvie." She smiled a little, a kind of resigned, fond smile that transformed her face into mildness. "Rusty's been tellin' us. Come on into the shade." She gestured toward some maple trees, where an assortment of metal and wooden chairs made a haphazard cluster. "Dorcas, honey, let go."

The child raised her hands higher, clutching at her mother's dress belt. "No now, I can't, the baby's too big, remember?" Evvie's soft laugh gentled the refusal, and when Rusty snatched the girl playfully, swinging her once before settling her on his hip, she looked altogether satisfied. "Go check on Nat, would you Rusty? He was pullin' his wagon down by the grapes, don't let him eat 'em green."

Rusty moved off with his sister, who soon got down, running ahead of him. Evvie pulled a cloth from a line as we headed toward the maples, swiping at the metal seat before letting me sit.

"Nat's only five," she explained. "Too little to keep up with Randy and Gabe, they're thick as thieves anyhow, won't have him unless I force it, and he gets kind of left to himself sometimes. Your roof holding up?"

I stayed a full hour. Mesmerized by her slow, husky speech, I fed her enough questions to keep her talking, which she seemed neither anxious nor reluctant to do. She told me more of the five boys, how Ellis, jealous of Rusty's job with us, had gone off on his own and got a job helping to milk for a nearby farmer. "We had trouble not laughing at him, he never liked to milk here, and goats a whole lot easier'n cows." Randy and Gabe were good help with the garden patches, but of course the most of the load around here fell on Rusty, with Morris gone all day. She hated to count on him so much and him so young, but there it was, she hadn't counted on another baby, though she hoped for a sister for Dorcas.

And the birds, Rusty was right about the birds. Their yard was more open than ours, so there were birds I hadn't seen – chimney swifts and swallows, gold finch, grackles, and a host I hadn't heard. She identified the song sparrow, the towhee, titmouse, nuthatch from my descriptions.

"Did you know my aunt?"

The merest shade of something disagreeable crossed her strong face, whether dislike or grief I couldn't tell, but when she replied her voice was warm, I thought. "They come up here for nearly ten years. Seemed to really love it, though you'd think it'd be hard, used to the city."

"Tell me, Rusty seems to think the friend, Leona, was younger. Is that so?"

"Younger? Why no – oh maybe a couple years. But you know, to a child Miss Armstrong must have seemed older."

"Why?"

"Didn't you know? She was crippled up so with rheumatism, she used two canes. Wonder she kept coming at all."

I decided that evening, looking again at the watercolors hanging in the upstairs room, that all the pictures were to bring the place inside. Not a lady's hobby, but a labor of love. I recognized now, besides the bridge in the woods, a corner of the dry-stone wall above the house, a bit of the rocky creek from the spring overflow. I would no doubt find the others if I looked. I felt the woman's sadness – she hardly ever laughed, Rusty had said – palpable in the strokes. Had she perhaps kept the pain of her friend's pain a secret, known only to the uncomprehending lad who carried her easel? For certainly it must have been hard to watch, that crippling. I thought again of the high spirited and tireless woman I met at LaSalle Street Station, the fearless pace at which she enjoyed the streets of Chicago and Indianapolis, the swimming at the lake. It must have been hard to see it all gnarl and stiffen. And I hadn't been there, hadn't even known it. Remorse closed around me with suffocating force, the very house itself seeming an accusation.

No, I hadn't been of such importance to her, it was vacuous self-dramatizing to think so. But she had been crucial to me, I saw it now, as I might have when I invited her, alone of all my family, to celebrate with me my new life in Chicago.

I thought again of the day at the lake, of the door I'd closed against the light my aunt shone around my father, around my parents' marriage, around the slot being ordained for me. No one had forced me, I'd wanted to join ranks with my father, keep my mother safe, against the disturbing openness of my aunt.

Whom I had loved, and needed as the very air. I could see that now. But at the time, she slipped out of my life without a murmur from me.

It had taken constant vigilance, to keep that door blocking the light. I thought it sadly: what a waste, as it hadn't worked in the end. Even more of a waste if it had, I supposed, but I was thinking not so much of end results as of the energy required to keep my own assumptions and presumptions inside acceptable boundaries, to keep believing my father had infallible knowledge of what would make me pure and good and happy, when all my instincts headed me in forbidden directions.

A scholar who read Latin and Greek, my father begrudged no expense on the boys' education, but was unshakably convinced that the pondering of history or philosophy or mathematics upset the delicate balance of nature in females. At fourteen, I was taken out of school and placed firmly on the right track: church socials, light verse, and domestic skills from the nursery to the sewing room to the kitchen to the parlor. I wanted desperately to study, and longed for my mother's gaze to rest on me a minute and focus, and see my need, and just for ten minutes to forget the endless household tasks. Ten minutes to plead my cause seemed the same as joy forever, so obvious did justice appear. If just once she would pause, and say And now Sarah, what about you?

But of course she never did. I did my reading on the sly. Once Father noticed a volume of Gibbon missing from his library and Harold covered for me, running upstairs to produce the book.

Father had been suspicious. "You?"

"I was about to put it back, sir."

There followed a lecture on no one being allowed in the library without supervision, delivered to the last person in the house who needed it. What Harold wanted was not to study. But no one turned to him, either, and asked What about you? So he took fate in his own hands.

"I'm off, Sally, I'm going."

I could have seen that coming, but I hadn't had the boldness to notice that he'd been serious about it, all the years of dreaming about Canada, Alaska, the sea.

"I'll get to Vancouver, sign on with a boat. You won't tell them?"

"Not even Mother?"

"Especially not Mother!" He was sixteen, but his face in my memory was that of a grown man, his understanding of the adult world complete. "She tells him everything, don't you know that?"

"Take me with you!"

"Oh no, Sally, it's no life for a girl."

I had felt the confusion of a blow to the stomach from no observed source. Surely not from my brother, my friend, Harold.

"I'll write, I promise. Soon as I'm out of reach. A minister! Good God, he's only got to look at me to see what a batty idea that is. But he doesn't. He doesn't actually ever see anybody."

Harold was still up there, ironically making a name for himself as a writer on Alaska's flora and fauna. I hadn't been quick to follow his example. When my mother died suddenly the next year, I threw myself into taking her place in the household, proud now of all my skills. I was dumbfounded when my older sister Celia came around and argued with Father.

"You've got to hire a housekeeper. Surely the church can afford that much."

"And ruin Sarah's chance?" He rocked a little on his feet, his voice carrying to every corner of his library, just as it fell to every pew in the church.

"It's not a chance, it's a needless sacrifice."

"She herself insists on it." And he looked at me, and I nodded.

Vigorously. But I was staring at Celia, drawn up so square and solid for this unprecedented act.

"And if you'll let her she'll fast, too," she fired back at him. "And walk barefoot through the snow."

"You have no right to scoff at your sister, just because she's come to righteousness late."

It was a clever trick, closing ranks with me against her interference, but it worked for only a year. When Father began all too clearly encouraging the attentions of his new assistant pastor, I thought a simple sentence from me would set him straight.

"I don't like him, Father."

"Surely I'm a better judge of men than you, Sarah."

"I don't mean to criticize his character, sir, I only mean –"

"We will talk more of this later."

My shoulder against the closed door was weakening. I looked at his assistant with new eyes, aware now that my father had a plan, but though I honestly tried, I could find no charm in the face, the figure, the conversation or aspirations of the young man. He began holding my hand a second or two too long after coming to dinner, but otherwise I saw no particular light in his tired eyes, and I tried again.

"Father, I don't think he's a bit more interested in me than I in him. I find this all very embarrassing."

"Your conduct is exemplary, but some feelings of modesty are only natural."

"No sir, this is not natural! There ought to be some – I mean, sir, isn't there supposed to be some, well: some sort of attraction?" I was in anguish, but determined to explain my true situation to him.

"He is being most considerate, I think."

I could feel a panic rising, I hadn't expected quite so deaf an ear. "You can't want me to marry without love!"

"Love can follow duty, as often as the other way around."

"My duty is here, to you and the boys, and Bea."

He smiled a little at that, pleased. "No, you have an even higher duty, to your own god-given womanhood. I have every hope, indeed I fully trust, that it will all fall into place for you in due course. You're still young, there's time. But Sarah, I do caution you to look with a clear eye at whatever expectations you have, that Charles seems to you to fall so short of. Do you understand me?"

I hesitated, but finally admitted it. "No, sir, I'm afraid I don't."

He hesitated in turn. "I mean that I would consider Charles an excellent suitor for you. An exceptionally lucky chance for you."

I still did not understand him, but could tell the conversation was over. When the light began to dawn as I mulled over his words, I was mortified. I began spilling things, dropping dishes. Glasses slipped from my grip, rugs caught my heel, corners bruised my arms. I had trouble looking at anyone's face, I avoided mirrors. I had never thought myself pretty, but had not known I was ugly; there had seemed to me a neutral ground. My mother had used to remark occasionally on my hair, with favor. Brush it well, Sarah, it's your best feature. I heard that now as a lament over the rest of me, and thought of my simple pleasure in my thick braid now as laughable. I was too tall, too thin, too flat, my nose too sharp, my mouth too straight and large. Probably I resembled nothing so much as a giraffe, stomping through polite society.

But surely, then, better not to marry. If I could not expect to be chosen for myself, did that mean I had to be party to a young man's ambition? Particularly a young man I didn't even like? And if I liked him, I realized with horror, it would be an even greater evil.

"Sarah, are you unwell?" Celia drew me aside from where the boys and Bea and I were waiting for Father to finish greeting parishioners, filing out of church.

I was a couple inches taller than Celia, and miserably aware of my gawkiness beside her full matronly beauty. I looked at the patterns in the bricks underfoot and tried to smile brightly. "No, of course not, I'm never sick."

"What's wrong then? You walk like an old lady, or as if your stomach hurt."

I blinked back tears, pushed down my longing to throw myself into her arms. "I'm sorry," I said instead.

Celia let out a sharp, exasperated sigh. "I didn't mean to scold, Sally. You're working too hard, aren't you? And bored with it? Sarah?"

But it was clear I wasn't going to open the door right there on the sidewalk in plain view of twenty people. Celia had an inspiration that changed my life. "I'll find you a replacement," she said. "You're coming home with me for a month."

"What? No, Celia, what about Bea?"

"Bea's not a baby anymore, she's nearly twelve. She looks perfectly happy to me, she'll be all right. I'll find you a *good* replacement."

She presented it to Father as a fait accompli, bringing the sturdy Bohemian woman around herself, installing her in the third storey room that had been empty since Horace and Harold had left, carting me off in a fog of bewilderment, pliable as a rag doll in her hands.

Two weeks later, with Father's grudging approval, I was on the train to Chicago, to employment for the summer as live-in nursery maid. The plan was for me to go home in September, but by that time I had plans of my own. If I hadn't learned to walk yet, I had at least found my feet. Although I had not been completely successful with their children, the family gave me recommendation to another household. The new position included some simple tutoring, while at the same time my employers were less concerned with the structure of the children's day. Heady with freedom and in love with the city I scarcely knew but already thought of as mine, I herded my three little charges to museums, to the lakeside, to fish stalls. Everything and anything fell under the rubric of education.

Celia urged me to come home for Christmas, and I did yearn to go. But my father would not welcome me unless penitent, and repentant was the furthest pole from what I felt. Finding it awkward sharing the holidays with my employers in spite of their kindness, I began to form notions of what a truly independent life might look like. I had no models, save one. I wrote to Celia for Aunt Anna's address, and she sent it, but was offended.

"I did not get you out of the way of Father's matchmaking to send you into the embrace of perversity. Take care, Sarah. The eccentricity of such women as our aunt exposes all women to ridicule, and surely is not the true or most satisfying goal of womanhood."

There was that word again, the same Father had used to define my highest calling. And perversity? I did wonder what that meant, but dismissed it as merely an element of my sister's melodramatic style. And anyway soon forgot my impulse. I had discovered the public library, and I was being courted by a dashing young man from the Episcopal Church I attended with my employers. The library had reawakened energy I had nearly forgotten I possessed, and transformed my rudimentary tutoring from chore to obsession. And the young man was a revelation. We were never alone, of course, but he was my passport from servant status into the ranks of carefree young adults, all unattached, all on the brink of momentous decisions. The Gay Nineties was not what we called it then, and I doubt that we would have quite counted to those who coined the phrase. My inclusion in the group was to me, however, like a rebirth.

Sleigh rides, ice skating, afternoon teas: every Sunday afternoon seemed like a highlight. Through the miserable slush and winds of the spring, through the summer and on around again into another winter, the group lost a couple to marriage, two or three to migration to the coasts, to colleges or trades, but picked up others and the circle wobbled on. These were not idle people; I hadn't ascended by magic to any high echelon of society. But they were of a class more comfortable with leisure and high spirits than anything I'd encountered before, and I felt such overwhelming gratitude and love I was sure I had made the last friends I'd ever have to meet. My own young man, whom I liked very well indeed, was still living at home, attending the brand new University of

Chicago, which was ironically both part of the attraction I felt for him and the circumstance that precipitated my slipping from the circle.

I saw some of his texts. His references to his classes and professors, though generally in jest or derogatory, fell on my ears like drops of water on fevered lips: my attention was always on the alert for more. I wasn't even sure what I was thinking. I had certainly no clear intention of becoming a student myself when I finally asked Vernon if there were women in any of his classes.

"If you can call them that."

I understood in that instant the fright I'd seen on my mother's face so many years ago, that fear I had stored away. My escape from my father's realm, and the surprising ease with which I was existing without his blessing, had fooled me into thinking I had broken out of such entanglement. But I understood then that the disapproval of the man you loved, or might love, the scorn of the people defining the rightness of the very air you breathed, and giving you permission to breathe it, was a matter more subtle, more serious, than I had imagined.

I did not challenge Vernon. I froze. I never brought it up again. That is, not until after his graduation, when he told me the plans were now firm for his going East to join his uncle's import business in Philadelphia.

"Sarah, you're not planning – are you?—to be nanny and tutor to other people's children all your life?"

I felt some confusion, suddenly aware both that I had not thought about it in those terms, so immersed in my evening hours of reading and my socializing that the day after tomorrow didn't impinge much on my consciousness, and that we were alone. We'd gone off on a side path in the gardens we were strolling, and were apart from the others.

"What I mean to say is . . . ." He hesitated, and I suddenly knew what he was going to say, stopped walking as if a crater had opened at my toes. I have never understood why it took me so by surprise, unless a part of my mind had known all along where I was headed.

He stopped, too, and took both my hands. "Do you care for me, Sarah?"

Yes, oh yes, my heart roared in my ears. I adore you, I revere you, you are a god. Handsome, and fun, and charming, serious about making his way in the world, courteous and well clothed: how could I not care for him?

"Yes," I managed finally to say, my voice a hoarse whisper. "But not – Vernon, you know I care for you."

He had heard the but, and both his grip and his expression tightened. "You have permitted my calling on you, Sarah."

"You never said – I didn't – Oh, Vernon, I don't know what I thought!"

"Have you – haven't you been enjoying it?"

"I've never been happier in my life. You must believe that, Vernon, it's absolutely true. And I do care for you, a great deal. A very great deal." As I found my tongue, my emotion too was let loose, and I hid my face and sobbed. Here was the path Celia had meant for me, lined with more roses than she could have imagined possible. It led out of tedious employment right into the bustle of Eastern culture, right into the security of a solid income and an impeccably respectable husband. A husband, furthermore, who had reached down for me – for me, not my father's daughter. A husband whom I liked, perhaps even loved.

What, then, was wrong with me?

To his credit, Vernon wrapped an arm around me and let me lean, chastely but gratefully, against him. "Don't cry, Sarah. We just misunderstood each other. I didn't mean to spring it on you like that."

"You'll think badly of me now." When I could look at him again, I felt like sobbing again, his face looked so forlorn. He was clearly near to tears himself. And he said the noble thing, which only made me feel worse.

"I shall never think of you with anything but fondness and respect," he said. "It has been a fine year. Sarah. Don't say this is final. I'm asking you to be my wife. But no! don't answer me now. I have to go East. I'll write. I'll ask again."

He pulled my arm around his, we began walking again, at a snail's pace.

"I do have to tell you," I said. "I'm going to University."

He could have been only slightly more surprised than I was. "What on earth for?"

"Why did you?"

He stared at me, dumbfounded. "It's an obligation. God knows it's all rudimentary enough, with me, I don't pretend to be a scholar. But men have to at least try to understand the culture's basic blocks of knowledge. I can see no reason for women to bother."

I made no reply, could think of none. I would cry again, I already knew that. Even while his words placed him beyond my reach, or pushed me beyond his, I knew that I wanted him more than I'd ever wanted anything before. But for the moment my tears were stopped. I was lining them up: Father. Harold. Vernon. They all loved me, but as a kind of abstraction. Once, women were thought not to have souls, or not quite; now, we were not to have individual being, or not quite.

I could not turn to Vernon, of course, for help with the puzzle of applying to the university, but discovered an unexpected ally in my employers. They were surprised to learn that Vernon went off without me, and though they were not given to prying into my life, they coaxed out of me my determination to become a student. By mid-summer they found me employment with a professor of languages, newly father of twins, whose wife needed help. There was actually less work in this situation, and also the relief of having a plan, and the bonus of getting explicit guidance. Far from seeing me as a freak or opportunist, Dr. Chadwell relished the task of preparing me for admission into the hallowed halls, and made sure my evenings were free for the course of study he laid out for me. He coached me through the admission forms and the required essays, and in May, 1900, I received a letter informing me of admission the following fall.

To save space in the car, I didn't go along with Ethan to meet our friends at the train, waiting instead with such impatience that when I heard the Nash laboring up the hill, I ran down the stone steps and stood in the road. With her usual high spirits, Agatha flung herself against me right there. I had forgotten how the sight of her could make my insides churn with delight. She was short, still petite, her head of cropped light curls not touched with gray, her rimless spectacles seeming to add to the sparkle of her wide eyes.

When we reached the yard, she dropped my arm and turned a slow circle, her face up toward the tops of the tall trees. "My God, just imagine this place in October. It must go insane with color."

"It's not bad for color right now," Timothy said. "What are those blazing things called?"

"Black-eyed Susans," Ethan answered. "They're the only bit of nature I can name, so thanks for noticing them."

Timothy let out his wonderful guffaw. "Thanks for mentioning them, you mean. No one could fail to notice them."

"Which is not accidental," I told them. "Ethan actually weeds and clips along that edge, so they stand out like that."

"*Ethan?*" They said it together, as shocked as I'd expected.

It had been only a month since we'd left Chicago, but it felt much longer, as if there must be years to cover. The stack of mail they brought reinforced the feeling.

"Next summer we'll get a post office box and have everything forwarded." Ethan took the bundle, leading Tim into the study-hut.

Agatha cocked an eyebrow at me, and I shrugged. "First I heard of it," I admitted. "His work is going well, though, so I'm not surprised."

"And you? What about you?"

I shrugged again, which for some reason made us both laugh. We settled on the porch, took cigarettes from the packet on the little table between us, and laughed again when I lit them with long kitchen matches.

"It's enchanting," Agatha said. "The whole place. The study is a perfect touch. This porch, these chairs. Your letter was a good description, but I didn't really believe you. Wait a second." She jumped up and went inside, up the stairs. "You have glasses?" she called from the kitchen, and I went in to find her opening a bottle of red wine.

I took Aunt Anna's four wine glasses out of the built-in corner cupboard.

"We brought – will you believe this – we brought six bottles. Tim, my brave and stalwart Tim, was terrified there'd be nothing to do here."

"Wherever did you –?"

"Oh, this crazy country. You can get wine a dozen places a block."

We toasted the wine makers. "For our own use!"

"We have a treat for you, too," I said. "The real local liquor. We must have doubled the mysterious gentleman's sales since we've come."

"I wouldn't bet on that. Good, is it?"

"Smooth as a ribbon."

The evening was festive. I had been far more starved for company than I'd known. By the time we split up for sleep around midnight – the men in the study, Agatha and I upstairs – I was more than a little tipsy, and feeling that life was sweet, my own in particular.

We drove around a bit the next day, taking a picnic hamper to a spot by a tumbling brook we'd discovered earlier. We lay low in the afternoon heat. I showed Agatha the wild flowers I'd pressed, laughing with her over the impossibly erudite descriptions in my *Wildflowers You Should Know*.

"Apparently you should know them before you look them up," Agatha said.

We set out a full table of vegetables and fruit, noodles and deviled eggs, and settled on the porch with another bottle of wine. "Here's to prosperity," Timothy toasted. "Whichever corner it's just lurking behind."

"It's hard to believe in disaster out here," I said, "with a full belly and a glass of wine and books to read."

"And a job," Ethan added.

"Ah, there's the rub," Timothy agreed. "For you especially, Sarah."

"Why?"

"Haven't you noticed? Prosperity is just around the corner, we're over the worst, but meanwhile why *do* you married women keep jobs from the rightful breadwinners?"

"Oh, that. Newspapers love to run pictures of women marching against women, but I can't believe it's a general feeling. If I can teach, what does it matter if I'm married?"

"It won't," Agatha said. "Before this is over, your sex is all that will matter."

"I should get ready for the ax?"

"Yes," she said quietly. "And I'm not convinced that very many men, even on the left, will stand up for you."

"Aggie." Tim's voice was aggrieved.

"Didn't you just say so?" Agatha flared a little. "Are those only hopelessly conservative voices suggesting women crawl back into their kitchens? As if every woman had one, or as if there'd be anything in them if they leave their jobs."

"It's true," Ethan said. "I've heard it from the left side of the aisle."

"Hell," I said. "I may as well get drunk, then."

We went out the next morning on a walk I had charted on my ramblings. By crossing the road, stepping across the little creek joined by our spring overflow and climbing over a short stretch of rocky swamp, we came to an old road through the woods, now unused but still discernible. In a quarter mile or so the trace of it disappeared but the woods thinned into a meadow, which sloped sharply away, opening a vista of rolling farm lands, wooded knolls, and narrow valleys.

There was general, satisfying acclaim, as if I'd conjured the scene myself. Agatha headed for a rock outbreak a little further on. I drifted in her wake, but Timothy said he was hot, and anxious to start reading some of Ethan's drafts. "I'll go back with you, then," Ethan said.

I joined Agatha on the rock. She seemed unmindful of the sun we were facing, already warming the stone. "I'm going to Spain."

"It came through!"

She turned to me, smiling. "See? You congratulate me, as if an assignment from *The Nation*, no matter how vague and unlinked to promises, just might be something to feel good about."

"Hey. What's the matter?"

"I'm risking my marriage."

"No. Timothy knows how important this is."

"I'm being irresponsible."

"To whom? The girls are both in college now. Or will be, in the fall." Their younger was following her sister into Oberlin. "Can't you wait 'til fall?"

"I am. I leave September 10th. But I have no idea, you see, how ruthless men can be, determined to stop the flow of information. My Spanish is not up to snuff. I understand the American labor scene, but how can I see accurately all the complexities of syndicalism and anarchism and republicanism and Francoism and –"

"Wait. Stop. That can't be Timothy talking."

"It is. Sarah, it is."

In all our years together, I had never seen Agatha in this mood. In a rage, furious at still another deceitful ploy of the powerful, impatient with the recalcitrance of the ranks; elated, giddy, abstracted with the energy of her creative flow, thoughtful, tired, funny; I'd seen all of that, but not this. I had seen her weep with frustration and weariness, had seen whole groups of people aching with laughter at her parodies and quips, but not this. Her collection of reporting, interviews, and essays was due to be published this winter, her work was finally coming to the attention of the pundits, earning her a nod from a national journal. She was clearly beginning a whole new phase of her career, and depression was tearing her apart.

"He's just scared for you."

"I'm scared for me, too. But how can I not take a chance like this? Why can't he prop me up a little, instead of whacking away at what little confidence I have? I'm tired of the fights, Sarah."

"He'll be so glad to see you when you get back, there won't be any more fights."

She was quiet for so long I finally touched her arm, sought out her face, and realized she was crying. "I don't know when I'm coming back."

"What does it matter when? The point is he'll be ecstatic with relief, I don't see –"

"I'm going with someone, Sarah."

"Jeffrey." Tears were in my voice, too, but it sounded nothing like the keening in my soul. You can't. You can't, there cannot be another, I can't give you up.

"How did you know?"

"I didn't."

"It didn't sound like a wild guess."

"I mean I didn't until this moment. I've heard him talk about wanting to go to Spain. But I still don't know what it is I know."

"I don't either. I feel sure of something, but not sure what it is."

"Does Timothy know?"

"No. Yes. Maybe."

We had to laugh a little, in spite of the pain. I pulled her into a hug, where we both cried a little more. But I felt a nudge of hope. If it was all a tightly guarded secret, maybe it wasn't as real as the present, maybe it would go away.

"Jeffrey's going over next month." Agatha wiped at her face, shifted on the rock, looking resigned now, her voice more matter-of-fact. "Tim knows that, everyone knows that. I mean, if you've been in the City."

"I didn't know a month would put me so out of touch."

"He gave a reading, to help raise the money. Read from his new poems on Cuba, which are coming out, by the way. In fact his editor is kicking in some money for this trip, hoping for another book."

"Well. He deserves some success." My soul was throwing a minor tantrum, but I meant my words. "He works hard, and he's a fine poet."

"We've been . . . seeing each other a bit. Just that, Sarah. Lunches, walks. Tim knows that. But maybe not how I feel about it."

"Maybe he does, though. Maybe that's why he's being so dead set against your going to Spain. Maybe you should talk to him about it."

"And say what? We've always been able to negotiate, before. But there's never been a complication for me, there's never been a part of me thinking well, maybe I don't want to negotiate this one." She went quiet, and I waited, not knowing what to say. "He says if I go I shouldn't think I can just come back, that sort of thing."

"That's nonsense. If he wants you to stay, why wouldn't he want you to come back?"

"You lived with your father, and you can ask that?"

"Timothy Barnes is not the Reverend Bradford Collings, he's not even close."

"Granted."

We sat in silence for several minutes, as if we really were watching the little black ants running errands across the rock. Agatha polished her glasses on her skirt, pushed sweat from her temples. "I'm going to Spain, Sarah, I already know that. The rest I don't know. So how can I make promises about what I don't know?"

On the walk back to the house, I agreed not to bring the subject up, and it wasn't as hard as I feared. A couple times in the next days I caught Ethan regarding me thoughtfully, and wondered if Tim had talked to him about the whole thing. But the week slipped by in pleasant diversions. Riotous rummy games, crazed moths finding the oil lamp, singeing wings at the candles; and quieter moments of chess and reading; walks and meals and wine on the porch late into the night. We had baths in the yard, in the little bathhouse Ethan had devised, comfortable in the heat of the day. Guy stopped the van, as delighted for the bit of news our having company provided as we were for the cheese and crackers, and flour. Not wanting to throw some kink in the works, I urged Agatha and Tim off the truck, leaving Ethan behind "to pay the bill."

But we were just scarcely home from seeing them off on the train, when I could hoard the topic no longer. "Did Timothy tell you Agatha's going to Spain this fall?"

"Spain! Why on earth didn't she say so?"

"Timothy doesn't want her to go, she was afraid of an argument."

Ethan looked gravely out over the railing, finishing his cigarette. "Timothy knows a lot about the situation in Europe."

"She wants the story right from the streets, you know that."

"But if he says she shouldn't be on those streets, he's no doubt right."

"Ethan. Agatha's a journalist."

"Journalist or not, there are some places a woman shouldn't go."

No life for a girl. I waited until my pulse calmed. "*The Nation* apparently thinks this woman should go."

I was gratified by his quick pleased smile. "It *is* about time they noticed her. I only meant that it's easy to see why Timothy would object."

"But not to forbid, surely."

Ethan shrugged, looking troubled again. "She's his wife."

Did you promise to obey this chap? I rubbed my neck, to ease the ache. "Wife or not, I'm afraid she's going to Spain."

"And will do a first-rate job. But I admit, I wish she wouldn't."

"I wish she wouldn't, too. But then she wouldn't be Agatha, would she?"

"For how long?"

"She's not sure." I felt guilty then at my evasion. Though my words were true, they weren't the whole truth I could have spoken. "She's leaving it open, with the girls both in college."

"And where does that leave Timothy?"

"Alone," I said sadly.

The fall hardened into winter. Agatha's "correspondence" began appearing not only in *The Nation* but in papers as well, mainstream as well as radical. She was, by all reports, safe. A bout with sickness had not developed into anything serious; though caught near some nasty clashes, she reported no pitched battles. She mentioned Jeffrey only casually in her letters to me, but did a feature on him, interview with expatriot poet, that appeared just before Christmas. She wrote movingly of workers' struggles to organize, of the fervor and idealism spreading through the ranks; she castigated the ineptitude and corruption and squabbling of leaders, but stayed hopeful that communists and anarchists would unite to keep the country from Franco's heel.

Time with Timothy was an agony for me. He would not talk of Agatha, not with praise or anger or concern. He buried himself so deeply in university work and politics that even Ethan scarcely saw him. He declined our invitation for Christmas dinner, taking his daughters instead to the home of a wealthy colleague. It was an uncharacteristic move, but he was more his old self when he admitted his mistake on New Year's Day.

His older daughter Miranda rolled her eyes. "Mistake is an understatement, Dad, but thanks for the material. I ought to be able to get a couple decent English essays out of it."

Her sister Leticia reached toward the bowl of nuts as if encased in armor, and like some mechanical device plucked a single peanut, offering it to Miranda. Randa lay back languishing on the sofa. "Why no *thank you*, darling, I couldn't possibly touch another morsel." Letitia ate the peanut herself.

"That bad, eh?" Ethan said.

"Worse!" both young women assured us, and Timothy laughed with them.

"I only wanted to be sure you weren't being deprived of the best society and all that, you know."

"Ethan," I said when they had gone, "what's going on in Timothy's head? Since when is he concerned about the 'best' society?"

"Sarah, he was joking."

"But he took them there, when we both know he despises that man."

"What are you getting at?"

"Does he ever talk about Agatha to you?"

Ethan frowned. "No, he doesn't. Now that you mention it, he doesn't."

"Is he after some sort of sea-change, or something?"

I had only a general delivery address for Agatha, launching my letters with a wish and a prayer. At the end of February, a reply came to my New Year's letter.

"You ask me to level with you," she wrote, "and so, my dearest friend, I will tell you. I'm crying as I write it, but I can't come back to Chicago, or to Timothy. When I come back – and I will come back, there's something truly evil in the air over here – it will be either alone or with Jeffrey. And I or we will stay on the East Coast, New York probably or possibly D.C. I can't be specific, I still have some assignments and have made some new contacts over here. I have already written to the girls, and to Timothy. I hate what I'm doing to him, but we wouldn't be able to make it work, now.

"Please Sarah, forgive me. Don't forsake me."

119

Ethan had a pass to the Democratic Party convention the next summer. Roosevelt flew out to Chicago, which at the time caused more stir than his speech, but his promise of a new deal for us all was duly recorded. So we didn't come to our log house until July. We rested only a day before setting out again for Washington, D.C., eager to see the camps of the Bonus Expeditionary Force before the veterans gave up and drifted away. The Senate, in spite of the House's vote to release the promised money, had sided with Hoover against it, and according to reports, the disillusioned men were fading from their camps.

We found our way to the Mall, saw the empty structures on B Street obviously once occupied by the men, went a few miles over to a camp on some donated wooded land, and across the river to the most famous camp, on the Anacostia flats, which still included women and children.

"I would rather have seen them," I murmured, "when they were still full of hope."

For these clusters of people, though orderly and friendly, were clearly dispirited. A few leaders were vowing to stay until the government changed its mind, but the people I saw looked caught in limbo between one idea and the next.

When Ethan approached two men and was immediately able to engage them, I decided to try the same with a group of women peeling potatoes in front of a cooking fire. Their smiles of greeting were shy, or weary, except for the oldest, who showed a flash of gold in a wide welcoming grin.

"You a writer, honey?"

"No, I'm afraid I'm not. But I do think your cause is just," I added, to make amends for my uselessness.

"Just or not," she said, tossing a spud into a pan of water and reaching for another. "hit's lost." The metal dishpan of peelings sat square on her broad lap. "Set down, if you don't mind the box."

I looked across the path to Ethan, still interested in his conversation, and accepted the packing crate a younger woman rose from.

"What will you do now?"

A low ripple of bitter laughter flowed through the women. "Starve here or starve t'home, it's pretty much the same, ain't it," said one. Her accent was so different from the older woman's I looked at her in some surprise.

"You're not all from the same place?"

"It don't pay to be clannish," the older woman said. "These is all my young'uns, every one."

The other women shifted self-consciously, then began to tell me where they had journeyed from, what the trains had been like. Nebraska, Iowa, Kentucky, Tennessee. Their voices held me spell-bound, as if caught in some powerful liturgy. But there was no shaking the sadness that filled me. It was not a liturgy of hope.

"Reason I thought you was maybe a writer," the mothering figure said, "there was one come just yesterday. Didn't look like you, but was sort of like you, know what I mean? Said she wrote for magazines, little bit of a thing, light hair."

"Short bobbed," a younger woman said. "I'm gettin' mine lopped if I have to do it myself."

"She about my age?" It couldn't be, of course, she was in New York.

"I'd say so. Why?"

"I know a writer would be interested, but I don't think she's here."

"Wait now, she give me a card." The woman reached under her apron for the pocket of her worn cotton dress. "Said if I wrote her an address when I get back to one, she'd see I got what she wrote. Think she really would?"

I looked at the card, gave it back. "Yes, I'm certain of it. Agatha Barnes means what she says. Just yesterday, this was?"

The next two days I looked for her in every restaurant we visited, every street corner we passed. We even called a few hotels, then gave it up.

We had a box in the village post office now, which had moved from the railroad depot to a house across from the grocery store, but July passed without the letter I hoped for, from Agatha. I hadn't heard from her since May, when she'd written to say she and Jeffrey were in New York; she'd found work there with a new magazine as well as writing free lance. Even Life Magazine was turning a blind eye to her known political leanings and asking for text. She'd sounded happy, and my reply had been happy, skirting the question of ever seeing her again, ignoring the burning loneliness I felt for her.

Agatha and I had met thirty years before, in an early-American literature class at the University. It was impossible not to spot each other, the only blouses among the curving rising rows of jackets and ties. We had both tried to emphasize our seriousness by dressing sternly, with the result that Agatha looked like a tiny under-age mill girl, and I like a half-starved one. By the middle of that first term, we were laughing together at our naïveté in supposing we could blend in, and then laughing again over the fact we neither of us had many wardrobe options. We took a room together in a mostly Jewish immigrant community just south of the university. I got a job in a Center there, teaching evening English classes, feeling very much like I had found my vocation for life.

I was tired most of the time, and cold a lot, and often frightened by the harshness of the streets, the desperate squalor of the tenements. But I recognized my freedom in the very otherness that frightened. If the experience in the comfortable suburbs had been a rebirth, I didn't know what to call this, an awakening of an entirely different sort. Old assumptions dropped away as painlessly as molted feathers. I learned far more from my students than they from me. The vivid images they drew for me of their "old" countries and home villages, in their brave English, would have tipped the balance without anything more, but there was more, much more. Released at last from the claustrophobia of the crowded parsonage, which I had come so close to exchanging for a different confinement, I discovered an explosion of idea in the air, and I began thinking about larger pictures of social and economic justice than had ever crossed my vision before.

As my confidence in my abilities grew, so did my frustration. I sat through classes as if shrouded in invisibility, received the barest nods for exams and essays returned with passing grades and no comment, and in spite of loving the work, the libraries, the very Gothic halls themselves, never lost the feeling that I looked upon it all with an outsider's oblique gaze. The yearning for full membership sometimes boiled into a rage, deftly smoothed by Agatha. She taught me to study the offending professor or student closely enough to devise one well-aimed curse. One pompous ego I sent into obscurity, another into obesity, a third into baldness. I had no way to check on these consignments but was comforted by them nonetheless.

Though closer to the goal than I, and a more apt scholar, Agatha dropped out of classes to write full time, piecing together a precarious living from reporting. She was in the thick of every police action at labor rallies, she wrote firsthand accounts of thugs breaking up meetings, she seemed right beside every arrested organizer, every threatened women's rights advocate. We went together to hear Emma Goldman and Mother Jones; she took me along for an interview with Jane Addams. I got so motivated toward "settlement" work I withdrew from classes, too, and worked for a year teaching in various centers, socialist halls, working girls' clubs and evening schools.

Agatha was patient with my infatuation, supported my commitment to the work, but cautioned against hanging any hopes on it. "A hundred Hull Houses would not make a difference in the reason we need Hull Houses."

"They'll learn to read union newspapers," I pointed out. "And your Emma's speeches."

"Not if your Jane catches them at it."

We'd laugh, and then grow giddy imagining encounters, lacing the scenes with the silly puffery of melodrama, handling our own fervor by tying it to earth with irreverence, just as we kept each other in check by squaring off our heroes.

The year stretched into three, before I decided to go back for the college degree and teach in the public schools. I happened to be taking a course with a young teaching fellow in economics the semester Agatha got arrested. Against all her own preachments, she slugged a cop with her purse at a National Woman's Party rally, throwing every one of her sixty inches and hundred pounds behind the swing. Desperation overcame shyness, and I approached Dr. Barnes for help. He bailed her out, and fell in love.

That didn't surprise me. What stunned me was the realization, barely a month later, that they were lovers.

Not that the idea of free love was new to me. It was in the air, and I was breathing in every available idea. In 1906 it was nowhere near a commonplace, but I felt no uneasiness about Agatha and Tim. No, what startled me was the surprise itself, that I had for a third time been caught flat-footed while people streamed past me at a brisk trot. My father's plan for me, Vernon's plan for me, and now Timothy's plan for Agatha, had all caught me completely by surprise.

Timothy – Dr. Barnes – was affable, and I loved him, in part precisely because he had the wit to adore Agatha. His face and figure gave him at first a rather Mr. Macawber appearance, but the impression was short lived, as he had no tinge of the fool in him. Quick-humored, intelligent, keenly observant, he masked the extent of his pessimism by working tirelessly for the socialistic ideals he saw as the only hope for the country.

But I was grief stricken. Officially, Agatha still shared our apartment, but was rarely there. If I scarcely had time to miss her, with courses and meetings and the three evening English classes, if in fact I saw her almost as regularly as before, at rallies and discussions, still I had fallen into thinking of Agatha as mine. Joining her and Timothy for late suppers, meeting them at gatherings, was not the same as rushing out with her to catch some touring speaker, or sharing a midnight omelet, confessing longings for steak and wine and warm, carpeted rooms.

I kept a brave face through the news of pregnancy, cheerfully witnessed their marriage, and resignedly began the search for a roommate to help pay for the apartment. There was a succession of young women, none of them memorable, over the years until I finished my degree and began teaching second grade and could afford the luxury of both rooms to myself. In the spring of 1910 I was still teaching one evening English class, so was late joining the group at Agatha and Tim's house to meet Eugene Debs. Hanging my coat in the narrow hallway, I could see that the living room was packed; a voice from somewhere among the sprawled bodies on the rug was asking Debs about the compatibility of foreign policy and pacifism. It surprised me that I didn't know the voice, as this wasn't a public meeting. While I hesitated in the doorway to scout out some possible square foot to park myself in, Agatha looked around and smiled at me, patting the broad arm of her chair, and so did the stranger look up, and I looked smack into Ethan Bakeley's face.

In the twenty years since then, the possibility there would come a time in my life without the four of us together had until last summer never entered my thoughts.

On the last Friday in July we found the little post office buzzing with controversy between two clusters of men. One man in each group held a copy of the county newspaper, which seemed to be passing from one hand to another. The voices quieted as we approached the counter, but at our backs, the conversations began again.

"I don't care what you think about the bonus, this is a shameful thing."

"And I say you can't have the capitol of the greatest country in the world full of people camping in the streets. What else was he s'posed to do?"

Ethan and I looked at each other, turned toward the men, not hiding our eavesdropping now.

"Well, he could've talked to 'em, for one thing."

"Mr. Hoover he might as well start packin' his duds, man, and lookin' for room to rent."

"Right or wrong," a heavy man agreed, "he done joined the army of the unemployed, come November."

Hoover's supporter shook the newspaper. "Can't you read? Says here they was only foreigners left."

"Now think about it, Duke. How the hell could a veteran be a foreigner?"

Duke consulted the paper. "Maybe not foreign then, but . . . here it is: 'subversive influences,' that's the President's words. He ought to know. And subversive means foreign, don't it? Communists and such."

"It ain't Communist to want a fair shake, I don't think."

Ethan could stand it no longer. "What's happened?"

"Hoover called out the army." A younger man, who hadn't spoken before, handed Ethan his paper, looking glum and disgusted.

"Marched tanks and cavalry right down Pennsylvania Avenue, it says."

"MacArthur went across the river, burned 'em out, every shack and tent, I guess."

"American soldiers against Americans. It ain't right." The glum young man, his voice breaking with emotion, shouldered past a couple men, toward the door. "This country's done gone to hell."

"Headed for trouble, that one." A wiry grandfather frowned at the screen door.

"Carl's right about it, though," the heavy man said softly. "It's a sorry day when a government fights its own people."

I was reading over Ethan's arm, my mind full of the people we had seen, stung with the image of the old woman with the gold tooth being driven from her cook fire by horsemen swinging sabres. And then I thought of Agatha and my heart fairly stopped. She wouldn't have stayed a month, I told myself, but knew very well she might have.

That evening I wrote to her New York address again, wrote on into the night, at the rough table in the living room, by lamp light. Ethan came in from the study and read awhile, then quietly kissed the top of my head, his hand lingering a moment on my neck, knowing my worry. He went upstairs, the ceiling creaking with his steps in the bedroom, and I wrote on.

I wrote to her without reserve, of our jaunt to the city, my joy and frustration at discovering she was so close, my terror that she was still there, perhaps caught in MacArthur's brutal sweep. I wanted very much to see her, it was a nearly physical need like hunger or thirst. I invited her to the cabin, but confessed I hadn't discussed this with Ethan.

Two weeks passed before the reply came. She had been in D.C., had just gotten back, unarrested and unharmed, though badly shaken by the spectacle. She missed me terribly, but she couldn't take any break now, there were too many deadlines, but sometime we would meet again. "But I doubt it would work very well to meet at the cabin just now, if you are that afraid of Ethan's feelings."

I was rebuked. Justly or unjustly, I couldn't quite sort out.

A colleague from the university who had recently moved to D.C. to enter law school, brought his wife and son and daughter out for a long weekend. Fifteen-year-old Ben disappeared immediately into the woods, climbing the hill, shrugging off our warning that a storm was brewing. The rest of us took a brief walk around the yard.

"There could be a lovely rock garden there," said Barbara, impressing me as older than the usual early adolescent. "With paths going up among the lilies, up between those two big trees. Look, you could circle up and meet that path."

"That path," said Ethan, "is incidentally a crucial component of this tour." We walked to the small clear space above the house, to show them the outhouse and the little bathhouse with its rainwater cistern.

"Ingenious," Dick said.

"All the amenities of home," Ethan declared. "Just in slightly different forms."

"I don't know where Barbara gets it," Lisbeth commented to me. "She'd garden the world. Every youngster ought to have a garden, really."

"When I take my second graders to the park, they bring me bouquets of grass," I said, sadly.

Ben returned minutes after the first sheets of rain drove us inside. "There's a great rock at the very top," he announced.

We flinched at a flash and crack, the thunder shaking the house. "Makes me more glad than sorry there's nothing electrical in here," Dick admitted.

I enjoyed the weekend's festive air. The place was meant to share. Parcheesi games and chess matches were taken up, abandoned and taken up again. We walked up to Ben's rock, which as he'd promised afforded a view of miles of wooded hills. Meals stretched into unstructured nibbling and grazing. In the study, Ethan and Dick hatched plans to form an association of radical academics and lawyers to support and publish progressive ideas.

"Ethan!" Dick was struck with an idea late Sunday night. "We should have the meeting here next summer."

Ethan laughed. "But why would Bergman, for instance, come all the way from Boston?"

"Tell him about this stuff." Dick raised his glass, a sample from the flour sack.

"How many people do you have in mind?" I asked.

"Just the planning committee. Half a dozen, eight."

"Look around you," I suggested.

We laughed it off as an impossible conference site, after all. But they left with promises that they, at least, would return.

1933 seemed possibly the beginning of some sort of end. Unionized labor had fallen off by nearly half what it had been a decade ago, while unemployment approached twelve million, a figure impossible to hold in the mind, no matter how graphic the bread lines became. Two hundred corporations controlled half the country's industry; entrepreneurism, which Hoover had called on to save us all, was a rotting corpse. Our bank joined the four thousand others to close in the first two months of the year. Our mortgage was safe and we managed not to default on it, but our meager savings disappeared, just when I lost my job, as Timothy had predicted.

I grieved for my children, I ranted at the unfairness, I wrote the school board, the governor and finally to Mr. Roosevelt himself. But I had no special case, and I knew it. Unable to be idle, uninterested in inventing housework to fill the time, uncalled to any artistic vocation, with no craft I'd been waiting for time to learn, I went back to the settlement houses where I'd begun, but I wasn't happy about it now.

"There's a dreadful irony in Jane Addams winning the Nobel Prize," I complained to Ethan, "when our government ignores not only her work but the whole problem. And volunteer work is a shameful prop for the failures of capitalism, I don't care what Eleanor says."

"I thought you admired Mrs. Roosevelt."

"I do. She can still be wrong. The truth is, it's different now at Halstead Street. Am I getting old?"

"No. You're teaching people who have had hopes smashed."

It was not hard for me to abandon those people for the summer, when we made the trek to the cabin. With a mixture of guilt and

bravado I looked forward to the leisure and peace of our retreat as much
as I'd dreaded it the summer before. The place felt unreal after Chicago,
where the Depression was so visible. The green woods and untidy but
productive farmsteads, so unlike the pictures of dust-choked homes in
Arkansas and Oklahoma, made suffering in this county harder to see.
The county bank had avoided collapse. The canning factory, Warren
at the Inn assured us, was due to open for cherry canning as usual in
July, and everyone was expecting a good apple harvest. We finished our
chicken pot-pies and headed up the back road to the cabin, with the
usual quart jar rolled in Ethan's jacket. Prohibition was over, but that
was no reason to drop allegiances.

"Mrs. Bakeley, here, let me do that."

I turned, my foot still on the shovel. "Rusty! Hello." I regarded him
with surprise: suddenly taller than I, and with a man's voice.

"Making a garden?" He reached for the shovel handle, and I let
go.

"Some flowers, I thought. There isn't much sun, but if those black-
eyed Susans can thrive, other things can bloom as well. Do you think
so?"

He shrugged, glancing around the narrow open space with a critical
eye. We were standing in morning sun. He pointed to the two tall
walnut trees beside the study. "They'll block the afternoon sun, but
maybe that's just as well, if it gets hot as last summer. How much should
I dig up?"

"You sure you came to work?"

He blushed, his easy manner disappearing. "I didn't mean – maybe
you don't want –"

"Of course we do," I interrupted him quickly. We'd find the extra
dollars somewhere. "Mr. Bakeley's buried in the study already, and look
at this grass, you'll need a scythe to cut it. There's not enough wood for
the summer, and as you can see I'm not a great hand with a shovel. Yes,
I'd say we need you."

"They're taking me on at the plant, in July."

"Good for you! For the cherry season, you mean. That'll be better than picking, will it?"

He kicked a worn brogan against a clod from my shallow digging. "I guess on into apples, too."

"Oh."

"It don't matter." He waved off the regret in my voice. "Ellis he's the scholar, we'll keep him in school."

I searched a moment for names. "And how are Randy and Gabriel?"

"Them two don't care about nothing but hunting. Dad's given them guns already, and Randy barely twelve."

"That's pretty young," I agreed.

"But they're putting rabbit in the stew," he added. "And I can't pretend I don't eat it, same as the rest."

He made an idle stab with the shovel. "Be nice, wouldn't it, to make a curve, like this." He sketched a quarter moon with his hands. "Or maybe two slight curves, like a wave. Do you like lilacs? A lilac 'd be nice there on the slope, this side the lilies."

"It would be splendid. Where would we get a lilac, though?"

"Could try a sprout of ours. Sometimes that works."

"And what flowers?"

He looked uncertain at first. "Maybe coral bells? They like the shade. Four o'clocks?" He warmed to his theme, gesturing from where we stood. "Fox glove, over there where they won't burn, out of the sun altogether. Marigolds? Zinnias? I wouldn't try hollyhocks, with this north side of the slope you just won't get enough sun for 'em."

My head was already reeling from the list. "You know a lot of plants."

"Not like Miss Anna, though. She was a botanist. But I guess you know that."

"A botanist?" I didn't know which surprised me more, the fact or the word on his tongue. "But she was a librarian."

"Yes, ma'am, she told me 'bout that."

Well, yes, I thought, you can be more than one thing.

He nodded toward the bank of day lilies beginning to bloom, at the bottom of the yard, behind the line of plants that would be, later, the bright yellow black-eyed Susans. "The roads 'll be solid orange with them, soon. That was Miss Leona's idea, to get some started here. You know they gave the place a name?"

I shook my head.

"Ragged Edge, they called it. Miss Anna she always laughed at that. Ragged but right, she'd say." When he saw no recognition in my eyes, he added, "That's a song she got my daddy to sing for her once."

"Morris? He's a singer?"

"No ma'am, not much." He offered no more, and I left him to his digging and went back to the house, upstairs to the desk. I had brought a notebook, a rather nice dark red one that lay flat, with three rings that snapped smartly open and shut. The pages lay ready, several inches thick. I filled my pen and wrote in large script: Ragged Edge. And sat for half an hour, looking out the window over the porch roof, watching Rusty dig.

The scene was ironic, an illusion of tranquility. A red-haired boy headed for the factory, digging a flower bed for a city schoolteacher with no classroom, while a scholar of Western history contemplated the very possible advent of a Dark Era. All set in the perfect serenity of the gently surrounding woodland green, everyone as apparently content and peaceful as the scene implied one should be. Depression settled like an ugly-voiced crow on my neck. I felt like squawking, flapping black wings in rage, but the weight was encompassing, innervating. And inside the weight, nothing. My stomach was hollow, and floating in air.

A hummingbird materialized, hovering at the window, tested a few buds of the trumpet vine, and vanished.

I smoothed the page, and wrote: hummingbird at the trumpet vine. Then capped the pen and closed the notebook, giving up. I knew what was wrong, and knew I would do nothing about it. I was lonesome for Ethan, for the marriage. With work of my own, I hadn't noticed how we'd become like two friends sharing a house. Well. We were still married, and him about twenty paces away. His absorption in his work was precisely what I'd always loved most about him, and I saw no reason to change that now.

I sat watching Rusty dig, until he suddenly stooped to pick something out of the earth, something interesting enough to make him drop the shovel and come toward the house, a study in contradiction: he wanted to hurry, but he also needed to pause every fourth step to examine the object. I met him on the porch, and he handed it to me, a perfect arrowhead, with chiseled point and notches still intact.

"This is marvelous."

"What's up, here?" Ethan appeared in the open study door.

"Look at this."

Taking it, he whistled, an admiring glissando. "This is in practically mint condition."

"As it were," I said, mindful of my duty.

Ethan laughed. "Right. It's a fine specimen, Rusty, congratulations."

He held it out, but Rusty shook his head. "No, sir, it goes with the place."

Ethan went still, regarding the boy more closely, his fingers moving slowly over the artifact in his palm. "What a fine historian you'd make," he said softly, and held the arrowhead out again. "You keep it, son. You're a part of this place, too."

The grass was a perfect carpet, wood stacked shoulder high in the little shed, flower beds planted and neat with seeds and seedlings, by the time the sour cherry harvest began in early July. I daily watered the lilac sprig, the coral bells and fox glove, all filched – I hoped with permission – from Evvie's yard. The daylilies, as splendid as Rusty had promised, were over, the trumpet vine in full bloom, and hummingbirds became a regular sight.

We went mid-week to check our post office box, and came home with a stack of mail. I opened the large envelope from New York. Agatha had sent a copy of a new newspaper, The Catholic Worker. Alarmed at first, I soon understood from her letter there had been no conversion, rather the acquaintance of a remarkable activist, Dorothy Day. Jeffrey had finished a book of poems on Spain, which his editor wasn't thrilled about but willing to gamble on; he'd be teaching this fall at NYU, convenient for Agatha, as she planned to take on fewer assignments, to work on a second collection of essays. Her daughters Miranda and Leticia had visited them this summer, they'd had a terrific time.

A friend of Ethan's, working now in the New Deal, wondered if he and an architect friend could come up for a few days. A reporter from Pittsburgh wanted to come do an interview for an article on the History and Law Conference planned for the fall.

"We better get organized fast, we don't even really have a name yet."

"How about: Historians and Lawyers' Organization."

Ethan noticed the mischievous glint in my eye, and worked it out. "Halo. I think not."

"Are all these folks coming at once?"

"You know," Ethan said, looking around the clear space above the house, "I wonder if next summer we should put up not only a mailbox but a guest lodge as well."

My amazement was complete. He wasn't joking. From a lark to a vacation to a three-month home to gathering place, it had happened so fast I still had trouble fitting us and the place together.

"Just a simple sort of bunkhouse," he said.

I nodded, and felt something in me stir enough to begin cracking the weight encasing me. A different vocation than I'd planned, but perhaps a calling, nonetheless.

Morris and his sons cut the logs during the fall and winter, and asked to bring in an old carpenter to help with the raising of the walls. "Tucker he's mostly quit working now, but he still knows more about getting a building up than I ever will." We agreed to it, and when the walls were up Muley Wilkes and Charlie Miller came with shingles and helped lay the roof. By the time Timothy and his new wife Paulina came for a week over the Fourth, the door was hung, the windows screened. We used no glass, but Morris made wooden shutters that opened in, hinged at the top so they could be hooked open or lowered against rain. He had built two bed platforms, a double and a single, advising against real beds, as mice and chipmunks would find their way in during the winters.

As I feared, Paulina appeared the first morning limping.

"Sleep all right?" I said brightly, feeling wicked and unable to stop myself.

Paulina pressed a hand against the back of her tiny waist, carefully, I thought, so that the perfection of her nails showed against the sleek blue dress. "Well, to be honest, that's a bit hard, even with both bedrolls."

Relenting, I apologized. "We'll find some way to soften it. Coffee?"

I opened the iron lid and slid two more thick sticks into the range, covered the flames, slid the heavy skillet into place, all the while aware of Paulina's wide-eyed stare, aware too of the irony of my feeling dexterous in a kitchen. Paulina was known for her dinners. I poured her a cup of coffee from the blue enamel pot, one of our recent finds.

"Marvelous," she murmured. "Where are the men?"

"They're already out strolling." I laughed, then felt irritated: Paulina didn't get it. Agatha would have, and followed it with something equally inappropriate. One "strolled" in English countryside or in city parks. I would bet no one ever used the word here, ever, within a hundred mile radius.

I filled the skillet with bacon, willing this woman out of the kitchen. It wasn't fair, my irritation at everything she did or didn't do, but the only way I seemed ever free of it was with her out of my sight. If part of me congratulated Timothy's wisdom in not trying to replicate his first wife, another part howled in derision and protest. But I had to admit Paulina met some need of Tim's, and was devoted to him. And it couldn't be easy for her, I kept reminding myself. And was irritated, nonetheless.

The little building acquired a life of its own furnished with all manner of things scoured from the countryside or brought by guests. Wash basins and stoneware pitchers, a handsome old walnut wardrobe, a carved folding screen, cots, an antique wash stand for fifty cents, a night stand for a dollar. Braided and woven rugs lay in motley assortment and colors across the rough floor planks. A little washroom was added to the side, its slanting roof nearly touching the hill. The building seemed to disturb very little: the branches of wild cherry, poplar, locust, and walnut still laced together over the roof, the limbs still full of birds and squirrels.

An increasingly steady stream of friends, and friends of friends, drove up the dusty or muddy road, or were met at the station. They came for a day, a weekend, a week. They came to rest, to study, to work with Ethan. Men fussy at home about the proper consistency of a sauce or the lint in a sock, here rolled their trousers carelessly, wore the same shirt for days, feasted happily on fresh corn, fried chicken, plain sliced cucumbers and boiled potatoes.

I felt a real friendship with Evvie Sharrah now, a kind of chef's partnership. Fascinated with the needs of feeding an ever-changing array of guests, and justly proud of her own larder and skills, she shared for a pittance her jams and pickles, preserves and sauces, as well as fresh produce in season. We got all our eggs and bread there, and fresh goat's milk and its lovely soft, spreadable cheese. I learned also from her children where to look for wild raspberries, wineberries, blackberries, elderberries, all in their successive seasons.

Two more girls had followed Dorcas; the last pregnancy had been difficult, and Evvie's once robust figure was thin, and carried as if a heavy weight. I worried about her, but couldn't budge her refusal to see a doctor.

Guy's grocery van stopped mid-morning every Tuesday, with cuts of meat in his ice box, with staples of sugar and salt and flour. Not every week but regularly, Ethan went aboard for a chat, a sweater over his arm; none of our guests but Timothy ever knew where the weekend shots of local liquor came from, and we ourselves never learned the source.

I asked Evvie about getting a good hard cheese.

"That would be up at Forrest and Hazel's."

"Can I get there from here?"

She laughed. "Yes. Just up the road a couple miles."

I'd never been up that way, and wanted her along, but didn't see how we'd manage the three girls, with all the boys working together in the cherries down near the village. So I listened carefully to Evvie's verbal map. Loathe to give up any of his rare solitary afternoons, Ethan nonetheless agreed to take a break, and we set out. I recited the map as best I could.

After the steep hill, heavily wooded on both sides, we passed a lane leading off to the left. "That's Mattie-something. Remember the cane I borrowed? That's the granddaughter, back that lane. Now we bear to the left, this is Mertz Hollow."

The way here was less heavily wooded, with some small orchards and fields of corn and oats. We passed between a big frame house and a large but sorry-looking barn, an adjoining pasture with a small herd of steers. "This is the Mertz place. He's not much of a farmer, according to

Evvie, but he's got the best team around, he's good with animals. When he's sober, anyhow."

"He have a family?"

"Four boys, all but the youngest gone off to the coal fields."

We passed a little school, abandoned a year ago. "And here's where our roof shingles come from." True to Evvie's description, every patch of ground was cluttered with all manner of tools and machinery, and with half a dozen scattered sheds tilting and over-full. "And she says he'll probably have anything you need."

"But could he find it?"

"So Evvie says."

A quarter mile further, we drove onto a lane hedged with forsythia gone wild, which wound through an array of buildings and various vegetable patches. Evvie had directed me to drive around the side of the impressive stone farmhouse; we stopped parallel to a porch along an added wing. A black collie came tearing out of a corn patch, a young girl in overalls and white blouse appeared at the end of a row, and a young woman came onto the porch, hushing the dog.

"Hello." Ethan got out but stood by the car. "We're staying at a place down the hill, Mrs. Sharrah said we might be able to buy some cheese here. Is this the right place?"

"Why yessir. But some Swiss style all we have just now."

"That would be perfect," I assured her, coming around the front of the car.

"Come on up in the shade. Louisa! Can you run fetch a round? We don't have but a little bit in the house," she added, to us.

I'd forgotten the youngster from the corn patch, and turned to see her literally run off toward a stone springhouse, the collie running circles, crossing her path.

"Come up in the shade," the young woman repeated. "I'll just tell Mama you're here."

"We don't want to bother –"

"She'll be sore if I don't." She cut off my protest with a light laugh.

So we stepped up on the long porch and accepted the offered metal chairs, and within minutes the screen door opened again. "No now, don't get up. I'm Hazel, pleased to meet you."

"Ethan Bakeley," Ethan said. "My wife, Sarah."

We were both taken off guard, because Hazel Miller was startlingly beautiful. Nearly as tall as I, she was trim and graceful in a way my hard boniness would never achieve. Heavy gray hair was pulled back in a careless bun, her face was weathered, with full lips and large cheerful eyes. And she had the sense not to apologize for the crumpled dampness of her apron, the sweat at her brow, the limp utility of her simple housedress. I suspected the broken lowheeled shoes had been slipped on a minute before. By nature curious and friendly, she had neither the reticence of Evvie nor the garrulousness of Amelia at the Inn. She introduced her daughter Hannah, and easily got out of us the history of my inheritance, the brief visits expanding to summer, the stream of visitors.

"We'd heard of the ladies from Baltimore," she said. "But never crossed paths."

Louisa came with the round of cheese. I gave over the sixty cents Hazel Miller claimed was enough, and there was no reason to linger. "I'm sorry Forrest's not around," Hazel said. "He'd want to meet you. Stop in again."

The cheese was handy excuse, and in a few weeks, after generously sending bits of the cheese home with guests, I drove up the mountain again, on my own this time. Hazel was on the porch pitting cherries for pies, and motioned me up to her. Someone was playing Beethoven well on a good piano. I looked the question at her as I sat down.

She nodded, obviously pleased with the playing and my notice of it. "Louisa," she said softly, but the playing stopped and a moment later the youngster appeared at the door.

"Oh," she said, surprised. "Hello."

"I'm sorry to disturb your playing. Please do go on."

"Should I get some cheese first? We've some nice cheddar ready."

"Yes, but –"

She was already off the porch. Hazel gave a low laugh. "She's not in one place very long at a time, that one."

"I *am* sorry to interrupt her."

"She'll go back to it."

"Would she? I'd like to hear more."

"She's not shy, just doesn't like to miss anything. Have lots of guests, do you?"

"Only two university friends coming this weekend. I'm glad for your cheese, it's very good."

"I'm thinking to give it up. Forrest's gone so into fruit the cows are really more bother than profit. And my dairy help's all growing up and sprouting wings."

"Evvie did tell me you've raised a large family."

Hazel laughed again. "She's hardly one to talk, she has just the same. Louisa's the last of eight."

"The only one left?"

"No, Hannah and Charlie seem settled here, 'course that can change anytime. Esther and Philip still live here too, but Esther plans to board in town this year for high school, and Philip's off soon to Philadelphia to a photography school. Wendell and Mary both in Colorado, he's teaching, she's got a family, and Corie's married in Virginia. That's the lot."

Louisa came back. The round was larger, and I asked if I could have half. "Come on in the kitchen," Hazel said. "I'll cut and wrap it for you. Louisa, Mrs. Bakeley would like to hear some more piano."

The girl turned to me, interested. She had her mother's direct gaze; not yet past childhood, she nonetheless struck me as likely to be as beautiful as her mother, in a darker way. "What would you like?"

"No, you choose what you like. I'm not a musician."

"Most people here want hymns."

My heart sank a little but I was determined not to direct her. "If that's what you like, I don't –"

"I hate them."

"Lou!"

"Good," I said. "How about more Beethoven?"

I related the scene to Ethan, the incongruity of the barefooted dungareed girl suddenly serious and self-contained, playing a perfect Beethoven rondo at a little Chickering grand. "Honestly, she seemed not to know it was any more extraordinary than picking corn for supper, or breathing."

The next summer – a real coup for Ethan and for the new association – Eb Bergman came for a week to help draft some by-laws. The law professor's world for the most part began and ended at Boston's city limits, and though an easy enough guest, he seemed hardly to notice where he was. His wife Liza noticed everything. She fell in love with the place, declared herself ready to move in.

A large, gracious woman with the round, strong face of an Old World peasant matriarch, she impressed me with a kind of awe I seldom felt. I loved her presence. Fascinated by everything around her, even the nuance of breezes, she made me aware of the quality of attention. She seemed always so still, and always in motion. "Of course, it wouldn't do," she admitted. "Where would I put the piano? Where would my students come from? How would they find me?"

"I know where there's a pretty little Chickering grand with carved legs," I said. "And a very unusual student, who could use you."

"Lead on."

"Yes. We need some cheese anyway."

CHAPTER 3.

Mattie

Mattie and Louisa were taking shirts off the line when Sarah Bakeley came with her guest. Louisa recognized the tan-colored car and ran to greet her; Mattie was glad to stay at the washline. She'd heard all about the visits, from Louisa's chatter, and knew she had no part in such company. She peeked a little, to see if Mrs. Bakeley was really as tall and straight as Louisa claimed, decided she was, and thought no more about it. With the shirts rolled damp for ironing, she went in quietly by the back kitchen door, and could hear the voices from the front parlor.

The ironing board was set up to catch breezes from the open windows and door, the irons already hot on the range. Mattie worked quietly as possible, hoping for the piano, which was the only reason anyone went in that room, and smiled when she recognized one of Louisa's pieces. A waltz, though Mattie could never remember the man's name. She searched for the word. Composer, that was it, composer. She didn't mind not remembering the strange names.

There was a pause, then a low murmur. Mattie could hear the warmth in the strange accent, even without the words. "Thank you." Louisa's voice was higher, and carried into the kitchen. "But would you play for me? Please?"

Curious, Mattie moved to the doorway. Still out of sight, she was closer to the hallway into the front room, and could tell now that it was not the tall Mrs. Bakeley but the old-fashioned looking visitor who was settling at the instrument.

"I see you have a book of Beethoven. Here's a later work, you should get to it in a year maybe less. I'll just do a bit, it's called the Pathetique. Full of feeling, you know? But not too much."

Mattie stood riveted in place by the suspenseful opening chords, felt buffeted by the sudden release into rivers of sound, a kind of melody but like nothing she'd ever heard a piano make.

"Oh," was all Louisa said, into the following silence. And then with a small laugh, "Oh my, Mrs. Bergman, I'll never do anything like that."

"Indeed you will. Trust me, child, you will. You have it already."

The women, with Louisa, moved into the hallway past the kitchen and out onto the porch. "Thank you for playing, Mrs. Bergman."

"And thank you, Louisa, it was a pleasure to meet you, to hear you. You will keep it up?"

Louisa must have nodded, unusually tongue-tied.

"Good, then. Remember to ask your teacher for some Bach, you're ready for him."

Louisa came into the kitchen, sinking into a chair, subdued as Mattie had never seen her. "Do you think it's true, Mattie?"

"Is what true?"

"I'll never play like that." Louisa answered her own question.

"Could be she's a better judge of that than you."

When she looked up at Mattie her eyes were full of tears. "Oh I hope so. I do hope so."

Carl had worked at the cannery instead of finishing high school, and got promoted to assistant to Morris Sharrah. "He knows how every machine in that place works," he told his admiring brothers. "And if something breaks he can't fix he tells Amos Lynn and he tells Mr. Casey up in the office what to buy."

Mattie was proud of him, but he seemed too young for this, in spite of his broad shoulders and serious face. And she was lonesome for him. By a twist of fate, he boarded at the Inn, now a thriving business.

In the spring Ed Lakin sent a letter urging Hazel to come help Corie, dangerously ill with a second pregnancy. Hannah quit her job and went with her, while Mattie tried to keep up spirits in the house, walking home with Jem and Duane only after the supper dishes were washed and put away. She was glad to feel useful again. She'd worked only occasionally through the winter, enjoying the new freedom, visiting Benjamin several times a week, but uneasy over the free rent, without the work.

Harry Kane came by, as he did about once a month, to drink a bit and sit in easy friendship by the fire, which still felt welcome in the cool April nights. He was, Mattie thought sadly, old before his time. He played no harmonica anymore, at least in company he didn't. She told him that Forrest was terracing the hillside here, where the sheep had grazed in that other lifetime, to plant rows of York and Goldens.

"His back pains him these days. Hazel she blames the tractor."

"Wouldn't surprise me none if she's right. Walkin' behind horses never hurt as much. Charlie ever fixin' to marry?"

"What makes you ask that? Lands, I don't know, don't think so."

"Hannah would've had the school teacher, I know."

Mattie nodded. "Maybe so. But she's not one to pine, and she'd die for Corie, I can tell you that."

He poured himself another tiny shot from his flask. He didn't like to drink from it directly, in company. Mattie laid another apple log and settled back with the sock she was darning.

"Jem up with the hermit?"

Mattie looked up, but he stared into the fire.

"That what folks say?"

"He don't exactly hide it, him and that whittlin'."

"Well then. It's true, he's taken a shine to him."

"Which way you mean that?"

"I mean Jem has, of course. How would I know what the hermit thinks?"

This time it was Mattie who didn't look, knowing he was watching her. She pulled the sock off her fist. "You ought to bring me yer mending, Harry, I'd be glad to do it."

It was a deal, and they both knew it. With anyone but Harry she would feel the panic she has known before. But Benjamin was too engrained a habit now, and Harry too familiar a friend.

"Charlie he'd want this place, I reckon, if he was sparkin' anyone." His sad eyes met her shock as he moved toward the door, and his slow smile softened it. "But I ain't heard he is." He meant just to give her warning, and she saw, gratefully, she had not been paying attention. To a lot of things.

Corie's baby boy was healthy, and her condition stabilized. Hazel came home, and Esther after graduating went to relieve Hannah, who had written of homesickness, of not liking the city. When she got home, however, she so tearfully missed Corie and little Elsie that Hazel teased her for not knowing her own mind. They were capping strawberries, as usual working on the long side porch.

"They'd ought'nt to live in such a noisy place, is all," Hannah said. "Esther she'll like it, she hankers for city life. But it ain't the place for me."

The Bakeleys visited again in the summer; they came in the evenings now, and visited with both Hazel and Forrest, and Mattie still never met them directly. Hazel in spite of her threat had not given up the dairy, and the cheese was still the given cause for the visits, but Louisa gave spirited accounts of the conversations on the porch.

"I have to go to Chicago, Mattie! They make fun of it and pretend it's better here, but anybody can see through that."

She thought Ethan Bakeley the handsomest man in the world.

"After Papa, maybe," Hannah concurred.

"Is Papa handsome?" Louisa was brought up short. "Yes, I suppose he is. But —"

"And Duane?" her sister teased. "What about your pal Duane?"

The porch swing slowed to a standstill. Mattie looked up from the pan of beans in her lap, to find Louisa frowning across the drive toward the barn as if to catch Duane coming from his work hefting hay bales, as if to have a closer look.

The Bergmans came again to the little log house everyone knew now as Ragged Edge, and again Louisa played for Liza. She had indeed studied some Bach, and played three of the two-part Inventions, to Mrs. Bergman's praise. The pianist played a Schubert nocturne, which again reduced Louisa to tears.

One evening late in the summer, Morris Sharrah's truck pulled in the lane to the big farmhouse, and Mary with her two little girls climbed out. Morris helped Charlie bring in the two steamer trunks, Mary hugged her astonished mother, and broke into tears, the girls clinging to her dress. She and Lloyd were divorced.

So the house seemed to fill up again. Ed and Corie came for a week, with Esther, who was to begin nursing soon. Mattie was shocked at the sight of Corie. Always slight, she was now fragile, her skin nearly transparent. She was not bedridden but often fatigued, and the women became as adept as Esther at protecting her. Ed was often by her, a hand always in some contact, lightly, unobtrusively. He was more skilled with the care of his toddler son, more patient with little Elsie, than any man Mattie had known before, and was the same polite and friendly guest they all remembered. But the gentle school teacher had aged, bowed with debt and worry.

Esther explained the disease as simply and truthfully as she could to her parents. "It's called Bright's disease, it's a kidney condition. There's nothing – Oh, mama, don't cry." She grasped Hazel's hand on the kitchen table and Hazel held on. "She'll go on, she may even get better, but she needs lots of rest, well you can see that. And no more children."

Four-year-old Elsie was entranced with all the relatives, especially the cousins from Colorado, who spirited her off to their room or improvised playhouse in the barn for hours at a time. Both school age, Marlene and Barbara were still shy of the newly discovered family, still missing the other life and friends they'd known, and were happy to have someone even newer to the household than they were. But evenings, Elsie latched onto Hannah as if remembering her infancy. Aunt Esther was a given, a second mother; Aunt Hannah was harbor.

Philip came for the weekend; even inside, the Kodak was close to his hand. He posed the intrigued little girls in this window and that door, his attention tuned to the light, his manner just beginning to learn the skills of relaxing his subjects he would in time perfect. In Saturday's sunlight he grouped his family in every conceivable pattern of males, females, children, parents, grandparents. He included Mattie, by paying no attention to her protests, and Jem and Duane, and Louisa's friend Emma Lynn from the village, who had somehow got added to the crowd. He prowled through the afternoon croquet game.

Mattie carried the picture in its stiff paper frame up to Benjamin's cabin. He folded back the cardboard to make a stand, and set the picture on the table. "A pity Carl wasn't there, this is a wonderful picture."

He drew her out into the slanting autumn sun, back from the cabin to the spring, a pretty little pool with rocky seats around it, ringed with ferns. "Mattie."

She waited, puzzled by the troubled tone.

"In that picture, Mattie. . . . It hits me now, I've wronged you. Terribly."

"What? It ain't wrong, there's nothing wrong in – there's nobody hurt by it."

"Yes, you. In that picture: you have a right to have someone there, beside you."

"I got sons beside me."

"You're young yet, you might have – I can't marry you, Mattie. I didn't give enough thought to this. Forgive me."

"I never. . . . I ain't forgiving you, there's nothing to forgive. Unless. . . . You don't want me to come anymore?"

"Oh Mattie, no, not that. But I'm standing in your way, you could –"

She reached over and stopped his words with firm fingers on his lips. Forgive him? Might as well forgive those ferns there for growing on the bank.

That winter, tragedy beyond anyone's worst fears struck the light from Mabel Mertz's eyes. A week after a mine collapse, Dorsey brought the bodies of their two oldest sons home, in sealed coffins. Grant Simpson had to give in to pressure and allow the burial in the churchyard. He used the occasion to make a call to the altar, but no one moved. Stiff-shouldered, Sam and Mabel stared at the ground; Dorsey watched a spot in the snowy woods as if to see his boys passing by. Petey had survived, but was brought home an invalid, a month later, with twisted back and missing leg.

Nearly every morning, Mattie would stop at Mabel's. When school let out for the summer, Duane would go on ahead to whatever work Charlie had for him, but Jem would pause to be with Sam a bit, hitching the pair of handsome Belgians to plow or mow. Setting out coffee, Mabel would sink to a chair at the table, and Mattie would for a quarter hour or so share whatever talk she could glean from her previous day, as Mabel was tied to her son's bedside.

"Them's the prettiest horses," Mattie murmured, as Sam and Jem happened to lead them by the open doorway one morning.

"Dorsey's talkin' about getting a tractor this summer."

"Be a shame, though, wouldn't it, in a way?"

Mabel shrugged. "I'd like to know where he'll come up with that kind of money, but it's his business. Not mine. His and Sam's. Sam he's doin' the work around here these days."

Mattie merely nodded. It was an open secret that Dorsey now spent as much time away from his home as he could, and was his own best customer now.

"Jem says Sam's the best shot. But Mabel, you don't have to be sharin' the rabbits he gets."

"Least we can do, with all the help Jem is here."

"He'd do a sight more, if he could."

"If I could pay him, I'd hire him steady, he's a good friend to Sam."

Sometimes Mattie would talk with Petey, in his narrow bed in the front room where he could watch the road, but increasingly as the summer passed, he refused her visits. Only a year older than Carl, the broken, helpless figure wrung her heart beyond concealing.

"He's given up, Mattie, don't think I don't know it." Mabel walked one morning with Mattie out to the road and past the barn, away from the open window. "And I'll tell you this too, what I wouldn't to another living soul: he might as well die."

"No, you don't mean that, Mabel."

"I've fought for him, with him and for him, nigh unto a year now. I'd fight for fifty more, believe me, if he wanted me to. He was the sweetest and quickest of the four, it's simple fact, nothing against the others, but it's so. But Petey's gone, Mattie. It's the shell of my boy layin' in there, and the bitter hate comes out of his mouth ain't from my Petey, he's gone."

As if cruelly determined to wound, Petey suddenly asked for Grant Simpson. Mabel overrode Dorsey's refusal, and sent Sam to summon the preacher.

"Simpson!" Mabel spat the name, walking with Mattie again outside the house.

"He's the only preacher hereabouts," Mattie offered.

Mabel shook her head. "Dorsey told him he'd fetch him a minister, a priest, anyone from anywhere he wanted. Had to be Grant Simpson." Mabel rubbed her big hands against her cheeks as if to wipe away the grime that had blown into her once solid flesh. "So I finally said, what the hell, if he'll come, you don't have to talk to him."

"What does he do, when he comes?"

"Pete says they pray, that's all he says. And he's comin' back, every week. The Lord does move in mysterious ways for sure, to put a Simpson and a Mertz in the same room every week, of their own accord."

Mary moved with her girls into a little house near the school in Potter's Corner, and began doing business as a seamstress, with seasonal work in the factory. She pretended indifference to the raised eyebrows and awkward silences her unprecedented divorce created around her, coached her girls in patience, and by Thanksgiving was an accepted and stolid member of the school and church groups.

And at Thanksgiving Carl was laid off at the cannery, with all but a bare bones staff. The winter before he'd been one of the few kept on for machinery and carpentry work, but this year there had been losses. That was the official word; the village talk was that rumors of union organizing had come too close. Rusty and Carl bought a Chevy together and made plans to go find work.

"Forrest he'd give you work."

"I'm a factory man, Mama. Damn it a man needs more'n ten cents an hour, and something worthwhile to do."

"Food's pretty important." Mattie eyed the bowl on the table with a wry smile. Its meal of chicken and dumplings was disappearing fast.

But Carl ignored that, as she'd known he would. "Rusty's got a name from his priest, an address of a parish priest up in Detroit."

"Detroit? Michigan?" Duane's fork stopped midair. "You're going clean up to Detroit?"

"What's up there?" Jem wanted to know.

"There's factories up there, makin' cars and trucks and stuff."

"What good's a priest for that?" Jem said.

"Rusty says he'll help us get hired on. And put us up, maybe."

"You stay out of the mines." Mattie was crumbling her biscuit, her appetite gone.

"This ain't nothin' to do with the mines." Carl said it gently. Petey had been laid beside his brothers a week ago. "Listen. When I get a place, a job and a place, you'uns come with me. Come on away from here."

"Away from here?" Mattie repeated it as if by rote, another language.

Jem shook his head. "I wouldn't take to a city much, I don't think."

But Duane stared at Carl, his eyes bright. "Really? You think you'd have room? Man, they must have really big schools, a place like that."

Carl gave him a light punch on the arm. "Schools, libraries, museums full of stuff to learn. Whatever you want, buddy."

"Can we, mama, really?"

"Let's not go crossin' bridges 'til we get to 'em. Carl ain't even out of the county, yet."

Hazel Miller began having fainty spells. She swore Mattie to secrecy and for the winter hid her weakness from the family, but with the spring garden work Forrest was more at hand, and saw it himself. For the first time in their married life he disregarded her objections, and young Dr. Carlisle came calling. He brought in a specialist, who confirmed his suspicion of heart disease, and the prescription for bed rest. Forrest and Charlie brought down one of the narrow beds, setting it up in the bay window of the parlor. Hazel refused to be kept in it, but when she did rest, she could watch much of the activity in the gardens, visit easily, hear Louisa practice.

When Jem heard Forrest was planning to sell the cows, he brought Sam Mertz along one morning to the farm. They found Charlie first, just turning the milk cows out of the barn, and presented their idea. They found Forrest coming out of the springhouse. He heard them out, asked a few questions, and nodded. Knowing Sam's care for the old Belgian work horses, and knowing Jem for a careful worker, he approved their plan.

"You pick out two, Jem, and soon as you're ready you can take 'em." The boys would thin peaches and pick cherries for him, and anything left owing would wait until they sold their first calves next year.

Mary came up and opened a package to show Hazel. "You like this material, Mother? For a dress?"

"Lands, I told you, I don't need a new dress."

"Nonsense, of course you do. Philip's getting married, big wedding in town and all."

"You let me pay you, then, and not be taking out of your own."

Mary laughed. "Mattie, what am I to do with her? Mother, I want to make you a dress, can't I show off for you, a little, once?"

"I never meant – I know you're good, I get comments from people I barely know. I'd be proud of a dress of yours, I just don't –"

"Good. Let's get started."

The Bakeleys came by as before, even without the excuse of buying cheese. Hazel told them only that she was "having a bit of trouble," and taking things easier now that the family was practically grown, and if they suspected more, they went along with the fiction.

The new dress was made, Philip got married and began a household of his own, above his studio in town. The apple cannery had re-opened for the cherry harvest as usual and ran full shifts for peaches and apples.

Sam and Jem both quit school and worked together in the apple harvest for Forrest, and together to bring in Sam's field corn. Sam persuaded his father to help them cut logs from their woodlot, to sell for firewood, and Dorsey stayed sober for most of the winter, with sudden new pride in his horses.

Charlie drove Louisa and Duane down the hill, where they piled in Morris's truck with three of his boys, to ride to Potter's Corner, where a bus now took students on to the high school in town. Louisa had by now outstripped the piano teacher in the village, and began staying in town after school twice a week, staying overnight with the aging Aunt Millie.

Carl and Rusty had found work in Detroit. After a year of sleeping on bedrolls in borrowed rooms and crowded tenements, they had found a half-house they could afford to rent together, and now Rusty had taken a wife, who also had work in a restaurant, which helped out. Carl wrote at Christmas that Mattie should come, Rusty and Eula were looking for a place of their own, and there would be plenty of space soon.

Well over a hundred people passed through the farm, the afternoon after Hazel's funeral at the church. Charlie took Mattie almost forcibly from the kitchen, out to the little bench by the springhouse. They sat in a silence which was easy, and for which, with the coolness, she was more grateful than she had any idea how to express. Louisa and Emma, Jem and Duane, came upon them.

"Oh, Charlie," Louisa said, looking guilty. "It's all right, don't you think? We were just going off a little while, there's so many –"

"Of course it's all right."

Mattie watched the youngsters walk away, saw Jem bend his head to catch something Emma said, saw him smile and nod, and for a moment, for the first moment that day or even all summer, suddenly thought not of Hazel but of lives moving on. Jem was to leave for the army in a couple weeks, but she thought less of that than of the grace of his slight gesture to Emma.

And when he did board the train, waving once through the open window, his face pale but excited before disappearing into the dimness of the car's interior, he didn't look much like his father, but still the memory was evoked so strongly that Mattie at home dug a hand into the chest, to touch the fiddle case. There was no talk of war here, on this side of the ocean, but she felt a vague reassurance anyway, remembering that other soldier who had come home. Then not distant grief but fresh bereavement overcame her, and she sank with tears to the floor. She thought confusedly she must tell David, and Hazel, about Jem's stepping so brave up into the train.

After the sour cherries were picked, Mattie began leaving the Miller farm after the noon meal. One day, when she had hurried with the last of the dishes, to get home before a threatening thunderstorm could gather itself, she noticed Charlie waiting on the porch outside the kitchen door.

"Well, Charlie," she teased him gently, "you thinkin' about the last piece of pie?"

"I'm thinking – I'll walk a ways with you."

"No, now. How come would you?"

"I want to talk to you."

Mattie suppressed a smile of surprise. She doubted if Charlie had ever "wanted to talk" to anyone in his life before. Her heart went out to him. Perhaps he had talked to his mother more than she knew, and now needed someone. They had already passed the cluttered, battered looking Wilkes place, the abandoned schoolhouse, and the Mertz barn, and turned up the footpath along the old rail fence that angled across the hillside, before he said anything.

"Do you think – I mean, would you be able, would you –?"

As he abandoned one question after another, Mattie stopped walking and turned to face him. She cast one brief glance back to the west, behind them, but the storm rumbling was still behind the hills, and she gave him her attention. He looked miserable, but she held her tongue, to let him take his own good time. He looked remarkably like Forrest, she realized, with his earnest, open round face and the lock of hair that fell apart from the others, across his forehead. Much more than Wendell, who looked more like Hazel, a grander look somehow, like what Louisa would have someday.

"Mattie." His voice brought her mind back from its wandering. "Mattie, would you marry me?"

Her hand flew out to the locust post beside her. She didn't actually stagger, but felt as if she had. He went a deep, beet red, looking away, and she realized finally she had to say something.

"Charlie, you can't. . . . You don't want to marry me."

"Yes."

She shook her head, marveling. Then thought she knew what was happening. "Charlie, you want it all back together," she said softly. "But I can't bring Hazel back, I can't make it all right again."

"I'm not wanting that." He stood straighter, looked right into her eyes. "I love you."

"But you're –" A boy, she meant to say, but caught herself in time. He was no child, after all.

"I've been loving you, this long time."

"You *can't!*" she cried, and looked up into such anguish she began to tremble, and hugged her arms across her front like a cloak. "Oh, Charlie," she whispered, "no, don't."

"It ain't as if we're strangers."

For one insane moment her mind clutched at the possibility: the farm hers again, or maybe Jem's. And then her world, what was left of it, crashed at her feet.

No going back now, and no going on. It was Hazel, she saw with light so sudden and blinding Charlie disappeared. Hazel who had held it all in place, and all of it – the big farm kitchen, the work so unrelenting

155

and purposeful, the rustle close around her of all these people's lives, and the love of Benjamin – all of it was lost to her now.

Mattie told him simply. "We're going to Detroit, to Carl's. Duane and me."

They were sitting on the porch edge, and she heard Benjamin's breath catch sharply, beside her. She was staring at her feet. She wore shoes these days, sturdy laced shoes she found in the new second-hand section of Guy's store, and her feet felt miserably hot. There was terrible pain all through her, as if acid lay against her bones, and then, as the pain flowed out in wrenching sobs, she lay close in his embrace, struggling to be closer.

"What's happened?"

"I – it don't matter." She cried some more before she was able to look at him. "With Hazel gone, there's no place for me at the farm. Hannah's really managing everything, she even does the books for Forrest now. Carl's needing me, and Duane's crazy to go."

"Mattie. Can I – if I –?"

They stared at each other, and around at the clearing, the corn, beans, squash, berries, roses. Mattie's eyes filled again, but she laughed a little against his chest.

"It ain't something to transplant. Our lovin' ain't an apple tree."

She pushed away from him, stepping to the end of the porch, touching several of the dark red climber roses. "And I can't stay. Don't ask me, it's just so, is all. If we go soon, Duane can get settled in before school."

They went inside, to the blankets he kept neat in the corner. "And I'll be back sometimes," she said. "Once Jem gets home, I expect he'll settle here, and I'll be back."

Part Two

CHAPTER I.

Sarah

Parking the car on the little flat space across the road from the cabin, I closed my eyes against the surrounding green and bowed my head against the steering wheel, giving body and soul to a moment's meditation. I gave a silent prayer of thanks to the little Studebaker for my safe delivery over the thousand miles from Chicago, with every inch of its seats, floors, and trunk packed full. Even more than gratitude, the thought of all the carrying to unpack made me immobile.

Eventually I needed to stretch. Outside the car, birdsong surrounded me; nothing calm about it, it had an urgent chaotic sound at first, notes flung every which way among the canopy of green, like the cacophony of an orchestra warming up before that eerie A of the oboe. In spite of my exhaustion, in spite of the years without practice, my ear began to separate the songs. I had arrived here, at our summer retreat, now my home, on the summer solstice, so although the worst of the day's heat was tempering into evening, the sun was still high above the hill rising from the house.

A Carolina wren lit suddenly on a rock only a step from my side, threw a three-note jubilation at me, and flew away, in a hurry. I stood still. Oriole, cardinal, thrush, flicker, towhee, titmouse. But the surprise and pleasure of finding the names broke into alarm and pain. Evvie was gone, defeated by the cancer we suspected. And Rusty and Ellis both lost in the War, in the Pacific. My images of them all were here, of course, and linked with Ethan. As if struck I tottered against the dusty green car. Ethan. Felled by a heart attack, five years ago.

This was going to be even harder than I had thought.

With two bags slung across my shoulders, a box from the back seat in my arms, I started moving in.

The yard was a ruin, but the years of abandonment seemed to have made little mark on the log house. The swollen door yielded to my shoulder, the kitchen linoleum didn't look worse than it always had. I set down my load and went through the doorway into the other room. Every surface was thick with dust, every angle draped with cobwebs, including the heavy beams spanning the ceiling. Dead flies, moths, crickets, junebugs littered the window sills. The room smelled of mold and mildew and mice. I worked off the latch at the bottom of a window, and the two halves swung out, precisely as they had for Ethan that first visit. The one kitchen window wouldn't open, but the ones upstairs did, and soon the house was airing nicely with a cool woods breeze.

With vacant doggedness, I unloaded the car, unpacking only enough to find some sheets for the bed, a plate and glass, the bread and cheese I'd bought on the way. The little pump in the kitchen had lost its prime, so I made one last trek across the road to the spring for water. When I finally settled with wine and my cold supper on the porch, in one of the two bent-hickory chairs, it was nearly dark. The bird song had faded like the end of Haydn's famous symphony, one musician after another leaving the stage. But unlike that stage, this one was immediately filled with the next act. "Something is making every one of those sounds," I could hear Ethan say.

With an irritated gesture, I wiped my cheek. That way lay madness,

160

or the useless waste of self-pity. But oh, that empty chair. I couldn't remove it, I'd want it, sometime. But how could I bear it? I wondered when I'd be able to open the study door. I had no idea what he might have left there.

Sell the summer place, Timothy had advised. You don't belong out there in the woods.

It's worth ten times as much to me in the saving I'll make living there as in the money it would bring. You know that.

Agatha and Jeffrey invited me to New York. And do what, I'd answered. You have your work, it's your city. At sixty-six, I'm not about to break into the work force there, even without all the veterans looking for jobs.

Besides, if I'd wanted a city, I would have found a way to stay in Chicago. But the city began to weary me. It was spinning out of my reach, not feeling like mine.

But I sat now, aware of the soothing, exquisite evening, and thought there was no bearing this loneliness. I'd have to go home, where at least I was used to it. I had assumed the place would be a buffer, that here I would devise a life of my own, separate from the loss of Ethan to death and Agatha to the vagaries of fortune. I had expected the place to call both to mind, of course. Agatha had sat with me here, watching the fireflies ascend from the grass until vanishing – where? – into the night. It took hours. We never left our seats, until no more lights flashed. And Ethan, well Ethan was in every chair, every tree, every path, every inch of the house.

I had expected that, but was unprepared for the pain of it.

I went to bed early, in no mood to find a book much less read one. Besides, the kerosene lamp was flickering and smoking. The bed felt comfortable, the dark quiet of the little house felt oddly familiar, but I lay sleepless for well over an hour, wondering what I'd done. I'd have to drive into the village in the morning, to see if my two trunks and the boxes of books were arrived. Passenger service had been discontinued during the War, but the freight train still stopped because of the cannery. I'd have to talk to Morris, or someone, about having it all brought up. I'd have to find out how the Millers were doing, what had become of Louisa. We had tried to keep contact with the family but it had never worked very well after Hazel's death, she'd been the real force there. And since Ethan's death, I hadn't been back or in touch at all.

"Is there freight for me?"

"Name?"

I smiled sadly. But astonishing as it seemed, I no more recognized the stout young man than he me.

"Bakeley. Two trunks from Chicago."

"Oh, yes ma'am, come in last night."

"I'll have to arrange. . . . How late are you here?"

"Six tonight, 'til two tomorrow."

"Tell me, does Guy Deardorff still have the store?"

"He'll be there."

The agent looked at me from under his cap, a closer look, but offered no more. The grocery store was where it had been, in the middle of the little string town, and Guy was there as promised, not inside but warming the philosopher's bench outside by the door.

"Miz Bakeley." He hailed me without a missed beat and labored to his feet. "I'll be." He was heavier and his breath pulled hard at his chest.

"Hello, Guy."

"I heard. Morris told us. I'm sorry for it, Miz Bakeley."

"Yes. Thank you." The formula felt awkward, but I could think of none other.

"And now you're comin' back through? Been a good while."

I forced a smile. "Would you have ever guessed it? I'm moving in."

I had the satisfaction of seeing the news was new. The freight agent was apparently not the town crier type.

"Here? Well now, that's one on Morris. He seen your car this morning, and told Marlin. That's Warren's boy," he reminded me. "He's runnin' the Inn now, him and Ruth Jean, just like Seth and Martha doin' this place. We can't hang on forever, I guess."

"You're retired?"

"Oh, I help out, you know how it is, they can't be hangin' over the counter all the time." Like we done, he might as well have said, but didn't.

"And Warren and Amelia?"

"Amelia still does the pies. But Marlin and Ruth Jean, they open early now, before the factory, and lots of fellows like to stop in for coffee, and Morris he says this morning how he seen your car and you should've called him, the place is a mess, he'd 've cleaned it up some."

"That's awfully nice of him, but I'll have plenty of time to clean. I even got the kitchen pump primed this morning, me who's never fixed a thing in my life. So Morris is still at the cannery? Can I get a message to him? Could he bring up my things from the depot, do you think?"

Guy nodded. "I'll go over at lunch. He's still got his truck, I imagine he'd be happy to drop your things off. You know, I guess, about . . . ."

"Yes."

We stood staring at the empty street. A car passed, turning into the lane to the factory, over the tracks. A pickup rattled by, Guy lifting his chin in greeting.

"No wagons anymore," I said.

"Nope. No wagons, no blacksmith, no stable, no carriage shop, no hat shop. No passenger train." When he turned to me with amusement edging out the sadness, I knew he was thinking of that first step, the twisted ankle. "And. No. Moonshine."

"Why, whyever would you think I'd know anything about that?"

His chesty guffaws were contagious, and helped to ease the pain of

Ethan's image with the folded jacket. "It's all strictly legal now, bar at the Inn with license and all."

"No local stuff?"

"Well. I wouldn't know about that."

"I see. Does Seth still make the rounds with the grocery truck?"

"He does, as a matter of fact. Go give an order, he'll be up your way Tuesday."

"Does the store still have ice?"

"Yep, plenty of folks still needin' ice. The rural electric's come in, though, you want to check that out."

"Really?"

"Clear up into Mertz Hollow. Get yourself a refrigerator. I got one now, wouldn't give it up for no amount of money."

I was upstairs late that afternoon when I heard the truck stop in the road, and heavy boots on the porch. I hurried down the steep stairs, and motioned the two men in through the open door. "Hello, Morris!" He looked much the same, with gray hair showing now under his cap. I couldn't place the younger, taller man.

"This is Nathan."

"Of course. I see it now. You were about half that tall, last I saw you."

They got the trunk upstairs, with a little trouble at the bend in the narrow steps. The second trunk I had them leave in the living room. "Morris. I am so sorry for your terrible losses. Guy told me."

Nat shuffled a foot and clenched a hand. Morris looked stricken but recovered quickly. "And you. He was a good man."

"Yes."

"Eula's up here now, her and the boy." He looked about to say more, but stopped, and I didn't press. There would be time to fill in other names, other news.

I fished in my dress pocket for the bills I had ready.

"No, now, no need for that. We were comin' right by."

I tried to protest, but they were outside. "Eula's right handy with the garden," Morris said over his shoulder. "I'll send one of the girls down with some early greens, if you'd like."

"I'd be delighted. She'll find me in, anytime."

Deciding to ignore the trunks, I poured some wine and lit a cigarette on the porch, looking idly over the railing down across the narrow yard. A few sassafras and wild cherry saplings were already starting, among the berries that had found their way in. I could see, because I knew where to look, the traces of Rusty's flower beds. The forsythia cuttings from the Miller farm we had planted along the top of the bank had become a wild tangled wall hiding the road. Iris were blooming bravely but almost invisibly among clumps of grass. The wild orange daylilies had spread up into the woods from the bottom corner of the yard, while the still unopened black-eyed Susans had spread the other way, out into the sun.

And here, just off the upper end of the porch, here just three steps away, was the study-hut. I finished the cigarette and pulled open the heavy door. Already steeped in grief, I was prepared for the sorrow that washed over me. There was a finality to the moment that embedded my loss as if a physical part of sinew, nerve, bone. The mourning as verb was over. The mourning as noun would live on with me.

There were still ashes in the fireplace, but Ethan had cleared the room carefully, no papers or books left behind.

I sat for awhile on the couch. A long one so Ethan could stretch out, it extended nearly from the fireplace to the door. The light from the window by my head was now nearly blocked by trumpet vine and ivy. I moved to the desk chair, looking out the other window, up the slope into the woods, past the edge of the little guest house. I sat for a while longer, and traced a finger in slow circles in the table's dust.

So. So my exile had begun.

Every Saturday afternoon, Morris came. No matter what the weather, he would stamp his boots on my porch shortly after one o'clock, and I'd tug open the stubborn door.

"Come in."

"Nah, better stack you some wood here, first."

Or saw a fallen tree limb, cut the grass, pick up all this litter from last night's storm. It was a ritual we both accepted, as if he couldn't do the task before stamping, nor I accept the help without first opening the door.

He protested at first, about the dollar I offered, but I stood firm. "Consider it a retainer."

"A what?"

"A salary, of sorts."

"It's too much for packin' in a bit of wood."

"And the new spouts? Cleaning the chimney, putting up a mail box? Fixing that window in the study?"

"You're a neighbor."

"Take it for Eula, then."

The local electrician and his apprentice son came with fuses and meter box, drills and wires. The Rural Electric Co-operative line men strung wires to the house from the tall poles across the road, and by August the kerosene lamps were for decoration, and for the power outages I was told to expect with winter storms. Two lively men, cursing softly, lugged in my new Frigidaire, set it purring where the icebox had been. Filling the trays, I looked forward to real ice cubes in my Scotch with a pleasure that amused me, and brought tears to my eyes. There was that "we" again, two glasses set out, in my mind.

I would have liked to have added plumbing, have a real soak, but my resources were alarmingly limited. We hadn't had time to rebuild much, I had little in the way of assets or pension. The house sold quickly, and the furniture, but the little left after taxes and moving must last, who knows how long? Anyway, the little kitchen pump worked well enough, the range was easy to heat water on, the outhouse was convenient enough. It was exactly like in every other house up here, with the addition of the collapsing summer bathhouse, which intrigued Morris. He shored up the sides, patched the oak cistern, secured its platform, replaced its rusty spigot.

"Won't do, come winter," he said. "Nor in a dry spell neither. But clever, ain't it?"

After Dorcas's first delivery of lettuce and radishes, spinach and spring onions, I arranged to walk back to their place myself, every Thursday afternoon, to fill a shallow basket with whatever was on offer. Young Thaddeus ran to greet me as I crossed the creek and came up the steep lane, out of the woods. Two rangy black and tan hounds ran with him but they knew me now and gave only soft barks of greeting. Thaddy's bare shoulders under the overall straps were peeling and freckled; his shaggy hair was a delicate light red. As always, there was the sharp edge of grief in my throat for the father before delight in the son.

"How old are you this week, Thaddy?"

"Just five, today." He grinned, happy with our joke. Once sure I knew he was five, he had begun suggesting he might be eight, or four, or even ten.

No one was on the porch or in the yard. "Where's your Aunt Dorcas today?"

"Her and Aunt Flo got jobs now."

"Picking cherries?"

"Punching."

"What do they punch?" I stepped onto the porch and helped myself to one of the metal chairs. I glanced with a little twist of loss at the deep shade under the maples. Evvie and I had enjoyed Liza Bergman's gift, the first edition of Peterson's field guide to the birds, checking the pictures and descriptions of the ones we knew, wondering how there could be so many we'd never heard of, marveling at the maps of their migrations. It seemed no longer anyone's special spot.

"The tickets!" Surprise made his voice rise on a laugh. "You know, to count the buckets."

"Oh, I see. But Thaddy, I've never seen it, this punching."

He stopped bouncing my basket against his knee, struck speechless. I watched him trying to work out how to explain something so familiar it has never needed words. "In the crates," he said after a moment. "You pick in a bucket and dump it out into a crate and get your ticket punched."

The screen door opened. "Oh, hello, Mrs. Bakeley, I thought I heard voices. I was dustin' upstairs, whyn't you call me, Thaddy?"

"Hello, Eula. I had him busy explaining cherry picking to me."

She gave me the ghost of a smile, reaching for the basket, her eyes as usual off to the side. She was thin, strong but round-shouldered, her long hair tied back with a ribbon, untidy, disregarded, unbrushed. She was young yet, but looked a grandmother. I knew the signs of deep depression, but had no power to heal it, and no way to get past her reserve. "Some early corn's in."

"That would be lovely, a few ears. No eggs today, I still have some."

"Run bring up some beans, Thaddy, from where Stella's picking." Eula disappeared back into the house, bare feet as soundless as the soft cotton dress. I had not yet gotten far enough through her reserve to get myself invited into the kitchen, and I waited, content, on the porch. Thaddy came tearing back and inside, and then they were both with me, the basket full. Six ears of corn, a cucumber, a mound of green beans, a few small new potatoes, a round loaf of soda bread, a pint jar of rich goat's milk. Fifty cents for the lot.

I went back the way I'd come, with Thaddy escorting. The goats moved with us along the fence, Thaddy reciting the names. Shasta was the old one, which I recognized only because she was the only white one. Olive and Sweetpea were black, and horned; Mickey the buck stood higher than the females, a scruffy but dignified mottled brown, aloof. The winter kids had all been sold but one, still bumping Shasta for snacks.

"What's the little one's name?"

"Stella wants to call her Natalie. She seen it in a book, or something, one of them movie magazines, prob'ly. You ever hear such a name?"

He was off before I could answer, darting to the side or stopping to pick up a stone or feather. We left the goats as the pasture rose up a hillside, while the lane descended into the woods. We stood together on the plank bridge to watch the water flow. There were trout, but we didn't see any today. He turned back toward the house with a wave. Walking on, I glanced back just before the bend, and either by chance or by hitting after repeated misses, he turned at the same moment, to share one last wave.

Bringing a cot and two night stands in from the abandoned lodge, I made the room at the top of the stairs into a second bedroom. "I would like to bring in the wardrobe as well."

"Not without we bust a hole in the wall," Morris replied, "and haul it up with ropes."

"Never mind."

"I could make a closet there in the corner, for your friend coming."

The closet was finished two days before Agatha's promised visit, the first of September. The road was now graded and "improved," but still with so little traffic there was no mistaking their car pulling in beside mine. I hurried down the broad stone steps.

The curls were thinner, whiter, the cut more shaped, her spectacles rimmed with a soft brown. With nylon stockings and low pumps, a straight skirt and ruffled blouse, matching jacket over her arm, Agatha looked the New Yorker she was, and for an instant I felt already gone dowdy in my simple dress and flat shoes.

"Sarah."

We reached both hands for each other, and then were tight. We pulled back, and hugged again.

"Hello, Jeffrey." I cleared my throat, relinquishing my hold on Agatha. "You're both looking gorgeous."

"Hold your tongue," Agatha scolded. "We're the old folks, now. Gorgeous, if it ever was, is past by forty years."

Neither of them had the least air of old folks. Receding hairline, a slight stoop, a bit of a paunch, detracted nothing from Jeffrey's air of distinction, any more than the lines in Agatha's face made her look less sharp or smart. Her commentary appeared regularly still in national journals, and Jeffrey's poems in quarterlies and slim, handsome volumes. Not quite in the light he enjoyed before the War, he nonetheless held a niche I suspected would be permanent. Teaching now at Columbia, he was staying only the night, leaving Agatha with me for ten days.

There were fresh beans to snap, from Eula's fall garden. Agatha and I settled to it on the porch, for all the world as if we did it every day. Jeffrey reappeared.

"Nice walk?" Agatha handed him a bean.

"Lovely." He chewed the bean, absently. "That's an intriguing stone wall."

"It's like a poem," I said, and immediately regretted the impulse, better left for my notebook. But Jeffrey picked up the simile without any hesitation.

"Yes. Now that it's there, it looks the most natural way to put the rocks together, each one fits as if obviously, just where it is." He finished the bean, tossing the tip over the railing into the grass. "And yet there's nothing natural about it at all."

And with that he was gone, inside the house, up the stairs. Agatha sighed. "Looking for his notebook. Hope he packed it, I didn't. It's like talking to a silkworm, sometimes. Anything you say is just another mulberry leaf, munch, munch."

We laughed, quietly. Lighting the kindling in the range, I soon

170

added larger chunks, and began the beef bits simmering for a stew. We started in on the supply of Scotch they brought me, Agatha gratifyingly impressed by the real ice cubes. I was aware of the happiness enveloping me, the special kind of content I hadn't felt all summer. Jeffrey rejoined us, handing me a sturdy little green book, the poems of Robert Frost.

"'Something there is that doesn't love a wall,'" he quoted. "'That wants it down. I could say Elves to him, but it's not elves exactly.'"

The evening was perfect. Wrapped in a shawl, I did not have to give up, yet, the summer habit of sitting up for hours doing nothing. Inside, I could not sit for five minutes without a book or a pen, but outside the night was entertainment enough. The scattered remnants of the firefly population dotted the yard, no longer like stars, more like the lonely lights of farms on a prairie.

"Where do they go?" Agatha asked, and Jeffrey reached for his notebook, ignoring or not even hearing our laughter.

In the morning we waved to Jeffrey's car until it disappeared. If the next days seemed busy, in fact we did very little. We made a brief attempt at reconstructing the paths and flower beds, but it was the wrong season to think about gardens. "The spirit is willing, but the flesh is weak." I leaned on the big tulip poplar tree surrounded by brown stems of day lilies. "God, Agatha, I'm as old as my father got."

"What brought that on?"

"I just quoted him, don't you know anything?"

We made a few sorties out into the countryside, searching for bargains. In the living room we hung two beautiful wall candleholders with polished reflectors; at an auction we found a little pot-bellied stove – Firefly No.22, Philadelphia, Penna – which Morris installed in the living room, with a double-walled pipe up through the bedroom and out the roof, a fetching little cap at its top.

"You should get a dog."

"Think so? It hadn't occurred to me."

"I think it's mighty dark and big out there," she said.

"Oh. You mean I should be afraid? That hadn't occurred to me either."

We spent a rainy day reading inside. Agatha read to me from Orwell's essays, but she was thinking less of Marrakesh than of currents at home. "Just as well you're out of the fray," she commented. "It's getting ugly. They'd be going after Ethan."

"What about yourself? And Jeffrey – or don't the rabid types read poetry?"

She shrugged, but looked suddenly weary. "So far, Columbia hasn't caved in."

Another day we walked again down the path on the other side of the road, across the creek, and climbed to the rocky bluff where once she had wept in my arms. If she thought of that day, there was no mention of it, though she spoke again of Jeffrey, of the political climate endangering his career as well as hers.

"You'd think anyone writing that early about the evils of fascism would be a hero."

She shook her head. "Suddenly you can't tell the truth about Franco."

"It's hard for me to understand why the Senate and the universities and the churches don't simply say no to this nonsense."

"That's exactly what scares me most. The people who ought to be setting the demagogues straight are scrambling to get in line to plead their innocence."

"Of what?"

"Exactly. Of what? Of criticizing capitalism, primarily."

"But isn't it true there's always been a fine line for radicals to walk?"

"I know. I hope I'm wrong. The thought of a whole new fight to fight doesn't set my juices flowing anymore."

I took her to meet Hannah Miller and show her some of the farm. Neither Hannah nor Charlie had married, but there were youngsters almost always there, Forrest's grandchildren visiting or working for the summer. Louisa, to my disappointment, was gone, taking a course at Peabody. She had graduated from the Boston Conservatory and would begin teaching, Hannah told us, at Oberlin. Hannah was surprised and pleased that we knew of the Ohio school; Agatha's Leticia had graduated from there, also in music though not in performance.

We went to the county fair, ate the sticky cotton candy and gazed as if entranced at the rows of preserves, canned fruit, pies and cakes. "How can any one of these be better than any of the others?" Agatha wondered. "The ribbons must be by lottery."

We looked at the prizewinning penmanship samples from each of the grades, we shared the looping sugared circles of a funnel cake, admired the dashing painted horses of the carousel. Sitting on a bench near the ferris wheel, we were reminded of the World's Fairs we had seen, mine in Chicago, hers in New York. We outdid each other with the absurdities of modern hubris, the ironies of bad timing.

"'A Century of Progress!' Just like Chicago to boast of that, right at the worst of the Depression."

"But that's nothing beside New York's gigantic cash register. Behold thy God!"

We shuddered but laughed anyway, moved from worldly to local affairs as we paced slowly through the craft barn, where Agatha fell in love with the second prize quilt, and bought it. We whiled away the rest of the afternoon in the animal barns, then collected the quilt when the fair closed at five. We stopped at the Inn in Potter's Corner for supper.

Formica tables and bright lights had replaced the heavy wooden furniture and lamps, giving the place a shiny, modern look. There was a real bar now, as Guy had told me, with stools on polished metal pedestals. Two men having pints at the end of it regarded us curiously but without greeting. Otherwise, the place was empty, and we chose a table at the hearth end, by a window. Ruth Jean heard the little bell over the door, and hurried to us from the kitchen.

"Where is everybody?" I asked.

"Early yet," she said cheerfully. "Get you something to drink?"

I shook my head, with a warning glance to Agatha. The wine here was short of her standard, by a good bit. "We're ready for dinner. Supper," I corrected myself. Dinner still meant the noon meal here, whether large or small. I glanced at the chalkboard propped near the unlit fireplace, but there was only a list of pies there.

"Got fresh vegetable soup, or chicken platter," Ruth Jean offered.

We chose the chicken, and enjoyed the crisp fried meat, mounds of potatoes with dark rich gravy, little side dishes of fresh corn. I bought a half pie to take home.

"We're fixin' to make a kettle of chicken corn soup next week, you come get some, hear?"

"Save me a jar."

As soon as we got in the house, Agatha took the quilt upstairs and spread it on my bed. Its star pattern burst from the center in reds and golds. "Perfect."

"Agatha, that's yours."

"It goes with the place."

"Oh, my." I sank onto the bed, overcome with the memory, and told her as best I could of Rusty, the arrowhead, Ethan's solemn praise. "And now they're both gone. Gone. How can it be?"

My friend sat close, held me. The grief rose in waves as if brand new, threatening to pull me under. It passed – a minute or ten, I had no idea. It passed, but was never gone. I willed myself out of the waves, but knew they were no more gone than the ocean at my back.

Recovered, I cleaned my face and opened my best sherry, and we settled on the porch, to celebrate the quilt. The hickory chairs were cocked toward each other, my ash tray on a little table between us, our feet sharing an upturned apple crate.

"Sarah, would you have us for awhile next summer, a couple weeks? Both of us?"

"Have you! Yes and yes. Why on earth wouldn't I?"

"Well. Jeffrey didn't want to presume."

"But I'd love it. Really."

"He wants to come, he says I didn't tell him the truth about this place. As if I'm to know that after never suggesting even a day in the park, he now needs – that's his word, needs – two weeks here."

"To work?"

"Yes, to work. Who wants you underfoot, I asked him. I'll live in the guesthouse, he says. Or in that perfect den."

"Study-hut." I felt the wave rising again, and was grateful for her voice pulling me back, safe in the present, among the living.

"Leave bread and water, he says. You'll never see me, you won't trip over me."

I smiled. "He could have wine occasionally, don't you think?"

"Oh, I suppose."

"And really we could let him out sometimes."

A screech owl, so close the eerie cry made us jump, was answered by another from below the road. "Why do they do that?" Agatha says. "If they're hunting, why give themselves away?"

"According to my sources, it sometimes makes things bolt in panic."

I got us more sherry, the owl moved further off, the night fell deeply, moonlessly, dark. Agatha, not a smoker, accepted a Pall Mall, and we were silent for some moments.

"Sarah, are you sure you know what you're doing? Do you have to do this?"

Waiting until the flicker of panic subsided, I answered her calmly. "I'm under the delusion that I both need and want to do this."

"Do you need money?"

"It'll stretch."

175

"I mean, would you have stayed, if –"

"Possibly. But Agatha, just possibly."

"Why? Why this?"

I waited so long this time she started to apologize, but I assured her I wasn't offended, merely stumped. "I've no good answer. Without Ethan, Chicago was beginning to feel like a treadmill, the same grooves, round and round. But like a downward spiral, narrower and narrower, more and more repetitive." This felt like the wrong mood, and I shook it off with a laugh. "Just sounds like life, doesn't it?"

Agatha lifted her glass. "Here's to the spiral." She sighed, softly. "And this will be different?"

"Well. It will be mine."

It was true that I wasn't afraid at Ragged Edge, not in the way Agatha implied, but it was also true that the first winter I lived with a soft hum of terror. It was like some sort of low-grade fever, not enough to make one crumble, but still an undeniable presence. Especially after a stretch of sunless days, when the sky was a gray shroud among the dark denuded trees, I could find myself in a panic, my breath held, fingers clenched white around a book I couldn't remember the title of. There were sleepless nights, when I listened until dawn to the fires in the stoves, the wind roaring in the chimneys, sorting out the smells of smoke blowing back in through leaks in the walls. There were unexplained noises outside, and inside the spectre of loneliness turning into madness. Interminable afternoons of no arm to touch, no voice to answer, were suddenly nights dense with heartbreaking memories, all recollection of the day or how I spent it, gone.

It was, fortunately, not the only hum within me. The smell of coffee was sometimes almost companionable, as was the busy fire in the little potbelly. My rocker drawn close, I could see past its pipe to the frost on the window and finally, noticing the exquisite patterns, think of Liza

Bergman. Listen, oh just listen to that! Suddenly Liza would be vivid before me, the pleasant alert face attentive to the thrush, the flash of oriole, the sun on a fern. She would enjoy the frost on the window, the warmth of the heavy mug against the palm, the hiss of a damp log, the creak of a floor board as I rocked.

It's morning, have you ever seen such a morning!

No, and this one will not come again.

But my grumping would only make her toss her head with a laugh, amused as if I had said something clever. When the thunk of the fire falling in on itself dispelled the vision, I was smiling. My coffee was cold, my left hip slightly stiff. Liza Bergman was dead. But something in the room felt precious to me in a new way.

Another sustaining note keeping the hum of terror at bay was the mail. Around noon every day Josh Mickley banged shut the mailbox door and drove on up the hill. I crossed the road to collect the tight roll of the New York *Times*, a gift from Agatha. It came a day late, of course, but that hardly mattered; I'd settle with it for an hour or more, a daily dose of the outside world as the male establishment saw it. More irregularly, other journals offered antidote to that perspective.

And an occasional letter. But already in Chicago I had begun to lose the contacts, the people who had trooped in and out of the log lodge, and by now the hiatus in the use of this place as summer retreat had changed it, irrevocably. Will you revive the visiting? Agatha had wondered. I thought not, with mixed feelings.

I found a solace from time to time in the notebook which had lain in its drawer all my years away. With Roger Tory Peterson to describe the birds, I had long ago stopped jotting notes; with conversation to satisfy my need for words, and enough activity to push me toward laziness rather than exertion, I had nearly forgotten it. Now, in fits and starts, I wrote through the terror. One January storm, when the power was broken by heavy snows and high winds, I lit a kerosene lamp, set candles around the living room, and wrote at the table for three hours, losing all trace of anxiety in the narrative of my winter. And I was conscious, as I wrote, that the heaviest balance against the terror was my neighbor Morris.

In the summer, Morris always paused on the porch when his task was done; with colder weather he started coming inside to take his leave, pulling off his heavy cap, combing thick gray hair self-consciously with his fingers. At least ten years younger than I, he might have been mistaken for my peer, or older, so deeply etched was his face with the elements and grief.

"I've chipped the ice off the path," he said. "Not that it'll do much good, I expect this sleet to turn to snow by dark."

"I have the kettle on. Do you like tea?"

"I do. But look here, my boots are thawing out all over your floor."

"Never mind. Come in by the Firefly." I tossed yesterday's *Times* on the floor, and – to my surprise – he hung his dark wool coat on a peg and stepped into the living room and stood on the paper, warming by the stove. I poured water, carried in the porcelain teapot with cups and sugar to the table under the window. While the tea steeped I offered him a cigarette. He shook his head, but drew a pipe from the pocket of his shirt, tobacco from his hip pocket.

"Dorcas tells us the phone company's planning a line out here," he said. "Maybe next spring."

"Will you get a phone?"

"With her workin' for 'em, she seems to think I have to. Now how would that look, she says, us not havin' a phone."

"But she doesn't live at home," I pointed out.

"That's just what I said. All the more reason, she says, I can talk to you."

I laughed. "Better give up, Morris, sounds like she has all the angles covered."

"The girls pester for it. Be a party line, I reminded them, you want everybody knowing everything you say to all the beaus? They know already, Flo says."

When I poured the tea, he moved to the table, stirring sugar into his cup before picking it up, standing again by the stove. I motioned to a chair by the table, but he shook his head, shrugging a little. One step at a time, I thought, placing my own cup on the lamp table by my rocker, where I settled. He stood easily, and handled the cup and pipe like one accustomed to it, with a grace I wasn't expecting.

Thus our Saturday ritual expanded to include hot tea, a smoke, talk of his daughters and absent sons. Morris was angry at that absence, a little ashamed of it, as if somehow to blame. He showed me the Christmas card from Pittsburgh, where Randy and Gabe had gone, working in a steel mill. Inside the standard snowy scene with archaic horse and sleigh Randy had written, Doing fine. Merry Christmas to all. Gabe says hi. Sincerely, Nat. P.S. You heard about the G.I.Bill?

"Is one of them thinking of going on to college?" I asked. All his sons had enlisted during the War, even Nat, who had walked off during the night to enlist in secret on his eighteenth birthday, the summer his brothers were killed.

"School never done Ellis any good."

I could not answer his bitterness, and was stopped by my own sadness from trying to draw Morris out of his.

I still walked up to buy a basket of apples or potatoes or baked things from Eula if the weather was not too cold or wet. I enjoyed the excursion, the slight pull in my legs from the hill, the burn in my chest from the cold air. I always paused on the plank bridge; first the reflection of autumn leaves in the shallow creek, then the crystals of ice along the rocky edges, and now a cold snap in January froze a skim across all but the most turbulent little waterfalls. Thaddeus was not in the yard this day, too cold even for the snowsuit and mittens his mother bundled him into most days, but he came sprinting to the side door, letting me in to the kitchen, to which I had gained access with the passing of seasons.

The hot room smelled of bread, apples, and cinnamon. Urging me out of my coat, Eula pulled a chair out from the formica table.

"Can we have pie now?" Thaddy plopped onto a chair opposite me, ready.

"Is that what I told you to say?"

"Oh." The child grinned at me, showing the gap of a lost tooth. "Want some pie?"

Eula sighed, shaking her head at him. "Would you like some pie, Mrs. Bakeley?" she coached, but Thaddy waited for me, rather than saying his lines. His mother and I exchanged hopeless looks.

"I would be very glad for some pie, thank you."

"Me too," Thaddy said, making Eula laugh outright, so redundant was the announcement.

He had milk with his, bought milk, for the goats were resting, pregnant. Eula poured us cups of strong black coffee.

"Flo got a whipping."

Eula's caught breath was her only sign of embarrassment. "Never mind that now, finish your pie."

"I'm full."

"I'm not surprised, with the plate of potatoes you packed away at lunch. Leave it then. Go get the picture you done this morning, show Mrs. Bakeley."

"What's Flo done?" Before I could stop the question, it was out, as the boy ran from the kitchen. My mind recoiled from the image of Morris with a belt in his hand.

"Oh." Eula went a deep red, but waved off her distress. "You know how Flo is."

I wanted to protest that I did not know, but Thaddy was back. I took the tablet. "Well, say, isn't this nice! Did you get new crayons for Christmas?"

"See, there's the pigs." He was afraid I couldn't tell, but in fact the animals around the central red barn were all clear to me, and I named the chickens, goats, dogs and cats, to reassure him. I glanced up to find Eula watching him with the tenderest expression I had yet caught in her dark eyes, the lines of her thin face softened into a fleeting beauty. Never harsh with him, she was sometimes mild to the point of seeming indifferent, clearly not the case.

"I guess I know now what you'll need for your birthday this spring."

"What?"

"Paper, of course."

Delighted, he looked at the picture with a new attention, surprised that it told me that. Eula got up to warm our coffee. She waited until Thaddy left the room, until we heard a muffled crash of blocks, then leaned toward me, her voice low. "It's a hard time for Flo, I don't know what to do."

"What did she do?"

"It's not so much what she done as what she wants. And the way she's never learned how to handle her dad."

"Is Morris so hard?"

She smiled a little, shook her head. "Seems like those two can't see eye to eye, they can argue about the weather. Dorcas now, she's got what she wanted, a steady job, a room in town."

"Was that ever a problem? Morris seems proud of her."

"He worries about her, but she comes home about every weekend. But Flo, no, Flo can't wait. Can't bide her time, like Dorcas did. No patience at all, none. She comes charging at him, like a train off the tracks, and tells him things instead of asking or giving him time."

"What does she want?"

"A job at Woolworth's, after school. She's got it all worked out, to stay with Dorcas, and by the way, they'll take her full-time in the spring so she's quitting school after this year."

"Even his boys all went through school."

"Exactly. Oh no you ain't, he says. And you're not sleepin' on no couch, neither. Dorcas can't look after herself and you both. I can look after my own self, she says, just like she don't know better than to talk back to him like that."

"And he hit her?"

"Not for that. She turns to go upstairs and he grabs her arm and her purse falls and spills, and she's got cigarettes in there, and he's got his belt off and four-five licks in before I can get to him."

"You stopped him."

She looked up at me, her face granite. "I won't have it, I don't care what she done. I growed up with that, Daddy beating this one and that one, and my mother too if she was in the way. Not here. I'll take Thaddy and live on the dole before I'll let him see that. I got brothers just like my daddy, I figure it's learned."

"Eula. Have you stopped him often?"

She relaxed, her fist unclenched. "No. Like I said, I'd be out of here if it was a habit. Morris has got a temper, but he holds his hand, mostly."

She must have seen the question in my eyes. "Rusty never hit a soul." It was the first mention of him between us. She smiled, looking both bleak and proud. "But still I made him promise, every year on my birthday. He done it too, just to please me. Listen, don't be hard on Morris. He's scared for Flo, is what's the matter. He seen them smokes and just had to hit something."

I winced. "Is he so against women smoking?"

She looked bewildered, then began to laugh, which so released us from the tale she had just told that I joined in. "Oh Lordy," Eula said, shaking her head at me. "You ain't sixteen, and his daughter."

"Can I have my pie now?" Thaddy said.

"My girl Flo's in some powerful hurry." Morris's voice was mournful. "I don't know how to fix the brakes on her."

"She wants a job, Eula told me."

"Wants a job, wants to quit school, wants to be in town, wants to be twenty-four."

"Can't Dorcas talk some sense into her?"

"She tried. Now she says let her do it, she'll be tired of the job in a week."

"That's maybe good advice."

"Too many ways for a girl like that to get in trouble in town. I want her on that bus after school."

"But maybe at work she'll see for herself that any decent job these days takes a high school diploma. Especially for girls. The war's over."

"She don't need the money anyhow for anything but foolishness."

"But Morris, you were young once, don't you remember how important the foolish things were?"

"Not floosy stuff. Her mother's turnin' in her grave."

"Oh, Morris. Of course the girl's wrong, but –"

"I've told her no. That'll have to be the end of it."

"Well, let's hope it is, then. Odd, isn't it, how things change? My father absolutely forbade me going to school."

Morris looked pointedly at the floor-to-ceiling shelves he himself had built for me, filled with books. "Didn't do much good, did it?"

"No." I left it at that. "What does Stella think of all this?"

"Stella, now there's a serious one. Ain't *enough* foolishness in her."

"Still going to be a missionary?"

"No, it's a nurse now. She's even written to Esther Miller, down in Virginia, acting all grown up."

"Morris, they do grow up, you know."

Spring came more dramatically here than in Chicago, with fewer false starts. Winds broken here by the mountains and ridges still bent the trees in March and whistled in the cracks of the old house, but seemed not to bear the menace of Chicago gales, nor the persistent iciness. It was true that the early flowers had snow to contend with, true that the first Sunday in April dawned with a coating of ice on every twig and bud, but winter was over in a way one couldn't count on in Chicago. The days when it was spring were purely perfect. A day too cool for sitting outside would turn suddenly balmy, like the touch of some large and soft being, leaving me dizzy with an unfocused joy even while I shivered again, and went inside.

I had expected a more sedate gladness, some heartfelt gratitude and relief, not this heady euphoria. I had simply not anticipated the profusion, the profligacy of the season here. Cherry trees bloomed, wild in the woods, tame in the orchards. Then peaches, and plums, and apples. Solid backdrops of dogwood and redbud made a pattern of color which changed with each bend in the road. Eula one day showed me a patch of wild orchids, or lady's slippers as she called them, in the woods by their lane. I began to wander with new purpose through my own. I never spotted any orchids, but I watched at close hand wild azalea and carpets of trailing arbutus give way to mountain laurel, rhododendron and spring beauty. Bloodroot and anemone bloomed among the fiddleheads of the ferns.

For the first time I looked again at the folder of drawings I had found in the desk, and saw now that every one of the flowers drawn was on the place. They must have come very early, sometimes.

Full of plans now for gardens, I wished I had planted bulbs in the fall. I made mental diagrams of where the tulips, daffodils, snowdrop and aconite, crocus and hyacinth, should go.

Telephone poles came marching up the road. I grumbled in letters about the growing clutter in the countryside but in fact my eye soon disregarded the lines, and I felt more glad than I admitted when the magic unit went up on my wall. Just inside the living room door, with a little crank on the right, earphone of a hook, it rang for five households. My ring was a long and two shorts. The others sounded with rather annoying regularity while mine went unused, but I nonetheless felt connected, and the hum of fear which the uncurling leaves had nearly extinguished went silent altogether.

With the storm windows off and stored in the cellar, I decided in early May to do a major cleaning, and started with the windows. Kneeling on the sill, leaning out the open half of the living room window to wash the other half, I listened to the phone jangling. Only after its repeating did it register as mine.

"Oh, Mrs. Bakeley." Eula's voice greeted me without introduction, urgent. "Can I leave Thaddy with you for a bit? I hate to ask, but –"

"Of course. What's the matter?"

"It's Flo. The hospital called. I got hold of Morris, he's comin' up to get me."

"What's wrong?"

"She fainted at school. It's more'n that, they don't take you to no hospital for fainting."

Thaddy was frightened, subdued. Eula had thought to send his crayons along, and after a short walk around the yard which held nothing to interest him, I gave him a stack of typing paper, at the table.

"Here, I'll open the window, it's almost like being on the porch that way. I like open windows when I work."

"You draw too? Here?"

"No, but sometimes I write letters here." Struck by his implication that drawing was his work, a serious task, I went back to the vinegar water to finish polishing the window, but watched him as closely as I could. He watched me, too, alarmed.

"Mind you don't fall!"

"Don't you worry, I'll be as careful as . . . ." I looked around at him. "What's really careful?"

It took him only a second or two. "A turtle."

"Turtle? Why do you say that?"

"I never seen a turtle fall." Chuckling now, the tension relaxed from

185

his face, he selected some crayons with new energy and began to draw. He was a happy mix of his parents, prettier than either, with Rusty's fair skin and large eyes, Eula's sharply featured face. His absorption in the drawing was enviable. By the time I finished the tedious eight little panes and clambered down from the sill, he had a picture to show me.

I laughed aloud, so surprised by the wit of it I had to sit down by him and study it. There was the window, with even the stove pipe encroaching on the corner, and on the sill a turtle, up on hind legs, a cloth in the front paw, a marvelous wide grin on the head stretched humorously far from the shell.

"It's just silly," he said, perhaps afraid I'd take offense.

"It's just wonderfully silly," I agreed, and we both laughed.

With the novelty of a grilled cheese sandwich at my house, however, he remembered that something terrible had happened to Flo. "Are hospitals where people die?"

"This is a brand new hospital." I was not about to answer his question directly. "With good doctors, and nurses."

"Stella wants to be a nurse."

"Yes."

"But is Flo all right?"

That one I couldn't evade. "I don't know, Thaddy."

He played outside for awhile, collecting pine cones, wandering through the traces of the paths I intended to reconstruct, then came in, wanting to see what was inside "that building." I opened the study door latch, and his eyes widened with the surprise of finding a real room, outside the house. Trying out the desk chair, he looked at me shyly. "Can I be here?"

"Why yes, if you like. But look at the dust. Let's clean, first."

I got fresh water and tackled the window while he turned a willing hand to wiping the table and chair. "What do you do here?"

"Nothing. But it's time someone used it. Are you going to draw some more?"

As he followed me to collect his crayons and papers, we heard the car stop down by the road. We stood as if netted at the edge of the porch, afraid to rush down, afraid to wait. When Morris appeared at the steps, Thaddy ran a few paces toward him but stopped, halted by the force field of sorrow his grandfather pushed ahead of his weary approach.

"Come on home now. Your mom's in the car."

The boy flung an arm across his eyes and started to sob. "Where's Flo?"

"Flo's very very sick. But you be brave, now, your mom's pretty wore out."

Thaddy nodded, struggling for control, and turned back to the house for his crayons. Morris looked at me with a helpless slight shake of his head. "They say she's all tore up inside." He was weeping. My own horror was a vile taste at the base of my throat. "We're going back in. Dorcas is with her, and we pulled Stella out of school."

"Thaddy can stay here, if you want."

"Eula wants him near. Ready, boy?"

The call came just before midnight. Flo had died, never regaining consciousness, never naming either her back alley murderer nor the heedless father.

There was no way to help. I drove alone to the beautiful stone Catholic Chapel in the valley beyond Potter's Corner, sat in the back through the mass. I felt neither aloof nor involved, simply there, a witness. The family filed out behind the coffin. Nat was there, but the middle two sons had not been reached. Morris gave me a nod of acknowledgment, his precociously austere youngest at his side, staring ahead of her as if at a future too personal and serious to share. Dorcas and Eula were both weeping, Dorcas with her face hidden, Eula's bowed and unseeing. When Thaddeus caught my eye and his face, without smiling, registered a gladness to see me, the poignancy nearly overcame my control.

"I didn't go along to the grave," I told Agatha later that summer. "Nor stay for the funeral meal. I went back, though, about a week later, and then I did cry. I stood there at the marker, the stone wasn't ready yet, stood there with the most awful rage, and cried."

We were walking, slowly, up the hill along the stone wall, toward the big rock. Once a well worn path, there were now some patches overgrown, but the wall was guidance enough. "How is Morris?"

"Blaming himself. Not the politicians or priests."

We fell silent for the last, steep, fifty paces or so, where the rocky footing took all our attention. We gained the top of the rock, a shelf large enough for half a dozen people, and sat, catching our breath. The view was not panoramic, narrowed by the slopes on either side, but was pleasing. Hillsides rolled away diminishing to the east, with some cuts of orchards and fields, and one bit of barn roof, placed as if by a painter's eye.

"Eula is grieving for the girl. Not raging at causes. Takes me, an outsider, to do that."

"Don't be so sure."

"You think I'm underestimating her, but what I mean is my own separation."

We began to feel the rock too hard and cool, and picked our way cautiously back down the hill. By the time we came to the circle of ferns and could hear Jeffrey's typewriter through the open study window, I was ready as any old woman for the porch, a smoke and a drink.

We had not banned Jeffrey from our midst. Agatha joined him at night in the guest house, and we all spent a day in town window shopping, browsing through a used-book store, stopping at the Inn for a supper. Evenings, when he tired of reading by the dim lamplight in the study, he joined us on the porch. Our meals were drawn-out affairs. For the most part of the day, however, Jeffrey was as intent on his work as Agatha was on the vacation from hers.

The two weeks were like an orgy of words for me. The first nights

I scarcely slept, not only keyed up from the talk but preoccupied with planning meals, fearful of their discomfort or boredom, aware of all the shortcomings of the place. But after the first few days, I was so attuned to my friends' presence I would fall immediately into sound sleep, wake relaxed, thinking of no detail but the joy of Agatha's good morning. She was almost always up before me, sitting in a patch of sunlight in the center of the little yard, the coffee already warming on the new electric hot plate they found for me.

There was hell to pay, when they left. The terror returned with a deeper hum. With nothing unfamiliar to me now to face about the house or its seasons, I was left with only interior demons, a depression frightening in its depth and breadth. With no specific cause, everything became cause, whether material or abstract.

Not completely paralyzed by it, I struggled to take hold of diversion. I concentrated, some days with minor success, on the beauty of the late summer. Buying a new notebook, I hoped to turn the occasional scribbling into regular habit. But both the summer's glory and any need to record it eluded me. Like all the roads of the empire, every sentence led me back to my own center, and my center was a dump.

One Thursday in August when Thaddy walked with me as usual to the bridge, he hesitated instead of running off. I paused a moment, shifting the basket from one arm to the other. "Do you think – Could I come draw in that place sometimes?"

"'That place'? Oh, the study. Why, yes, Thaddy, I'd like that very much. It's empty again. We'll have to dust it."

"I'll do it."

"Why don't you come with your granddad, Saturday?"

He started to run up the lane, whirled and shouted a thank you. I waved, laughing. I was standing in my own kitchen before I realized I was still smiling, with tears in my eyes.

So another dimension was added to the Saturday ritual. Morris came now in the wake of Thaddy, whom I was ready to greet with a dust cloth for the study table. At first he came laden with his crayons and tablet, but I told him I have plenty of paper. I bought a supply of crayons and colored pencils as well. "Save yours for home," I told him. Morris tried to object, but I ignored him.

As the days got chillier, I tried to warm the little room with fire in the fireplace, but by November he agreed to come inside the house unless trailing after Morris. I watched with a worried eye, meanwhile, as Eula showed me the inane color-this-green work sheets from school. She was justly pleased that he was getting off to a good start.

"Mrs. Roberts says he colors better 'n some third graders already."

"But, Eula, does she ever let him draw?"

"Oh, well, I don't know about that. Maybe that's not a school thing. It's the numbers and letters is the real business, don't you think?"

Sure enough, Thaddy was soon self-conscious about his drawing, frustrated that his imitative efforts didn't match the coloring books. Launching a counter-offensive, one Saturday in December I spread the *Times* on the table, and greeted him with a new tin of twelve watercolors, a large pad of heavy paper, three sizes of brush, a tin cup of water.

"Do you draw the picture first?"

"You can do whatever you want."

"Show me."

I pulled another chair close, wet a brush, stroked the red, swiped a rainbow arch. I washed the brush, made a yellow streak, then a blue copy of the red. I knew absolutely nothing about watercoloring, but his eyes followed my brush as if watching magic. When he picked up a brush and made a few tentative strokes, the amazement and barely suppressed excitement made his face itself a picture I would have recorded if I could have. I got up to leave him alone.

"Aren't you going to finish it?"

I sat back down.

"It's a rainbow," he said.

"No, it's just a design. Just colors."

"*Mine's* a rainbow. In a pond."

For the first and only time in my life, I played with colors, beside an artist.

Morris dumped an armload of wood in the kitchen box, stepped into the living room and stopped in his tracks with an abruptness that startled me. "What's wrong?"

He shrugged, laughing a little. "I just wasn't expecting to see that."

"Look, granddad, I can paint!"

But Morris barely looked at the rainbow reflected in the pond. "'Bout ready to go, are you?"

"No time for tea?"

Since Flo's funeral, whether he would stay or not was uncertain, week by week. He had not spoken a word to me about the girl's death, or life, and with that reserve the accord between us had become strained. He did stay, some Saturdays, but this was not to be one of them.

"Starting to snow," he said. "We better go pack in some wood for ourselves."

The next Thursday I walked up for eggs, and the picture was taped to the refrigerator door. "That was kind of you, to get paints," Eula said. "You be sure to say, though, when he gets to be a bother."

"I love to have him."

"He loves to go." Her smile was, I thought, even fainter than usual, and I was searching for some possible reason when she suddenly walked to the doorway and gestured to me. "Come upstairs once. I want to show you something."

I followed to her bedroom, where she tugged a box out from under the bed, hefting it onto the quilt. "Look here." Untying the string, pushing off the lid, she stood a moment as if not sure, now, whether to go on or not, but I couldn't resist picking up the book lying on top. The lettering on the brown cover was nearly worn away, with the word Plants near the center. On the blank flyleaf inside was my aunt's name, in the old ornate lettering, with the date, February 16, 1873. And under that: To my friend Rusty Sharrah, June 20, 1927. The title page proclaimed the book "A Botany for Young People and Common Schools," with the title in bold print: **How Plants Grow.** Written by one Asa Gray, M.D., in 1862. The pages were brown and brittle with age.

But it was not the book Eula wanted to show me. Carefully stacked in cardboard, were several dozen watercolors. Some faded, some creased or wrinkled, some torn at the edges: methodically, she laid them edge to edge on the bed.

My eyes filled with tears. "He never told us," I said. "Never said a word about it, only that he carried Miss Leona's easel sometimes." This, then, was the root of Evvie's uneasiness, that frown. An ambition introduced by strangers, taking him at best beyond her boundaries and at worst into the pain of the unattainable.

"They made fun of him, some of the others, sometimes. Said it wasn't fitting. But look here, and him just a boy."

A blue ribbon from the county fair, 1930: a pleasing bit of dry-stone wall, framed by the grape arbor in his mother's yard. He never told us, I thought again. But he tried, he did try. Here was the key to him we never found, because we hadn't known to look.

"There was a painter lived near us, in Detroit," Eula said. "I begged him to go meet him, but he wouldn't hear of it. But oh, he did love it so, I knew he did. Never had much time for it . . . ."

I picked up one of the paintings, trying to place the familiar scene – the big rock. Of course. Rusty would have been all over that hill, as a boy. Later ones, of the city and a different countryside, showed surer execution, more detail, a growing expertise with shadow and light. I walked entranced around the bed, feeling I would never get my fill of this singular showing. "Have you shown this to Thaddy?"

Eula shook her head. "Soon. When he's big enough."

We stood several minutes more before her hand moved to gather up the paintings. I picked up the rock one, to help, folding the tissue paper back in place, and noticed the arrowhead, in a corner of the box. I pressed it gently in my palm, unable to speak.

"That was his," Eula said. "I guess he found it somewhere."

"He did, indeed." I told her about the flower bed, and Ethan's praise.

"Would you like it? You have it."

"I wasn't asking —"

"No, I know that. But if you want it."

"I would cherish it, Eula, a great deal."

CHAPTER 2.

Carrie

The barn, the springhouse and its overflow pond, the meadow, all seemed different, unfamiliar without her brother beside her. Even after it was hard to remember a time without his leaving on the long yellow bus every morning, even after she trusted his returning every afternoon, Carrie wandered through the fall days with a sensation of loss. She reassured herself with repeated visits to the creatures, as her mother called them: the two hogs growing to alarming size in the sty built off the side of the barn; the chickens and the rooster she must keep a wary eye on; the new litter of kittens in a corner of the empty stall beside Nell's, also empty since the cow spent her days outside. Carrie liked to stand quiet beside her father when he milked, if she got up early enough, but was a little frightened of the cow, who often swung her head toward her. Her brother Jarrett was already learning to milk, but Carrie was content with watching.

The fall was wet, hampering the apple harvest that looked to be a bumper crop. Forrest and Charlie, with Carrie's father Jem and another worker, Skip, took refuge one afternoon in the kitchen. Carrie's mother poured coffee for all of them, and laid out sliced bread and butter.

"Here's to October's sunny skies!" Skip raised his cup.

"How's Verta doin'?"

"Well, Emma, she's out to here."

Even Carrie, leaning shyly against Jem, had to smile at the image. Verta was a large woman, even without the baby which Carrie understood was inside her, like Nell's calf last spring.

"Trouble at Sam's over the weekend," Charlie said. Carrie and her brother called him uncle, though he wasn't a real one; she loved the low murmur of his voice, which she had never heard raised even in a shout among the trees. He was a thick man, not as tall as her father or Uncle Forrest but strong. Somehow Carrie knew that even though he wasn't the sort to lift you around. Skip, who looked too small and wiry to be much good at lifting, was actually fun for that, swinging you up onto tractors and wagons, helping you spring much farther than you'd dare alone, catching you when you jumped down. Uncle Forrest might carry you, not in play but comfortably, as easily as he might cradle a pup, the slight tremor in his left hand not noticeable when he worked, though it was here, at the table.

"Oh, dear." Emma sighed. "Sam drinking with Farley again?"

"I always heard his dad hit the bottle pretty hard," Skip said. "That true?"

Forrest nodded, looking weary. "Died of it, some say. But I don't know what's got into Sam. He talk to you, Jem? You used to be thick, as youngsters."

"Not so much lately, since he got in with Farley and his friends. Since Mabel died, seems like he goes on a spree every weekend."

"Poor Dora," Emma said. "I think I'd lock the door to Farley, but guess you can't, your own brother."

"What happened this time?" Jem asked.

"What I heard," Charlie said, "they got to swappin' ghost stories with the Leathermen boys, and then somehow got into tradin' insults."

Forrest shook his head, his voice scornful. "Fighting over ghosts."

But Skip's eyes were lively with interest. "Ghosts 're either there or they ain't, what's to fight over?"

"Over the proof, I'd guess," Jem said.

"You'd ought to know," Skip said, "livin' right here in the thick of 'em."

"Skip," Emma scolded, but she was too late.

"There ghosts here?" Carrie straightened up to look in her father's face.

"Nah." Jem raised an arm to pull her into a quick hug. "Them's just stories, to pass the time. I been livin' here all my life, ain't seen a one."

"Not this close to the house, anyway," Skip added.

"Skip!" Emma's voice was genuinely irritated, now. "Stop that nonsense. She's not old enough to sort it out from true, and you know it."

In November, a few inches of heavy wet snow drew Carrie outside, for the first time unmindful of Jarrett's separate life in school. Her feet snug in the boots that buckled in three black latches, she packed snow into a big lopsided ball, until her mittens were so wet she let them dangle from their strings and walked on under the clothesline to the springhouse to investigate tracks. She tried going up the roof, but it was too slippery to climb, and she turned her back on it. Hypnotically, she counted her steps to the slope, got to a hundred and forgot to stop. She got to ninety-nine again, and stopped, trying to remember Jarrett's lesson. "*Two* hundred!" she shouted, and looking around for his approval was brought with a jolt back to the present.

She had walked down into a little pocket, so that the springhouse and the yard were gone. Pine boughs laced over her head, and trying to see a tree's top made her dizzy and she staggered against a low limb. Snow spilled down inside her scarf, chilling her and making her suddenly afraid.

She heard the voices then. Far off and close beside her, the pines were talking.

With pounding heart, she knew the stories they were telling. She had heard them for years, a jumble in her head of Indian phantoms, mothers crying for lost children, a maniac with an axe looking for the Rebel soldier run off with his daughter or wife or somebody. A whole camp of Rebel soldiers was seen somewhere back up in there, but couldn't anybody find it again. And there was a hermit too, somewhere, with a foreign name. Brustein. Somewhere, without a road, so how would you find him? The pines can move, shifting paths and ridges so that people get lost.

Was she in Pine Mountain? How far had she come? Not this close to the house, Skip had said, but how close was she?

The cry of a blue jay covered her own sob of terror, and released her into a run. But after only a few steps in the clumsy boots she tripped and sprawled. Forced to look at the ground, she realized that she made tracks too, just like the animals at the spring.

She stood in the kitchen, stunned by the warmth of the wood range, by the return of the familiar, by her mother's voice coaxing the answer impossible to her constricted throat.

"Were you lost? Get too cold?" Emma knelt to unbuckle the boots, and Carrie laid stiff fingers against the thick hair held back by the combs that wouldn't stay in her own. Her mother looked up, smiling.

"Landssake, you're near froze. Why poor darlin', what's the matter, you been cryin'? Your hands ache?" She cupped Carrie's hands and blew on them. "You'll be all better soon, stay close to the stove awhile."

Somewhere there were words, or songs, that would explain everything to her and to this beautiful mother with the breathtaking hair and large warm hands and questioning blue eyes, but Carrie couldn't hear them, and could only wait for some future chance.

Her grandmother Mattie, visiting for a full month between Thanksgiving and Christmas, looked up from her crocheting. "How you happen to hear of him?"

Carrie shrugged. "He's s'posed to be up on Pine Mountain, but I'm not sure. Is he real?" She repeated her original question.

Mattie raised her crocheting. Carrie heard Jarrett dump out the brick-blocks in the hallway at the foot of the stairs, but she stood still, leaning on the empty armchair, looking across the hearth at Mattie in the rocker. The fire snapped, but the spark flew harmless onto the stone facing, and neither of them moved to stamp it out. Carrie waited, watching the needle, how the end of it made little circles in the air as the crooked end made the loops that will be a shawl. Her grandmother's thin gray hair was pulled in a tight bun against her neck, her navy blue dress had large buttons down the front and a narrow belt, her feet in laced dark shoes were crossed at the ankles. In spite of the year's absence since the last visit, she felt familiar to Carrie; though the crocheting was new, it did not seem strange.

"Yes, he's real. I mean, was real."

"You ever see him?"

"Yes. I seen him."

"When?"

"Long since, child. Back when I used to live here, when your daddy was little."

"What's he look like?"

"He ain't up there no more, Carrie."

"Where'd he go?"

The needle stopped. Mattie was looking into the fire. The wind had risen, and sleet pinged against the windows. Jarrett came into the room, holding something half-fashioned from the red blocks. His light hair fell thick around his ears, shaggy on his neck.

"What did he look like, Gramma?"

"Look like? Oh, well, he was tall. Longish hair . . . ."

"Was it black?"

"Did he have a beard?"

"He wore a beard, yes. Usually suspenders. Heavy shirts, seems like it was always cool enough back in there for flannel shirts."

Carrie and Jarrett looked at each other, bewildered. She was describing an ordinary man.

"But wasn't he mean?" Jarrett prompted, as if she were holding back the best parts. "Wasn't he sort of, you know, a wild man?"

"Is that what you heard?"

"Well, yeah." Jarrett looked at Carrie, uncertain. "And that he was awful rich."

"Had a treasure," Carrie agreed. "But can't nobody find it, 'cause the place is haunted."

"Pooh! I don't believe that, do you, Gramma? If it was real, it'd be there."

"And that he grows roses," Carrie added, undaunted. "By magic."

"There just ain't no such thing! Is there, Gramma?"

"How's he get stuff to grow up in the woods, then?" Carrie challenged him. "Skip says –"

"Roses?" Mattie looked across at them sharply, from one to the other almost as if trying to place them, then leaned back against the rocker's high back, staring again at the fire. Even Jarrett was silent this time. "I had no idea," she said finally, "that folks still talked of such things, or of him." She began her work once more. "Whether it was magic or if there's any such thing, Jarrett, I can't say. But he growed roses up there, sure enough. Wild ones like is beside any road, and little dark red climbers, and a bush of yellow ones."

"You seen 'em?" Jarrett's voice was high with surprise.

"I seen 'em."

They stared at her, digesting that. "Well?" Carrie said. "Was there a treasure there?"

"I guess that got started because he didn't have a job, not like most people."

"What did he do?" Jarrett wanted to know.

"Oh dear." Mattie's hands rested again in her lap. "It's hard to explain. He was . . . just there."

"But it ain't true about the spells and magic, is it?"

"No, Jarrett, it ain't. And he wasn't wild nor mean. I don't know why folks believed that. I suppose I did, myself, at first."

"How come?" Carrie asked, something like grief in her throat.

And something unknown passed over her grandmother's face, something alarming and painful, so that Carrie raised a hand to pull it away, but Jarrett's voice interrupted the gesture.

"Where'd he come from?"

"New York City, I believe."

"How come?"

"I don't know that part."

"Part of what?" Their father was in the room. "I interrupt a story?" He added wood to the fire, standing close to it; Carrie could smell the damp in his clothes. He smoothed back straight dark hair with both hands, and moved his shoulders wearily. "Christ, what a rotten day out."

"Daddy, you ever see that old man Brustein?" Jarrett asked. "Gramma did!"

"'Old man Brustein'?" Jem took papers and tobacco off the mantel. "That what you're talkin' about? Yeah, I seen him. He was Mr. Brustein to me." The correction in his voice was clear, and Jarrett was subdued.

"Oh. How come did you see him?"

"They been full of how-comes this afternoon," Mattie told him.

"Skip been tellin' you tales, that it? Listen, there's plenty of crazy tales about lots of people, it's one of the favorite pastimes around here. Remember that."

"But how come did he come here?"

"I don't know, never asked."

"Was he hidin' out?"

"What did I just tell you about them stories?" Jem licked the edge of the thin paper, finishing the roll. "How could you hide out with everybody knowin' where you're at? He was a hermit, he liked it that way, that's all."

"Where'd he go?" Carrie asked.

Her father moved to the armchair, the children making way for him. He lit his cigarette, tossed the match into the fire. "Leave it. Mr. Brustein's nothin' to you kids, don't pester Gramma."

"But Daddy —"

"Carrie, I said leave it. Go wash up for supper."

Jarrett had just gotten out of his coat, from school, and was settled on the couch to show Carrie his papers and read his lessons to her, as he always did, when there was a light tap at the kitchen door. Their mother was upstairs cleaning the bathroom, their grandmother resting in the little room beyond the stairs, but the children made a dash for the door lest one of the grownups beat them there. Jarrett tugged at the stubborn door, then stood confused. There was a stranger at the door, not Charlie or Skip or Dora Mertz. He had no formula for dealing with a stranger. And Carrie thought there was something oddly familiar about the man, which made it even more confusing.

"Hello. Jarrett, isn't it? Can I come in, do you think?"

Jarrett stepped back from the door, leaving the visitor to open it or not. "I'll go get Mom," he said, and was gone before Carrie could think what she should do. The man moved in enough to close the door and stood quietly. His dark overcoat, carelessly open at the throat, looked too big for him, and was ripped under one sleeve, muddy at a hip.

Carrie took in the black hair and thick beard. "Are you Mr. Brustein?" she blurted out.

"Mr. Bru – Good god." He stood returning her stare for a moment, then covered his eyes with one hand, smoothed away the surprised laugh. "No, I'm your Uncle Duane, Carrie. But you were just a baby still, last time you saw me."

Her mouth dropped open, and she blushed. Of course. She had seen the pictures, pasted in the book with gray pages. In an army uniform, then posed beside a car with a taxi sign on its roof, then one with other men dwarfed by a huge tractor along a muddy track going to be a highway. That was why he looked familiar, but in none of those pictures did he have a beard, and there hadn't been any new ones in Carrie's memory.

Emma rushed into the kitchen, and pulled up short. "Duane!"

"Hi, Emm. Sorry if I gave you a scare."

"I couldn't really believe there was a stranger in the kitchen." Emma laughed and went to him. "Give me your coat. Why, you're soaked. Did you walk here?"

"Pretty much. More or less."

"Whatever that means. Hungry, I bet."

"I can wait."

She hung the coat behind the stove, and moved to poke up the fire. Duane sat at the table.

"Did you know your mother's here?"

"Here?"

Emma poured him coffee from the pot, looking at it dubiously. "Carrie, honey, get him some milk from the 'fridge. I don't think you'll want this straight." She smiled, handing him the cup. Carrie brought the heavy white pitcher, carefully.

"I'm sure I've had worse."

"Where you coming from?" Emma took a loaf from the bread box, sliced a thick slab. "How long can you stay?"

"Thanks." Ignoring the questions, he concentrated on spreading jam, so intently that Carrie's mouth watered though she wasn't hungry. He felt her watching him, and looked up. "You pick these blackberries?"

She nodded, then looked uncertainly at her mother: she picked berries, but maybe not those. Emma smiled. "She sure did. Both of 'em are real helpers around here. Jarrett milks already."

Jarrett grinned in response to Duane's glance, and moved an inch into the room. "You travelin'?"

Duane chewed, cocking his head, considering. "Yeah. The word will do. I'm travelin'."

"You'd ought to have a suitcase, then."

"Where you learnin' all these words?"

"Gramma brings a suitcase."

"Ah. Of course." Duane turned to Emma. "She's just visiting, then?"

"Comes at Thanksgiving, this is the third year now."

"And Carl?"

"He'll come at Christmas, take her home. She rides the bus down, if you can believe it. I swear, she seems to enjoy it."

"How is she?"

"She's fine, you'll see for yourself. Takes a rest this time of day, but I think just to get some time to herself."

"She ain't that old, really, come to think of it." Duane looked surprised as he said it. "Well, in fact, Jarrett, I do have a suitcase. Of sorts. Left it on the porch." He got up, but swayed, grabbing the back of the chair. With a cry, Emma was at his side. "No, I'm all right, I just –"

"Jarrett, go on and see can you get in his bag."

"Just a little dizzy, a bit of a cold."

The habit of mothering strong, Emma touched a hand to his forehead. "You're burnin' up, this is no 'bit of a cold.' You come on upstairs. We've got hot water now, since the electric came out here, we're modern as all get out. Thank you, Jarrett." But she looked doubtfully at the grimy dufflebag. "Leave it here, I'll get out some things of Jem's for you."

Duane gave her a lopsided grin. "You're right, however did you guess? There's nothing clean in there. Look, Emma, I'm sorry to bust in on you like this."

"Nonsense. Come on."

"It's just I was –"

"Hush, come on."

Mattie heard the voices in the hall, and opened the door to the little catch-all room she slept in. She took a quick breath in surprise. "Duane!"

He turned from the bottom step and she came to him. "You're here!" She laughed a little through the tears brimming, at the needless comment, and he hugged her again.

"And you're here," he said. "I don't know which of us is the more surprised."

"You're sick."

"Nah, just a little wore out."

"Go on, get yourself warm and clean." She turned him toward the stairs, but drew him back into another embrace before releasing him, so he could follow Emma.

Jarrett, entrusted to bring the mail in from the box after school, generally had nothing to show, but the next day handed Emma a stiff brown envelope.

"What's – Oh, Duane, look!" She hurried into the living room. "Mattie! Duane, it's a letter from Louisa!"

Duane, wrapped in a blanket on the couch, took the glossy photo from her, and Emma unfolded the letter, sitting on the very edge of the armchair.

"Who's Louisa?" Jarrett asked. He tugged off his coat, and dropped it on the floor in the kitchen, to hurry after Emma. "Who's Louisa?"

Duane sat up, motioned to Jarrett and pulled him down beside him on the couch. "This is Louisa."

Carrie edged close, too, to look over his arm at the photo of a woman at a piano. She wasn't playing the keys, but turned toward the camera, smiling slightly, one arm lying easily on the music rack. Her dress had long tight sleeves, but her neck was bare, showing a delicate chin and locket; full waves of hair fell back to her shoulders. This was so clearly a creature from another world that Carrie drew a sharp breath, and looked with new wonder at her once-familiar mother, uncle, grandmother. "You *know* her?"

They laughed, but Emma explained. "That's a Miller, sweetheart, she grew up right here, up at the farm."

"She was born," Mattie said, "on the very same day as Duane here, same Sunday, it was."

Carrie, distracted by the picture still in Duane's hands, and by her own thoughts trying to put that lady together with Duane in a cradle, did not really follow the details of the letter her mother was reading to the others. It was about someplace in Ohio, about Louisa's studies and teaching – Carrie couldn't hold both those images at once. There was a daughter, Diana, there were concerts, and there was something called a grant which was going to send Louisa to Europe. Or take her, maybe it was a boat. Sometime or maybe already had.

"Jarrett," Mattie said, "can you bring me the picture?"

"You better frame that," Duane said, handing it over and lying back on the cushions again. He covered his eyes with his arm, as if the light hurt. "She'll be famous someday."

"What's she do?" Jarrett asked.

"She's a pianist," Emma said with some impatience. "Weren't you listening? Can't you tell from the picture?"

"Oh. Yeah."

Carrie was glad he asked, as that helped explain some things, if not others.

Duane slept on the couch, and for the next week remained there, wrapped in a blanket, for most of the days. Carrie liked him, but preferred to listen to others talk to him. He didn't push her, accepting a shrug or a nod as answer enough if he asked her something. So she was nearly as surprised as he was to hear herself say her thought out loud, when he declined Emma's invitation to go along to church.

"But don't you want to see it?"

"See what?"

"Daddy made it."

Jem waved off Duane's surprised look. "She means the crèche. I carved out some pieces, over the years. Nothin' much."

"Is so, too," Emma declared. "Hannah saw 'em last year, we had it set out here, and this year asked could the church borrow it, and there it is now."

"They're pretty rough pieces, really," Jem insisted.

"Wonder whatever happened to . . . ." Duane let his musing fall off, as he got up from the table to get the coffee pot.

"To what?" Jarrett asked.

"You know, I would like to see that, of course," Duane said. "You got an extra tie, Jem?"

No one urged Gramma to come. Carrie was used to that. She had wondered about it at first, since everyone else she knew went to church at least sometimes, but by now it seemed natural, that Mattie would settle by the fireplace and crochet. Though her shawls and scarves usually went to be sold at a store in Detroit, Carrie knew that the blue one she was working on was to be a gift for Emma.

Duane made no move to get out of the car when Jem parked in the muddy lot. "I been gone a couple days, is all?"

Jem laughed. "Now, there must be a change or two."

"Newer cars," Duane said.

They filed behind Emma into their usual pew, about halfway back on the left side of the aisle. Sammy Mertz, two rows up with his mother, his brother Jimmie and the baby Donnamae, turned around to grin at Jarrett. He noticed the stranger and nudged his mother. She leaned toward his whisper and turned enough to smile hello to Emma, her gaze curious as it brushed over Duane. Carrie became aware, then, of other faces turning, felt a current of surprise. The church was nearly full; Carrie felt the excitement of the season, but this was something new. She sought out the table at the front, laden with the Christmas figures, and leaned forward to look across her father at Duane, at the end of the pew. He smiled and nodded at her, and she sat back, satisfied.

Just as Miss Bream, limping slightly, went to the piano and arranged her hymn book, Forrest and Hannah and Charlie came in, and Hannah gave a little gasp of delight. Duane looked up as she squeezed his shoulder, leaped to his feet and hugged her right there in the aisle. Forrest grasped his hand, pressing his other hand against Duane's neck in a near-hug that astonished Carrie. Charlie grinned and pumped Duane's hand too, as the piano began Hark the Herald and everyone stood up. Duane pulled out a handkerchief and blew his nose in the general bustle. He had a cold, Carrie remembered.

On the last afternoon of June, Carrie and Jarrett finished their assigned chore of sorting the cherry crates. It had taken a week, bringing each one out of the barn, stacking them again, which was tricky on the slope of the bank. They separated out any broken ones. Tricky, too, to tear down the elaborate castle/fort the crates had become over the winter: the oblong boxes were perfect for overlapping into winding stairs, for making walkways and rooms with windows overlooking medieval Europe or Western plains. The edifice was the reason for their chore, as Skip had refused to have a wall of crates tumble on him again, as had happened the summer before.

"They're big enough to build it, they're big enough to tear it down," he'd declared, and Jem had agreed and they had grumbled and taken their time, never admitting that their dawdling was in good part to prolong a curious pleasure in the task. In fact their new stack looked suspiciously, in parts, like a rampart.

They checked once more for any stray crates in the dim cavern of the barn, mindful of broken planks in the floor. A few of last year's hay and straw bales remained on the other side of the open center, and Jarrett climbed up the heavy wooden rails, pretending to fire at the pigeons fussing on the high beams; he stepped onto the lower beam and jumped onto the hay. The drop wasn't far, and Carrie had done it too, but the bales were hard, not cushioning like the piles of loose hay she liked to imagine from the days before tractors and balers. She turned to the outside, and Jarrett came behind her. They stood, between ideas, watching as Uncle Forrest's spray rig moved across the top of the terraced block of young Golden Delicious trees. The round tank was still enough of a novelty to watch, as most still had men riding, to hold the hoses.

And suddenly they grabbed each other's arms, cries caught in their throats. The tractor had gone wild. At an angle over a terrace, smashing the small trees, it was pulled by the sprayer into a roll, and they saw the driver a tiny fleeting figure flung against the sky. The tractor slid over another terrace, skidding to a smoky halt on its side.

Screaming then, they sprinted to the house.

The first few mornings after, Carrie clung to Jem. "Honey, it wasn't the tractor." He'd pull her hands off, hold them, repeating it patiently, morning after morning. "It wasn't the tractor nor the sprayer. Uncle Forrest had a stroke, that's what the doctors say. It wasn't the tractor's fault. I'll be okay."

And night after night, Emma came to her bed to allay the terror, holding her tight, murmuring memories of Forrest alive. They would cry together, and Jarrett too, slipping from his bed onto hers. "But we can't ever see him now," he said, the night after the funeral. "I want to *see* him."

Their mother had no answer.

They were at the big farmhouse with Emma most of the days before the funeral, and some after. Their own house was full, with Mattie and Carl come from Detroit, and Duane from his apartment in town, but the Miller house was even more packed. Wendell, whom Carrie had never met or known of, was a tall man who kept quietly off mostly with Ed Lakin, alone now; all the others were home as well, most with children too confusing to keep track of. Jarrett made some friends but Carrie wandered mostly on her own, glad to be unnoticed. Her mother and grandmother were busy. Aunt Hannah, who everyone said had borne up so well at her sister Corie's death, crumbled at this one, and was kept mostly in a darkened room upstairs, with one or more siblings or friends by her.

Most of it Carrie saw through a haze of terror and confusion. Uncle Carl – a real uncle, she knew the difference now – she got no more sense of than during his brief Christmas visits. He was a heavy man, powerful looking in a way her father was not. He didn't talk much; at home he drank beer from brown bottles, and her father had some with him. But Carl also went evenings down to the Inn, which her father never did.

But Louisa: they finally met Aunt Lou. And she was beautiful, better than the picture, even, which hadn't shown that her eyes and face were constantly changing, hadn't shown that she could look at you like you were the only other person in the room, that she had a voice that came from way deep in her throat and stroked the air, like a thrush song.

"And this is Carrie." Emma drew her into the circle of women in the kitchen during a brief lull in their work.

Louisa turned that look on her, the lovely hair with its red highlights swinging softly. "You look a great deal like your grandmother."

"Go on!" Mattie waved a hand. "She's too pretty a thing for that."

"Diana's about your age," Louisa said, touching her lightly on the shoulder. "When's your birthday?"

Carrie leaned harder against Emma, who answered for her. "June. Just turned six."

"School for you, then. Diana started last year, but she's only six still, 'til December.

"She here?" Carrie finally found a voice.

"She's with her dad."

"Why?"

But Emma turned her gently away from the table. "Go on, now, let us visit, okay?"

She wandered around by the big grape arbor for awhile but not finding any of the other children, went to the barn to check on the kittens. She knew she was taking a chance, still in her good dress, but she knew her way around the barn without getting too dirty, and there was a new litter under the stairs that led to the main floor from behind the first big box stall. The litter wasn't there. She crawled out from under the first step and lingered to touch the leather harness hanging on the wall, and a halter, a bridle with the reins looped neatly. Everything was covered with layers of dust, gone hard over the years. She would have liked to have known the horses, and was idly imagining that other time when two figures appeared silhouetted against the outside light.

Carrie opened her mouth to say the mother had moved the kittens, but when she saw it was Louisa and Duane, she was struck mute with shyness, and stood unmoving in her dark corner. They'd come in for the cool, not the kittens, and stood leaning in the doorway without glancing toward the back.

"It's hot," Louisa said. "Like Mother's funeral. Remember?"

He let out a single coughing sound.

"Duane." Her voice was husky. "Duane, why did Mattie and you move away? Did she ever say?"

"No. She said Carl needed us."

"*I* needed her," Louisa said, then shook her head, pushing a hand as if impatiently through her hair. "Never mind that. But I missed her, horribly."

Duane said nothing. Louisa turned from looking out over the yard, and looked at him. "And I missed you. Horribly."

He still said nothing. And then it was not so much that they moved toward each other as that the sky between them left. Their mouths touched lightly, then again, then harder; and then their bodies did move, their arms lifting, circling, pulling. They leaned against each other a long moment, then he leaned back against the wall.

"And now you're going to Europe."

"Finally. Diana and me. And you're going to college."

"Finally."

"I don't see Barclay anymore. Ever. What a stupid misalliance that was. Except for Diana. She has his perfect pitch."

He drew her face to his again, and she pressed tight against him, then pushed gently apart. "Don't look at me," she said. "When we go in, don't look at me."

"Come into town tonight."

Whether she agreed or not, Carrie couldn't tell, as they moved off. But she did know where "into town" meant. When Duane had first moved into town last winter, she had fretted about what a basement apartment was, until they all went in after church in March, and she saw for herself that it was nothing like the cement and dirt floored cellar at home with wash tubs and tools. It was a rare excursion, and both she and Jarrett had to be reminded not to bounce on the car seat, not to shout at everything they saw. And Carrie loved the apartment. Aside from pictures of igloos and African huts she'd seen in Aunt Hannah's missionary pamphlets, this was her first real evidence that not everyone lived in houses surrounded by yards and gardens and woods and orchards. It was only a narrow room, with a sink, refrigerator, and electric stove at the back, the window over the sink looking out on an alley. There were two doors, which he opened to show, one to a closet and the other to a bedroom not much bigger. They stood for a while by the single armchair and table cluttered with books and papers, before walking out and up the street, to a diner. Duane was working at a hardware store then, and treated them all to dinner.

Carrie touched the dusty leather collar of the harness, a pretend final pat to the horse, and climbed the uneven steps to look for the kittens among the apple crates.

By the end of the second day she knew it was hopeless. Two days in that bolted down desk, waiting for something to happen, waiting for knowing to begin – she was a failure. The bus ride from school was forty minutes long. Jarrett tossed pennies with Sammy, Jimmy had nothing to say to her, and she had plenty of time to make up her mind. She told Jarrett, on the walk in the lane.

"I ain't going back."

"What?"

"To school. I ain't going back."

"Carrie, you're crazy, what're you talkin' about? You got to go to school. It's a law, I think. And even if it ain't, Mom and Dad would make you."

"I ain't goin' home then!" And quickly, not looking at the house forever closed to her, she jumped the ditch and ran into the cherry orchard, dropping tablet and reader and lunch pail to fall where they would.

He caught up as she hesitated at the shallow creek below the pond, but she moved on, ignoring him. He grabbed her arm, and she lashed it away and back at him, and ran on: back the peach orchard road, into the woods, up the slope. She gave out just over the first little hill, and Jarrett came up to her as she sat weeping, leaning against a sticky pine trunk.

"Carrie, come on back."

She picked up a pine cone, pulling off the seeds.

"I'm sorry about recess," he said. "Come on now."

"I don't care about recess. It ain't your fault."

He sat facing her. "What's the matter, then?"

"It wasn't no different, Jarrett. Just like yesterday. I ain't fit for school, that's all."

"'Course you are. Lookit, you're a lot smarter'n a lot of kids. Like Sammy. He's my friend and all, but he still don't know the Psalm, and he just mutters through the Pledge, and you know all that."

"I know all that 'cause you told me. I ain't learned a thing in two whole days. You just keep goin', like before, and tell me, like before."

He shook his head. "I don't think that's allowed, Carrie."

Carrie started to cry again. "I don't understand nothin' she says, Jarrett. It won't do me no good to go, I'll just get dumber 'n dumber."

"But like what, Carrie? It ain't hard. Hey come on, don't cry. Please, Carrie, come on."

Desperate, he pulled on her arm, pulling her to her feet. She pushed back at him. "Leave me be!"

He stepped away from her, hesitated a moment, then turned and scrambled out of the shallow pocket.

A calming sense of things gone crept into her misery. Gone was the school yard with its milling groups, swinging ropes and chasing balls. Gone the lines of Red Rover, where Jarrett was a captain but she was afraid of the game. What's wrong with yer sister? Jason had asked, and Jarrett had shrugged, avoiding her. Gone the awful mystery of the order inside and the puzzle of her proper place, learning the numbers and letters she already knew, the words to the flag already familiar. Was she wrong to know? Was it too late now, she already caught in the lie of pretending not to know?

And now she had fought with Jarrett, who didn't like her anymore, anyway. Her dress was torn, her new shoes dirty and scuffed, she had broken her promise never to go into the woods in her school clothes. They wouldn't want her back.

She began to walk, and as she walked, was overcome with longing for her grandmother. *She* would never urge her to pass out pencils without explaining what she meant, never expect her to walk among rows of strangers, or answer questions she hadn't heard because she'd been watching the sunlight dance on the window sills. Gramma Mattie wouldn't make her go at all, Carrie was sure of it. Carrie looked around her, and headed straight for the steepest part of the slope. If she went right over the mountain, and out the other side where no one knew her to send her home, she could ask the way to Detroit.

She was pleased to remember the name of the city, at least. She couldn't picture it; even with the snapshot of the house, with its two little stoops side by side, she kept imagining it as some sort of mix of her own house and Uncle Duane's apartment. Which wasn't his now. She had to use her hands to crawl up a steep bank, and when it leveled off a bit she sat and let the tears come, frightened and tired. People kept moving around. Or dying. What if Gramma –

She caught her breath and looked behind her, up another ridge. She didn't seem to be getting over the mountain. And suddenly realized where she was. *The* mountain. She must be near Brustein's ridge, in fact there were a couple pines, just up a little way. She'd stop at his place. If he tried to run her off, she'd just ask the way to Gramma's, and could she stay the night, then he'd be nice, he'd remember Gramma since she used to visit him.

She was brought up short by the used to. What was it Gramma had said? She hadn't said he was dead, but he wasn't up there anymore. Well, he could have come back.

Carrie hurried along a little trail, but lost it and turned another direction. Another path ended. She hesitated, without her earlier sense of which way to go. She was hungry, which brought vivid image of her mother, the kitchen, Jarrett scooping out a gravy lake in his potatoes.

Maybe they'd take her back, give her a second chance, maybe she should go home after all.

She looked around, and was struck to her knees with panic. She had no idea which way home was.

She stayed on her knees, panting, until the fear subsided. Down. She'd have to go down. None of the ways down looked familiar, but all must lead somewhere, eventually. She'd just rest a bit, first. She crawled in under a small hemlock, its lower limbs a friendly shelter.

She woke to hear the pines sighing, calling her name, and gave a shrill cry of terror before scrambling out of the dark into the slightly more inviting dusk. She moved downhill, as fast as she was able, crying, stumbling, suddenly hearing her name again. Not the trees, but a voice, a real voice. She held her breath until she heard it again, faint, below her, off to her left.

"Daddy!" In a panic that he would miss her she tried to move faster, but ran into a berry bramble and turned frantically to get around it. Her foot rolled on a loose stone and she pitched headlong down a bank. Pain in her left arm was nauseating, and she lay still. "Daddy!"

"Carrie? Carrie?" The voice seemed closer, and she forced an answer through her throat aching with sobs.

He dropped to his knees and hugged her close, saw the ugly blue knot swelling on her wrist. He took off his shirt and tied it around her, binding her arm tight to her chest, and lifted her carefully. His white undershirt was damp with sweat. Trying hard to stop her crying, she held tight around his neck as he angled down across the slope.

"Hush now, it ain't the end of the world. How come was you runnin' away?"

"I can't go to school."

"Why would that be?"

"Jarrett he don't like me anymore."

"Hey. Jarrett's your friend."

"Not at school he ain't."

"Never mind, hush now."

She broke into fresh tears at the sight of her mother's. Emma sat in the back of the car with her, Jarrett in front as they went into town, to Dr. Carlisle.

Carrie was allowed to stay home the next day. She tried to protest against a nap after lunch but Emma was firm, tucking her with a light quilt on the couch, propping the cast on a pillow, then moving Carrie's legs to sit with her. "Carrie, why would you run away like that? No, honey, don't cry, I ain't mad at you. Just tell me how come."

"I hate school."

"Ah. Listen, it'll get better. Where was you running to?"

"Gramma."

"Oh, dear. Carrie, Detroit's an awful ways off. How would you find it?"

"I thought . . . I thought he'd help me. Maybe."

"Who?"

"Mr. Brustein. He knows Gramma, she said so. I think."

Her mother said nothing, and Carrie felt herself drifting drowsily. The couch was soft and comforting, in spite of her being too old for naps.

She was sent back to school, with a note of excuse and to be kept in at recess. Mrs. Roberts sat with her and in their little talk discovered Carrie could read, had already read several times the soft, worn reader. The next day the teacher handed her a blue hard cover book, The Fairy Find-Out Book, and school changed for Carrie.

On Sunday morning, to her surprise, Jem said he'd stay home with her. She was feeling fine and wanted to protest, a little disappointed not to show her cast, but saw her mother nod, and knew it had already been decided. Jem took a cup of coffee to the porch after Emma and Jarrett left, settling in the sun with his knife and a long piece of hickory he was smoothing for a walking stick.

"You going to make designs, like the ones we seen at the fair?"

"Good idea. We'll see." He shaved the branch in silence for several minutes and then, just as Carrie began to think she should go get her new reader, he pulled something from his pocket. "Look here."

She took it, marveling. "How'd you do that?" She turned the links of wooden chain around, looking for seams. The circles were smooth as marbles to her fingers.

"I didn't. Mr. Brustein done that."

"He *is* up there!"

"No. No, Carrie, he ain't, and I want you to get it straight now. He give me that when I was just about your age. So that's a long time ago, you know? Not now. He's gone, this long time, way before you was even born."

"Where'd he go?" Carrie blinked back sudden tears, a loss sharp and bewildering in her.

"I don't know."

"Didn't nobody see him go? Didn't he say goodbye to you?"

"I wasn't here. I was in the army. And the others were up at Carl's, wasn't none of us here. Then your mom and I come here, but he never came back, Carrie, and he ain't a ghost. Don't pay attention to what Skip says, they're just stories."

"But he's still livin' someplace?"

"No, Carrie, he ain't, that's what I'm telling you. Your gramma got a letter some years back, a notice from New Jersey someplace, by the ocean, that he was dead."

"Why?"

"He was an old man."

"But why did Gramma –?"

"That don't matter." He reached for the wooden chain and slipped it back in his pocket. "Can you leave it alone, now? Don't go that far up there alone. And you do have to go to school."

CHAPTER 3.

Sarah

Thad picked up the snapshot, tilting it toward the window to see it better.

"My friend Agatha's twin granddaughters," I told him. "In England."

"They live there?"

"So does my friend."

"Well, I know that." He gave me a look, offended that I would think he had forgotten such an established fact, since I'd been giving him the stamps for years now. He was thirteen, no longer painted at my table, but still visited nearly every weekend. He had wandered in today, a gray Sunday afternoon in February, like a lost soul. "How come do they live in England?"

"Those children, you mean? Their mother –"

"They're not children," he interrupted me. "They're as old as me, at least."

"You're right." I spoke with emphasis, hoping to coax the frown off his face. "They were born right before the War, they're fourteen."

"So they didn't move there, they were born there?"

"Yes, they're English. Their mother is a composer, went to England to study and married."

"A composer? You mean like men who write music?"

"Composers aren't all men."

"In music class they are."

"No doubt."

"You know some women composers? Really?"

"Not personally." I told him of Liza Bergman, dredging up from nearly buried memory the names she had championed in her playing: Clara Schumann, Fanny Mendelssohn, Amy Beach. We sat in silence for some moments, he by the table under the window, I in my rocker by the stove. "Is art class getting any better?"

He hissed through his teeth. "She made us do valentines."

I had to laugh at his dreadful voice, and the dreadful idea, which made him smile. "I put a Cupid's arrow right through a deer's heart."

"Here's one for you, my dear."

"She give me a C."

"Oh, never mind her, Thad."

"Wish we'd do some more wood blocks, that was okay. But she says we're done with that." He picked up the photo again. "What's their names?"

"Clarissa and Norman."

"She's awful pretty, isn't she?"

"You should have known her grandmother fifty years ago."

He gave me a grin, finally, but went back to studying the photo. "Must be different, having a twin. Or even just brothers and sisters."

"You had the girls, almost like sisters."

He shrugged, not to argue.

"Does it seem lonesome at home, with Stella gone now too?"

"No, I don't mind."

219

But he was frowning again, and now I could wait no longer. "Thaddy, what's troubling you today?"

He considered before he answered. "Mom says we might move."

Though I'd known since Christmas that Eula had a suitor, I was taken by surprise. I had thought I would know of any change before Thad. "So you'd have a sister, and two little brothers. Is that so bad?"

He managed to shrug and shake his head at the same time. "I just don't see why I can't make up my own mind, that's all."

"Your mother would never leave without you, Thad."

"But I'll have to change schools, and everything. He don't even come to our church, he's a Quaker."

"That will be a change, I grant you. From mass to silent meeting. Have you been?"

He shook his head. "I seen it though. It's ugly."

I smiled at his loyalty to the little stone chapel. "And what does your mother say about it?"

"She says there's nothing wrong with setting still for an hour a week." He gave me a grudging little smile and got up to feed the fire. "I could stay with Granddad. Somebody should."

"You do like him all right, though? What's his name, Damon is it?"

He nodded. "Big fruit grower, other side of town. Yeah, he's all right. His kids 're okay."

"It's not very far, not these days."

"I like it *here*."

"Yes. Well." I could think of no encouraging way to talk about it. That we didn't go howling into each other's arms was a marvel.

I complained to Morris the next weekend. "You've been keeping secrets."

"Eula just now told us."

"It's definite, then."

"Early April."

"At your church?"

He stopped packing his pipe, and shot me a surprised look. "Father couldn't do that."

"Oh. Is Eula joining the Friends?"

"They'll marry in town."

"A concession from each to each. A good start, I should think."

Morris lit his pipe, and smoked quietly for several minutes. "Eula says she'll probably join the Meeting, as they call it. Eventually. She says she don't want Damon to change."

"Thad seems to think Damon's church isn't as pretty as yours."

"Well, it ain't." He accepted more tea, stirring in the sugar slowly. "The boy's taking this kind of hard. Even asked me could he stay."

"He's very loyal, Thad is."

"Loyal? I hadn't thought of it that way. He says he won't fit in there."

"I suspect he'll do just fine."

Morris nodded. "He will. I know what he meant, though."

"Is this Damon the critical sort?"

"No, not a hard man, I don't think."

"And Eula's happy?"

"Anybody can see that."

"Yes, I thought so. She must not be too worried about fitting in."

Morris knocked his pipe against his palm, the spent tobacco falling on the stove's skirt. "Still and all, they're different people, the Tylers and them. College people, every one of them. It's bound to change Thaddy."

"You don't need to worry he'll ever forget you."

"It's just the way of life, ain't it? The very things I want for him will change him. Like Nat."

"Nat's still your son." With a hard-won college degree, Morris's youngest son now had a new house, pretty wife, and accounting business in town.

"But I don't know how to set right at his table."

"Ah." You're talking about class, I wanted to tell him; Americans don't talk about class. But I felt a wave of sadness, a kind of weariness that washed over me more and more often, and I didn't say it.

We talked then of his other sons, lumberjacks now in the Pacific Northwest, still living within shouting distance of each other, both married with children. To my surprise, Morris was thinking of visiting.

"It ain't right, not knowing your own grandkids. They're after me to come. Not to stay, I wouldn't. But to see it, see them. I might."

I fried a chop for my supper, with a bit of Eula's canned corn, feeling already nostalgic for the Thursday visits. I washed up the dishes and went to the outhouse, tossing the pork bone into the bare space in front of the old guesthouse, where I had twice glimpsed a fox this winter. Back in the house, I stoked the fire and settled at the table with pen and notebook.

I wrote of the conversation with Morris, about his facing the spectre of aloneness. It's just the way of life, he said, and I thought about that. I had not had a houseful of children disperse, nor the heartbreak of burying any, but of course there was the unused study, the empty guesthouse, and all the loss of community and support that implied. I thought of the invitations Morris would continue to get from his sons, from Eula, how he would have to juggle them now with his own needs, and his demons. I had deflected similar offers, almost without thought.

During the despicable Congressional Hearings after the War, Agatha and Jeffrey had decided to shake the dust from their sandals, and accepted a timely invitation from the London School of Economics. With Agatha's daughter Leticia already settled in England, the choice was easy and had worked out well. By now, in 1954, the ugliness here had subsided. The ACLU was still busy with contempt-of-Congress charges, but Agatha and Jeffrey could have come back. But they needed nothing here. Jeffrey was in enough demand in Europe to feel not retired at all, and Agatha was still publishing occasional pieces of social and political acumen, enjoying her semi-retirement and her grandchildren.

"Eastbourne has become a home to me," she wrote to me several years ago. "Please Sarah, can't you come to us?"

I had gone as far as to inquire at an agency, but a steamer ticket cost more than I spent here in several months, and I had given it up with mixed feelings, mostly relief.

Timothy had come from Chicago to testify, narrowly escaping an indictment but eloquently holding to his ideals. He had stopped at Ragged Edge on his way home, haggard and defeated. Once portly, he had lost weight too quickly, the flesh loose around his face and neck. I had hid my alarm, persuading myself the gray tinge was my imagination, or merely fatigue.

"Timothy, we've always known the stuff of which governments are made. Why is this so devastating?"

"It's so blatantly cynical. Suddenly it's impossible to support the need for any change whatsoever."

"It's always been 'American' to blame the poor for poverty, the colored people for racism."

"And there have always been a few corrective voices, even at the top. Now silent as a tomb."

"No, Timothy, there's your voice. And others, surely. Not everyone has joined in the madness."

"But the madness controls the discourse."

In the morning he had looked a little better, complimenting the comfort of the couch, but I searched in vain for the familiar sparkle in his eye.

"Do you ever think," he had asked me, "about coming back?"

"To Chicago? No."

"But how will you manage here? When you can't drive, for instance."

I had shrugged. "It's a topic I try not to think about."

"We would have room. We could look after each other."

"A latter-day commune!"

Timothy had joined in my laugh, but I wondered if I'd hurt him. "I don't mean to be flippant. I'm touched you'd think of such a thing. But. No."

I had written one spring to my brothers Harold and Amos, and my sister Beatrice, for any memories they had of Aunt Anna. I hadn't really expected any, and was right about that, but surprised that from all three siblings came invitations to travel, offers of companionship, temporary or permanent. Amos and his wife still lived in Indianapolis, and I was sure his invitation was merely polite form. But Harold wrote with apparent earnestness. Retired from his tramping around Alaska, he had an apartment in a small town in British Columbia. He told me the adjoining rooms were empty; he declared the charms and conveniences and affordability of the town. I had seen his picture on his book jackets, we had written each other sporadically over the years, but we had not met since Father's funeral, nearly fifty years ago. I was glad for the renewed correspondence, but I never even mentioned the invitation to join him.

And then was floored by a similar suggestion from Bea. Widowed too, she lived in Arizona, and extolled its virtues, invited me to come see it all, think about moving. There were three "adorable" adobes available, all within walking distance of her own cottage.

The unspoken but clearly assumed condition behind her offer was that my entire adult life be stricken from the record. How had I earned such condescension? For a few days I had stalked angrily around my rough little cabin, then abruptly one afternoon found the image of me – too tall, too thin, too boney and gravelly-voiced and ill-clad, with my unremarkable white hair still my best feature – in some "adorable" cottage learning bridge and serving tiny sandwiches, overwhelmingly funny, and had written it all out in my notebook.

So here I remained, a transplant with memory of past places and offers of other possible places. This was not home: home was with Ethan, home was where one had some purpose, some goal, even if just the tautology of creating the home. But it was familiar. Every surface of the house, every rock of the yard, every turn of the path and treacherous place in the steps, was known to me now as not even the Chicago house had been.

Listing the options I had so thoughtlessly turned down, I thought again of Morris, his more honest facing of the future. Was I to lose another friendship? For that it was a friendship, and a strong one, I suddenly saw clearly. The length of the acquaintance stunned me. It was twenty-four years since that first ride to the station, and already eight years since he and Nat had hefted my trunks and boxes up the stone steps.

I wondered now what I had had in mind then. I had come because it had seemed to me I must: to get my stopped life out of its downward spiral and onto a simpler, more level, horizontal, plane. Not to begin again; I had not then and did not now have any expectation of that. But as I filled the last page of the notebook and carried it by flashlight out to its place beside the others in the study-hut, I knew with a bewildered happiness that I had not merely waited out the last eight years. I had lived them. I opened the notebook and wrote in a margin: A transplant, even a potted plant, is different than a bouquet.

CHAPTER 4.

Carrie *Mattie*

Carrie's tenth birthday fell on the last day of school, a ritualistic half-day. She and Jarrett hurried in the lane, the hound Casey Jones bounding out of the cherry orchard at the bend, ecstatic as they.

"Casey, Casey," Carrie shouted. "Guess what! It's *summer*!" He barked and ran circles in an abandon of joy, making them laugh. "Silly," Carrie said, "you'd do that no matter what I said. You don't have to go to school, what's vacation to you?"

They ran, bursting into the kitchen to slam the report cards down on the table.

"We passed," Jarrett yelled, before realizing the kitchen was empty. Carrie went stiff with the distress she felt so often these days, since her mother turned sick, since Carrie had caught her crying, time after time. Emma always denied it, sent her away, but Carrie knew weeping when she saw it, goodness she wasn't a baby any more.

"Hi, kids." Emma's voice from the other room came hoarse and weak, but with relief they grabbed their cards and went in. Emma was lying back against pillows propped on the couch's arm. "You had lunch?"

"We just got home," Jarrett said, frowning. "Here." He handed her his card, and Carrie did the same. Emma glanced at them and smiled. "Well, Carrie, you don't have to frown so, nobody can scold you for this. And Jarrett, good for you, straight A's!"

Carrie sat gingerly by her mother's feet. She hadn't been thinking of grades, but searching Emma's face for signs of tears, or pain. It looked a little puffy, but Carrie decided she was just resting, this time.

"Can you get lunch for yourselves? I left everything out. There's strawberries, too, and some shortcake if Skip left you any."

"Mama," Carrie said, "when is the baby coming?"

"Not 'til August. I've told you that often enough now."

"And you'll be okay then?"

"I expect so, Carrie. Don't you worry about that. I'm okay now. I just have to rest more, is all, to keep the baby safe."

"We'll do the dishes."

"That's my girl. Change your clothes first."

The children had never known their other grandmother, and Emma tried to make them familiar with her father, but without much success. Emma's brother, a career army man, had survived the War but died in Korea, and Amos Lynn tumbled with grief into irritable senility. Her only sister had married before Emma and moved South, where he refused to go. He refused, in fact, even to move as far as Emma's, glued by some terror and need of his own to the street of Potter's Corner. He fretted even for a Sunday afternoon, and wouldn't hear of her assurances of space for him.

"There's this room, here, look." She opened the door by the stairs.

"Looks full up to me. How would I get to Guy's?"

Found wandering along the tracks, he was finally taken to the

County Home. Emma was humiliated by the move, and thought others judged her harshly for it, but knew him to be happier there, where other old men sufficed as village, in a way the farm could not have matched. She visited, but gave up taking Carrie and Jarrett. Amos had no interest in the present tense.

And now Dr. Carlisle said Emma must positively have help, if the baby was to be saved. So the little room just past the stairs, by the backdoor, had been turned from makeshift visiting space into a real room for Mattie. The sewing machine stayed, but all the trucks and blocks were packed upstairs or stowed on the back porch.

The day she came, Casey heard it first, of course, raising his big head from the packed earth in front of the porch, cool from the shade of the two big pines. Jarrett stopped shelling peas and looked at him. "Somebody's comin'."

They abandoned their pans and ran to the side of the house just in time to see a gray car pull out of the woods, turn the bend, coming toward the house. "Suppose it's them?" Carrie whispered.

"Must be. It's nobody's car around here."

Casey started barking, and the car came close enough to see it had two people in it. "It is! It is!" Carrie bounded for the door. "Mama! Gramma's here! Mama!"

She got halfway up the stairs before her mother's voice answered. "Yes, all right, go and greet them."

Carrie turned and tore back through the kitchen but halted abruptly on the porch, standing a little behind Jarrett as the strange car stopped. Duane got out, stretched, moved to the trunk of the car. "You two for hire?" he said, and released from their shyness they both rushed to help, as their grandmother Mattie came around the car toward them.

With Gramma here, the summer tasks, the endless weeding and hoeing and picking and washing and fetching and sweeping, all seemed less dreary. Even Emma got better, though Dr. Carlisle still didn't want her out of bed much and reminded the children not to let her lift so much as a book. Aunt Hannah came at least one afternoon a week, driving the Buick carefully over the rocks and potholes of the lane and helping with some chore or sitting with her embroidery, chatting with Emma to pass the time. Carrie liked to hang around the edges of the talk, especially when the three women rested on the porch.

"And Mattie here," Emma said, "she thought she got away from all this."

They would laugh, those soft chuckles of sharing a truth that didn't need to be spoken. Carrie glanced around from the step she was squatting on to reassure herself that her grandmother was not unhappy here. Mattie was smiling with the others. Jars of sweet cherries bubbled inside the big kettle of water inside, on the new combination stove. Half of it was electric, but for the canning the wood box was stoked, and the house was hot.

"You go to Duane's graduation?"

"Id 've give my eye teeth to go," Mattie said. "But even Duane didn't go, said he had to be in New York that week."

"New York?" Emma was astonished. "*City?*"

"My lands." Hannah sighed. "Folks sure do go traipsin' all over, these days. Wendell's always in some new place out West, one park or another, I don't know when he gets any work done. And there's Louisa, just back from France and off again to Colorado, not even time to stop by."

"That's where Uncle Duane's at now," Carrie said.

"No, honey," Emma corrected her. "He's in Chicago, the university there."

"Oh." Carrie didn't argue, but was sure she'd heard Duane tell her father that he was going to go see what Colorado looked like, before school.

"Is he really?" Hannah was pleased. "Well, he was always the bright one. How many degrees does a person need, these days?"

If the afternoon was hot and not threatening a storm, Carrie and Jarrett would sometimes walk over to Mertz Hollow, where a dammed up creek was the nearest swimming hole. Jarrett whistled as they walked down from the woods along the field always called the cornfield, though it was in clover now. He was whistling a jumble of the fiddle tunes he was learning from Skip.

Dora Mertz hailed them from the porch. "They're all already down at the creek."

Four-year-old Kenny John dropped the handle of a tiny wagon and set up a wail to go along, but Dora waved them on. "You're too little, KenJohn, you stay with me."

Carrie and Jarrett ran past the rotting picket fence, climbed the rail fence and ran on through the pasture, an eye out for Sam's steers. Over the fence again, through a few trees, and they were at the creek.

"Hey!" Sammy's close-shorn head surfaced in the middle of the pool. "Where you been?"

Jarrett flung off t-shirt and jeans, and did a belly-flop off the bank. Jimmie was astride the twisted oak that hung over the water. "Watch out, Carrie, the alligators 're hungry today!"

"Yeah? Says who?" Carrie shivered as a breeze touched her sweaty back. "Hi, Donnamae."

"Hi." Donnamae was trying to fashion a castle out of the wet mud.

"Says me," Jimmie yelled back. "And I'm king of the bridge!"

"Maybe, and maybe not." Carrie ran out the trunk, and in a second they were both splashing in the water. Sammy swung up in their place, Jarrett said his name was Little John and ordered Sammy off, winning the struggle but lost his balance and had to jump off. The water was just up to Carrie's chin.

"Hey, Donnamae, you learn to swim yet?" Jarrett called to the younger girl.

"Shit, she's so dumb she'd drown in a thimble."

"I am not, Sammy, you shut up."

Carrie laughed with the boys, but felt a tug of sympathy. She liked it better, generally, when Donnamae wasn't around.

"Come in and show us, then," Jimmie taunted.

"Nah, don't wanna."

"Sissy!"

"Aw, forget it, Jimmie." Sammy dove under, picked a stone and skipped it across to the far bank. "Swimmin' ain't what girls is good for, anyhow. Come on, Carrie, let's show 'em what girls is good for!"

Without warning, he grabbed her arm. Off balance from the smooth rocks underfoot, and caught by surprise, she fell against him. Her free arm swung for balance and collided with his mouth though she hadn't really meant that, and he let go with a cry. She went under the water, and when she came up, Sammy was spitting blood, holding his mouth.

"What the hell 'd you do that for?"

"What 'd you shove her for?" Jarrett demanded.

"I didn't shove her, stupid. What's the matter, ain't you never kissed?"

Jimmie was staring at them both, wide-eyed. "Kissin' makes babies."

Carrie turned her rage on him. "Nah it don't, you don't know nothin'."

"Oh yeah? How do you know so much?"

"Because I seen –" Carrie stopped, astonished. She felt her body go suddenly hot with undefined shame, and cold from the water. Her hand hurt. She looked, frantic, for her pile of clothes.

"Hey, come on," Sammy called to her back. "I didn't mean nothin', Jesus Christ."

"Carrie?" Jarrett called too. "Carrie, come on, we don't have to go yet."

"Don't then!" On the bank, she scooped her clothes tight against the hurt in her chest. "And anyway," she yelled at Sammy, "that ain't the way you kiss!" She moved behind a tree to tug on her jeans over wet underpants. The jeans were hot and sticky against her wet skin, with dirt from her feet scratching all along her legs. She jammed her feet into her sneakers, stuffing socks into a hip pocket.

Jimmie was mystified, and came crashing out of the water. "Carrie, you hurt?"

"Shut up!" Crumpling her t-shirt in her fist she climbed the fence, and ran all the way across the pasture. She had to stop then for breath. She put on the shirt and moving more slowly now had time to think about the whole bewildering moment. Finally, the image of the kiss and how she knew about kissing, came clear. From so long ago it seemed like a part of some other self, but so powerful it was without a doubt part of her. She had never told even Jarrett, had never really thought about it all this time.

"Why, hello, Carrie." Her grandmother looked up from the sink, her arms up to her elbows in suds. "You all done swimmin'?"

Carrie slumped into a chair, and shrugged. She watched Mattie's hands moving up and down, open and close, in the water. "I ain't never goin' swimmin' no more."

The hands paused. "How come is that?"

"Don't want to." She watched as her grandmother pressed the suds from the slips and put them in a basin of clear water. "Wish I'd 've hit him for real. I mean hard. But I don't care. They can have their stinkin' old hole, I don't care."

She kept her chin up for a second or two longer, then hid her face in her arms, stifling sobs. Her grandmother came to her, drew fingers gently through Carrie's short tangled hair. "You have a fight, that it?"

"No. Well, sort of."

"What about?"

Carrie had to cry again, the scene hateful inside her. Mattie moved her chair closer and handed her a handkerchief from her apron pocket, and waited.

"I don't know. Nothing. It was just Sammy being stupid."

"What'd he say?"

"He tried to – he said girls ain't good for swimmin' and he tried to kiss me and I fell and my fist smacked him and I wish I'd 've had a rock in it." She bit her lip, afraid of rebuke, but her grandmother said nothing. Carrie wiped at her face and felt the rage building in her again. "He thinks he can push me around just 'cause I'm a girl! Who needs *him*, anyhow?"

Her grandmother after a moment gently covered Carrie's fist, smoothed open the fingers. "You can go swimmin' again. You will."

"I ain't! I don't want to."

"But you will want to, sometime. Never let the other fellow call yer shot."

"What?"

Mattie smiled, gave a quick flick of her hand. "That's city talk, I guess. I mean, don't let Sammy decide whether you swim or not."

Carrie slumped again, with sudden weariness and confusion, longing at the same time for the swimming hole and friends, and for the solitude of the dimmest corner of the barn. Her grandmother caressed her neck before pushing back from the table. "I didn't mean you have to decide right this minute. But you got a right to swim. We all of us forget that, from time to time. Can you hang these things out for me?"

Carrie took the pan of clothes and trudged out to the clothesline. When she came back she heard her grandmother's voice in the kitchen. "I don't mean to meddle, Emma, but I think maybe Carrie's ready for a swimsuit."

Her mother gave a short laugh. "Lands, I suppose you're right. And the room ought to be divided. How do they stop bein' babies so fast?"

Each trailing a shirt from a careless fist, Carrie and Jarrett walked into the yard from the cherry orchard. Even now at the end of the afternoon, the July heat was so intense the walking itself brought sweat. Their grandmother was gathering clothes from the line; they met her in the shade of the maple, and she set down the basket. "How'd it go today?"

"Oh, Gramma, I'm sick to death of them damn cherries!" Jarrett dropped to the grass.

Carrie cast a worried glance at her grandmother, but when no rebuke came, sat down to pull off sneakers and socks. "Wish there was a thousand pickers and zoom! We'd be done."

"You wouldn't make much money then," Mattie reminded her. "You only been at it a week."

"A *week*?" Jarrett shoved sun-bleached hair back from his forehead with a sticky hand, leaving a smudge. "Seems like so long I can't remember back so far."

"Only be another week or so, won't it?"

"Yeah, we should go up to the other farm soon," Jarrett said. "If I don't get killed 'fore then."

"Jarrett, you ain't . . . ." Carrie trailed off.

"What might you two be talkin' about, I wonder?"

"Jarrett fell off his ladder today."

"I did not fall off no ladder," he corrected, flaring. "The ladder turned on me, it was Skip's fault, he set it, and the next tree was a great big one and Daddy made us take it just for meanness. I mean a great big one."

"He don't want to play favorites, the others –"

"That ain't no call to jerk my arm like he done, lookit!" Jarrett held out his arm for her to see, and she touched the bruise on his upper arm lightly, clucking her tongue.

"He's a bit worried these days, he wasn't –"

"And make me go clean to the top for a half dozen stupid cherries. I tell you one thing, I ain't bein' no farmer. I'm goin' to college, like Uncle

Duane." He jumped up and stomped off, to the hand pump behind the house.

"Here, honey, you take this towel and go wash up, too, you'll feel better."

Carrie took the towel, averting her eyes to keep back tears, picked up her shoes and socks and shirt and started after Jarrett.

"Carrie!" Her mother's call from the porch stopped her. "Carrie you get that shirt right back on, what did I tell you?"

Startled into confusion, Carrie froze, too many things in her hands and on her mind. Her grandmother, passing her, touched her lightly. "It's all right, Emma, she's only going to wash up a bit first."

One morning soon after the cherry harvest was finished, Mattie interrupted their bean picking. "Go get your daddy, he's mowin' somewhere up on the hill back of the barn."

They hesitated, questioning, but when she said, "Run!" they tore out of the garden and off around the barn, with sudden comprehension.

At the car door, Emma turned to Mattie. "Would you come along?"

Mattie was already handing her apron to Carrie. "You two be okay? Stay here close by the house. You better get in the back, Emma."

"Don't cry, stupid," Jarrett growled at Carrie as the car disappeared around the bend. "Women have babies every day. Look at Verta and Skip, they have one every year, about."

"I'm not crying."

They finished picking the row of green beans, made themselves sandwiches. "We should have a phone," Jarrett complained.

"Maybe they'll call Aunt Hannah."

They threw the baseball for awhile, then Jarrett got a book and pretended to read under the maple tree. "We could build the fort back up now," Carrie said. "The cherry crates are back."

Jarrett only glanced vaguely toward the barn, and she felt rebuked, as if something had changed while she wasn't paying attention. "Are you going to college, really, Jarrett?"

"Yep."

"You couldn't stay here, then."

"Who wants to stay here?"

"I like our place!"

"It ain't ours, you know, and it won't never be. The Millers just let us live here, 'cause Daddy works for them."

"I don't care who owns it," Carrie said, but felt unsure about that. "I wonder who owns Pine Mountain now that the hermit is gone."

He looked up, impatient with her. "What's that got to do with anything?"

"We never found the cabin." She meant, you can't leave yet. But she didn't really know what anything had to do with anything, especially with Mama off in some hospital.

"It's prob'ly not there, never was."

"What? Don't you remember? Didn't Gramma tell us it was?"

"Carrie, for pete's sake, I'm trying to read."

She was stung into silence, and rolled over onto her stomach. Casey came and licked her face so she giggled and hid it; he pushed his nose under her arm to try to get to it, and she rolled over to push him away, when he suddenly barked and ran toward the house. It was Charlie, in a pickup.

"It's twins!" he called to them through the window.

"*Two* of 'em?" Jarrett said, then blushed at such dumbness, but Charlie only laughed.

"Yep, two of 'em. Boy and girl. Hannah says to come on over for supper, till your dad gets back."

"Where's Mama?" Carrie asked. She could hold no image of baby, much less babies, only kept seeing her mother's frightened face turned to Mattie at the car door.

"She's fine. Wore out, but she'll be all right. Come on, Casey!"

The dog sprang up into the bed, which had no tail gate, and barked all the way out the lane, first to one side then the other. Carrie and Jarrett sat up in the dusty, cluttered cab, Carrie in the middle with her feet tucked up under her so Charlie could shift the gears. There were twins now, she kept telling herself, two new babies. But she couldn't picture the hospital, couldn't picture the babies at home, hard as she tried, and the two blanketed lumps floated as if unattached through a whole series of other thoughts that wouldn't stay away. The swimming hole, the shadowy stall in the barn, the cherry orchard, the crazily spinning tractor, and roses, something about roses; and her father whittling on the porch, the ridge of pine trees, a broken wrist – the two babies got mixed up in it all.

"Skip said we're all to come over," Jarrett said. "To celebrate getting through another cherry season."

"Daddy said we could, too," Carrie added.

"And so you can," Emma said, "soon as you do the dishes."

"Don't you want to go?" Jarrett's tone was full of disbelief.

"You go on, I'll wait for daddy to get back from the factory. Anyhow, these two are too much a handful to go visiting with." She held Nathan's foot from banging his high chair tray; instead of protesting he threw back his head with a belly laugh, and his twin Naomi shouted and banged her plastic cup.

"Look out, Gramma!"

Jarrett's yell was too late. Omie stared in surprise at the white liquid filling her tray, running across her arm, cold on her bare front. Their grandmother jumped up, untying her apron for a towel. "A drum's one thing, Naomi Brown, and a cup of milk's another, entirely."

"And if you two can't learn not to laugh at them, the rate of destruction at this table's going to rise 'til it'll be safer eatin' out with Clover."

Jarrett, his mouth clamped obediently shut, nearly choked. "At least the milk 'd be handy," he said, and Carrie had to laugh, and then again at Nathan chuckling as if he got the joke. While she and Jarrett complained to each other that the twins have practically pushed them out of the house, she could sometimes scarcely contain her love for them. There was no getting her mother's attention anymore, for anything, but on the other hand because of the twins Gramma Mattie was here all summer again. And now that Jarrett was so little interested in their old pursuits, she found herself drifting for company often into the range of the babies.

"You can go on over to Skip's," Mattie said. "I can wash up the dishes this once, guess it won't hurt you."

"No!" Carrie shouted. "You got to come, Gramma!"

"Skip's awful good, Gramma," Jarrett said. "You ever hear fiddle?"

Mattie's hands, reaching for Omie, suddenly rested on the tray. Omie, thinking it a game, patted them with her own. Nathan kicked his tray again, fussing until Emma lifted him down.

"Yes, I've heard fiddling," Mattie said. "Fair amount of it." She reached again for Omie, who was standing on her seat and fairly leaped into her arms.

"It ain't far to Skip's," Jarrett said. "You could come along with us."

"Jarrett, don't pester Gramma."

"Please, Gramma."

"Carrie!" Emma scolded sharply. "They can go by themselves, Mattie, don't you be forced into it."

But Mattie suddenly smiled. "I think I'll go along, after all. Let's clean up here."

"No, you go on, I can manage here. Listen, watch out for any wine of Skip's. He'll declare it's harmless, but it ain't."

Skip lived on the Jack Road, which at the other end came out far up the ridge beyond the Miller farm, but at this end lay just a half mile from the peach orchard. The little frame house, in want of paint and with no sign of grass in front, stood neatly for all that just off the graveled road, behind a huge pin-oak. A series of sheds climbed the partly cleared slope behind, with garden patches in long rows on the other side of the road. Skip hailed them from the porch, which seemed to release two little boys. Jarrett grabbed Alvin and slung him head-down over his shoulder, and Carrie side-stepped the larger Clyde, letting him chase her to the house.

"The fudge is ploppin'," he told her.

"Boilin', you mean."

"It don't boil, it plops."

The toddler Violet let go of the porch post to clap her hands. Verta looked through the open doorway, a wooden spoon in one hand, a baby cradled in the other arm.

"Hiya, kids! And Mattie Brown! Clydey, go in and get a chair out for Miz Brown."

Mattie smiled and held her arms out for the baby, whose tiny bare limbs were elfish, unlikely, against the startling expanse of the mother's bosom. Verta transferred him with the deftness of long practice, and Clydey pushed a plank-bottom chair out from the kitchen.

"I declare," Verta said, settling beside her, "I was saying just the other day to Skip why here the summer's half over and I've seen you exactly once, just by accident at Guy's, and your place our nearest neighbor."

"As the crow flies, anyhow," Skip said. He sent Jarrett inside to get the fiddle. Carrie watched approvingly as he knelt and opened the battered case, took out the bow, tightened the end screw, drew the hairs across a cake of rosin, before giving it and the violin to Skip. It had the importance of ritual, the beginning of a moment, the proper beginning, that would not slide past haphazardly or take you by surprise. There would be the first short strokes across each string, a little tuning, the beginnings of a few shuffles, the nod that the bow and strings are suiting him, and then always sudden and loud, a real beginning, and Carrie would release her held breath in a shout that made Skip grin and stamp his foot.

And so it was. The tentative notes and bits of scales and chords broke into Bill Cheat'em, and Carrie's Ooo-*ee* rang over the tune. Skip began to beat time on the porch boards, the children grabbed each other and swung around the yard in giddy reckless abandon. The tune changed with scarcely a pause into June Apple, into Miller's Reel. The baby, astonishingly, fell asleep. Verta took him inside and came out with the fudge, cool enough to eat. Laying the fiddle down disregardful of its safety, taking it for granted, Skip went around the corner of the house to the cellar door. The children passed around the bottle of orange soda he brought, and Verta got glasses for the dark wine he poured from a gallon jug.

In only a few minutes, Skip straightened from the post he was leaning against, and picked up the fiddle. "It's a fiddle night," he announced, "no stoppin' it now."

Verta laughed shrilly and hugged Violet. "Yer papa now, he's something!"

Skip winked at her and sawed into Sugar in the Gourd, and Verta shrieked again. The children ran past him down the two steps and began their dancing with fresh energy.

> Met a little girl, met her on the road,
> Tune up my fiddle, give her sugar in the gourd;
> Sugar in the gourd and I can't get it out,
> And the way to get the sugar out is roll the gourd about!

Skip sang in a high powerful voice that carried out over the instrument, over the shouts of the children, moving his lips but little, the words seeming to come from some mysterious place so much larger than his wiry frame could possibly hold. He finished the verses but played the tune several times more, faster and faster, until the children flopped on the porch steps at his feet. Skip laughed at them, wiping his forehead, and held up his empty glass.

"What d'you say, Mom? Give the fiddler a dram!"

"Yep, looks like you won, sure enough."

"No more for me," Mattie said. "It's a hot night, and I been warned."

Skip laughed again. "Why, ma'am, that stuff's harmless as a little ol' blacksnake warmin' in the sun."

"I don't aim to step on him, neither."

He topped up his glass again and sat quietly, almost absently, brushing his fingers across the fiddle in his lap. Carrie sat cross-legged near Mattie's chair and watched him with eagerness, studying his face for the signs of softening that could mean he was getting ready for a ballad. Violet yawned. Jarrett took her into his lap, where she lay back against his shoulder with a sigh. Alvin looked at her jealously, then realized his mother's lap was free for a change, and settled there. Clydey lay down of the porch beside Carrie.

"Well, man," Verta said, her voice unusually soft, "you best be singin' a story, to stop all this wigglin' on my lap."

Skip raised the fiddle. As if all joy was gone from it, it yielded rather than offered its melody, it sighed and mourned, muted in lonesome drones. "Down in the willow garden, my love and I did meet . . . . ."

There seemed to be no one doing the song, the notes of instrument and voice rose and fell as if without effort, twining of their own volition. The tale and tune were one, an entity that wrapped around Skip and listener, child and adult alike, a force that transformed the gory murder and hopeless repentance into universal, chilling truth.

"My race is run beneath the sun, all hell now waits for me . . . ."

The lament wailed high, dipped an octave, ended simply. The fiddle repeated the cry, and trailed off in a whisper.

Released from the spell by Verta's heavy sigh, Carrie unwound her legs to rub a foot that was tingling. She looked at her grandmother to share the pleasure, but Mattie was watching Skip.

"Where'd you learn to sing and play like that?"

"Why, ma'am, it ain't much of a tale. A fellow name of Roger. We never found out any more, no matter how my ma wheedled and pried."

"You mean when you was little?" Carrie struggled to imagine it. "Here?"

"Down in Maryland. Place called Jacob's Hollow, after the fellow wrestled with an angel, that's what farmin' there was like. My dad used to say he'd ought to sell the cows and open a quarry and get rich. 'Course, he never done neither one."

"So who was Roger?" Jarrett prompted.

"He was a tramp come by. Along in the fall, it was, not cold yet. Me and Sis we're out throwing a ball and I says, Bet I can throw it clean over the barn and I rared back and give it a pitch in spite of her yellin not to, we'll lose it in the spout. She always did have more sense than me. So it gets over the peak and off we go 'round the barn. But what was I thinking? We don't see no ball, and it's comin on dark and we walk around in the thistle and milkweed and dock pretending there's some way we're gonna find that ball, when out comes this voice from the barn. You'all a'lookin' for this?

"Well. I don't need to tell you, the back of my neck bristled up like a porky-pine. Neither one of us could move, we turned bloodless as a cake of salt. Finally Sis she reaches out real slow and grabs my arm and the both of us turn our heads, eyes big as meat platters, to look at that barn. God knows what we figured we'd see. Here was this old man, hunkered down against the barn wall, and when he sees pretty plain we ain't comin' to take no ball outa his hand, he gives it a little toss. My hand goes up, just by habit, you know, and I catch it and that breaks the spell and we like to fall over one another gettin' over the fence and down to the house screamin' for Daddy like the whole Rebel army was at our heels.

"He's out lookin' at the grapes. We get it out that there's this man at the barn. By this time Mama comes out from the back kitchen, trailin' Josh and Bessie and Howie and holding Mary, and the whole bunch of us just stand there starin' at the barn. And Daddy, he sets his cap on square and starts out.

"You get the gun, Mama says. You don't know what he is. Hell, I don't need no gun, he says, and takes about a dozen steps and pulls up short. There's the old fellow, comin' out around the barn.

"He's one of them tramps, Mama says. You git rid of him. And Daddy he looks at her kind of funny. More'n likely about half-starved, he says, and Mama looks like she's workin' up towards mad, and then she says, He can sure as hell-fire eat it out there, then. She herds all us kids back in the house and then sends Sis and me out with a pan of hash and a big hunk of bread and a mug of coffee."

Skip crushed out his cigarette on his work boot. "Well. By that time, Daddy and him were settin' together on old boxes in front of the horses' stall, and Daddy he's turnin' over a beat-up fiddle in his hands. When he see us he lays it down and says, You put away that food, I'll just go see if my banjo's got any strings. Which don't make no kind of sense, that banjo's hangin' on the wall in first rate shape, he plays it about every evening. So Sis and I just sort of back up and hang around. He eats, real quiet, lookin' comfy and even happy. Shirt that dirty you can't tell its color, his hair and beard all raggedy, gray and white mixed."

As if the story were over, Skip picked up the fiddle and bow, and handed them to Jarrett. "Here, you play it some."

Jarrett lifted the sleepy Violet off his legs and took the fiddle. "So what happened?"

"Why, them two played 'most all night. And then the old man stayed all winter. Mama she grumbled some at first, but she must've known she'd lost when she seen Daddy take down the banjo. Uncle

Roger, we called him. He was from the South, somewhere. Cleaned up and fed he didn't look so old as we thought at first. He knowed more tunes even than Daddy. I took to it natural, but I ain't the musician he was. He had the gift."

"Where'd he go?"

Skip shook his head. "He up and left, that's all I know. What you going to play?"

Jarrett glanced at his grandmother. "I ain't much to listen to."

"Now, you go on," Verta said. "Ain't no judges settin' here, that I can see."

So Jarrett began a quick, stiff Old Joe Clark, and then Carrie was singing along, a verse and then another. Skip clapped time and joined in the chorus:

Get out the way, Old Joe Clark, hide that jug o' wine!

Get out the way, Old Joe Clark, Ain't no friend of mine!

The fiddle began to swoop and soar a little, with some shuffling and double stops that made Skip nod and grin, as Jarrett's arm lost its shyness.

And then it was time to go. They crossed the wooden bridge just down the hill from the house, and turned into the woods, following an old logging trail.

"You like it all right, Gramma?"

"You done fine, Jarrett. I didn't know you could play like that."

"No, I mean Skip. He's awful good, ain't he?"

"Indeed he is. I ain't heard nothin' like that for a good many years."

"Wish I could practice more."

"Jarrett!" Carrie swung her arms wide, struck with an idea. "We could use our cherry money. How much do fiddles cost, Gramma?"

"I don't know, child. A good bit, I'd think."

The path even in the woods was speckled with moonlight, and when they reached the peach orchard they stopped of one accord. "Look at it," Carrie whispered, as if the scene were timid, and might vanish. The moon hung lopsided just above the swamp on their right, bright enough to throw shadows from the trees and light up the white blooms of Queen Anne's Lace.

Just as the children were ready to move again, Mattie's voice held them. "Listen. Back at home, I mean back in Detroit at your Uncle Carl's, there's a fiddle. Layin' in a box."

She began walking again, and Carrie and Jarrett moved close on either side. "Just layin' there. All this time. The strings wouldn't be no good, I don't imagine, but outside of that there wouldn't be nothin' wrong with it. You should have it, Jarrett."

"Why?"

"It's no use in a box."

"No, I mean how come you got a fiddle? You used to play?"

"Oh. No, I never. It was your granddaddy's."

"What?" Carrie shook her head. "Granddaddy never played a fiddle. All kinds of things he done, people talked at the funeral but nobody said —"

"Wait." Jarrett stopped her. "Gramma means Daddy's dad."

"Where's he at?" Carrie demanded, feeling bewildered. She had never heard of this grandfather.

"Gone, long since, child."

"How come Daddy never —"

"He wouldn't remember him. Nor the fiddle."

"Why?"

Mattie paused, then moved on along the rows of trees. "You've had enough tale for one night."

They went through another short stretch of woods, came through the meadow, past the pond where frogs hushed just ahead of their stepping, past the little stone springhouse. At the clothesline they could see the truck in the driveway, and Jarrett broke into a run. His shout from the porch carried back to Mattie and Carrie.

"Daddy! Guess what!"

But Carrie, feeling an odd sense of loss, wanted to linger in the dusk, to kick around in the weeds looking for the ball. "Did you know Skip's old man the fiddler?"

"No. That's a different story."

"And Mr. Brustein, did he play the fiddle?"

Her grandmother gave a short laugh of surprise, then regarded her a long moment. "You want it all connected, don't you? Well, maybe it is. That's what he used to say."

"Who?"

"But not in the way you think."

"*Tell me.*"

Mattie drew a long breath. "Someday. Jarrett the fiddle and you the tale. Fair enough?"

At the edge of the porch, her grandmother stopped again. "But listen, Carrie: just parts, is all anyone can give you."

She went inside. Carrie turned for one last look at the dusk becoming night. She didn't believe her grandmother, not yet, hearing the promise but not the disclaimer, seeing the fiddle in Jarrett's hands, the lost ball in the tramp's fist, and all contained somehow in her grandmother's firm grasp.

"Carrie?" Her mother is at the screen door. "Come in now, let me check you over for ticks."

"I don't have any ticks."

"How you know?"

Carrie took a deep breath, to take in something of what was left, to pull it inside with her. But her mother was right, the day was over, and she felt a kind of relief to step into the kichen, where her father was pushing back his chair from his supper, stretching his arms high over his head.

"Hey," he said, through a yawn.

"How'd we do today?" Carrie asked.

"Inspection? Ninety, not bad for end of season. What'll you do tomorrow, with a whole day to yourself?"

She shrugged, but there was a cheer from Jarrett. "Finally! I did think cherries would never end."

Carrie submitted her head, her back and arms, to Emma's check. "Where's Gramma?"

"Gone to bed already, you wore her out. You wash your feet good before you touch a sheet."

Her grandmother's door, beyond the stairway, was indeed shut tight. Carrie hesitated on the bottom step, enclosed by the surrounding lives of the house but feeling again the hollow loss, hearing now the warning in her grandmother's voice. Just parts. Watching the door, she went up a step backwards, and another. But the door did not open, and she turned and climbed the stairs.

Hannah Miller called the next Saturday, just as they were finishing lunch. Jem always let Emma deal with the new contraption on the kitchen wall. "You'd never guess who just drove in!"

Emma couldn't.

"Ed and Elsie and Thomas, all the way from Virginina. Can you'uns all come on over?"

"Listen, it's the twins' birthday. Bring everybody over here for cake tonight."

Mattie caught her breath at first sight of the young woman straightening from the car. With a dress instead of slacks, with tied back curls instead of bobbed ones, Elsie might have been Corie come back. She even had Corie's diffident way of drawing you into a special circle. The teenager Thomas had on principle to be more sullen, barely masking his boredom with a shell of politeness, intimidating even Jarrett into unusual bashfulness. Ed Lakin, now with steel gray hair and

247

some slackening around the jaw and waist, had still the good looks that draw second glance, and seemed as unaware of that as always.

"Where's Charlie?" Emma asked.

"Said he had paper work," Hannah said with a slight smile that added, never mind, you know how Charlie is.

Oh, Charlie. Mattie saw him with sharp sadness. His reticence was so part of the landscape no one would notice, and there no doubt really was paperwork, but she realized that but for her he would have come.

A card table had been set up on the porch. When Jarrett and Carrie brought out the two high chairs, Mattie and Jem plopped the two surprised babies in them, as Emma brought out the layer cake slowly so as not to put out the two candles. Hannah started everyone in a hearty round of the birthday song. The twins stared solemnly at the candles and then at each other as if to consult. Emma coaxed them to blow, and the candle flames wavered at their attempts until Jarrett took over.

The cake was served, the twins washed and set down to wander. Ed, sitting on an up-turned apple crate, gave Nathan a ride on his foot: This is the way the ladies ride, nippity-nippity-nip. And Mattie drew a hand over her face, taken off guard by the sudden image of Hazel there, right there, sitting astride the pretty horse.

She set her little caned rocker going, to anchor herself, and might have given Charlie a sympathetic smile. What's past ain't always over, is it?

Young Elsie pointed to the chairs Emma and Hannah were sitting in. "There's a chair up at the farm like those." Everyone did always refer to the Miller place as the farm, no matter how many other farms there were.

"They been here since before me," Emma said. "Gramma, you know about 'em?"

"What?" Mattie was startled, and embarrassed. "Sorry, my mind was wandering."

"Where?"

"Elsie." Her father rebuked her gently, but Mattie thought it a fair question.

"Why, truth to tell, I was seeing your gran there, about where Ed's got Nathan, she was settin' up on the prettiest little dark mare you'd ever see. First time I ever met her, to talk to."

It was a long bit of talk, for Mattie, and a vivid image. The insatiable Elsie recovered first. "What did she want?"

"Give me a job. That was during the War, the First one, I mean, there was no men around to help get the field corn in. We had a team of mules then."

"We?"

But this time Hannah intervened. "Elsie was asking about the bent-hickory chairs, Mattie."

"Those? Harry Kane used to make 'em. Before he lost an arm. They're prob'ly all over the county, still."

Hannah ran her hand over the smooth saplings of the arm. "There's two down at Mrs. Bakeley's, the ladies from Baltimore must've got them."

Then Elsie had to be told that story, with so many questions no one could answer Hannah finally teased her out of the subject. "Elsie, you're that curious you'd think we lived in a museum, all of us. You know why they come, Emma? You won't believe this. Elsie drug her daddy up here to show her his old school room!"

"And it's wonderful, too," Elsie declared. "I can just see him standing up there, in front of those little seats. Can't you?"

"Not only can," Jem said. "Did."

Elsie looked confused for a moment, then realized the age difference. "Of course! Oh listen, I've got to talk to you before we go back. In private." She blushed. "I mean, without Dad around."

"What for?"

"I've got this paper to do, for a composition course, has to be on a relative, and I chose Dad."

"You staying for church?" Emma suggested. "There'd be others there with a tale or two, I'd bet."

"Including Reverend Simpson," Hannah added.

"He still preaching?" Ed groaned. "Now there's a man did try my soul."

"They say Paul's comin' back to take over," Emma said. "Him and his wife."

"Like a dynasty?" Ed gave Nathan a final bounce and set him on his feet. "Didn't know Methodists did that."

On Sunday after the others left for church, Mattie finished up the meal's dishes and went out to the porch. The day was already hot, but the breeze there was perfect, and the rocking felt peaceful. More peaceful than her bed the night before, where she'd been restless. Mattie rocked, thinking wryly that even if not yet sixty, she felt old enough to spend the whole morning watching the shade move.

There was no transition, no moment of decision that she could ever remember, as if her body did it without her, and she caught up somewhere nearly back to the peach orchard. The path she had worn entered the woods nearly at the top of the orchard rows; she had always wondered, but never asked, whether Jem had found the path or had just happened on Benjamin's cabin while hunting squirrels, as he claimed. It wasn't really a distinct trail, even then, and now was only a trace. There were moments when she hesitated. She never worried in the slightest, however, that she might miss the clearing.

Pushing through a thick patch of laurel and spicebush, she found the trail again and came upon a ruffed grouse which ran ahead of her, making her laugh, until it finally did the sensible thing and turned off into the underbrush. Over a steep rise, her feet sliding a little down the rocky side, she came into one of the thick stands of pine so unusual to the area. She stood a moment in surprise. She must have lost track of time, for she was here already.

How could she have left it?

How could he?

It had seemed so clear at the time, a necessity so without question. And he had never blamed her for it, his letters made that clear. She had given up her right to the swimming hole, all right, and betrayed his love at the same time. But if there had ever been moments of thinking she could somehow get hold of him again, un-do the wrong, surely she had gotten over such foolishness years ago. So what was she doing standing here in the middle of the woods?

There had been letters, two of them. But her answer to the first had come back to her, and his second had come from a hospital in New Jersey, a single paragraph she knew by heart; she carried the image of it just behind her vision, the uneven penciled lines written with such care. *My Mattie, I love you. I meant only to come see the ocean once more and bring you back a perfect shell. I won't be back. Remember we make up the limits It is so fine mattie to think of you.*

She had figured out, during that awful afternoon, how to place a call to Atlantic City, to the hospital that someone, a nurse perhaps, had written on the envelope – but she had been several days too late. And then the letter from the lawyer had come.

At the clearing, a doe and fawn sprang up from the berry brambles and sassafras and bounded off. The rotting porch roof was hanging askew, the steps were gone, the door had fallen in; so much chinking had fallen out of the walls they looked skeletal.

Roses climbed and bloomed in a tangle of color. Mattie moved through the overgrown garden patches, right up to them, and sat on the porch edge with dark red flowers touching her shoulder, the scent nearly overwhelming. "Limits to what?" she whispered. Maybe there are no limits, he said. What if everything is connected, I mean every possible concept and thing is connected, infinite possibilities of connections, everything in the universe a single web, what if it's as simple as that?

Mattie went inside. Jem had cleaned out the little cabin, as she'd asked him to. Leaves and twigs made something's nest in the fireplace, two of the six little panes in the window were broken, the jagged edges breaking the sunlight like prisms. In the middle of the back wall was the narrow sill, below a square door hinged at the side: the joke of a wooden window. Mattie lifted the rusty hook, pushed gently with her fingers. With Virginia creeper and poison ivy climbing up against the outside, it didn't swing open as it had to his touch, and she first drew back, and then pushed hard. The window broke through the vines far enough to evoke a gasp of satisfaction from her throat.

For the effect was as always: the woods were immediate, and the dense layer of pine needles created a park. Why is it different than being out there, Benjamin? We humans like things framed, we like beginnings and endings to things, boundaries. But, she said, that's just a pretend frame, it ain't really holding anything in.

Mattie leaned on the sill. "Oh Benjamin. It is so fine to think of you." She felt something open in her, like the vine-choked wooden window. The foolishness was not in coming here, after all; the foolishness was in trying so hard to live without him. And without David, and Hazel and Mabel. They were all like the pine trees, right there in the frame. If she opened the window.

Someday, soon, she would be ready to start the telling, however Carrie wanted it. And she should tell Jem, too: That window, in the back of the cabin? It still opens.

Part Three

CHAPTER 1.

Carrie

Mattie brought Jarrett the fiddle for Christmas, and when she came the next summer she declared herself well satisfied with the gift. "You've been practicing."

"It still doesn't sound like Skip's," Jarrett said.

"Yer fiddle arm's only but fourteen, you'll catch him up soon enough."

He practiced nearly every evening; the twins began assuming it was part of bedtime. Sometimes he walked back to Skip's, and usually Carrie went along, soaking up the songs and stories. Carrie thought some about the fiddle's rescue from Mattie's closet, her grandmother's promise tucked in her mind, but the real event of the summer was the advent of Diana into their lives.

Aunt Hannah came to announce it while Carrie and Emma were clearing lunch and Mattie was putting the twins down for their nap. It was her custom to lie with them on the mattress for her own rest. "Now Emma, what do you think of this? Hannah laid the letter in its envelope

255

on the table. "Lou says can she leave Diana for the summer, July and August. What on earth am I to do?"

"Do? Why Hannah, you say yes, of course. Why? Are you having a houseful of others?"

"No, that's just the problem. There'll be the usual crowd for the Fourth, I suppose, but other than that it's just Charlie and me, rattling away in that big house. We've never even met the child, and her used to Paris and London and who knows what all."

"Why does she want to leave her?"

"She has some sort of work most of the summer, concerts and workshops at some fancy place. The farm was Duane's suggestion, he's off to a dig or whatever you call it somewhere in Central America, and can't stay with her. And bless me, the child's begging to come to the farm."

"And her father?"

"I take it he's been pretty much out of the picture since they went to Europe that year, maybe even before that."

"She's around Carrie's age, isn't she?" Emma nodded at her own question, the problem settled. "There you go, that's plenty of company, they're practically cousins, with Duane and Louisa together now."

Carrie felt the silence and looked around from the sink, to intercept a glance her way, Hannah's pleasant face troubled. Emma reached across the table to touch Hannah's arm. "Carrie knows about that," she said gently. "And she knows we don't approve. But Hannah, they're family."

"Why don't they marry, Emma?" Hannah whispered, close to tears.

"I don't know." Emma's voice was low, too. "They spend so much time apart, maybe they don't think – I don't know. But, you know, that ain't Diana's fault. Let her come, Hannah. Carrie and Jarrett will keep her busy."

Duane called first, then came over with Louisa and Diana. Carrie felt like bolting, especially when she saw the long-legged beauty right off the Ward's catalogue page. A plastic hair band held perfect hair perfectly in place; she wore not sneakers but soft shoes scarcely more than slippers; and worst of all, a neatly belted summer dress with wide neck and tiny cap sleeves. She looked completely at home in her body and clothes, a feeling Carrie only had alone, sitting by the spring. And her level gaze betrayed none of the shy awkwardness Carrie could not seem to grow out of. She smiled through the introductions, accepted the glass of lemonade with a firm grace, obviously not at all anxious about spilling or drinking it too fast or too slow. The grown-ups chatted on, about the summer plans, about the farms.

The twins were pushing trucks on the packed dirt by the porch, a little behind the chairs Jem and Duane had placed to face the others on the porch. As if on cue, they both abruptly abandoned the toys and came onto the porch. Duane laughed a little. "They always do that?"

"Pretty near always," Emma answered. "There's some kind of invisible thread between them."

Nathan patted Jarrett's knee. "Fiddle."

"No sir, not tonight." Jarrett tried to lift him up on his lap, but Nathan squirmed away.

"Fiddle," he repeated.

"Nathan, we have company." Jarrett was trying to keep his voice apart from that company, but there seemed suddenly a quiet space on the porch. Carrie saw his flush, but could think of no way to cover for him. To suggest bedtime would only introduce mayhem. Anyway it was too late to run interference.

"I've heard about this fiddle," Duane said. "Hannah said something about you playing. Can I see it?"

Jarrett looked surprised, then went to fetch it. Carrie suddenly made the connection she hadn't really thought of before, and looked at her grandmother and her father. Jem was studying his hands, Mattie's face was set, blank as a plate. *He wouldn't remember him, nor the fiddle.*

257

"Fiddle," Nathan said, satisfied, and maneuvered onto Jem's knees. Naomi looked at Mattie; the porch swing was already crowded with her and Emma and Louisa, but the women all nodded to the unspoken question and Emma helped her up.

"They're used to it at bedtime," Emma said, some apology in her voice.

"So then let's have some of it," Louisa said, the velvety voice striking another thrill of memory through Carrie just as Jarrett came out the screen door. He glanced at Louisa, smiling a little but shaking his head. He handed the instrument to Duane. Duane plucked a string, turned the violin in his hands to study the curly-maple back.

"It's a pretty one. Where you think it's from?" he asked Mattie.

Mattie was taken aback, and had to clear her throat a little before answering. "I never knowed that."

He handed it back to Jarrett. "Go on, now. Where's your bow?"

But Jarrett was firm. "At the Fourth, I will. Skip'll be there."

"You got to play!" Nathan raised his voice this time. "You got –"

"How about a song?" Diana's voice stopped him, and Omie too sat up in surprise.

"What song?"

"You know about the fly?"

The twins shook their heads, both leaning now toward this unexpected treat.

"I know an old woman who swallowed a fly." Diana began the simple song without preamble; she seemed to be sending her voice precisely to the children. "I don't know why she swallowed a fly: perhaps she'll die."

Omie snapped her head around to stare at Emma, but was reassured by her mother's smile, and fell into the weird magic of the song.

"I know an old woman who swallowed a spider, that wriggled and jiggled and tickled inside her. She swallowed the spider to catch the fly, I don't know why . . . ." and on the song went. The rat, the cat, the dog to catch the cat, to catch the rat to catch the spider, and with every "tickled" Jem and Emma both got into the act, reducing the mesmerized twins to giggles which they stifled to hear the next impossible feat.

"I know an old woman who swallowed a horse – She's dead of course."

There were two full beats of silence before everyone broke into laughs and applause, which Omie and Nathan loved as well as the song. They demanded more, but Diana was too clever for that. "Next time. I'll have to think about another one."

"Right. We'll go on back now," Louisa said, approving her strategy. "Goodnight, sweet." She planted a kiss on Omie's cheek and rose to do the same for Nathan. He caught her blouse and pulled her down to return the favor.

"Oh ho." Duane gave Jem a nudge. "Better watch that one, brother."

"And what do you say to Diana?" Emma coaxed, as everyone was standing up. "Can you say thank you?"

The twins, shy now but safe in their parents' arms, parroted the thanks. In the general exodus, Diana came to Jarrett and Carrie. "By the 'Fourth,' do you mean at Uncle Charlie's?"

"Yeah."

"Good!" Somehow she included them both. "By the way, can you call me Dee?"

Jarrett asked several times in the next few days if he shouldn't go over and help Hannah get ready for the picnic and each time Emma would remind him how much help she had. "She's got Charlie and Skip and your dad, besides all the folks starting to arrive."

"But all that company –"

"They'll all help. They're family."

"I think –"

"Here. Go get me another half bucket of cherries. We'll need more pies."

"I could maybe find some sweet cherries, over at Uncle Forrest's."

"Jarrett. I want pie cherries. Right there beside the yard. Sweet cherries been over for weeks. Now git."

Carrie watched his arguing with some tension in her stomach. Emma didn't much allow that kind of talk. But when he finally took the pail and went out the back door, and Emma went back to washing lettuce, Carrie saw with astonishment that her mother was smiling. Faintly, secretly, but smiling.

"Are they all coming?"

Emma glanced around at her, still smiling. "All but Wendell and Esther, I guess."

Jarrett was so restless the holiday morning, Emma relented. "Go on, walk on over if you want. We'll remember the fiddle."

He grabbed his baseball cap and practically leaped off the porch, then stopped. Carrie was coming out with a broom to sweep the porch, and he turned to her. "Carrie? Um, you ready to go too?"

Carrie had finally figured out her brother was anxious to meet Diana again, so now hesitated, unsure of her welcome. But he was waiting with an unmistakable plea in his eyes, and she saw he was afraid to do it alone. "Sure."

They walked without talking much, going the way they usually did, not out to the road but up behind the barn and across the apple orchard. They walked along the top of Sam's field. "Think Jimmie and Sammy'll come,too?"

"God, I hope not. You never know what Sammy's liable to do these days."

"Yeah." Carrie watched the house below them; things were uncomfortably uncertain there since Dora Mertz had died the previous winter, from complications after a miscarriage. And though it wasn't the official story, some said her trouble started after a fight there, between her brother and husband, that she got in the middle of. "Poor Sammy.

Me and Jimmie we've caught up to him in school. He's not dumb, why don't he study just a little bit?"

"He ain't – he isn't thinking clear, that's all."

And Carrie got the real message, the Mertz boys forgotten: mind your grammar today.

They were the first besides family there, and they felt a shyness as they walked, hesitant now, through the empty front yard to the side. Charlie was there, with Philip and one of his sons, unloading the church's folding chairs from the pickup.

"Just in time!" Philip hailed them. "Here, Jarrett, give us a hand."

"Hi, Allan." Jarrett knew Philip's son from school in town, and grabbed two chairs.

"Take 'em anywhere you want, spread 'em all around under the trees."

Charlie told Carrie there was corn to husk, if she had a mind to, and she moved on. She looked around her with an anxious love at the yards and flower beds, the long rows of tasselling sweet corn, the huge stone barn with its dozen empty stalls, the handsome farmhouse with its balconies and porches, the flagstone walk. Was Diana – Dee – finding it all as lovely as she should? For some reason, that felt important.

Not on the long porch but in a cluster off the end of it, Carrie saw three women sitting around two baskets of corn. She had to stop on the way, to greet Mary's two daughters, both grown and married but home for this day and seeming mostly interested in catching up with each other, so they didn't keep her long. Mary, at the corn, saw her first and waved, and Dee looked around and jumped up to greet her.

"Hi, Carrie. I'm glad you came early." Her voice was as direct and unaffected as Carrie remembered it, and her answering grin was genuine.

"Jarrett got drafted already into setting out chairs."

Dee's glance took in the spreading yard, and lit on him. "He's there, beyond the picnic table. He bring the violin?"

Carrie went stupidly blank for a moment, then nodded, relieved she hadn't asked. "The folks'll bring it. We walked over."

"Carrie!" Mary called from the corn. "You're just who we need. Here, take my chair, I'll go help Hannah with the potato salad."

Giving a quick greeting hug, she hurried off, taking a large platter of corn with her. Philip's wife Fern also got up to give Carrie a hug before settling back to the task. "We need an expert, is what Mary meant."

Dee laughed. Carrie slipped into the middle chair with a protest. "Anybody can husk corn." She liked Dee's laugh. In pale blue pedal pushers and well worn sneakers, an oversize shirt with the tails tied at her waist, she still looked more like something from a book than Carrie would ever, with her rolled up jeans and cotton shirt. But she looked more possibly a friend than she had the other night. Her hair was unruly in the heat, tied back carelessly with a rubber band.

And she didn't know how to husk corn. Fern was not much better, pulling at the sides of the husks. Carrie scarcely noticed the older woman, but felt a rush of affection for Dee.

"Here, look." Carrie separated the silk at the top, pulling a third of the husk off in a motion; the rest peeled off easily.

Dee laughed again, a real laugh, and Carrie had to join in. She noticed then Fern's difficulty, the stiffened and misshapen fingers. "We can manage this, if you want."

Fern didn't try to hide it. "Some things don't go so well." She stood up, shaking silk from her skirt.

"You did your share, looks like."

When Fern was gone, Carrie felt shy again, but Dee, still with laughter in her voice, said, "Do that again. One-two-three-GO!" and soon they were clowning together over the task. Carrie was a good audience for Dee's mock-serious comments about the occasional worm, or a recalcitrant unyielding husk or the silks that clung. Husking corn had never been to her anything but husking corn.

Jarrett came by with some chairs and paused, blushing a little but put at ease by Carrie's obvious good time.

"Are you as fast as Carrie?" Dee asked, frowning at her ear of corn.

"Of course."

"Then come back. There's half a basket yet."

"I'll just deliver these to the horseshoe field," he said, and hurried off.

"What's that?" Dee asked.

Again Carrie had the moment of blank. "For horseshoes," she said finally. Seeing Dee's puzzled look, this time she herself burst out laughing. "You'll see. It's too silly to explain."

"Try."

"Men throw horseshoes at iron stakes in the ground."

"Oh." Dee held up her half-husked ear of corn and addressed it. "She's right. It's too silly to explain."

With Jarrett back, they finished the corn in short order. Jarrett cleaned up the husks and went with them to the garden; the girls took the corn into the kitchen, were thanked and dismissed, and they made their escape quickly.

Skip's old white Chevy pulled up. Dee and Carrie walked over to it by the corn field as four youngsters piled out of the back seat, all out the same door. Clydey and Alvin, skinny, barefoot, and shirtless, didn't wait for greetings, running off on an immediate mission, but Violet hugged Carrie tightly. She was a pretty sprite with big smile and wispy blond hair nearly white in the sun. She hid her face from Dee, who held her hands out to the toddler trying to get out past his mother in the front seat. He let her lift him out, regarding her in silence. Verta lumbered out of the car, a baby carried as if weightless on her big arm.

"This must be Diana!" she declared, robust as always. "Skip said about yer comin'."

"Dee, this is Verta."

"Hello." When she spoke, the toddler looked surprised and stretched toward his mother. Verta took him with her free arm and set him down. He grabbed a fistful of dress, still staring at Dee.

"Hi, kids," Skip called across the car. "You all ready for tomorrow?"

"I hope so," Dee said.

Carrie looked at her, astonished. "You picking?"

"Didn't she tell you?" Skip said. "She ain't the lazy sort as some I know."

Carrie ignored him. "But that's great, Dee. Jarrett's working with the men this year, you can pick with me. If you want," she added quickly.

"Oh, yes, *thanks*." Dee looked so relieved Carrie had a fleeting question about her poised manner. "I don't know the first thing about it. Like husking corn," she said, and they laughed and moved on together.

Jem and Emma, Mattie and the twins, came in the station wagon and the girls helped carry pies and salads and chips and pickles, a big casserole of scalloped potatoes. All of this joined more of the same on the picnic tables, and Hannah and Mattie led a procession of women out of the kitchen with platter after platter of hot corn and cold chicken. The picnic was officially begun.

There was no formal meal, folks gathered and shifted, children swiped chips and ears of corn throughout the afternoon. There was some softball play, not teams but men taking turns hitting grounders and fly balls for each other and the children. Dee and Carrie and Jarrett wandered over together to watch the horseshoe pitch. Dee asked Charlie if she could try it, and he let her have his turn, which cost him. It had never occurred to Carrie to ask that, a child simply didn't. She glanced at Jarrett, watching Dee with some mixture of admiration and embarrassment. He'd never played, either. Dee, laughing and coming away toward them, had maybe never seen herself as a child.

The bonfire was lit, Charlie whittled points on long green sticks for roasting hot dogs; there were slivers of watermelon, cool from the spring. Then a table was moved, to make way for a reel. Skip was on a table, so his instrument and voice carried over the yard. "Eat, drink, and be merry, folks," he called, "for tomorrow we pick cherries!" He shuffled some chords, yelling over the strings. "Fellas get a move on, now, get your ladies over here, it's a Miller's reel!" Laughing at his own joke, he started into the lively tune.

Charlie started the line, facing one of Philip's daughters, a college student. Jem and Emma joined them as Philip chose Louisa. Duane headed toward Carrie and Dee, but Jarrett had laid his fiddle down on the bench behind Skip, and ran to claim Dee's hand.

"Wait! I don't know how."

"It ain't hard, come on!"

Carrie heard the slip, but they were off at a run for the double line. Duane kept coming toward her, but suddenly his nephew Allan darted between them. "Oh no you don't, sir! This 'n's mine!"

He grabbed Carrie's hand with a laugh and they ran after Jarrett and Dee. Duane without a pause veered off and invited Mary to the dance. Beside Carrie, Dee was clapping rhythm with the others but looking a little frightened. "It's easy," Carrie assured her. "Just watch, you'll learn it before you're head couple."

All the do-si-does and elbow swings were easy enough, the repetitions unvaried. Charlie and his partner started the reel, each swinging a waiting partner in the line, then back to each other, off to the next, hand-in-hand back up to the head with a lively sliding sashay. The lines followed them around to the bottom of the set, through their arch and back up, where Jem and Emma became the head couple and the whole thing began again. And sure enough, by the time Jarrett and Dee were head couple, she knew the figures perfectly. And by the time Allan was swinging Carrie in the middle as they danced from partner to partner down the lines, Carrie felt she could dance forever. She and

Allan made their arch, the others filed through, Duane and Mary did the last reel and the dance was over, with a final swing-your-partner.

"Thanks, Jarrett. What fun."

"I think I'm supposed to thank you."

"Yeah, like this." Allan, facing Carrie, swept an imaginary feathered cap from his head and gave her a deep bow, one leg cocked smartly a little behind. Carrie laughed and dipped a tiny curtsey, not nearly as convincing.

"Aren't you playing?" Dee asked Jarrett.

"I don't know that tune yet. Yeah, I will now." He looked pulled two ways, but gathered his fiddle and bow and stepped up by Skip. They played June Apple, and Sugar Hill, Skip's voice ringing clear above the fiddles, then he called for some squares. "Duck for the oyster, folks!"

Allan took Carrie's hand again and but for his impetuous move to the open, she would have been rooted to the spot in surprise. She scarcely knew this boy, she wouldn't start the school in town until this fall, and what was the butterfly doing in her stomach? But he knew the dance, and led her nicely through it, one just complicated enough to have to concentrate and active enough to take her mind off his attention.

Jarrett and Skip played on, after the dance, to a shifting audience, until Skip broke into a waltz. Allan this time found his sister, Duane and Louisa joined then, and the two couples did the graceful steps as if oblivious to the watching, admiring faces around them in the twilight. Skip then shook hands all around, Verta collected her tribe and with a parting, "See ya tomorrow," the Wilkeses drove off. Everyone else, reluctant to let go of the day, gathered slowly into a cluster of chairs to watch the end of the bonfire. Carrie and Jarrett were sitting with Dee in the ragged line of folks watching the glowing remains of the fire when the twins materialized in front of Dee's chair.

"Another song?" Omie's voice raised in a question, but still with something imperial in the tone.

"The fly!" Nathan said.

"No," Dee said softly. "How about a lullaby?"

Omie and Nathan fell to the grass like rag dolls, then sat up, ready and waiting.

"When at night I go to sleep –" Again, Dee began without fuss, as simply as if by herself under the big walnut. ". . . fourteen angels watch do keep."

The spell was immediate, the hum of voices fell silent, and as the count went on, two by two, Carrie became aware of a soft harmony in a hum underlying the words. It was Louisa, a couple chairs away and so unobtrusive as to seem part of the air itself. "Two my feet attending, Two to wake me bending, Two to guard 'til I arrive in heaven's paradise."

Omie drew a breath in the silence, a shudder almost like a sob. "Sing it again," she whispered. "Please."

Dee's gaze sought her mother, and Carrie saw the smile and slight nod. As if the two had spoken, they began the song again, Louisa with words too this time, singing it through to the end. It was a hard spell to break, but finally the circle stirred.

"I should've got a picture of that," Philip murmured. "Never saw those two so still."

Emma sighed a soft, "Oh, Lou," and laid a hand tight on her friend's arm, but spoke to Dee. "You're a singer, sure enough."

Dee smiled her thanks, but shook her head. "I hope to be, someday."

Carrie rode with Jarrett in the back of Jem's pickup over to the farm at six the next morning. There were cherries at the very top of that farm, and Charlie wanted to pick them first, before the larger block at their place. She pulled her flannel shirt tight against the chill, knowing but scarcely believing how hot it would be soon. Hannah and Diana met them at the tractor shed and rode up the hill with them to the first checking station, where Hannah would punch tickets. Skip and Charlie drove tractors up, with long trailers piled with ladders and buckets, and cherry season began.

"And keep them buckets in the shade." Skip gave a final instruction as he set two ladders for Carrie and Dee. "Don't go trying to move these, I'll be back."

Carrie taught Dee to pick from the inside of a twig toward the end, to pull without squeezing, to fill a bucket half full and set it under the tree; when each had filled two buckets from a third, they set off to turn them in. Hannah punched their tickets, they set the buckets in line for Jarrett to dump, took a drink from the water barrel, picked up two empty buckets, and trudged back to their tree again.

There were about twenty pickers, most of them local teenagers or whole families, with half a dozen Black migrant men, who had come North early. Charlie, needing more help as local patterns shifted away from seasonal work, hurriedly opened the apple season cabins and let them stay. Carrie noted their full tickets with jealous awe, and tried harder, but never did much better than half their thirty buckets a day.

Dee caught on quickly, and never complained, even when the afternoon heat slowed her to nearly a standstill.

"You okay?" Carrie asked her once, noticing that she was standing very still, a cluster of cherries in her hand.

"What? Yes, I was just – oh, I don't know. It's so pretty up here."

There was little to distinguish the days, except the one at the end of the first week with the frightening thunderstorm, coming over the ridge so quickly only a lucky few got to their cars or a building before getting soaked. The girls had to crawl under the trailer with Jarrett, where they tried to squirm away from the leaking cracks, getting dirtier and nearly as wet as if they'd stayed in the downpour. Jimmie Mertz joined them.

"How come Sammy's not picking this year?" Jarrett wanted to know. "He get a better job?"

"Guess so."

"Don't you know?"

Lined up as they were on their stomachs, peering out at the rain, it was hard to see each other's faces, but Jimmie was quiet so long that Carrie curled a little sideways to look over Jarrett at him. "Why don't you know?"

"Well, because he's gone, that's why."

As best they could, all three of them stared at him then.

"Pop says he'll be back, but I don't think so, he's been gone since last Sunday. Why would he come back and get a lickin'?"

"How do you know he's all right?" Jarrett asked.

"He's all right."

"Jimmie, how come would he go off?" Carrie saw the back of Sammy's head disappearing down the hill below Mertz Hollow.

Jimmie snorted. "You don't need to ask that, you know damn well him and Daddy's been fighting since forever."

"Where'd he go?"

"How should I know? Uncle Farley's, I figure."

"Farley's?" Jarrett voiced his disbelief. "But he's –"

"Yeah, Farley's," Jimmie snarled. "What do you know about it? I'm goin' home." He pulled himself out into the rain and walked away.

"What's wrong with him?" Dee wondered.

Jarrett sighed. "My fault. You don't talk about the fight, around Jimmie. His dad and his uncle got into it one night and somehow his mother got in the middle and . . . well, got hurt. The baby died and . . . and then she did."

"Wow," Dee said, very softly.

"Yeah."

"And now his brother's run away?"

"Sounds like it."

"Why would he go there, to that uncle?"

"Getting even. Jimmie's right, it's something Sammy would do."

They went back to their work reluctantly after the storm,

269

uncomfortable in their muddy clothes, soaked anew by the dripping trees, and uneasy with thoughts of death and running away.

"You ever run away?"

Carrie was startled by Dee's question the next day, and had to consider it, taking her time to come around the ladder and empty her bucket. "Yeah, once. I meant to anyway, didn't get very far. You ever?"

Dee joined her on the ground. "Never. Did you really?"

"I hardly remember it. I was just little, pretty mixed up."

"I'd never leave my mom."

"You miss her?"

"Well, yes, but I'm used to it."

"You were sure great together, yesterday."

"Did you like it, really?"

"*Like* it? How can you even ask that?"

"It's kind of a corny song, in a way."

"Yes but – no it's not, it was just perfect, that's all."

"It's from an opera, can you believe that? An opera about Hansel and Gretel: now, that's corny."

"The twins are fixed on it now," Carrie told her. "They have to have a song every night *and* Jarrett's fiddle."

By the middle of the next week, the orchard at the Miller farm was done, and the crew shifted to the big orchard near the house at Carrie's. For two more weeks the steady progress continued, broken only by one afternoon's heat, when Charlie called a halt to save the fruit from turning to mush in the crates. And then finally, suddenly, there were no more trees to pick; the cherry harvest was done.

Carrie suddenly felt herself restless, at sea. Jarrett continued working at the farm, and was learning about the tractors, hauling trailers of crates, even mowing with the long cutter-bar that had to be raised and lowered around the trees. He went to the work without his usual resistance, partly because of the driving but partly . . . . In her first real dose of jealousy, Carrie imagined him happily shoulder to shoulder with Dee all day long. She knew the image was wrong, Jarrett wasn't there to sit around or even be around the house, and probably Dee wasn't one to wander around or ride on trailers. But Hannah kept to the old way of setting out a noon dinner, and he'd have his lunch in the big kitchen.

It seemed unfair, even if she couldn't have said why. The twins and the garden kept her busy, she had plenty to do and her grandmother's company was precious as always. But still. Something in her had got unsettled at the picnic. She even caught herself looking forward to the frightening shift to the town school, with Allan's grin in her mind's eye. Both things were so entirely new she blocked them out and felt even more restless. And something had been given her during the days with Dee in the cherry orchard she'd never known she was missing.

Mattie was resting with the twins. Carrie was helping Emma pick some corn for supper, when the image of husking corn at the picnic made her longing too much to bear. "Mama, you think Dee might be lonesome?"

"I'm not sure, but I think *you* might be."

Carrie stared at her in surprise. She hadn't said anything about that.

"Shall I call Hannah? You could go over there tomorrow if it suits. If you want."

Carrie nearly dropped the corn in her hand. "Yes! I mean, if Dee wants me to."

"Well, we'll find out."

Hannah invited Carrie over warmly, when Emma called. "In fact, I thought about calling you, Dee was wondering if Carrie might have time to come over. Can you spare her?"

"Tell you what," Emma said. "I'll spare her a day if you'll spare Dee a day. You keep 'em busy there and I'll have 'em here a day."

"That's a deal, send her over."

271

So Carrie walked over to the farm mid-morning. She felt shy about it now. Used only to the rowdy games at recess, with no special playmate but Jarrett, she wasn't sure now why she'd wanted to come. What did visiting a friend look like? What were you supposed to do?

But as she had guessed, Dee had not explored much of the farm and agreed eagerly to a walk before lunch. She remembered to ask Hannah if there was work, but Hannah shooed them away. Dee was a good walker, and with her long legs and years of dance classes, set a challenging pace before drooping a little in the heat.

"Aunt Hannah told Mama you play the piano."

"A little."

"You never said."

"Have you heard my mother? You don't need to hear me."

"No. Yes," Carrie said, and they both laughed, easy with each other again. They went around the corn patch and away from the house; Carrie led her up a tractor path nearly as far as the cherry orchard, but at the crest of a hill turning left away from that section and down into a little ravine, across a narrow brook, to one of her favorite spots. Three large hemlock trees and as many smaller ones had created a sanctuary. She felt nervous now that Dee would see nothing remarkable in it, but she need not have worried.

"Oh, my." Dee sank to her knees, then sat down on the woods floor. She had become nearly as unmindful of her slacks and blouses as if they were farm clothes. Today she was wearing shorts, but didn't seem to notice the prickly twigs and needles against her legs. Carrie settled quietly beside her, satisfied with her gift. Neither spoke. Carrie picked up a twig full of the tiny hemlock cones, examining them idly until some motion of Dee's made her look up. Dee was crying, and at Carrie's startled reaching out a hand to her, she let out her breath in a sob.

"Dee?"

"It's nothing." Dee wiped at her face, struggling for control. "Only, I don't want to go back."

For a moment Carrie thought she meant to the house, then realized what she meant. "Is it so bad at home?"

"Bad? No, it's not that. I just never . . . . never knew summer could be like this."

"You're not bored?"

Dee shook her head, emphatically.

Carrie searched for comforting thoughts. "Seems like your mom's really nice."

"My mother's the best. She has to be away a lot and she has to practice a lot and has bunches of pupils but I know all about that, I'm used to it, I understand it."

"But you don't like it?"

Dee sighed. She poured a fistful of crumbly soil from one hand to another. "Everything is so on a schedule at home," she said finally. "Time for this, time for that. There's hardly time to think, or to watch things, like there is here."

"But it's like that here, too," Carrie objected, and mimicked her own mother's voice. "Time to get the clothes in, Carrie; Jarrett, time for more wood in here, time to pick the beans, time to wash up, kids; time to set the table, time to clean –"

"Stop!" Dee was laughing now and gave her a friendly shove. "Okay, but it's not the same. Believe me, it's not the same."

They contemplated that a moment or two. "Dee, what if – couldn't you come every summer? I bet Aunt Hannah would love it. I would, Jarrett would."

"Jarrett's nice, I like him. Do you? Most of my friends at home hate their brothers but you don't seem to."

"Hate *Jarrett*? He don't – he doesn't like me as much as he used to, he's in the big school now and has got other things to think about, I guess. But I'd never not like him, I don't think." Carrie frowned, the idea new to her. "And he'd stand up for me, no matter what."

"Anyway, I can't come next summer. I'm going to Interlochen."

273

"What's that?"

Dee's surprise was obvious, but she made nothing of it. "A music camp."

"Oh." Reminded of Dee's differences, her knowing of things Carrie had never imagined, she lost all words entirely.

They took off their shoes and waded in the shallow creek, sat on a log until their feet were dry, pulled sneakers back on and were home in time to help Hannah set out the meal. Neither Jem nor Charlie was by nature talkative, but Jarrett asked Dee about her morning. She answered, without a trace now of her sadness, that Carrie had shown her the most beautiful spot on earth. Jarrett looked puzzled, but before Carrie could explain, he thought of it himself.

"The hemlocks?"

She nodded, pleased that he too remembered a childhood pretend spot. They'd had the whole farm at home to play in but were at this farm enough to have explored it, and had used to – when they were children and bored with the grownups – have several special spots.

"She tell you who lives there?" Jarrett said, clearly laughing at that childhood, and Carrie had to laugh too, it was so preposterous.

"No. Tell me."

"Robin Hood, of course. That is, when the Band wasn't in our barn."

"Making a mess of the cherry crates," Jem added.

They helped Hannah clean up the kitchen, pull out some rows of beans, and pick the first tomatoes, then she insisted the afternoon was too hot, they should stay in the house.

"Play something, Dee," Carrie said.

Dee shrugged a little. "Honest, Carrie, I'm not very good. It's not really my instrument."

"What is?"

Dee shrugged again. "My voice, I think. It's hard to know for sure."

"I really wish you would play."

So they went into the front parlor, and Dee played. A Chopin waltz, part of the brooding Moonlight Sonata, and something she called Golliwog's Cakewalk, which made them both laugh. Carrie knew she was out of her depth here, but also knew that what Dee did was out of the ordinary, no matter how much better her mother might be at it. She pushed into the softness of the davenport, feeling content and proud, almost as if the accomplishment were hers.

The weather turned stormy, and Dee didn't come for the reciprocal visit that week. Carrie was eager for church, to see her again, and was gratified there by Dee's warm smile. But she felt uncommonly restless during the service. Occupied as usual with keeping the twins quiet, drawing, making babies in Jem's handkerchief, dividing up the animal crackers, nonetheless her attention flew in all directions, but always bumping against the confines of the little church and the now dreary succession of prayers and hymns and scripture.

She felt for the first time embarrassed for the empty pews and the shuffling slowness of the congregation. How could Dee stand to come? She'd never said anything about the church, or religion at all. Except to ask once why Gramma Mattie didn't go, which Carrie couldn't answer. She just never did, was all. But now, looking not at people she'd known all her life but a rag-tag mumbling bunch of strangers, Carrie blushed deeply, mortified. If the church were packed, full of the joyful noise God commanded, with shouting and singing and clapping of hands, well, that would be one thing. Then never mind the ill-fitting suits, the awkward blunt haircuts, the hand-me-down dresses too tight or not yet grown into, never mind the awful gossips like the preacher's wife, or poor Isaac Burns who was nearly twenty and had to be led by the hand and given sweets to suck and once had wet his pants and cried in a horrible snuffling wail. She'd love them all, she *would*, just like God commanded. But this.

She concentrated fiercely on Reverend Paul's words. Sweating, with his usual scowl, his paunch firmly vested in spite of the heat, the preacher was too familiar to her, his cadences too predictable, to hold her interest, especially this morning when she was impatient to get back to the farm. But on and on he went, about the Tower of Babel, a story she could have told in three minutes, without all the paper shuffling and page turning going on up there. Carrie shivered, and folded her arms tight against her chest, hating both the docile dull ignorant people and all the empty spaces. No wonder Jarrett tried sometimes to stay at home, claiming he had homework, or a headache. She shivered again, and suddenly her misery turned physical, with a strange cramp in her lower belly. Her hips ached, and her back felt odd, as if something had come disconnected. Sweat prickled her neck.

When she touched Emma's arm, her mother bent her head slightly. "I'm gonna be sick," Carrie whispered. Emma looked at her quickly.

"Go on out." Emma moved her knees to make a path but Carrie hesitated, bewildered by her sudden pains and cringing from the thought of the old outhouse. Emma looked at her again, then whispered something to Jem. He dug in his pocket, and handed her the car keys. "Come on," Emma whispered to her.

Meekly, Carrie followed, avoiding Jarrett's surprised look as she stepped past his feet at the center aisle. He and Jem deftly swept the twins back onto the pew and Carrie concentrated on her mother's back, as mystified as her brother. If she was sick enough to be taken home, why wasn't her mother worried? There was, to be sure, a slight flush on Emma's face, but there was nothing angry or exasperated in her eyes, even the hint of a smile. She said not a word all the way across the ridge and when they turned off the hard road into the lane, Carrie thought she heard her mother humming. Humming!

Only after she stopped the car by the two pines did Emma turn to her. Her light blue eyes held no censure, but Carrie's chest tightened with the alarming sense that her mother was about to cry. "Your friend's come, I think."

Carrie could think only of Dee, or the hymn about Jesus, and looked at her mother blankly.

"Never mind, come on, I'll show you what to do."

As her foot hit the porch boards, Carrie's brain fitted together the odd bits of talk with school friends, the explanation her mother had tried to give her months before. It hadn't seemed to have anything to do with her.

"Well, Mattie, you'd never guess."

Her grandmother gave her a rare, broad smile. "Bless your heart, child, it's nothing to be so scared of."

Carrie nodded, not daring to speak around the lump in her throat, and followed her mother upstairs. She accepted the belt and pad with trembling fingers, followed the instructions in silence. She rinsed her underwear in the prescribed cold water, scrubbing until not a trace of the friend remained.

"Feel better?" Emma came back into the bathroom.

"Everyone will know," Carrie said, and burst into tears.

Emma drew Carrie against her, a gesture as rare as Gramma's smile. "It's nothing shameful," she said, but her voice shook, and Carrie could not quite believe her. "Go on and change into jeans, lay down a little, you'll feel all right in ten minutes, I promise you."

"I'm not comin' down for dinner."

"Yes, now, don't be silly."

"I'm not comin'." Tears welled over, she couldn't help it.

Emma stroked Carrie's sweaty bangs back from her forehead, her hand startlingly cool and tender. "Carrie. Don't be scared, you're a healthy girl . . . . But all right, I don't suppose a missed meal ever hurt anybody."

Carrie wasn't scared, now that she knew she wasn't dying, but something had collapsed, crumbled like the sand castles she made for the twins, like the cherry crate forts and secret places Jarrett laughed at now. She lay on her bed in a limbo between mourning and celebration.

Later in the week, Hannah brought Dee over. Carrie showed her the barn and springhouse, neither as interesting as the Millers'. But where the hens roosted at night in the low white coop was a novelty, as Hannah no longer kept chickens. They picked tomatoes and the last of the corn and beans, entertained the twins in the big sandbox. Dee came up with the idea of a marble race track, which after many failures stood two feet high with a spiraling raceway. They found two unmatched marbles and let the kids play, then settled to the Chinese checkers board themselves. It was an unhurried, pleasant, almost dreamy, time, and with a lucidity that made her feel odd, Carrie longed for it even while still in it.

She made a shy attempt to persuade Dee back next summer. "I mean, if you don't really want to go to that camp, then why –?"

"Oh, but I do. To sing and sing and sing, with all new teachers . . . . Carrie, don't you feel it, that having to have something, like if you don't get it you won't be able to breathe?"

Dee stayed for supper and eventually everyone gathered on the porch sharing a hope for a passing breeze.

"Look at the pines," Emma said. "Not a needle moving."

"Hope it don't hail," Jem said. "I don't like it this still and hot, and peaches just comin' in."

Jarrett raised his bow and started with the usual double-stop shuffles. "Let's do June Apple," he said to Carrie.

"Are you crazy? I can't sing."

He lowered the fiddle. "You sing all the time."

"But not –"

"Go on, Carrie," Dee urged her. "I'd like to hear it. What's a June Apple, anyway?"

They laughed: nobody knew. Jarrett lit into the tune and Carrie sang the silly verses, forgetting her shyness in the infectious rhythms of the song and Jarrett's runs, more intricate and pleasing than a year ago.

Wisht I was a June Apple

Hangin' on a tree;

Every time my true love passed,

Take a little bite of me.

The tune was in a major key but had an almost sad feeling in spite of the pace, with what Skip called a mountain minor.

Over the river to feed your sheep,

Over the river, Charlie;

Over the river to feed your sheep,

Feed 'em all on barley.

Two more verses, a final run-through on the fiddle, and Jarrett ended with a flourish. Dee clapped, which the twins picked up on and thought a good addition to the evening's ritual. They were sprawled on the glider between Emma and Mattie. Naomi raised an imperious finger. "Some more."

Jarrett grinned at her. "Give me a minute, your majesty, to dry the sweat."

Nathan, in spite of the heat, crawled onto Mattie's lap and patted her cheek. "A story, Gramma."

"What story might that be, now? I don't know no stories."

"Story," Nathan repeated, leaning back against her shoulder, every bit as royal, in his quieter way, as his twin.

Carrie drew her feet up to sit crosslegged, her back to a post. "You got to now, Gramma, you been chosen."

"Carrie," Emma objected. "No need for everyone to give in to their every whim."

Encouraged by her mild tone, Carrie persisted. "Something from the Inn, maybe?"

Emma did cluck her tongue then, and looked a dark warning at her so clear that Carrie shrank a little, embarrassed. It had been a bad place for Gramma, she knew or had somehow guessed that. But Mattie suddenly chuckled. "Why yes, I do remember a fellow. A stranger, come walkin' in one afternoon with a pocketful of money and –"

"What'd he look like?" Omie asked.

"Oh, I hardly remember."

"He had green teeth," Jarrett said. "And yellow eyes."

Omie squealed, Nathan cried No,no! Mattie agreed with Nathan. "No, wasn't like that, I'm sure I'd remember that. It was along in the fall, he had a jacket on, heavy shoes. No hat or scarf, it wasn't that cold. The grapes were still hanging. He did have one eye didn't quite follow the other, that got worse as the day wore on."

"Why?"

"Because he kept pullin' bills out-a his pocket and buyin' beer, that's why. One after another, a whiskey and then a beer. Just settin' there, quiet as can be. A whiskey and then a beer. Come evening he bought some soup and bread. Bought a whole pie. And just kept at it, ate and ate and drank and drank. And then he run out of money, near eleven dollars I think it was. A lot of money in them days."

"And then what?" Nathan asked.

"Why, then he went out. None too steady, but still he could walk, somehow. We figured he'd gone away. And not ten minutes later, in come three men from Claysville, and here one was a policeman, a deputy of some kind, and he –"

"He have a gun?" Nathan asked.

"I suppose he did, but he didn't use it. Didn't need to. He asked, Did we see a stranger anytime today. Yessir, we did, but he left. Could they just look around? Well, yessir, of course. And you know what?"

"What?" said both twins.

"That poor fellow was curled up under the grape arbor fast asleep. That's all the farther he got. Turned out the money wasn't his, he'd taken it from a store. Walked all day, and then spent it, every penny. Went to jail for a month, and worked off the debt. End of story."

There was only a moment's quiet before Naomi remembered Dee was with them. "Song now," she said as if consulting an agenda.

"Golly, I'm out of ideas."

"You know Down in the Valley?" Jarrett suggested.

"I've heard it."

"Carrie can teach you the words, there's a lot of repetition."

He played a slow, sweet version of the tune. Carrie joined him, and repeated the verse for Dee to join, and even the twins had learned it by then: Down in the valley, the valley so low, Hang your head over, hear the wind blow. At three, repetition was a glorious bit of fun: Hear the wind blow, love, hear the wind blow; hang your head over, hear the wind blow. And every verse had the repeat. Will you be mine, love, will you be mine? Answer my question, will you be mine?

. . . Know I love you, love, know I love you; angels in heaven, know I love you.

They went back to the first – Down in the valley, the valley so low – and the twins made the most of it.

When it was time to drive Dee home, the twins begged for a ride in the pickup. It was past their bedtime but Emma relented and sent along some blankets to soften the bed. "Mind you don't let them stand up."

Jarrett and Carrie and Dee joined them; they asked for songs all the way and with rising hilarity the three "big kids" thought of every game and nursery song they could. Itsy bitsy spider; teapot; blind mice; Willie Boy – even Tennessee Ford's old house and sixteen tons from the radio. Jem drove without any hurry, but even so, Dee waved a farewell way too soon.

And the next week Louisa was there. Carrie saw with some wistfulness the joy of Dee's reunion, the hugs and casual touching between the two, but felt too a gladness that apparently Dee would be all right.

Then summer was over, and even Mattie was gone. Carrie weathered the panicky confusion of the switch to junior high, struck mute by the crowds, the jostling around lockers in the halls, the bewildering array of rooms and hallways. Familiar faces from the little school disappeared and reappeared but with no recess for talk. Sammy Mertz had stayed with his uncle in Claysville and Jimmie sat with Jarrett now on the bus. Carrie always had little Donnamae with her, as far as Potter's Corner, waving her off with an aching heart.

For some weeks, then, the novelty of the notebooks, the strange texts, the book covers that had to be folded just so, the fearsome science room, all occupied her attention. In early October, however, she began reading *Silas Marner* and wondered with new intensity about the hermit close at hand. She resolved, one Saturday, to find the cabin. She'd helped peel apples for sauce, had played with the twins and sung to them to start their naps, and the rest of the day was hers. She determined not to get sidetracked this time.

Maneuvering around honeysuckle and greenbriar, she pushed through spicebush and a path of laurel, to pause on an open rock break. Here and there a tree was bright with color, but some of the summer's green still lingered, and the air even here felt close and humid. She followed a deer path, and entered one of the pine stands the mountain was named for, but she knew it was not the one she sought. It was cool and dark, but not big enough: she walked out of it in minutes.

Skip told tales, still, about the tricks the mountain could play, to keep you wandering. She hadn't been paying much attention to landmarks, and felt a surge of fright, but it passed. She was in the woods, was all. This wasn't a wilderness, she'd come out somewhere, she had hours yet before dark. Turning again she headed at an angle up another steep rise, and intersected a path too good to resist. When it dipped into a little ravine, she noticed she was in another stand of pine.

There was no longer a path, but back along a level space through the pines, there seemed to be light. With her heart beginning to pound, she walked at first furtively, from tree to tree, as if someone might see her, and scold. And then suddenly the clearing was right there, curving away from her and there was nothing at all frightening about it. She decided to cross it; it was lighter out in the open, but noisier. She hadn't noticed the pines while under them, but they seemed all around her here. And in spite of the light, she stumbled, so hard and unexpectedly she barely got her arms out in time to break her fall.

When she sat up she saw the cabin, in the angle of the clearing. He came down the broken steps, out from under the shadow of the askew porch roof, raised a hand toward her: Listen!

The sounds of her own heart and blood and mind went silent. Her very being was lifted from the boundaries of skin and suspended in the enveloping rush and drone of the meadow, the sighing pines, the air and earth itself. There was no happiness or sorrow or fear that was hers separate, hers alone. And the hermit stood there forever, broad suspenders fraying against a heavy shirt, baggy denims faded and patched, unruly gray hair framing the bearded jaw, dark eyes, heavy brow. Listen!

Getting up, Carrie looked down to free her jeans from a blackberry cane, and when she looked up, he was gone.

There was no longer any sign of corn, but the roses were there, real as her own hand, gone wild over one end of the cabin, some still blooming on the roof. Carrie trod carefully on the rotting porch boards and went in through the doorway without disturbing the door, hanging crookedly on one hinge.

The dank air smelled of mice. Some stones had fallen in from the chimney, there was light coming in through the log walls, but Carrie stood easily in the center, still infused with the sense of welcome the vision's greeting had given her.

There was nothing at all in the room. Someone, or something, had pushed open a little door in the back wall, like a window. Carrie leaned on the rotting sill, breathing deep of the fresher air, laden with mingled scents, as the pines pressed close. A chipmunk with an indignant whistle hurtled off a log.

She went outside again, feeling as familiar with the place as with her own yard. Taking out her pocket knife, she climbed a few steps up on the log ends and cut four roses. She wouldn't need to be carried weeping from the mountain this time.

Helping Emma wash the storm windows lined up against the house, Carrie decided to try some questions. The twins were napping, Jarrett with Jem in the apple harvest. "How come you came up here?"

"What a question. Your father never had any notion of being anywhere else."

"But he was born here. I mean, how did *you* get here."

Carrie looked around to see a soft look come on Emma's face; she was absently rinsing her cloth in the vinegar water, with none of her usual briskness. "That was Louisa's doing, really. We rode the bus together into high school, and I'd come home with her sometimes."

"Dad never went to high school?"

"He went, never finished. Times were different, then. He needed to work, and the Millers needed him."

"And Gramma, too."

"Her place, Louisa's place, was so much grander than mine, with that big house and all the barns and the dairy they had then. Even two riding mares."

"You went riding?"

Emma laughed then, swiping almost gaily at a window. "Well, I wasn't always fat. But I never was as good as Lou, she was fearless. She and Duane used to do some daring things with those horses. Until her mother died."

"What happened then?"

"I don't know. It all . . . changed. Mattie and Duane moved away,

Lou got serious about the piano. And she left too, but then of course I always knew she would."

"How did you know?"

"People go where life leads 'em. Here, polish this quick before it dries."

Approaching the house after hunting wild strawberries in early June, Carrie was in earshot before the women on the porch saw her.

"Why, I scarcely know Ada Simpson," her grandmother was saying. "Paul and her come back here after I left."

"Exactly," Emma said, her voice a little high with irritation. "What's it matter to her? Every Sunday all summer she'll be after Jem, about you comin' to church."

"I guess there's no other witch come along for her to save."

Emma laughed, but looked up to see Carrie frozen in shock with one foot on the porch. "Oh, Lord. It's just a joke, Carrie."

Mattie's thin face blushed faintly, but her dark eyes showed amusement. "Be careful where you walk in them woods, girl, folks 'round here liable to say anything."

"I been to Mr. Brustein's cabin. I found it." Carrie nearly turned and ran, stunned at her own words. This was not the way she had meant to bring the subject up.

Mattie surprised her. "Did you really, though? Just now lately?"

"Last fall."

"A marvel it's still there." Mattie picked a sock out of the mending basket, but held it absently. "I wonder, could I still make it."

"I wouldn't remember the way," Carrie admitted.

"Oh, I would, child, I would." She replaced the sock and stood, looking suddenly tired. She reached for Carrie's pail. "You got enough here for two batches, you must know where to look." She went into the house.

Carrie felt as if she should apologize to her mother for something, but didn't know what, so she backed off the porch and headed for the garden. With Mattie and Emma in the house, and Jarrett in the orchards, and Dee off at music camp whatever that was, the gardens were Carrie's domain, her curse and solace.

Emma's new freezer, a big double-doored behemoth that Charlie and Skip had helped wrestle into the cellar, began filling up. The corn came in, tomatoes began to turn; there were early Transparent apples to sauce and peaches to can, as well as slice and freeze, the new way. Carrie walked the roadways and edges of woods for blackberries, and worked patiently with Mattie pulling the tiny elderberries from their round heavy clusters. The flower beds went neglected, parts of the garden grew thick with weeds as the women concentrated on getting everything canned and frozen. More corn, more tomatoes, green peppers and broccoli and kale, more beans, limas, carrots and beets. Carrie grew almost tired of food, her only relief from the constant smells of it cooking seeming to be the smells of it growing. Neither she nor her grandmother said anything more about the cabin, until late in August.

"Maybe we'd ought to go on up the mountain," Mattie said one Saturday afternoon.

"Now?"

"Let's go tomorrow, before it gets hot."

To Carrie's surprise, no one objected to her staying home from church, and as soon as the breakfast dishes were cleared, the two of them set out. "This used to be pasture," Mattie told her, as they passed the springhouse. "We had the prettiest pair of mules. I'm sure I don't know where mules get their bad name, I don't recall any trouble with ours. Could be he just had a way with 'em."

"What was his name, Gramma?"

Mattie stopped. "Ain't I ever said? David."

"What did he look like?"

"Duane's the spittin' image of him. Only if he'd laugh more. It was that laugh . . . ."

Carrie was surprised when Mattie walked on past the spring, following the muddy track around the pond, around the base of the hill toward the peach orchard. "Right here's where David failed the worst." Mattie stopped halfway up the steep edge of the orchard. Carrie looked out over the lush, orderly rows, puzzled. "He cleared this bit, but the peaches never took, never even got started. We had a terrible drought that year, and then it poured. Too late, and too much."

"Wait. The farm was yours once?"

"Never rightly. Never paid for. But yes, I come here with David."

"But Dad's never said anything about the place ever being ours."

Mattie pursed her lips and walked on. "Well," she said, pausing again. "He may not even know of it, or like to think of it if he does. He was just a baby when David left."

"*Left?* Just left?"

"Prob'ly not 'just'." Mattie gave her a fleeting, small smile. "It cost him something, I guess."

"Is it hard for you, to talk like this?"

"Hard? It's always hard to talk about love, child."

As if she'd only said an ordinary thing, they walked on, but for Carrie the whole story shifted. Love. Following Mattie into the woods at a deer path, she nearly laughed at the simplicity of it. Love. Never mind that she had only the fuzziest notion of what that might mean, never mind that being fourteen was like treading water in an endless channel between high cliffs. She could be patient now, take the pieces as they came.

There was no vision this time, no pulse thundering in her ears. They went inside the cabin and stood at the back window. "Somebody must have cleaned it out," Carrie said.

"Your dad. I told him to. There wasn't much."

"It's like the woods is a framed picture."

"But it ain't a real frame. He liked to talk about that."

"About frames?"

"About limits, how we put them around life because life's too big."

They sat on the porch edge, shaded by the wall of climbing roses. "How'd you ever find him?"

"He found me, I have no idea why."

"But you loved him."

"Yes."

"Why did you leave?"

"There were . . . . It was time to leave. I'd be back, I thought. Maybe David thought that too, thought he'd be back."

"But he never. And you couldn't, not in time."

"No."

"A mistake."

Mattie leaned forward to massage a muscle in her calf. "I didn't mean to say it was a mistake. Didn't turn out like I'd imagined. But there's no knowing that in advance. Your own next step, that's all you can know."

"I'll never."

"You don't need to yet."

"Everybody else does. Jarrett knows what he's after, and Dee."

"You'll know."

"Gramma, who owns this now?"

"I do." Mattie touched her arm lightly, then stood and stretched. "Shall we go back a different way? There's a way comes out the other side, above the Mertz place." She stepped away from the cabin and headed off, as assuredly as if she walked the paths every day.

CHAPTER 2.

Sarah

When I brought home the traction device prescribed for the arthritis creeping into my neck and upper spine, Morris wanted to mount it from the living room doorway.

"Handy that way. You'll use it more."

"Upstairs," I said firmly. "There's a doorway just like this one."

He also wanted to see me use it, but I shooed him off. "You see me in this ridiculous collar, that's bad enough."

In a couple months the pain subsided. Though the doctor warned me to expect flare-ups, I could go days and then weeks without the meditative hour stretching my neck. I wore the collar brace only for gardening and driving the little blue Henry Jay which had replaced the Studebaker. And in the fall, regarding the untidy beds and overgrown pathways, the stalks of asters and marigolds and daisies all broken, fallen, gone to seed, I realized I was nearly done with all that. Even the little flower beds were beyond my endurance now, and the drive even to Potter's Corner was a draining task. Next year, I decided, I'd let the flowers all grow wild, or have Morris mow everything down with the new power mower he used now, and be grateful for it, noisy obnoxious thing that it was.

Guy Deardorff's funeral was the biggest affair I'd been to here. "It'll be crowded," Morris warned me. "Better let me drive you in, one less car to park."

I accepted gratefully, and was doubly glad when we saw the cars and pickups already jamming the sidewalks and side alleys of the town's one street. The church was near the east end, close to the school; the lot there was already packed. Morris let me off, saying he'd find a spot up at the Inn, the other end of town.

Men were busy setting up folding chairs in the aisles and corners of the sanctuary; a fairly large church, as country churches went, it would seat little over half the people. There must have been no one at work in the entire township. Fortunately it was one of those resplendent fall days that can happen here in October; men gave up their seats to women and the elderly, and stood in subdued clusters outside the open doors and windows, sons beside them looking startled at this novel way to hear hymns from the pump organ. I was motioned inside by an usher, who handed me a folded program while his eyes searched the pews for a spot. A distinguished looking man, whose white forehead and bronzed cheeks marked him for a farmer, touched my elbow and pointed discreetly to the far left wall, where I saw Eula, nodding in invitation. I recognized him then as Damon Tyler. Whispering a thanks to him I moved across the back of the church and up the far aisle to Eula's side. With a quick squeeze to her hand in greeting, and a nod to Damon's two younger sons, I settled to endure.

But I had little attention for the service. Neither the music nor the readings, not even the preacher's heartfelt eulogy, could divert me long from the disorderly sequence of my own thoughts. Is grief always so self-referential, I wondered. How could it not be? It is one's own grief, after all, always. As if Guy were taking with him my last link to Ethan in this place, countless images of the two together flipped like turning pages full of snapshots before my mind's eye. I did not join the line shuffling past the coffin, for I felt no need. The grocer-historian's face was vivid before me.

We moved, a powerful, sluggish wave, out of the church behind the coffin, across a dirt lane and into the expansive cemetery: this church had stood for over a century. Past stones nearly or wholly illegible, of various sizes but all modest, past heart-wrenchingly plain ones – Infant, Son – and the elaborately inscribed, we fanned out several hundred strong, lapping at the yawning edge of the clean hole. Stronger people than I broke down at the sight, at the beseeching note in the preacher's strong voice as he commended his friend's spirit into his God's care. In spite of the unclouded sunshine, I shivered with cold.

Eula stood with me until Morris got back with the car. Her slenderness now had an edge of style to it, her hair had been cut and permed; still slow to smile, her face was now fuller, softer, and her eyes more eager and forthright. She invited me to come with Morris for supper, but I said, truthfully, I was too tired for it.

"But tell me what you hear from Thad."

"He writes to you more than us," she said, smiling. "Morris tells us so."

"But you know he plans to come home for Christmas. And that he's thriving there." At a Quaker college in Indiana, Thad had hit a stride that surprised even me.

"He says Nancy should apply. Just imagine." Eula's voice was quiet with both pride and disbelief at her own involvement with such things.

Morris came in with me, and had the fires going by the time I came back from the path and hung up my coat.

"You ought to get a bathroom."

"Yes," I agreed. "Perhaps I'll write to Mr. Kennedy when he's settled in the White House, I'm sure he'll see my point."

"He ain't won yet."

"And won't, in this county," I warned him. "We're outnumbered five to one. Thank you for the fires, Morris. Stay for tea."

We reminisced quietly about Guy and Verna, who had died several years ago. She had refused to see a doctor about a stubborn cold.

"You suppose she knowed all along it was pneumonia?"

"The old person's friend," I said, but didn't attempt to answer the question. The kettle whistled and he helped me bring the pot and cups into the living room; I was not as steady with the tray as I once was.

"My very first talk with Guy was about my Aunt Anna. He was all full of her, really, as if she were his discovery. But it was your Evvie who told me she was nearly crippled, he never mentioned that."

"He might not have noticed."

"He saw her every summer."

"But he saw her here, only. It was her friend done the walking for her, like even to the van. I'd bring their mail, what little they got."

"But Guy made such a point of her snappy step. The arthritis must have come on very quickly."

"Seth he'll quit the van, now, I figure."

"Just when I'm needing it. But it's not the same anyway, is it, without Guy bringing the gossip with the goods."

We finished our tea, sat smoking in companionable silence. "Did you like her?" I asked.

The question surprised him, as it did me. He took his time with it, frowning at the bit of flame visible in the stove, where the two little sliding doors were open a crack. "I can't say I knowed either one of 'em very well. Young and busy as I was then, you know, I didn't see a whole lot of 'em really. Evvie –"

"Evvie?" I prompted when he broke off.

"She had a little problem sometimes with Rusty spending so much time with them." He glanced at me, looking apologetic. "He carried painting stuff for her friend, loved it."

"Yes, I remember him telling us that. Why would Evvie mind?"

292

"Well, you know. . . ." He rubbed his face briefly, clearly uncomfortable now. "They were a couple, like."

For an instant I was blank, thinking of course they were a couple, a couple of friends who lived amiably together for forty years or more. But in the next instant I understood. And also understood my father's rage, my mother's half-hearted defense, my sister's fear. Fifty years after the fact. Of course, I must have known. Suddenly I had to laugh. I coughed with the smoke and laughed again. Morris, bewildered at first, was finally powerless against the tide, and added his own snaps of laughter. The day had been too much for both of us, with its beauty surrounding the clean-sided hole in the earth, with the memories of our losses, the acknowledged fruitlessness of our passions and our cherished, crippling, categories and beliefs.

The letter from Agatha's daughter was gentle and loving, and grief-stricken. Jeffrey and Agatha were both in a plane that had gone down in the French Alps. Almost as if they'd planned it: the phrase was Leticia's, not mine, but I repeated it in my notebook, my handwriting even more spidery and uneven than usual. Most of the time I spent with the notebook now was not writing time; holding it closed or open I'd sit before the fire or staring out a window, as now, my arms heavy on the table, my back to the fire.

With Agatha's death I felt a core in me begin to crumble. I was quite alone now. Alone in a whole new way, I wrote slowly. Timothy was gone too, losing his battle with cancer years ago. I had outlived the brother and sister who once thought to look out for me, and Amos was bedridden in a nursing home. With Agatha gone, I was solitary as never before.

The chill on my neck reminded me it was winter, and heating the house was a manual task. Closing the notebook, I built up the fires and settled with the *Times*, pulling the light wool Black Watch shawl across my shoulders. It had been a gift from Agatha: I took a handful of the softness, pressing hard, abandoning the headlines. The world, just now, was no concern of mine.

Without the grocery van, I began to rely increasingly on Morris. Recently retired, he had a constant string of repair jobs, but cheerfully saved his Saturdays for me. The little store was still open in the village, and sometimes on clear days I drove my cautious way there, but more often traveled in with Morris, or let him pick up things for me. His patience was endless as I mulled over library choices, wended my tottery way through the new supermarket, hesitated between a blue and a black notebook, tried out every new-fangled pen in the stationery store.

Thad came, over the Christmas break, with a bulging portfolio of work from design and drawing classes. "My C.O. status has come through," he told me. "And I'm thinking of going ahead with alternative service next year."

"You have student deferment."

"I'm getting tired of school."

"Where will you go?"

He shrugged. "Wherever The Friends want me, I guess. Trouble is, what service can an artist do?"

"They'll find something," I assured him. "Something more useful than cleaning a gun." I regarded him with approval. His reddish hair was cut too short, as was the fashion now, but his lean good looks, the new dark-rimmed glasses, gave him a mature air beyond his years. "So you've found something of use in that ugly square church."

He grinned, remembering. "More literally than you think. Damon found me a wonderful used Rolleiflex for Christmas, I've already begun a series of photos of the meetinghouse. I'm taking a course next semester, be able to develop them myself."

"You won't give up painting!"

He shrugged, his eyes untroubled, as yet, by any necessity of choice. He did not look, to me, like a boy tired of school.

The winter was a dark one for me. Newspapers piled up unread around unread journals, the cold seemed a permanent fixture of every corner, my depression a permanent aspect of life. You've been here before, I reminded myself, and survived it. When the thaw began I even ventured into the study hut, searching the shelf of notebooks for record of the ecstatic spring still in my memory. Not knowing where to place the memory, however, I got lost in my rummaging. By the time I woke up to the folly of what I was doing, I was more sad and lonesome than ever, and chilled so badly I could barely walk the half dozen steps to the porch and inside. I lay down on the couch wrapped in a bright knitted afghan from Eula, and slept, and when Morris found me the house was cold, and I was sweating with fever.

I spent two weeks in the hospital in town. But apparently not ready to die after all, I was one day suddenly well, and completely fed up with the bed, the blank corridors, the mumbling old woman on the other side of the curtain. I had no more patience for the routines of nurses and doctors, the pills and needles and prying.

"You'll have to find someone to stay with you."

"Doctor, I'll be fine."

He shook his head. "You'll be right back in here if you don't eat regular meals and stay warm and rested."

I pleaded with Morris. "Get me out of here. Tell them anything. Tell them my daughter's coming from Minneapolis, promise them anything."

"All right," he said. "I will."

Weak but triumphant, I leaned heavily on his arm to leave. I was in some way humbled by my body's tenacity. Apparently it, not I, would decide certain things. I sank against the car seat as if into some priceless chariot summoned by a good fairy. I didn't even ask him what he had promised the meddling doctor, so homesick was I for the place and the solitude I had thought I couldn't stand. I watched the countryside go by, the traces of snow, the bleakly dormant trees, feeling resurrected from a sleep of months.

The kitchen was warm, and smelled of cooking, and a teenaged girl was stirring a thick stew in my deep skillet. I stopped so suddenly Morris had to nudge me to get the door closed.

"Hello," she said.

I looked helplessly at Morris. "But I can't have –"

"Give me your coat," he said. "Carrie's your ticket out of the hospital."

She looked about half my height, a mere baby. She also looked embarrassed, I realized, and mended my manners. "Hello, Carrie. I'm Sarah Bakeley."

She nodded, and I felt foolish. And miffed. What does one do with a tongue-tied adolescent underfoot? Aware that I was being less than gracious, I turned nonetheless toward the living room, feeling almost weepy with frustration and weariness.

"I've brought some pillows down." The girl's voice behind me made me jump. "And a blanket, for the couch. Or the water's hot for tea, if you don't need to lie down."

I turned for another look at her, which made her blush and bite her lower lip. Her short brown hair, tucked artlessly behind her ears, matched the carelessness of her jeans and loose flannel shirt; with no sign that trinkets or cosmetics were known phenomena to her, she seemed completely without the self-consciousness usual to her age, but at the same time nearly felled with shyness.

"Yes. Some tea." I put some warmth into my voice, forcing aside the sense of intrusion. If I was to be waited on like some poor old soul, I might as well enjoy it. "Thank you, some tea would be lovely. Good and strong, not that brown water they serve in town."

Her lips parted in a quiet laugh which lit her eyes and changed her whole face. "Morris can show me," she said, and it was as if we'd leaped over some barrier.

"This is Jem's girl," Morris explained. Carrie was sitting near the table, in the corner of bookshelves, not having tea but watching everything Morris did. I nodded, not really placing her but trusting it would all come clear in time. She helped me get comfortable on the couch. I fell into a light sleep and when I woke, Morris was gone, and Carrie was studying at the table.

"Oh, dear."

Carrie looked up. I realized I'd spoken out loud. I avoided her eye, feeling a turmoil of embarrassment and irritation and relief. No one should be witness to this dissolution of body, it took me a full four minutes to get my feet flat on the floor. My privacy, the privacy of over twenty years, had been appallingly invaded, but I was more grateful for the girl's presence, the warm fires and fragrant stew, than I could say.

I protested when she slipped into her own dark coat after helping me with mine, but she was undeterred. "It's still icy out," she said, as if anyone might need an arm for balance in such a case. "I'll carry the flashlight."

I had to relent, knowing myself too weak to navigate the uneven path. "Mind, Carrie, this is what comes of looking through old notebooks. Stay out of the study, the dust of the past is lethal."

The meal was delicious, the rich brown gravy faultless.

"How will you get home?"

Carrie had for a moment the startled shy look of her first greeting, then indicated the stack of school books at the table's corner, tight against the window sill. My own notebook, the pen and inkwell neatly by its side, was against the wall. "The bus will pick me up here, Morris arranged it."

"In the *morning*?"

Her shyness turned to dismay. "I thought you knew. I mean, that it was your plan. Morris told me a week, at least. Maybe more."

"Well." I was stunned by both the surprise and the obviousness of it.

"I'm glad to do it, Mrs. Bakeley." She blushed, but now met my gaze bravely. "I've always wanted to meet you."

"Well," I said again.

"I'll be gone all day," she pointed out, gently comforting me with a sensitivity to my distress that won me over.

It was a stubborn, reluctant spring, warming only to rain, clearing to be cold. On Easter Saturday, Carrie shook the night's snow from a dozen daffodils, set them in a little pitcher on the table, smiling at my compliment before going upstairs. The ceiling creaked with her footsteps as she changed my bed and started the vacuum cleaner.

For the first time in the month since I had come home, I went to the table and opened the notebook. It was dusted now, as everything was. Carrie came only on Saturdays now, but she was a whirlwind of energy.

The daffodils, I wrote. What makes them do it, year after year, struggling up through the snow only to flatten in the rain. But I too yearn for the sun, for doors and windows flung open to hot breezes; what makes me want it, year after year?

Not hearing the car by the road, I was surprised by Thad's knock. By the time I had the pen capped and the book closed, and was on my feet, Carrie was down and at the door. I took hold of the wall to brace against the force of the contradictions assailing me. In the split second stopped-frame of their greeting, the puzzlement and interest was clear as words on their faces. I had known him nearly all of his twenty years, known her only for one intimate month of her sixteen, but I carried an absolute conviction that each had a separate destiny that must not stumble against another's. I wanted to push my hand into the force between them, but my breath was stopped, in that same half-second, with the undeniable joy in its existence.

It wasn't I who noticed the roof was on fire, but Jem Brown, driving by with a load of apples for the cannery. Afterwards, I realized I had begun to register the smell of smoke, but in fall, scents fill the air and I hadn't yet comprehended what my senses were telling me. It was a sunny afternoon, I was reading on the porch, but the kitchen range was lit, as the house didn't warm up well from the autumn sun. When I heard the truck stop, its brakes protesting, I looked up and saw the top of the load of crates, red apples showing, then a lean man bounding up the stone steps toward me. Alarmed, though not nearly enough, I stood up and he shouted at me over the railing.

"Your roof's caught! Call up central, hurry, tell her to call the Valley truck."

He rushed past me and down into the cellar; it was weeks before I understood he'd gone to cut off the electricity. My call went through quickly, and my instructions were efficient. Jem was already upstairs. I could hear shingles crackling now. "Come down!" I cried to him. He came down carrying two of the desk drawers, into which he had dumped everything from the desk.

"Come on outside, Mrs. Bakeley – grab something."

Idiotically, considering its worth, I scooped together my notebook with two library books from the table, the shawl from the rocker, my winter coat and the shoulder bag from the kitchen pegs, and headed out for the yard.

"Don't!" I called to him again as he passed me, but he disappeared inside, reappeared bent under an enormous mound of clothing wrapped in a cover snatched from the bed. Swinging it off his shoulder, he dropped the bundle on the desk drawers beside where I stood, and scarcely pausing hurried back into the house. I didn't bother protesting again. The blaze was very small, at once harmless looking and heart-stopping, a slowly enlarging circle just this side of the roof peak. Jem came out with the rocker and two straight-back chairs.

I was never able to reconstruct with any accuracy the next hours. By the time the trucks came, the roof was nearly gone, and the upstairs engulfed in varying white, gray, and black clouds. I stood numbly hugging my coat and notebook until someone gently tugged me down into the rocker, incongruously comfortable. There was by then a small crowd, and all the living room furniture stood tipsy around me.

Oh, Ethan, *the books*. I thought the cry so plainly I might have spoken it. And then, a void.

I had no idea whose room I was in when my eyes opened, or why I wasn't on my own couch. In an instant, of course, the image of the house in flames was clear and overpowering; I closed my eyes against the vertigo. When I dared to look again, I recognized Morris's front room. The cover over me was the quilt Agatha had bought at the fair twenty years past, faded and fraying. Belatedly, I recognized it as the cover my neighbor – I was not then sure of his name – had bundled the clothes in, and my eyes filled with grateful tears. Lying very still, as if to keep them from spilling over, I waited, with no desire to sit up or stir.

Perhaps I made some sign of waking, however, for a heavy-set woman appeared from the kitchen. I recognized the braids, pinned up across her head: Carrie's mother, whom I'd met in passing several times in the summer. She paused far enough away so as not to hover above me, but near enough to be a solid and reassuring presence.

"How you feeling?" Her smile, her round face and whole bearing, was friendly but suffused with the seriousness of my situation.

"Is it gone?"

"The fire's out."

"The house."

"Oh, no, the house ain't gone. Those big old logs are about as good as rock. Well, but upstairs is fairly gone, though," she added sadly.

I plucked at the quilt, feeling the grief coming at me as if from a distance, with still time to sidestep it, still a few moments to breathe before it hit. "Who was it, came by? He saved my quilt."

"Why, that was Jem. My Jem. You know, Carrie's father."

"Oh." I did sit up then, amazed at how small I had kept my world. "Will you be sure to thank him for me? I must have . . . ."

"Yeah, you blacked out. And no wonder. He's just glad he come by in time."

I accepted a cup of coffee in a thick white mug. *Oh Ethan, the books.* The two rooms upstairs were lined with them; the ones downstairs spared by the fire would be ruined by the water. And suddenly I laughed. Emma looked alarmed, so I hurried to assure her I was not hysterical. "I just got surprised by a memory, is all. Is the stairway still there, do you know?"

"The stairs? Well, I guess so, yes. Most likely there's some damage, but the kitchen's not burned. Why?"

"My husband once cursed the lintel."

"Bumped his head? My husband's all the time doing that at home, and cusses at it too."

"I mean in Latin. Condemned it to eternal fire. No, ethereal fire, that was it."

I looked up, saw her shock, and knew that I had been unwise. "It was a joke," I added, lamely, but had to smile again, remembering the dramatic pose, hearing the cadence of the Latin though the words were gone. "It was some obscure Virgil, I think. Nothing really to do with doorways, of course. All inflated and biting at the same time. Sonorous. He didn't really teach Latin, he was a modern historian but he started out in the classics and he loved Virgil, who knows why. And he had a mind that kept hold of things he loved . . . ."

I felt a shiver, and Emma was beside me offering a light afghan. My

301

breath came unevenly, in painful gasps. Her arm lingered a moment across my shoulders.

"I'm sorry," she whispered. "It's so awful."

She offered no consolation, for Ethan or for the fire; gave me no platitudes, for which I was grateful. In a few minutes the shock wave passed, and the coffee revived me somewhat. By the time Morris and Jem came in, Emma and I were sitting at the kitchen table talking like old friends, about the living, not the dead.

It was a fairly large house, a little helter-skelter with additions. Morris and Evvie had added the kitchen onto the back, with the boys' room above. His parents before him had added another two-storey set of rooms off toward the barn. Morris led me up the stairs, and in spite of my exhaustion I remembered the only other time I had come up here, and wondered if the arrowhead was still in the drawers Jem had saved. Morris turned back a narrow hall, showing me first the bathroom, then my room beside it. On an unmade single bed lay the two desk drawers, my purse, notebook, shawl and coat, with a towel, flannel nightgown and long terrycloth robe. The double bed, under a window looking out the front of the house, was neatly made, my quilt now on top with a corner turned back, two pillows in cases so white they fairly shone.

"Who did all this?"

"Your dresses, what Jem could grab, are in the closet there. Listen, there's plenty of hot water, draw all you want for a bath, it'll maybe help you sleep."

When I nodded and sat on the bed, I must have looked as stunned and drained as I felt, for he moved a step closer. "Can you manage? I can call Emma back."

I straightened my back. "No, of course I can manage. A bath sounds wonderful. And Morris? I'm not an early riser. Don't worry, and don't wait for me."

"I'll be here," he said.

By the time I stretched under the clean sheets, I was certain of one thing. When I rebuilt Ragged Edge, there would be a big rectangle of a tub, and hot water coming right out of the wall.

And so for the third time in my life, I lived with a man. Father, husband, friend. We never quite resolved the business of schedule, though Morris had to finally agree that I could look after myself in the mornings just as well with him gone as there. He introduced me to television, which I found equal parts inane and seductive, and for us an oddly companionable way to pass the evenings. I tried to retire early, as he always did, but took to reading in bed, a pleasure I'd never discovered before. He expected me to do nothing whatever, and aside from making my own coffee and toast, I obliged.

With the insurance money, and what extra I could manage, Morris and Jem did most of the rebuilding, finding used windows, putting down plyboard flooring. They installed a new bathroom under the sloping roof, by the top of the stairs. A double sink and formica counter, with hot and cold running water, replaced the old pump and deep sink in the kitchen. I got a new hotplate, a toaster oven, and a small black-and-white TV.

The new roof was tin, ugly and safe.

People I scarcely knew appeared Christmas week, organized by Eula to paint the upstairs and scrub the downstairs. I made a deal with Carrie, a senior in high school now, to give her my car in return for her driving me places on weekends and doing errands. We prowled through dusty crowded stores where I picked out inelegant but useful things for the bathroom, and found a priceless old tub with claw feet, for ten dollars. We shopped together for used rugs, looked for sales for bedding and towels.

I moved back home in February. Carrie stopped almost every day on her drive home from school, but I wouldn't allow her to stay with me as she suggested. She was right that the house did spook me a bit, beloved and familiar as it was. The smell of smoke lingered in spite of the new paint and cleaning, and the new things, convenient as they were, put me off. And though Morris came down at least one evening a week, I missed the sounds of another in the house. But there was at the same time exquisite comfort in the solitude, and I would get through the other bits.

I pointed out to Ethan that the doorway lintel was not even charred. That fire, he replied, had nothing to do with the ethereal.

Chapter 3.

Carrie

Jarrett went on scholarship to the state university, as naturally as if passing one grade to another. Carrie applied because it seemed natural to follow in his steps, but rather hoping her mediocre grades would bar that gate. Her collection of wild flowers had been her only A in biology; an essay on the bird songs she'd heard in a half hour walk was one of her few successes in English; her term paper on the history of Potter's Corner got her noticed by the history teacher, who encouraged her to write features for the school newspaper but still gave her C's in the course.

When she was accepted, however, it seemed a good thing, and she followed Jarrett to the university town, not so much because he was there as because he'd made a path there. She had to go somewhere, and her imagination faltered at the idea of jumping track. She went through the first months in a daze, confessing her homesickness to no one, partly because she was ashamed of it and partly because it wasn't true. She didn't want to be home. She didn't hate it where she was, not like the four girls on her hall who disappeared by midterm. She merely went on with it.

Her parents did not probe for details, but Mrs. Bakeley was troubled by her lack of enthusiasm. "It should be more than just okay. Have you no interesting courses? Amusing professors? New friends, from places you never heard of?"

Carrie felt uncomfortably as if she'd been sleepwalking.

"Write to me," Mrs. Bakeley ordered.

Accepting the challenge, Carrie did discover during spring semester that the classes, the dining rooms and dorm halls all gave plenty of material to describe. She turned to letters almost as to a drug, discovering not only Mrs. Bakeley's interest but also a new dimension to the friendship with Dee. They both enjoyed writing, and both thought the other's letters far superior and more interesting than her own.

Jarrett got summer work on campus, but Carrie came back to her parents, happy to fall into the summer work, glad for the time with her grandmother, who still came summers, and looking forward to time with Dee, who was coming to the farm, if only for two weeks. Their reunion was immediate in spite of the years apart. They spent the two weeks nearly inseparable; almost daily, they ferried Naomi and Nathan to various activities in the village and even in town. Both twins were on softball teams, even if hardly taller than a bat; both were adamant about weekly trips to the county library; both were regularly invited to spend afternoons with friends. No one splashed in the swimming hole anymore, but learned to swim properly, in proper pools.

When Dee left, Carrie threw herself with a kind of panic into the garden work and time with the twins, and was overjoyed one Sunday afternoon to find Thad at Sarah Bakeley's. He had decided to finish his college degree, after all, and now was waiting for an appointment with the Friends Service Committee, for his alternative service. He filled his days with work at Philip Miller's photography studio, but met Carrie every week at Ragged Edge for tea and a walk.

In cherry season, Carrie took over the checking job from Hannah. Skip welcomed her with his usual noisy teasing, mournful over Jarrett's defection.

"Don't he know he has a job here?"

"I wouldn't expect Jarrett back here, Skip."

"He don't play anymore either, I bet."

"Oh yes, he does, I've heard him. There's a group gets together."

Skip's expression was a mixture of pride and hurt, but he turned to the task at hand. "You'll be busy, Charlie's bringin' in a whole crew of Porta-Ricans. You learn any Spanish at that fancy school?"

There were only eight men, it turned out, and none was from Puerto Rico. They were Jamaicans, with the jauntiest walks and most lilting voices ever known in the rows of cherry trees.

"Come hear them," Carrie urged Thad. "Bring your camera. Basil brings his buckets in two in each hand and one on his head, I'm not kidding. Ezekiel has a gold star on his front tooth. Milton's about eight feet tall. They're gorgeous, every last one of them."

"Would they mind?"

"They're all legal. I think."

Far from minding, the men were delighted. And Carrie noticed with a kind of proprietary pleasure the sure way Thad handled his camera. He never fumbled, never hurried, glancing at the light meter and changing settings with the ease and precision of a master. She had never seen him so lit with energy, and yet his manner with the men was a perfect mix of deferential and off-hand. He pushed for nothing, and she could see he was getting every shot he wanted.

He brought the pictures to Sarah's, with extra prints for each of the men. They had only one walk after the picking, and then suddenly he was gone, for what would turn into three years and a solid apprenticeship in photography. Carrie kept working for Charlie, in the peaches, with loneliness like an ache worse than the sore shoulder from hefting fruit. In spite of herself, she began looking forward to school.

307

"I got into a writing course this fall," she told Mattie one evening when the two of them were up later than the others. "I never expected to, it's one of those 'by permission' classes."

"How do you get permission?"

"You have to submit something you wrote."

"What did you write?"

"I hope you won't mind: I wrote about the story you told us once."

"I never —"

"The fellow asleep in the grapes."

Mattie gave a quick laugh. "And he got you in? If that don't beat all."

They sat on in the soft warmth, the pine trees out by the drive dipping their boughs with exaggerated grace.

"Gramma, would you mind if I — sometime — wrote about Mr. Brustein?"

Mattie watched the night's dark shapes for a long moment. "Well," she said finally. "I guess I don't tell Jarrett what tunes to play on his fiddle."

"I don't know much about him."

"Well," Mattie said again. "We can see about that."

Muted by shyness, Carrie disguised her lack of direction under a layer of calm that quite without her intention gained her a reputation for solid sense and clear purpose. Her roommate Barbara seemed to her on the other hand to be cloaking an iron will under a gauzy ditziness. She liked and admired Barbara, but was repeatedly irritated by the manipulative show of helplessness, unable to understand any reason for it.

Barbara's goal was to get in with the theater crowd, not a simple thing with hundreds of others nurturing the same goal, but she'd made significant progress her freshman year. Specifically, her sights were set this year on one Byron Maleski, a graduate student in English with such a passion for drama he practically ran the undergraduate drama program, according to Barbara. She pleaded for Carrie's help.

"I'm so nervous! Just come along to tryouts, please Carrie, please please *please*. Otherwise, I'll bolt at the door, I know I will."

"How am I supposed to keep you from it?"

"Just be there. Walk in with me. I'll play to you, forget about him. Oh, you don't understand."

"No, I don't."

Carrie laughed at her but went along, only a little worried that Barb was expecting something from her she had no idea how to give. Surely she knew better than to expect any such thing, and anyway, what would be necessary? If the poor fellow was available, and not blind, he had no reason to resist the flattery of Barb's desire. She was sexy, with a neat figure, long legs, gorgeous dark eyes she knew how to highlight. Furthermore, her interest in the theater and her talent on the stage were real. She'd already been in summer stock, she had a keen memory, and knew her way around more dramatic literature than Carrie knew existed. Carrie decided this fellow had already noticed, and Barb wanted an audience for her conquest.

He was rather magnificent, Carrie conceded. Tall, with a dancer's grace and disciplined body, a sharply boned face more striking than conventionally handsome, with straight brown hair pushed carelessly behind his ears and longer than the usual, he had an authority in the lab theater no one seemed to doubt a bit. He set up improv scenes and watched them with an intense engagement that Carrie suspected was drawing out the best in the auditioners. Then he assigned them all numbers for the set pieces they'd prepared, and to Carrie's discomfiture, came into her corner and sat beside her.

"You're just observing?"

"Is that okay?"

"Sure."

"Thanks." She gave him a smile she hoped was polite and not as stupid as she felt. He smiled back and turned a chair in front of them sideways to prop his legs. He tapped his pencil lightly on his notebook, occasionally making notes she forced herself not to read. He said nothing more to her through three Shakespeare soliloquies and something from Shaw. Barbara was number five. Carrie began to relax, and even smiled a little, anxious to tell her friend there had been a definite coming to attention when she stepped into the circle, and that her Hedda Gabler had been breathtaking. In fact, it got applause, which the director joined.

Barbara didn't need her anymore. She started to ease out of her chair when Byron touched her arm and tilted his notebook toward her.

Sorry, not Mother Courage, he had written. Would you help with the set?

She looked at him, baffled. The first words meant nothing to her, and surely there were plenty of theater people needing credits and experience. She shook her head. He wrote a word, tilted the book again, not watching her, ostensibly listening to an Antigone.

Coffee?

She went hot. What on earth was going on? She glanced desperately at Barb, who had joined the dozen or so other actors ranged in a far corner, but couldn't catch her eye. Then she saw the smallest hint of a smile on Byron's face, more in his eyes than on his face, but an unmistakable mischievous grin if it broke loose. Mortified for her friend, knowing the amusement and the invitation were meant to derail Barb's too transparent agenda, Carrie left as quietly as she could.

"Who's Mother Courage?"

"What? That's the play. Why?"

"Oh. Can I read it? Do you have it?'

"No, of course I don't have it. Scripts are given out to the cast."

"What's it about?" Carrie wasn't too alarmed at Barb's touchy mood. She got snappy when tired, and she had every right to be tired, it was nearly midnight.

"Something about a war, I think."

Now Carrie was alarmed. "Barb, you didn't read it?"

"Why? Carrie, one can either act or one can't. I can. Give me a part, I'll do it."

"But shouldn't you –"

"How many tryouts you been to?"

"Sorry. Good point. You're right. When will you know?"

"I've got a voice in the crowd part. I already know."

"But you were terrific!" She'd already said that twice, and every time, the note flashed in her mind.

"I can tell. He has Marjory in mind."

"Well. Shit. She the powerhouse one?"

"Draft horse, rather."

Carrie laughed, and kept her admiration for the other woman's stirring voice to herself. "Well then, it must be the part's fault, it isn't right for you. There are other productions, right?"

"Mmm." Her roommate agreed absently, still twirling a pen dejectedly in her fingers. "Carrie? Why were you sitting with Byron?"

"He came over. I couldn't very well get up and move. Barb listen, forget him, he's not . . . ."

"Not what?"

Carrie took a breath. "Not interested in dating, I think. He's probably one of those egomaniacs who thinks of nothing but his work."

"You left awful quick. What'd he say to you?"

"I thought your part was over. I thought you'd done so well that –"

"What'd he *say* to you?"

"Nothing. Why?"

"He asked me your name."

Carrie felt hot again, with the numb panic of being completely at sea. "How did he even know we were together?"

"He must have seen us come in together. Or you said something."

"I never – I asked him if it was okay if I watched, I never said a thing more than that. Barb, come on, why are you looking at me like that?"

"Because you double crossed me, that's why."

And with the fluid motion Carrie admired so much, Barb rose from the bed, plucked her wool plaid cape from the desk chair, swung it neatly around her, and strode out. The door closed behind her quietly, and in spite of her shock Carrie noticed that it was an infinitely more effective exit than slamming.

The same day Byron's note came to her campus mailbox, Barbara told her she'd found an apartment. Insisting it was coincidental, and more convenient for the rehearsals for the Albee play she'd got a part in, she waved off Carrie's attempt to clear the air. "I've never seen him, Barb. And I won't. Look." She tore the note in two.

"It doesn't matter. A stroke of luck, really. Albee's all the rage now, Brecht is – well, nobody's doing Brecht anymore."

"I'm trying to tell you I had nothing to do with it."

"With what?"

Carrie turned away from the wide innocent eyes in exasperation. "With whatever you're mad at me for."

"You're forgiven, how's that? I'll be late for bio lab, bye."

The next day Carrie came home after lunch to find Barb's side of the room empty. She fished the torn note out of the basket.

Delores moved in from a triple. "Barb's neurotic. Nobody blames you, I can assure you."

"What was I supposed to have done? All I did was sit there."

Delores gave her a fond look. "Surely you noticed, her motives weren't always that clear. I suspect you were to be some sort of foil, reflecting the light somehow. Anyway, it's too late. Angie already asked me who the guy is you've been meeting in the Dive."

In three weeks, Carrie was in love. "But *why?*" She was beginning to be able to talk about her feelings now, an exercise new to her. Especially with Delores, who was warm and easy-going, whose laughter and tears were genuine. "I mean what in the world does he keep wanting to see me for?"

"He likes you, idiot."

"He couldn't have liked me when he sent the first note, he'd only seen me once."

"Well? Love at first sight. It happens. But you want a reason? Because you're not using him for anything. That must be pretty rare, in his line of work."

Carrie thought guiltily of her pleasure at the notes, the flush of pride she felt when others noticed his attentions to her. She was using him, all right. "I'm not exactly seeing him for *his* sake."

She said little about him at home, over Christmas, but Emma caught onto something, and worried. "You say he's older? How much?"

"Mother." Carrie scattered more flour over the dough she was kneading on the table.

"I mean, does he respect you?"

"Yes, of course."

"You will be careful, won't you?"

"Mama, it's just – we're just good friends, is all. He's fun."

Mattie and Carl didn't come that Christmas, Mattie down with a new influenza. Disappointed, Carrie was no more alarmed than anyone else, but in February Emma wrote to her that Mattie had been hospitalized for some tests. Carrie called her uncle, and learned that Mattie was at home again, but going in for more tests.

"What kind of tests? Why?"

"There might be some heart damage, they think."

"Can I talk to her?"

"Gosh, hon, she's asleep right now."

"Will you tell her I called? Tell her –" But Carrie's throat closed, and there were no words there anyway.

"Hey, Carrie, it'll be all right, it's just tests."

One evening late in February, the hall buzzer gave her signal for a visitor in the lounge. Expecting Byron, she went rigid with panic at seeing Jarrett. His face struggling for control, he told her the only possible way.

"Gramma died."

They stood frozen for several seconds. He raised an arm toward her and she crushed against him, and they clung together unmindful of the public space. She cried, feeling his sobs against her, wishing she could burrow into him forever somehow, into the past, into something soft and protective, into any moment not this moment. She pulled him down with her to one of the hard-cushioned gray couches.

"Her heart gave out."

"Did she – did she know about this, Jarrett?"

"I don't think so, they said something about it being from the flu. I feel like smashing the fiddle."

She hid her face and cried again. "No, not that. You can't."

"I won't. I just feel like it."

She nodded. How would he ever play again, how could she ever hear him play, without more pain than it was worth?

They squeezed in with the ten-year-old twins in the back of the Rambler, and headed west across Ohio on the turnpike. At a motel in Indiana, Naomi and Nathan lost their grief in the excitement and wonder of it all, then cried inconsolably when Nathan said, "I want to tell Gramma."

The endless streets, the endless rows of houses, stunned them all, but Carl's street, when they finally found it, was not unlike a small town street, if you disregarded the fact there were hundreds more between you and any field. In the middle of a block of attached homes, with similar square little porches and the same squares of space behind, Carl's house was neither shabbier nor better than any of the others. Carl-and-Mattie's-house, Carrie reminded herself firmly, but looked around in vain for any sign of her grandmother. She was even no longer in the kitchen, where a solid-figured woman greeted them, wiping tears.

Carl introduced her as Tania, a neighbor and friend. She shook Jem's hand, but embraced Emma, with fresh tears. "Such a good woman," she murmured softly, her heavily accented voice gentle as a purr. She nodded to the younger ones. "Ach, she spoke of you all, all the time of all of you."

Understanding that she was more than neighbor, Carrie wanted to hate her as a usurper, but she was impossible not to like. She affirmed their loss and grief; without fuss and without apology, she drew out their sorrow. Unobtrusive, claiming nothing, she loved them simply because they were Carl's people, Mattie's people.

"And you." With a touch, Tania turned Carrie's head to look at her as she dried the dishes Emma was washing from supper. "You favor her almost like a copy."

"Duane's here," Carl announced, hanging up the phone. "With Louisa. Flew in from Denver."

"Oh!" Emma gave a little cry of joy. "I'm so glad she could come. I was hoping. She did love Mattie so."

"The Millers were all good to her," Carl said. "Give 'em that much."

Carrie looked at him with sudden interest. What would he not grant, she wondered. Did he remember his father, the farm that might have been his? Every inch an auto worker, had he left the land for more reasons than the wage?

"Hannah and Charlie are awful broke up," Jem said, his voice husky.

Emma herded the twins upstairs, where Carl had given over his room to Jem and Emma, with bedrolls on the floor for the youngsters. Mattie's room stood heartbreakingly empty, with a white crocheted bedspread and carefully ironed curtains in the window toward the street. A third room had cots for Jarrett and Carrie, Carl insisting he would be fine downstairs.

"And were your uncles like you remembered?" Byron asked her when she got back.

"My Uncle Duane was not quite like I remembered," she said, relishing every word. "He was better. I missed you particularly at that breakfast, Byron, I've never been able to imagine you with my family, but I tell you we were transformed. It could have been in a movie. The auto worker union man; the tractor driver father of four who's been in a restaurant maybe six times in his whole life and never to a barber; and the college prof radical anthropologist who spent a couple years riding the rails before realizing he could get paid to study. They all look so exactly what they are, and yet they all look alike. Carl's a little beefy, with sad eyes, and drinks beer, going a little bald; Dad's more wiry but the tallest, drinks coffee, straight black hair; Duane's gorgeous, and drinks wine. There you have it."

Carrie stopped herself, a little embarrassed, then flushed with surprise at Byron's expression. He was eating it up. He loved her, he wanted her to talk, and she'd never realized it before.

"And his hair? You have to balance it. Balding, straight, and –?"

"Curly. They're all dark-haired, but his just frames his face perfectly."

"And the face is perfect as well, I take it."

Confident now, she laced her fingers in his. "Perfect. Don't be jealous. He's nothing like *you*."

"I'm jealous of you, not him. I don't adore any of my uncles, that's for sure."

They laughed, and started out on the trek back to her dorm. Her mood sagged, the closer she got, and by the time they were on the steps, she was crying.

"Hey, babe." He kissed her eyes, holding her face. "Hey."

"It's that urn," she sobbed. "I know exactly where that urn should be buried. Dad knows it too, but it'll never get said, I bet. Oh, Byron, I want her back so much. No one's saying the right things, I can't deal with this, I can't."

He held her quietly. "Carrie, you want to come on back? I have a rehearsal, but you could bring your books and . . . and stay. If you want."

She plunged without a thought. "Oh yes, could I really? Yes, yes. Wait two seconds."

Later, much later that night, there was the thought, What will I tell Emma now? Then, with the realization she'd thought "Emma," not "my mother," and nothing of her father or Jarrett or the twins, she also realized there would be no questions to answer. She had slipped away.

For the next few weeks she relied solely on momentum, and like a wagon coasting to a stop, her habit of going to class, reading assignments, planning research papers, slowly dropped away. She began walking. Especially in the heavy snows of March, she found it nearly impossible to turn inside until the cold forced her in, and only then would she think of her schedule. With growing anger, she felt school to be a digression that had cost her the real goal, a roadblock between her and the true source of knowing, a source now gone. And as if she herself, sitting dutifully at the desks, listening politely to others, wasting time on her own limp themes and awkward stories, had caused Mattie's death, she hated herself. She was a fraud, neither contributing to nor gaining from the academic enterprise. She forsook the dorm entirely; her corner of Byron's rented room, and the kitchen table they shared with Hugh and Winston, was enough.

She still met Delores nearly every week, and it was she who heard her plan first.

"I'm quitting."

"Now? It's only a month left."

"Two. It's only March, Delores."

"Carrie, are you −?"

"What? Oh. No, no I'm not. This has nothing to do with Byron, actually. I don't think it does."

"You going home?"

Carrie shrugged, admitting that would be the simplest plan but not one that appealed much. "Surely there's a job around here somewhere."

When she told Byron she was quitting, that she'd found a job in a restaurant kitchen, he propped his chin, regarding her so long with his inquiring, steady gray eyes she thought he intended to dissuade her. "I could help you out with this place," she said. "I mean, if that's okay."

"You're serious about this."

"Yes."

He grinned at her. "You can sure stay here. But I got an even better idea." He reached for a letter stuck in a drama anthology and handed it to her, his face lit with excitement. "I wasn't sure what to do about this, but now I am. Remember me talking about how I'd like to get out of English lit and into more drama?"

She looked at the letterhead. "Chapel Hill? What is this?"

"Read on, babe, read on. I talked to this guy last fall, he was here. I'd nearly given up on it."

Carrie's frown disappeared in a shout as she read. "Byron!" The letter offered summer stock work and acceptance into the Master's program in Drama. "But you already have a Master's."

"In English. A handy little credential, depending what happens."

"The theater's in Durham, where's that?"

Byron shrugged. "Next town, he told me. I've never been there."

"Byron, this is fantastic. It sounds like exactly what you want."

"The fellowship or teaching assistantship isn't for sure yet."

"But once you're there – you are going, aren't you?"

"If you'll go with me."

"When do we leave?"

He caught her up in his arms, dancing circles with her in the narrow kitchen. "Look out, North Carolina, here we come!"

He tried the next day to persuade her to finish the term. But it seemed to her even more important now to keep working, and she felt not a single pang at turning her back to college life.

The two of them fit themselves and their entire earthly possessions in a green VW bug and headed South. They stopped for one uncomfortable night near Pittsburgh with Byron's disabled, bitter father. Grieving still for the slain President Kennedy, the old steel worker spent the evening assuring them the capitalists had had him killed, and there was no more of a future in the arts than in the mills.

"Don't come running to me, I done what I could for you."

"Hey, Pop, I told you, this is a paying job we're going to."

Carrie's stomach did a happy little lurch at the pronoun. She'd almost forgotten she existed, so determinedly had the old man ignored her. She had never felt such instant aversion to a person. His hack, his spitting, the hunch of his once-crushed shoulder, but particularly the anger he turned on his only son, all made her despise him.

"And get a haircut, for chrissake."

"Sure. Got five bucks for it?"

His father hissed impatiently. "You," he said to Carrie, "can't you cut it?"

She shook her head, and said her only sentence of the entire visit. "I like it the way it is."

"Figures."

They walked to a shabby, cluttered store in the next block for ice cream. "You took a big chance, didn't you? What if he'd said yes?"

"I know him pretty well."

"If he doesn't want you in the mills, and doesn't want you to act, what is it you're supposed to be doing?"

"Becoming a famous surgeon."

"Ah. Well, no wonder he's pissed." She tucked her arm in his. "You'll have to get famous on the boards, he can brag on that instead."

"Brag? No, it's the security he's after, not the achievement." Byron sighed, rubbing his neck, aching from holding his temper. "I can't blame him, really. But he's a pain in the neck, literally."

They didn't head east to the farmland she once thought she couldn't leave. Without a thought for the hills of her home, she charted their route down through West Virginia, into Virginia. There were other farmlands, other mountains and valleys, other forests, and they were all calling to her. Loudly, urgently.

They lived in a one-storey, redwood-shingled house in the woods with Joel and Roz. Unlike any woods she'd known, these were flat, mostly scrub pine with occasionally imposing, branched oaks. The house was hidden, but only twenty yards from the next, and a stone's throw from a major artery between Chapel Hill and Durham. They had found the place on a Laundromat billboard, took it without looking any further, and stayed four years.

Joel and Roz were English doctoral candidates at Chapel Hill, both studying for their oral comprehensives in August, both nearly insane with tension, smoking pot every other night. Carrie was at first shy of intruding, but with Byron gone nearly every evening, with the back screened porch a haven from the day's humid buggy heat, she soon accepted their offered friendship, and their grass. From New York, and wishing they were back there, they adopted Carrie rather like a pet and Byron like a trophy. Roz zeroxed a stack of articles on Becket, which Byron touched reverently, but shook his head with an apologetic smile.

"I can't right now. I'm stage managing the Synge, I can't be changing the way I wait for Godot now."

Roz let out her high ringing laugh. "What a luxury study is to the real world. Never mind, it's ninety percent verbiage, anyhow."

"Verbiage," Joel said, in their usual way of finishing each other's paragraphs. "Def one: composted crap."

"But keep them. There are a couple good ones. At least we hope they're good, we intend to spout from them if the right questions come up."

Their endless cynicism was equaled by boundless good-natured generosity. Making do with one car, an ancient Saab, they were always dropping off, picking up, waiting on each other, or going together on errands one could have done, and quickly extended the habit to Carrie, who learned to carry a book everywhere she went. Waiting became a way of life.

She found a job in a coffee shop she liked, but the hours became so complicated to keep she switched to kitchen work in a crossroads diner a short mile from home, so she could walk. It wasn't a particularly pleasant walk, and she missed going into Chapel Hill. The town, if you disregarded the surrounding miles of residential streets and the campus of thousands of students, seemed merely an enlarged and enriched Potter's Corner to her. But the diner was pleasant enough, the minimum wage bought groceries and beer, she got a free breakfast, and enjoyed the Black women she worked with, one large, one skinny as a spring rabbit.

Durham she never warmed to, despite Byron's love for its charm and energy. The theater, loosely connected with Duke University, was not on campus but in an old building on a once main but now off-track street. Particularly backstage, the place propelled her backward into some era she could only guess at.

She'd felt spell-bound, stupefied, the first afternoon Byron showed her around, down a creaking stairway into a dressing room-office with mirrors inside and his name –his name! – on the handsome solid oak door. He watched her face, cocked an eyebrow in question.

"I've always thought of you as avant-garde."

He smiled, his eyes flashing with excitement and love. "Oh, Babe." He drew her into a hug, turning her so they both looked into the tiny room, his chin against her hair. "This is so far out it leaves avant-garde in the dust."

She laughed at the image of sand and soil piling up on sparse, white-lit circular spaces, her only sense of experimental theater, and leaned back against him, happy for him, happy for herself, feeling complete, replete.

After an initial enthusiasm for marijuana, she took Byron's advice and avoided it as a habit, using it as he did, occasionally at parties or Sunday evenings breaking from his relentless schedule of rehearsals and productions. Too many actors he knew spent their precious mornings stoned; he studied scripts and production notebooks, and exercised. He discovered yoga, precisely the combination of physical and mental stretching and rest he needed.

Roz and Joel passed their orals, threw a huge party still going strong when Byron and Carrie got home at two in the morning from the troupe's final curtain call party. "Listen." Carrie clutched his arm in the dark of the trees. From behind the house, high over the babble and hum of voices, came the strains of a slow tune on the violin. She stood still in wonder. "That's 'Omie Wyse,' I know that song."

By the time they got to the back, a banjo had joined in. Two men sat on kitchen chairs under an oak, faintly lit by light from the porch. Meaning it only for Byron, Carrie started singing.

"Come all you good people, I'll tell you no lies . . ."

Thinking the shadows hid her sound as well as sight, thinking the party was too noisy to notice one more sound, she sang on, protected by Byron's light touch at her waist. She saw the banjo player look around, but didn't register it as search for her. She was watching Skip, she was back at his ramshackle house with the bodies of children sleeping wherever they fell, she was singing for a fat, adoring Verta, for her silent grandmother. Tuning in with perfect accord to the musicians' pacing, she had no idea of their attention to her.

"Then up spoke her mother, in her voice was a sting . . ."

She would quit wherever in the song they stopped playing; they must be enjoying the tune to keep it going so long. "Go hang him, go hang him was the judge's command, and throw him in deep water that runs through the land."

The instruments did a nice tag, and stopped. Carrie caught her breath in confusion; mortified, she realized she'd been singing not under other sounds but in a pocket of silence. There was scattered applause. Resisting the urge to bury her face against Byron like a child, she murmured a low, "Oh, dear," and moved tighter against him. Tugging her gently, he led her toward the musicians, the only polite thing to do, but she would never have managed it on her own.

Roz materialized beside her. "My God, that was fantastic."

"It's a neat song," Carrie said.

The banjo player, a hefty fellow with thick blond hair and beard, laughed. "To say nothing of the voice."

"Best to say nothing of that," Carrie said, wishing Roz would hurry and get the introductions over so they'd play some more.

"It's a perfect voice," the fiddler said. "You didn't learn that in any music class." He pushed up wire-rimmed glasses, appraising her with frank curiosity in his round, clean-shaven face.

"And you should know," someone commented.

Roz laughed. "This is Jeremy, A-B-D in music. And Rodney, soon to be A-B-D, philosophy. This is Carrie, and Byron."

"Ah-ha!" Rodney swung his banjo aside and extended a large hand. "The house mates. Going for letters, too?"

"I will be," Byron said, and Carrie grinned, relishing his last-minute luck. "A drama fellowship just came through at UNC."

"I'll drink to that!" Joel called from the porch. "Another poor sod. Welcome aboard."

Sober now, and thirsty, Carrie accepted a beer. Rodney and Jeremy played a final tune and packed up, but Rodney paused on the porch by Carrie's chair.

"You know a lot of them old tunes, do you, ma'am?"

She laughed lightly at his exaggerated drawl. "No. Not really. Some." She wished, for some reason, she'd changed into her usual jeans. Her skirt was tight, and short, and why she should be aware of that now, after several hours among all sorts of strangers, even dancing with theater folk trained to do it right, she was at a loss to explain. "Just, you know, what everybody knows."

And he laughed again, that gently rolling chuckle luscious as the summer night. "Like 'Omie Wyse.' Does singing interest you?"

"What?"

"We're playing some, around. You be interested in trying some material with us?"

"I don't play anything. I've never thought about it."

"Well, think about it. Joel's got my number."

"Gosh. Byron? I didn't mean to sing like that, I meant it just in your ear. I hope it wasn't too embarrassing."

"Embarrassing? Babe, I was proud fit to bust."

She rolled over, up on an elbow, to frown at him if he were teasing, but his smile was genuine. She smiled back, relieved it could all go behind her now. He curled around her. "It won't happen again," she said.

"Don't say that. Why not?"

"Just . . . No. It's not my thing. I must've been drunker than I thought."

"Sure didn't sound it. Um. . . . You really liked Rodney, though?"

Her eyes flew open as if to see his thought in the dark, then she dismissed the absurdity of any hidden meaning, and laughed softly, snuggling comfortably under his arm. "Yeah, he's like the big teddy bear I never had. And did you see his wife? Hair like a long shawl, gorgeous."

"That was his wife?"

"Yeah."

"I thought . . . . Oh, Carrie, I did think he was maybe coming on to you." Byron squeezed her a little tighter in apology.

"Me? Hardly. He was talking about songs, is all."

But Carrie smiled again, into the dark. So that's what it was, she'd been desired. Obliquely, faintly, not seriously, but still, desired. Well, Lordy. She tightened her own arm against Byron's. He needn't worry. That kind of warm wave was nothing, nothing, compared to the heat he offered.

They thought about moving into Chapel Hill, but soon realizing they were lucky to have a place at all, settled more completely into the house. Joel and Roz had one more year of teaching fellowships. With everyone now traveling the same direction, Carrie was able to take a slightly higher paying job at Lum's Snack Bar, across the street from The Wall, on which students perched at all hours. She loved the phenomenon of that, and the glorious fall weather that encouraged it. She felt no envy whatever. None of them could be feeling life was better than she knew it to be. She read Byron's texts and scripts, and typed his papers; learning her way around campus, she was often able to slip into movies for Joel's film course. Roz's work on the modern novel opened a world she knew she'd never get enough of. What better tutelage could any of those exhausted looking students be getting?

She entered another new world in the spring as posters and leaflets became ubiquitous, against U.S. military build-up in Southeast Asia. At the same time, the Black student caucus was finding its feet and its voice, and grad students from several disciplines formed a radical alliance that began making suggestions that the university change its course.

"Time to get out of here," Joel said, stroking his new droopy mustache.

"You don't agree with them?"

Roz laughed. "We're *in* with them. But it's going to get messy."

"Makes me tired," Joel said. "But I'm sure Skidmore will be more of the same."

"We'll be on the wrong side there," Roz reminded him. "Soon in the over-thirty crowd, and establishment to boot."

"We'll keep up our SDS membership."

Byron's father died, just before Easter.

"I can go with you, if you want."

"Of course I want. But no, it would be boring for you, just making it worse for me. Unless maybe you'd like to go home?"

"Now there's an idea." She was brought up short by the fact it hadn't occurred to her. Reveling in a town gone mad with bloom and mockingbirds, she'd scarcely given the familiar Pennsylvania spring a thought. It would be just starting there. She could take a bus straight east from Pittsburgh and be there in . . . . "No. I'll stay here and work."

She wrote her usual monthly letter home. She got only terse, hurt notes from her mother, variations on the same theme. What am I to tell the twins? If he loves you why aren't you married? Themes which Carrie never helped her out with. Her own thinking had begun finding a solid base as she had picked up pamphlets from some new tables appearing on the campus, and began dipping into suggested readings. Betty Friedan, Simone de Beauvoir, Olive Schriner, Virginia Woolf, Ruth Hirschberger, the Brontes. . . . Famous names and obscure ones jumbled together in a kind of stew, with one prominent flavor as base: women were better off on their own.

This was all as much a surprise to her as the singing had been. And like the singing, it seemed to rise not from outside but from something inside which had found the instruments others were playing. Her letters to Dee and Sarah Bakeley got tangled with lists, half-formed responses to her reading. Dee, in school in Boulder, was more interested in the party. "Wish I could have heard you!" she wrote. "You know, folk is a whole new big thing out here, maybe you should say yes to the teddy bear." Carrie felt no pull toward such a life, avidly engaged in her own awakening and in life with Byron.

Byron watched and listened, and by the end of summer was showing both pride and uneasiness. Her new confidence, her nascent comprehension of feminism as an historical and ever-evolving reality, helped him considerably with directing the theater's summer production of Ibsen's *Doll House*. He gave her too much credit really, since she never said anything original, mostly just asking questions that would turn his thinking in new directions. On the other hand, he looked askance at some of the more political and radical writings, the buttons and crude underground rags.

"Am I unfair to you?"

"Nothing even close," she assured him. "I'm not reading this stuff to break out of anything, more like to explain how I got here. I've never been happier in my life." She leaned over and whispered in his ear. "Can't you tell?"

It was true. She was soaring free. Unlike the singing, nothing in the women's writing made her recoil in fright. No matter how angry or clumsy some of the writing in that early renaissance was, she found it releasing, not depressing.

She began writing some of her feelings to Mrs. Bakeley, who was interested and sympathetic, but thought her stance on marriage was throwing the baby out with the water. "There is no intimacy quite like that in marriage," she wrote back. "Prince Charming is a myth, yes, and the institution has a dreadful history of abuse. But if his conversation is worth anything, he's your man. Don't be afraid of commitment."

"Why can't marriage be merely one form of intimacy?" Carrie returned. "I want to be with Byron the rest of my life, but do I have to marry to prove that?"

They were more in accord with their growing awareness of the horrors of Vietnam, the magnitude of the civil rights problems in the States. Sarah saluted Carrie's awakening to the complicity of capitalism in the world's injustices, and wondered if the contradictions in the present system would begin pushing the country toward needed change. "Maybe even a new New Deal of some sort."

Carrie, for her part, was becoming more convinced that the so-called women's issues were not a luxury but a key to unraveling the cat's cradle of social and economic inequities. She found no forum for that idea at the time, nor was she able to formulate how the key worked, but her letters stumbled toward articulation.

After two years away, Carrie went home for Jarrett's graduation. Seeing Jem and the twins waiting on the sidewalk as the bus swung into the alley, she was still blinking at tears and too choked to speak as she swept a weeping Omie into a hug. Nathan, a little stiffer but with the same adoration in his soft blue eyes, let himself be hugged, too. Jem nodded at her, his face friendly, his hands already picking up the suitcase and shopping bag.

"This it?"

She nodded, hanging on to the twins for ballast the block to the car, slipping an arm through Nathan's, stroking Omie's long silky hair. At nearly eleven, they were looking more alike than they'd used to, and stood up to her shoulder. "What happened to your babies, Dad?"

Jem looked a little startled, then gave her one of his rare broad smiles. "We got rid of 'em, they were no good."

"Heavens, there are new houses in Potter's Corner."

"New whole wing on the school," Jem pointed out.

"There's two fifth grades now," Nathan informed her.

"And Mr. Dillard retired and died," Omie added.

As the car began to climb through orchards and stretches of woods, Carrie felt affection rise like a tide in her. How could she not have missed these beautiful kids, this marvelous safe place? By the time they passed Sarah Bakeley's house, and driven up the hill to the farm's lane, she was ready to fall sobbing into her mother's arms and be whoever she was supposed to be.

By supper her defenses were back in place. There had been genuine love and welcome in Emma's hug, and emotional, happy tears between them, and then the yawning gulf. Emma was not going to forget or forgive her fall from grace, from the expected, and Carrie was not going to plead for understanding.

They spoke at the table of their neighbors.

"Be sure to go see Hannah," Jem said. "She asks about you all the time. And Morris and Mrs. Bakeley, of course."

"What's become of Jimmie Mertz?"

"You know, he's doing right well," Emma said. "Wife, new baby. Making a reputation as mechanic."

Jem nodded. "Different as night and day, him and Sammy."

"Sammy went back to 'Nam," Nathan said.

"Went *back*?"

"Finished one tour," Jem said. "Signed on again. Jimmie and his friend Jake they come back and stayed, both up around Claysville somewhere."

"Jake's the one Donnamae ran off with?"

Emma went to the stove for Jem's coffee. "At least he married her," she said.

By that night, Carrie lay a visitor in her bed, crying silently with impatience to be gone. It was so stupid. The constraints Emma had always put around their conversation, and her own absolute obedience about the limits, continued to rob them of any knowledge of each other.

They were allowed only a synopsis of each other's stories, and expurgated versions at that. Emma showed no curiosity about the particulars of Carrie's life, and encouraged none about her own. The message was clear and unrelenting. Until Carrie was a married woman, she could not join the conversation of married women.

By the time they drove up to State College and sat with thousands of other families through droning speeches and interminable lists, had done the usual meals out with Jarrett, posed him in cap and gown, met his friends and tied his trunk and boxes onto the Rambler's roof rack, Carrie was in a comfortable middle state, just waiting it out.

Jarrett, for all his distance the past four years, with only brief vacation visits home and sketchy reports of his life, was the hero of the hour, and Carrie relaxed gratefully, sharing her family's pride. Summa cum, no less, a new phrase to the twins and one which was to launch Nathan into his quirky love of Latin. And with full fellowship to Stanford, which made Emma's eyes tear with pride and grief. So smart and good looking, and so far away.

It was a cramped ride home, and the house seemed more crowded than it used to, but Carrie enjoyed the two days before she and Jarrett left. They didn't delve deeply into each other's lives, but did swap stories, about campus protests, frights and triumphs, plans for the future. He had no advice about their parents' hostility to Byron except patience. "They'll come around," was all he could offer.

As if already nostalgic for a passing way of life, they compared notes on the changes the twins had wrought on the homeplace, particularly the television in the living room. "Uncle Carl and Aunt Tania bought us that for Christmas," Omie explained proudly.

She and Jarrett walked over to Skip's for an evening of fiddling, and she sang with them. Telling them she'd once met Rodney Blake, who by now was fairly well known in the traditional music revival, she said nothing about singing to his banjo, or his offer. In truth, it scarcely entered her mind. This for her would always be the proper place for the old songs, the only place to sing them.

"Don't be such a stranger," Skip said to them as they set out for home, and all the way along the track through the woods, circling the peach orchard and up the big yard between the spring and the house, Carrie thought about that. He'd only meant, don't stay away so long. Hello, stranger! was the usual local greeting to anyone who managed to get away for more than a week. But that she was a stranger now, a visitor from unknown parts, was all too obvious.

Byron got his degree, and landed a year's fellowship with artist-in-residency at a University of California branch in San Diego. Carrie meant to go home before they left, but she wanted to bring Byron, and Emma objected. Her cause was not helped by Duane and Louisa marrying. Byron urged her to go alone, but she refused, and the next thing she knew they were driving across the country in an old Ford station wagon. Sleeping in the back, they ate hot dogs and beans, fried eggs and bacon, at roadside rests. They stopped a day in Denver, washing clothes and getting properly fed at Duane and Louisa's. Louisa kept plying Byron with food to watch him eat it.

"Where does it go?" She mimed her astonishment to Duane.

Their house, Carrie thought, was perfect. This was about as far as Louisa could have gone from the three-storey heavily furnished farm house, yet somehow the spare sunlit rooms on the single floor gave the same warmth and welcome. It was the sense of purposeful space, Carrie decided. Whatever the eye took in, whether the grand piano, the sofa and arm chair, the drop-leaf dining table, the door open to Duane's study, the body wanted to go to.

"I love them," Byron whispered, in the guest bed. He hadn't wanted to stop, wary both of the family connection and their position in high brow culture. She had nearly agreed, since Dee had graduated and was in Michigan now. "You're right, they're for real."

"Even more than I expected," Carrie admitted. She'd expected a welcome, but was unprepared for the warmth of it, and hadn't known the aura of fun Louisa created around her. Her light blue eyes were curious, completely without judgment. A lifetime of creating music by the sheer force of concentrated will had honed her attention, and one felt wholly within it, without any stray distractions.

"Actually, she reminds me of you," Carrie said as later on the road they rehashed the visit. "The way she's so totally there. You're like that, when you coach students. I bet her students, like yours, play better than they know how to."

He was pleased at the comparison, but looked abashed. "Thanks, but I'm not there yet. And your uncle – he'd be wonderful on the silver screen, with all that energy in his eyes."

Camping at Mesa Verde, she was awed both by the mesas and by the depth of Byron's response to them. On one climb he dashed to a mesa's edge. "'Blow winds, and crack your cheeks! Rage! Blow!'" His ranting contortions were like a dance, so perfectly was he in control of his body. "'You cataracts and hurricanes, spout till you have drenched our steeples, drowned the cocks! You sulphrous and thought-executing fires, vaunt couriers to oak-cleaving thunderbolts, singe my white head!'"

He turned a full circle, lowering his hands to rest calmly at his belt, his gaze sweeping the relentless blue arc of sky. "Wrong sky."

"The scale is right, though," she said.

"Indeed."

To their immense satisfaction, they found a loft apartment in a warehouse at the edge of the gas lamp district in San Diego. It also bordered the Bad Part of town, but Carrie said it that way, with capital letters, laughing. Bad to some, maybe, but to them and scores of artists of all stripes, a haven, a marvel, a dream if not quite come true at least bright with possibilities.

The heat was a bit of a shock, and the extent of pavement. It was a dry heat, however, just as everyone had told them it would be, not the mugginess of the East. And if they were surrounded by pavement, the single large space of the apartment was exactly what Byron needed for extra rehearsal space and the mime exercises he practiced daily. Carrie had no desire to fill it, settling happily at its edges. The chipped formica table at the kitchen end and the mattress and cushions under the big windows were furnishing enough.

The pervasive military presence was unnerving at first, but they soon found the pockets of community resisting its dominance passively or actively. As usual, Byron used everything as grist for the mill, studying body language, noting how people grouped, parted and regrouped.

"Like high grass in a wind," Carrie commented as they stood at the edge of a restive crowd at an anti-draft rally.

"Ripples. That's it!" He pulled her against him in an enthusiastic kiss. "You're a genius."

She laughed, understanding that he had just solved a blocking problem for a crowd scene.

Ripples of bodies was a little how she began to view their loft, too. It felt at times as if their entire generation had cut its moorings, and drifted or dashed with great purpose if little aim. Toward their pad. She and Byron both took to the mores of the time with the sense of being at the center of something, though they couldn't have said what, precisely. In any case, there were generally two or three sleeping bags parked in their space, and their lovemaking was snatched like a snack.

It seemed impossible to be any happier than they had been in Carolina, but it also seemed they were. She loved Byron more with each nuance of character she discovered in him, and loved the way he might seem entirely engrossed in the cluster around him and without missing a beat suddenly seek her out. For the instant of their glance they'd be alone, separated from the crowd. She found him more beautiful than ever, more fine-tuned and focused. There was nothing of the charlatan in him, no sham, no pose. Purely and simply, he loved what he did, and worked hard at it. And only at it. He would have begged, or starved, before spending an hour at anything unrelated.

She took a job in a fusty book store, which at first was more depressing than fun. She longed to sweep the piles of disintegrating paperbacks, the stacks of Readers Digest Condensed Books, out the side door, to pull down the dusty rows and clean the shelves, widen the aisles, bring in some armchairs. Enchanted now with sunlit space, she balked at the bad lighting and crammed shelves of the long narrow store. The place spoke to her more of greed and neglect than of eccentric passion or buried treasure. But she wouldn't have known where to start, even if cleaning had been in any way suggested or encouraged, and so she sat every afternoon on her high stool behind the antiquated cash register, accepting people's crumpled bills and planning the evening meal.

She did browse enough to get an inkling of the old man's system, such as it was, and the first time she was able to nod helpfully at a customer's request, the job took on a more pleasing aspect.

"You wouldn't happen to have *My Friend Flicka*, by any chance?" an older woman asked. "I think my grandson would like that book."

Carrie went straight to a set of Mary O'Hara's Wyoming trilogy, and the woman took all three, grateful as if Carrie had done her a personal favor. "They're not really children's books," she told Carrie, with a conspiratorial air. "But they're such grand stories."

Maybe it wasn't such a bad store after all, Carrie thought. She began tidying up, in tiny bites. It was hopeless, but made the hours more interesting, and the old man didn't seem to mind.

Her evenings were filled with plays and coffeehouses and rehearsals. Not drawn to the theater as performer but enthralled with the scene, she ran errands and filled in around the set or just sat in the shadows, watching Byron at his best. She juggled the demands of cooking, laundering, cleaning, shopping, around her job and the odd schedules of others, careful not to interrupt anything going on in the apartment or to miss any precious chance of being alone with Byron.

After San Diego, a sweltering summer in La Jolla. After a term in Vancouver, a spring in Boulder. Carrie despaired of ever seeing Dee again; from Michigan she'd gone to spend a year in Amsterdam, studying voice and harpsichord. And Carrie couldn't find a job in a city bursting its seams with unemployed youth.

"Just hang out." Byron swung an arm around her neck and got an oafish, stoned look on his face. "Hey, Babe, you can park your sandals under my bed anytime."

"It's on the floor."

"Oh. We'll think of somewhere to put 'em."

His clowning was without malice, and not far from the mark: the thinnest of veils separated them from the shiftless. Byron was teaching only one course, performing for no pay in a community theater, involved in a guerilla mime troupe. They lived in a crowded student co-op, a four-storey fire trap from some other era – from some other planet, Byron said. Carrie was not at all bored, discovering a knack for finding out what other people were studying. Or avoiding studying. There were teach-ins, be-ins, processions and vigils and study groups and protests and picket lines. Carrie took in as much as she could of it all. Byron's student deferment, through some snafu, kept coming through, but in those tense years they learned the route to Canada, and considered it seriously as an option.

"I think I'll check this out," Byron said one evening. "There's a church in Arvada, someone told me, planning to do a production of *J.B.*"

"Aren't you busy enough?"

"It's probably an in-house thing, but the play's interesting."

"Look good on your vitae."

"Don't smirk." He shook a finger at her. "If the church is going to support the arts, it's enough to make a Christian of anybody."

As seemed to happen regularly, his impulse was a good one. The minister of the church was so taken with him he asked him to direct the play, offering a small fee that was enough to keep them afloat.

As a favor, Carrie typed a history paper for one of the housemates, and soon had all the work she could handle. At first she took only gifts in return – some grass, a six-pack, a lunch or dinner; but others persuaded her she was crazy. She bought a new electric typewriter and went into business. Fascinated, she learned the intricacies of the MLA style sheet for references and footnotes in the various humanities and social sciences, and began to notice that the content of those courses was changing.

More than once she came across Duane's name in a quote. One week she'd follow leads into the writing of Howard Zinn or Noam Chomsky, the next into R.D.Laing or Edgar Cayce. She read the same way she typed, uncritically, with voracious appetite. It was when she discovered that feminist thought was becoming an academic subject that her reading began to focus.

That summer, Byron joined a troupe in Santa Fe, and from there got a faculty position, in his usual last-minute style, at a university in Texas. This time, instead of getting rid of everything, Carrie lugged the typewriter along. For the first time, they rented a whole house, a small one-storey adobe in an ugly but safe neighborhood, where yards were allowed to parch and half-hearted fences allowed to sag. Dogs wandered and several languages mingled. Carrie bought a used bicycle and found a job quickly, at a garden center with greenhouse and nursery, within biking distance.

Jarrett was by this time searching the market, and came to their city for an interview. He didn't get the position, but they had a fun couple of days. In spite of having written to her of the "mountains of sludgy weighty triviality" of academic work, Jarrett was in a good mood, nearly finished with his dissertation and looking forward to taking his brand of radical sociology into classes of his own. He congratulated Byron for his survival.

Byron was unsure it was a step in the right direction. "Academia seems an unhappy place, somehow."

"No question." Jarrett uncapped another beer. "It's peopled by cynics, dilettantes and moral cripples."

"Wait a minute, what about Uncle Duane?"

"Bingo." Jarrett smiled happily. "There are just enough hold-outs for the game to be worth playing, to keep on keeping on."

His stamina for keeping on was impressive to her. He'd protested regularly Stanford's involvement with the defense industry, been chased by police at the Oakland induction center and by angry right-wingers at anti-ROTC demonstrations. He worked summers organizing for health projects in East Palo Alto; he read widely, went to Black Power speeches and farmworkers' union rallies. And somehow kept up with his studies, and occasionally played his fiddle.

"And what's the prize?" Byron asked him. "I mean, for keeping on, what do you expect to get?"

Jarrett had an answer. "I want depth."

Carrie caught her breath. They were much the same words as Dee had written her once. "I can sing, but haven't yet got down to where the music must come from. Depth, or whatever the right word might be." Byron knew it, too, always diving for more and more in a scene. So she would probe, too, if only she knew where, and how.

"Byron. . . . Byron?"

He looked up from his plate, his eyes seeming to focus on her from something far away.

"You haven't said a word all evening."

"Sorry. It's this damned play. It's dull, I mean the production is dull. Wooden."

"Maybe it's a dull play. Not your fault."

"It is if I chose the play." His voice was cold, with none of the invitation to help she was used to. Used to be used to. Carrie felt a worry like a slender worm crawling up her rib cage. Had she known he chose the play? Was she supposed to have known? Was it her attention, not his, that was wandering away?

He gnawed on a chop, dropped the bone with an impatient gesture. "It's not a dull play. It's Pinter."

"Pinter? Pinter's not very –" She stopped, afraid of irritating him further.

"Not very what?"

His flatly uninterested tone made her hesitate. When had she started being shy of him? She used to be able to say anything, ask anything. He hadn't minded when she was wide of the mark, it helped him clarify, he'd say. "Political," she said weakly.

"Since when has everything got to relate to U.S. imperialism?"

She tried to laugh, over her wince. "I only meant you do your best with –"

"Pinter's one of the big guns, I ought to be able to bring him off the page."

"Even with children?"

But their standard joke about how students were getting younger didn't work. "If they don't know shit, whose fault is that?"

"Byron. Why are you being so hard on yourself?"

"I'm easily replaced."

So it was a harder job, Carrie decided. This has nothing to do with me, or with us. Times were changing, drama departments were tightening up their act. So to speak. The loose sorts of making do, the guerilla theater tactics of the past decade, were being codified; departments wanted not only those who could do but could explain what they did, in appropriate academic fashion. Byron was working hard on a series of articles, and now had only another year to finish his dissertation on Brecht, to get offered the tenure track position the powers were planning for him. He was working too hard. He needed her to be cool, not start fussing at him with questions and needs, which would sound like criticisms.

"Let's go somewhere over Christmas break."

"I should stay home and work," he said, but he was tempted. "Like where?"

"It might be fun to see Joel and Roz again. We could afford to fly, now." Their first housemates had wound up in Madison.

He was noncommittal for a week, then backed out. "You go, if you want."

"What fun would that be? You're the one –"

"What?"

She shrugged. You're the one likes big universities, she'd almost said, but it sounded wrong, as if she didn't like it here. She liked it wherever he was. "Well, you know, with shop talk and all that."

"You spent more time with them than I did."

"I don't want to go by myself. I want *us* to get away, somewhere."

"Well, I can't. Not this year." His face softened, and he came to sit by her on the couch. "Carrie, I'm sorry, it's not that I don't want to, believe me."

She did believe him. She shooed her worry away. He didn't mean he didn't want to go places with her, he was busy. Busy so they could be together. Surely she didn't want to stay hand-to-mouth, tumbling around the streets, forever, waiting for parts season by season. Easy enough for her, that life, but she wasn't the one working her tail off, depending on luck, the right role, the right review, the right audience.

But. He was working his tail off here. And where were the reviews now? The fits of brilliance that had gotten him noticed as a director had come on him because he lived and breathed the stage, and could recognize inspiration when it came. Here he was living and breathing something else: the job.

She shooed the worry away again. He was a marvelous teacher, she still loved watching him from the shadows, he was always still as surprising to her as that first evening in the lab theater. In a year, two at most, his reputation just for that would probably get him on tenure track. And his fall production of *The Homecoming*, in spite of his frustration with it, had been a resounding success. He knew what he was doing. It didn't mean anything that they no longer piled gleefully into a car and took off every six months like kids at recess. They were growing up, was all.

And like grownups, maybe they could do separate things sometimes. Instead of Wisconsin, she chose home. Emma's November letter told her of Skip's death. A truck with a load of apples had gone out of control and crashed into Skip's pickup, killing him and his daughter-in-law. The baby they'd been taking to a clinic for shots survived; Alvin moved with the baby girl back to his home on the Jack Road, and began working for the Millers, perhaps to keep the earth in its orbit. The letter reminded Carrie that anyone could die, anytime, and two days before Christmas she flew home.

The twins were sixteen now, lithe and poised. Nathan with shy pride admitted to being a straight-A student, and Naomi showed her an issue of LIFE magazine on midwifery that had set her sights on nursing. Nathan was also thinking of medicine, maybe research or therapy.

"They're so full of plans," Carrie commented to Emma one morning.

Emma gave her a sideways glance, her hands in the dishwater. "Nothing wrong with that."

"Wrong? No, I'm speechless with admiration. But they will play a little, won't they, along the way?"

"Those two? They seem to have a pretty good time."

"That's true, they do."

She and Emma were friendlier than before, accepting the limits. Sharing little but the actual days they moved through, they avoided the past, and sought no confidences about each other's lives. Carrie spent as much time as possible walking, or with Sarah Bakeley. There was usually something in the *Times* Mrs. Bakeley was anxious to discuss, and she had none of Emma's fears about quizzing Carrie.

"Your job is still fun?"

"I like it fine. I do kind of miss reading all those papers I used to type."

Mrs. Bakeley made a face. "They can't all have been very good."

"They were terrible, some of them. But every third one or so led me to an interesting book."

"And still no plans to marry your young man."

"As far as I'm concerned, I am married."

Carrie was with her the Sunday afternoon Thad came. He was as surprised as she, and before they had time to feel awkward they were hugging tight, swinging a circle in the kitchen. With all those transient musicians and actors, Carrie had learned to hug.

She thought of leaving, to allow Mrs. Bakeley to have him to herself, but the three of them together felt so much like a golden part of the past she'd nearly forgotten, that she stayed, and the next hour sped by. When Thad said he ought to be going, she pulled on her fleece-lined denim jacket and went out with him.

And somehow they passed his car, walked down the little path that crossed the creek. They climbed the gentle hill, talking all the way. He'd done an extra two years with the Friends and was back now with Philip Miller in town. There was a woman he'd met in Service; she was teaching in Cleveland now but wanted to start a school; and how was Byron?

She told him about San Diego and Boulder, the troupes and her reading and the jobs at this and that, and the crowded apartments.

"Even now, our house is like a way station. He's some sort of beacon. Bring me your tired, your poor, your busted, your brilliant."

"Do you mind?"

"Me? No, what's to mind? They're good people, most of them."

They sat on a rock outcropping, warm in the sun, the air mild.

"I keep being attracted to community ideas," Thad said. "But the truth seems to be I had enough of communal living during the AFSC years."

"You don't miss it?"

"In some ways."

"The alternative is so terrifying to me."

"What? You don't want a box like every fourth box on the street?"

"What makes it so oppressive, I wonder. Oh Thad, I do have a horror of it, of falling into a trench and sleeping through life."

"You don't seem the least bit nodding off, to me."

"Thank you." On impulse, she leaned against him and kissed his cheek. "Nor do you."

"Thank you," he answered, and kissed her back. Their eyes met, a surprised light in both their faces. Then there was her hand on his shirt, his arm under her jacket, a proper kiss. She felt the tiny sob in his throat as he ducked his face against her neck, she felt the sudden urgency in her, the decision to seek its source.

They lay very still, very tight, the air cold now on the sweat where their clothes had parted. He stirred in her, and she tightened against him as if protectively.

"Carrie."

"It's okay."

He raised his head to look at her.

"It's okay," she repeated, and drew his face down for one more kiss. Meaning, I'm on the pill; meaning, I love you; meaning, fare thee well. They walked holding hands, slowly, back to his car, where they embraced gently. Chastely.

"I'm sorry –"

She touched his lips. "Don't be. Don't ever be. Don't spoil it."

He caught her hand, kissed the palm, and waited while she walked the short distance to the stone steps. She turned and waved, he lifted a hand and climbed into his car.

She flew back to Byron the next day.

Among the young faculty that began mingling in their house with the students and the passing-throughs was a woman who went by the sole name of LeNae. Slim, unruffable, with a pixie face and a moxie air, LeNae hated Texas with a passion that never seemed to throw her out of humor. An anthropologist by training, in American Studies by accident, and teaching women's studies by design – on the sly, as she put it – she was fighting an uphill but tireless battle to get women's studies a recognized program at the university.

"Even though it'll be merely a bone thrown for the bitch to chew on."

"How can you say such things," Carrie wondered, "and still seem so happy?"

"Despair among the powerless is the establishment's heaviest club. Come to the women's caucus."

"I'm not a university woman."

"It's not just for campus politics."

Byron persuaded her to try it, and she was hooked at the first meeting. After a month of Monday night meetings in LeNae's efficiency, she wondered how she'd lived this long without such a group. She was the seventh member, and welcomed as the last.

"Seven's the perfect number," Kathy said, pushing up heavy glasses, her usually worried face looking content.

They talked of everything, of anything, they passed around drafts of their work, ideas for course syllabi. They discussed problem students, grading dilemmas, the difficulty of creating free and equal classroom climates.

"We hold all the power," LeNae would remind them. "We can talk egalitarian all we want, let us not fool ourselves by making them push their chairs in a circle."

Carrie was shocked at the tales of fending off unwanted attentions from senior male faculty. Her indignation was one of the few things she carried home.

"Some of that stuff gets made up," Byron said.

She felt almost as if he had hit her. "That's exactly what Melanie said they say. She went to the dean about her chair, and in essence he said she probably needed a good lay to quiet her imagination."

Byron laughed, then looked contrite. "I do see your point. Like complaining to the police about police brutality."

"Exactly."

She and LeNae started meeting for lunch on Wednesdays, when LeNae had a long enough break to drive out to a café close to the garden center where Carrie still worked.

"You ever think about having children?"

Carrie shrugged. "Not much. The theater's Byron's child."

"Do *you* ever think about having children?"

"No. Do you?"

"All the time. But god knows what I think I'd do with a baby."

At the end of term, on a rare leisurely Sunday night, Byron and Carrie were sharing a quiet pipe or two with Gregory, a Black jazz guitarist staying with them a few weeks. Byron got in the mood for some I-Ching, and they settled on the floor. It was later than Carrie should have been up; the wine or the hash or the combination felt suddenly odd. She excused herself and found the bedroom, the bed. Her abdomen cramped painfully. A house, a huge and sinister house, began settling on her chest, going to push her deeper and deeper into the earth where no one would think to look for her. It was not so much frightening as inexpressibly sad. She moaned.

"Hey man," she heard Greg say, "I think your old lady needs you."

"You don't walk away from a throw," came back her lover's voice.

Carrie had the earth in her mouth, but with a mental heave rolled the house off her. She lay still, panting. Everything ached. Struggling for control, for perspective, she told herself to cut out the dramatics, pressed hard against the self-pitying tears, and fell asleep.

Before dawn she woke, barely making it to the bathroom before vomiting. There was no question of getting up in the morning; this was a real sickness, not a bad mood. Byron called the garden nursery for her, kissed her, said he'd be back at lunch.

"Oh, don't bother, I can get some tea or something."

But his eyes were worried. "You have a fever."

"Just a bug, as the old folks say."

"I'll be back."

She nodded, grateful, as another wave of wretchedness wracked her body. When he came home at eleven, she was so feverish, with pain and repeated retching, she agreed to see a doctor, and by 4:00 she was being wheeled into surgery for an appendectomy.

She had no insurance, so the surgeon cut his bill in half. Her boss helped her to get six weeks of disability pay, and she worked out a year's payment with the hospital. She luxuriated in her convalescence, in Byron's attentions and concern, the empty days full of reading and sunning. Once up, she began baking bread, and started a new book of notes on her reading, on the children playing in the street, on the personalities passing through their house. Even story ideas began to fill some pages.

"If we were married," Byron said when the first hospital bill came, "you'd have been covered."

"Score one for the patriarchy," she said sourly, then grinned at him. "But score two for us, these are easy payments."

She went back to work, with a new urgency about earning money but also a new interest in the time to herself. She carried a notebook everywhere, snatching it from the bike basket for five minutes on a park bench, or eating lunch with a sandwich in one hand. The last half of that summer, Byron practically lived in his office, revising his dissertation. He'd pushed back his defense date to October, and his department was sure enough of him to offer the tenure track position even though he hadn't quite met their deadline.

One Friday when an unusual cool air gentled the normally brutal afternoon sun, she biked a different way home from work, discovering a small park with a duck pond and shade trees. She stopped just for a moment, pulling out her notebook to record a brief but to her enlightening conversation with a co-worker. He was gay, and cut off from his family.

"Completely?"

"It's not just my lover I can't take home," he'd told her. "The ban includes me."

The talk had left her saddened. Why all this need to control what people ate, what they wore, who they loved, how they loved? He was a lovely, Nureyev-type of man, a whiz at flower arrangements, cheerful at the most tedious or arduous tasks. Of course his parents loved him, how could they not?

She wrote all her sadness out, and sat on watching the ducks. No one came near her; even the traffic was muffled. Finally aware she was stiff, she got up and pedaled off. She was locking the bike to a back porch post when Byron appeared at the door.

"Where the hell have you been?"

Her smile froze. "Just riding around, why?"

"*Why?* We're due at the Olson's in five minutes. That's why."

"Oh god, I forgot." She sprinted for the shower. "Lucky I don't wear makeup," she said, ready in ten minutes, but he wasn't amused. Jeff

Olson was his staunchest backer in the department, a marvelous older man who did everything he could to smooth Byron's way.

"You should have just gone," she said as they waited at the umpteenth red light. "Made my excuses."

He gave her a dark look and said nothing.

As it turned out, they weren't the latest. One other couple was there, but a fourth was expected. They all started another round of cocktails, quite happily, it seemed to Carrie. Mrs. Olson, elegant in a simple blue silk dress, showed not a trace of anxiety about the dinner. Everyone seemed glad to meet Carrie, and she managed not to spill the gin and tonic Dr. Olson mixed for her. At dinner she was careful not to drink too much wine, a cabernet she could tell was in a price range she'd never tasted before. She ate the delicious lasagna and salad without betraying the ravenous hunger she felt, and without dropping any on the white tablecloth. She was glad she was at the end, at the corner by Dr. Olson's right, feeling protected by him and out of the rather brilliant banter at the table's center. She didn't know the other two couples, and didn't like them nearly as well as the Olsons, and thought with satisfaction and pride that Byron's steady understated wit outshone the strained efforts of his colleagues. Both of the wives had already made and abandoned efforts to find anything interesting in her, to her relief.

It was, in short, a perfectly happy occasion. She beamed her contented pride catty-corner across the candles at Byron, she followed the conversation attentively, even entering it occasionally. And yet it was immediately obvious to her, when they got back in the car, that her lapse was not entirely forgiven. Or was Byron's sullenness from a deeper dissatisfaction? She flashed back through the evening uneasily. Her hands looked a mess, she had noticed that, admiring the other women's graceful fingering of wineglasses, butter knives. Her smocked dress was okay, and her figure was fine, if nothing smashing. But it was true her arms had a funny tan line from the t-shirts she wore to work, and her sandals weren't the flimsy dressy kind.

Carrie frowned and feigned a drowsiness, struck mute with the horrible possibilities the white light in her mind opened to her. She didn't stack up well against the other women. Even the rather stout one had a professional air, and the younger could have walked unchallenged through the pages of *Vogue*. Assets. Those women were assets. She'd never be any such thing.

Alone with Byron the next evening, she tried to apologize again. "I just got carried away by the silence, it was such a lovely spot."

"You're lucky you didn't get mugged. This is a city, for chrissake."

"It's just . . . . I mean, you have your office, sometimes I hanker for a nook of my own."

There was an edge to his laugh. "Would that help you remember things?"

Stung, she tried to laugh, too. "Probably not."

"I suppose we could look for a bigger place."

Surprised, she glanced around. The kitchen was a big, sunny space opening nicely to the unkempt but still inviting back porch and square of yard. She often wrote or read here at the table rather than in the darker front room. Their bedroom and the bathroom and a large closet was all the rest. No wonder it seemed crowded, it probably wasn't as much total space as the San Diego loft. She liked the house, though, discovering at that moment she didn't want to move. She laughed again, meaning only to tease. "More space would just mean more sleeping bags."

"Look, you don't have to mother every motherless child crashes here."

"I didn't mean –"

"You let anyone cry on your shoulder at the drop of a hat. You've got to be responsible for creating your own space."

Well, I did, she wanted to remind him. And am being royally scolded for it. But she swallowed the retort, complaining to LeNae later that her apology hadn't cleared the air. "Everything I say makes him defensive. Or instructive."

"How do you feel?"

"I don't know what to feel. A little hurt, I guess. He doesn't seem very interested in why I was late, or in the fact that it's the first time it's ever happened, in ten years, or in how bad I felt about it."

"Are you afraid to say those things?"

"Scared?" Carrie took a deep breath. "I never thought of it that way. But yes, a little. LeNae, I'm still crazy about him, you know? And I'm beginning to see he's not letting me in close like he used to. Do you suppose –?"

"No. He knows what he's got, he's not stupid. Carrie, I think it's just a slump. Probably dissertation jitters, try not to worry. How are you ever going to get your own writing done with one eye and ear on him all the time?"

Carrie stared at her. "My own writing? What are you talking about?"

"I know you write. You've filled half a dozen notebooks since I've met you."

"That's not *writing*. You don't know what you're talking about."

"So show me something, and then I'll know what I'm talking about."

Carrie showed her a first draft of an essay on the women in *The Dollmaker* and *The Great Meadow*. LeNae persuaded her to pass it to the group, where there were enthusiastic suggestions. LeNae sent the revision to a new feminist journal in Portland, and the week Byron flew to Carolina to talk about Brecht, Carrie got an acceptance call from the editor. Byron's call came the next night, giddy with relief and buoyed with the encouragement he was getting to make the dissertation a book. She saved her news for when he got home.

His delight for her, and his obvious joy to be back, swept away the anxiety of the past months. It was as LeNae had predicted: he'd been working too hard, too much was riding on the dissertation, a hurdle he had to face alone. They could go back to being together, now.

Praising her prose, Byron was nonetheless a little put off by the article, which traced how the strengths of the two Kentucky women two centuries apart had been subverted from scholarly, political and artistic expression into invisible props for a dominant male culture.

"Men give up a lot for women, too, you know."

"I didn't mean it as a man-woman thing," she said, but had to wonder what she had meant. Realizing he was hurt that she'd shown the work to LeNae first, she showed him her rewrite of the drunken thief story, which he praised for its convincing dialogue.

When a letter from home brought the news that Sammy had been killed in Vietnam, she began a series of sketches about the Mertz family, and Byron seemed interested as he'd used to, in every detail of every memory.

"How about lunch tomorrow?"

Carrie looked up from her book. "Tomorrow's Wednesday. I have lunch with LeNae."

"Yeah, well, is it a private club? I have a free space tomorrow. I don't, very often, you know."

"Of course, let's meet."

But she had missed her cue by a crucial second, and he shook his head. "I can tell when I'm not invited."

"You just took me by surprise, is all."

"It's bound to happen, babe, at least once in any triangle."

"*What?*"

"Come on, Carrie, I've got nothing against lesbians but two lovers is two lovers."

She stared at him, the book open on her leg.

"I think you might have to choose."

"I'm not in love with anybody else, Byron."

"You're never really here. What else am I supposed to think? Someone else is filling your head."

"I am here," she protested. "I am. I try to stay out of your hair."

He stood still a moment, then dropped into the arm chair, his head back, eyes closed. "What the fuck is going on?" It was a murmur, and an anguished cry.

She couldn't tell him, she didn't know. She went and sat on the arm of his chair, waiting for him to open his eyes. His schedule this semester was another brutal one, with too much classroom, too many labs, too many admiring, ambitious students. And now a draining production of *Antigone,* staged in modern army fatigues. There had already been several "incidents" on campus. Perhaps her support, always absolute and fierce, had been too understated. She drew her knees up, nudged his leg with a bare foot. When he opened his eyes, she looked right into them.

"I love you. Only you."

No answering assurance came into the troubled gray eyes. For another moment he searched hers, then turned away. "She is gay, you know."

"Actually, I didn't."

"What? I thought she was your bosom buddy. As it were."

"She probably assumes I know a lot of things I don't. It never occurred to me, and doesn't matter to me. How do you know, anyhow?"

"Scuttlebutt."

"She's certainly not living with anyone, in that shoebox."

He went to the kitchen for a beer. "Could well be someone casting aspersions."

"It's not wrong."

"Won't do her chances any good."

"I thought this was an oasis of liberalism."

"Relative to what, is the question." They smiled at each other, some of their past in both their minds.

Her efforts to adopt a higher profile beside him, however, now met with some resistance. At first seeming to her merely generous, by summer his excusing her from department activities began to feel like deliberate exclusion. She swung in terror from admitting to herself the possibility of his involvement with someone else. There was no way she could confront him with it. Either he would be cruelly hurt by her lack of trust in him, or he would not deny it, and the world would end.

Fearing rebuff, she initiated lovemaking less. But his cues came often enough to reassure her, and they were good in bed, as always. Surely he loved her, to satisfy her so deeply. If she was aware, dimly, that they spoke little of themselves to each other, she felt the deep accord between them and dismissed the need for words.

She woke one morning to find him regarding her. The room was already hot. She threw back the sheet and reached for him, but he caught her hand, holding it against his cheek, "Marry me."

Her surprise gave way to an exhilaration she hadn't known in years. Drowning in love, she tried to pull him down to her. "We are married."

"I mean for real." He resisted her pull. "We could even, you know, have a kid."

"We can have a kid right now, if you truly really want one."

"And kiss tenure goodbye."

Slowly, she sat up, drawing the sheet up to her waist. "Is marriage some sort of prerequisite?"

"Carrie, no, I didn't mean it that way. I don't want just to be married. I want you."

"You've got me. Forever and ever. You know that."

He rubbed his hair. "I'm serious, Carrie."

"So am I." Her voice sounded dull, and hollow in her own ears, as if coming from a long way off. Her happiness was sinking like something physical, misery engulfing it like mud around a foot. "I don't want to be a faculty wife."

"What would it change? I think your thing against marriage is a little neurotic."

"You didn't use to think so. You used to say, when a couple married, you wondered what hole in the dike they were trying to plug."

Shocked at the sudden clear sense of an arrow on target, she rolled her face into a pillow, crying. He sat for a moment, then stroked her hair, his fingers combing it gently. He kissed her neck, at the spine, his hand lingering another moment on her shoulder. Then he got up to dress and make coffee.

There had been, he told her later that fall, a friendship, well, a very deep friendship, during the summer. It was nothing, she was gone now; sometimes friendship just took that turn, it had nothing to do with her, with their relationship. She pushed away her hurt as a conventional hang-up, and agreed with him, loving him for leveling. She took as implicit the assurance they were beyond all that, stronger than mere attraction. She knew, after all, about all that loose energy around the stage. As if released from the discipline that kept it controlled and useful on stage, sexuality fairly bounced off walls in the wings. In mostly harmless camaraderie, bodies collided, barriers were set aside; the sensual was a necessary component of the art.

She never mentioned her own suspicion, feeling at fault now for not bringing it up at the time and asking for clarification. She also never asked if his sudden yen to marry had had anything to do with being left. He didn't approach the subject again, and she didn't like the thought even occurring to her.

She didn't like it, either, that there were the next winter other friendships, as he called them. But she fell into a compliance she was powerless to break. To balk now seemed too heavy an admission of a flaw in the bond between them. And he seemed if anything more comfortable with that bond, not less. She persuaded herself they were doing the long distance run correctly, by not tying their legs together as if for a sack race.

With her belief in the relationship strengthened each time a "friendship" dissolved, her belief in herself shaken each time he formed another, Carrie held on. That she would ever stop loving him, ever not care, she knew to be impossible. The way others talked of relationships as "over" she now knew to be either false statements or something outside her experience. She would never be over Byron, if she lost him, any more than one would get over the loss of an arm or a leg.

But she had determined that control was wrong. She remembered clearly the day by the little duck pond when she had articulated that to herself. If she wanted Byron to be different than he was, then she was wrong.

In a year's time, however, the inevitable happened. A friendship did not dissolve, the woman's marriage came apart, instead. For months Carrie kept her distance, her balance on the high wire, asking only that he be up front with her. He was, which meant she found herself agreeing to some weekends alone. She also found herself opening the second bottle of wine, the second six pack, crying whole nights.

Taking only a suitcase, the typewriter, and enough money to get home, she had LeNae drive her to the train station, on New Year's Day, 1975.

Chapter 4.

Carrie

Carrie stands in the kitchen, glad to be out of the wind, relishing the sudden relative quiet. For three days now a fifty-mile-an-hour wind has buffeted a shocked landscape cruelly unprepared for such force. With gusts of eighty-miles-an-hour and two weeks of April rain, trees all over the wooded hillsides are crashing down, the big ones bringing down neighbors.

"Mrs. Bakeley?"

"Hello."

Frail and thin, as if spoken after breath rather than with it, the welcome still is hearty, with the echo of a voice once rich and deep. Shucking her knapsack, Carrie pegs her sweatshirt and steps into the other room, reprieved, from the anxiety she tries to ignore. Some evening, some morning, she will call to her friend and Sarah Bakeley will have left. Passed on, a term Carrie thinks curiously suited, though Mrs. Bakeley rejects it. Well then, the River Styx and all that, Carrie tries. Happy hunting in the perfect library.

But Mrs. Bakeley is having none of it. Die, is what I'll do. We can't know a thing more than that. Why even try?

Carrie crosses the narrow room to the couch as Mrs. Bakeley sits up. "Crum, it's cold in here. Sorry I'm so late." Carrie helps pull the blanket over Sarah's lap, arranges the dark woolen shawl around her shoulders.

"I'm fine."

"You are not, your lips are fairly gone to blue."

"It must be dangerous, you out walking like that."

Carrie laughs softly. "Safer than trying to drive the road. It's completely blocked between here and home, trees and power lines tangled up everywhere."

On her knees by the little parlor stove, Carrie lights some business pages from Sunday's New York *Times*. "You know, it's almost a kind of high to be out there, as if getting walloped by a tree might be some sort of fun. Maybe we weren't meant to be always so separate from the elements."

Sarah cocks an eyebrow, with a gesture toward the rattling, whistling window. "I'm happy enough, thank you, to be separate from that element."

"Well, I said 'always.'"

"And meant by whom?"

Carrie conceded with a smile. "It does imply volition, doesn't it?"

"You mean created, with definite intentions, by some god or other?" Sarah's words are slowly, precisely, spoken. "Is this god personal or indifferent?"

Carrie shrugs. She's used to not getting by with vague sentiments with this woman. "Or did I mean formed by biological forces? Destined by the accident of the spark? I have no idea what I meant by 'meant.'" She adds wood to the kindling and closes the little sliding doors. "Upstairs?"

Sarah nods, accepting Carrie's help to stand. When she is ready to move, they go together across the worn Oriental rug, Sarah's arm laid on Carrie's, her nearly transparent long hand on Carrie's harder, blunter one. Bent some now under her ninety-five years, she still stands a head taller than Carrie, and needs not so much support as steadying, like a new skater.

"I ought to move me upstairs, or the bathroom down."

"At least it's inside now."

"Yes, but the path worked whether the current was on or not. No need to carry water to it."

"Good point, but we'd maybe be carrying you to it."

"Two bedrooms and a path, Ethan used to tell our friends. They'd all be appalled, and came anyway. All summer long."

"Wish I could have been here. I could have cooked and cleaned and eavesdropped."

Sarah stops at the foot of the narrow stairs to look at her, for a moment disoriented in time.

"But alas, that was forty years ago," Carrie adds quickly. "And I'm only thirty."

With the railing along the wall, Sarah can manage the stairs herself, and Carrie stays below to build a fire in the handsome old range, start some rice, peel carrots and onions. There will come a time of more explicit nursing, when privacy will be at best an elaborate fiction, but neither speaks of that, yet.

When Sarah is downstairs and settled in her rocker by the parlor stove, Carrie fills the toilet tank, and takes the bucket and two plastic gallon jugs to get water before dark. The little stone springhouse in the woods across the road looks in the twilight forlorn, its door propped, one rusty hinge pulled loose from the rotting jamb. She pauses to contemplate it, a good project. Rebuild the door, replace hinges, fix the headers and frames, paint, repoint. She's not a carpenter, but the years working on Byron's sets have taught her a few things.

With an impatient kick at the door, she hurries in to the spring.

Carrie, you need to *plan*, her mother gripes at her, and Carrie has sidestepped any response, for four months now, numbed by her flight from Byron, by the obvious failure of plan. In her head, that is capitalized. Failure of Plan. She has no intention of getting caught up in another Failure of Plan.

The spring fills a cement and stone pool three feet deep and nearly as wide in a corner of the shelter, and overflows into a shallow channel intersecting the floor to the opposite end, where it skirts a stone fireplace and runs out through a hole in the wall. With gentle busy sounds the overflow stream ripples in miniature waterfalls into a creek which joins another a mile away, and travels on to Potter's Corner and eventually into the Chesapeake.

Carrie kneels to fill the jugs. Water flows, no big deal. Connection does not imply purpose.

"Don't you wish the wind would just stop, even for a minute?" Carrie sits on the rug, close to the stove. "Even in here, just listen to it."

"It got right into my sleep this afternoon." Sarah shakes her head at Carrie's curious look. "No, I've forgotten it."

"Meaning you won't tell it."

"Dreams are interesting only to the dreamer."

"Depends on the dream," Carrie says. "And the dreamer." But she knows better than to insist.

After Carrie has finished the washing up, she joins Mrs. Bakeley in the living room. Settling at the desk under the window, she starts a letter to Diana – she has gone back to her given name. Piercing through the wind's roar, the thin wail of a siren rises, and stops, still down the hill.

Sarah shudders. "Imagine a fire in this wind. And sounds like the truck can't get through."

Carrie waits a few minutes, then pushes back her chair. "I'll just walk down and see. Won't be long."

Down the three stone steps and out on the road, she is hit by a gust that makes her zip the sweatshirt and tie its hood. Clearing the litter of small branches as she walks, she feels a confused sense both of safety and peril. The trees press close, arching across the road, their thrashing shapes eerily unfamiliar and menacing in the dark; but they are the same trees, this the same darkness, the same road surrounded by the same slopes and ridges she's known all her life. Ten years away has eroded but not destroyed the habit of feeling protected here.

A quarter mile below the house, around a slight bend, the road dips into a small clearing where the fire truck comes suddenly into sight. This has been its destination, after all, as clusters of yellow-suited men are already reeling in the hose, shouting words whipped away by the wind. A half dozen cars and pickups tilt along the road. There is no house here, no sign of accident, but whiffs of pungent smoke. Carrie hesitates by the first vehicle, a compact station wagon; she can see that the back seat is folded, the space stacked as if permanently with boxes and equipment.

A man breaks away from the group by the fire truck, exchanging waves, and starts uphill, so hunched against the wind he doesn't see her. Something tugs at Carrie. She knows that walk, surely. Even bent, there is a familiar rhythm to the figure. Before she is aware enough of the feeling to place it, the man looks up toward his car and pauses at the sight of her. Thad.

He recognizes her, too, and they both hurry to cross the space. "It *is* you," he says.

"And it's you, too," Carrie says. Their laughs draw them into a quick hug. "It might not have been either one of us. What happened here?"

"A grass fire from a live wire."

"I should have known that was a photographer's wagon. You doing pictures for the paper?"

"No, just happened by. Meant to check on Granddad, and Mrs. Bakeley."

"Well, come on, then. Why are we shouting out here? You can drive up to Mrs. Bakeley's, but nobody's cut open Morris's lane yet. It's a mess up here."

"You picked a good time to visit," Thad says, when they settle in his car.

Carrie's stomach churns a little at the realization of how much time there is to cover. "I live here."

He looks at her sharply before pulling out on the road. I'm never coming back, she told him once. "With Mrs. Bakeley," she adds.

Thad parks, nose to the woods, beside a battered International pickup. "You didn't drive that from Texas."

"Hey. Don't cast aspersions, that's my dad's pride and joy."

Thad has to duck in the doorway, and in the living room his dark red hair nearly brushes the beams.

"Look who's here!" Carrie presents him as if he is her doing. The joy in Sarah's candlelit face, the sight of him so familiar in this room, fill her with such a turmoil of emotion she bends quickly to feed the stove.

Thad lays a wrapped package in Mrs. Bakeley's lap, taking her hands as he kisses her cheek. "Happy birthday. I know I'm late."

"How kind of you!"

"You look terrific."

"It's the light."

Carrie, straightening from the stove and looking over Mrs. Bakeley's shoulder, can appreciate the gasp of delight when she opens the present. It is a portrait of Sarah, in the same rocker, backlit with soft natural light from the window; hanging over the chair's arm, peering up at her, is a beautifully wistful girl just out of babyhood, her intently interested face suffused with the same soft light, wispy red hair floating in an uncombed cloud.

"Your daughter," Carrie says, for even without the red hair there is no mistaking the wide set eyes, high forehead, square chin.

"Thad, she's absolutely beautiful." Sarah raises the photo to catch more of the light.

"I'd say both of you are," he answers. "And it's not just the light."

"You obviously know what to do with light, though," Carrie says.

"I got lucky."

"What are you telling her?" Carrie asks Mrs. Bakeley. "She looks bound to remember it all her life."

"I haven't the faintest idea. When was this?"

Thad turns the chair from the desk, sits close to the stove. "Last fall. Sorry it took so long to get it to you."

"The studio keeps you busy."

"I've started teaching, too, a course at St. Mary's."

"You like it?"

"A lot. I'm getting a little tired of weddings and anniversaries."

"Yes," Sarah says. "After Laos and Cambodia, I can imagine."

"Mom told me you went back abroad for the Friends," Carrie says.

"Just briefly. They wanted pictures of Cambodia. But it's too dangerous now."

"At least we've got our bombers out."

"Leaving behind . . . Don't get me started on what we've left behind. When did you come here?"

"January. And I had a time selling myself for the position, let me tell you."

Sarah has a ready defense. "I can't imagine what she thinks she's doing, burying herself here."

"I can't afford an apartment. And this cabin is the wide world compared to my parents'."

Sarah's lips purse, her hand rising with an emphatic pointing finger. "By 'here' I mean more than this cabin."

"For right now, here is perfect."

"I'm glad of it," Thad says, then leans toward Sarah to make his meaning clear. "I'm glad someone's with you."

"And I'm grateful," Sarah assures him. "But there are plenty of people on this mountain would keep tabs on us old folk. How is Morris, by the way? Haven't seen him since the storm started."

"I'm just meaning to go find out. Carrie tells me I'll have to walk back."

A loud crack interrupts him. After a wrenching, splintering and crash of branches, the final deep thud of a large tree hitting ground shakes the cabin.

"My, how we do cling, we rooted things," Sarah says.

"Your car!" Carrie grabs a flashlight on her dash out of the kitchen, with Thad close behind. The vehicles are all right, but a large walnut has fallen just opposite the steps, fortunately away from the road. They stand at the edge of the crater where its roots had been, Carrie shining the light over the dark circle of earth rising twice her height.

"I feel like we ought to somehow to able to pull it back up, tamp it into place," Thad says, just as there is another crash, on the hill behind the house.

"It's that whomp at the end gets me," Carrie says. "It's so final."

They stand a moment more, then Thad tightens his jacket. "I might as well head up. Can I borrow the flashlight?"

"Can I come with you?"

"Of course. Will she be all right?"

"She's a rock. But I'll ask."

Sarah urges them away, anxious for news of her friend. "And stop back in," she says to Thad, "for a glass of sherry."

They walk quickly up the steep road, not needing the flashlight until well back the lane. Carefull to avoid any wires, they find their way around and over fallen trees and brush, murmuring dismay at the tangle. The bridge over the creek is intact, and beyond that the woods thin. At the top of the rise, light shines from the frame house.

Thad laughs in relief. "He's still got some kerosene, apparently."

"Funny how the old ways do better in storms."

They go, as everyone does, around the side to the kitchen door. Their knock is unanswered.

"He's a bit deaf," Carrie reminds him. "Let's just go in and shout."

Morris answers Thad's call from the front room, and is struggling up out of a recliner as they come in. Greeting them warmly, he apologizes for the flickering lamp. "Seems like I can't get it trimmed good like I used to could. The devil, getting old."

"But it's nice and cozy in here," Thad says. "You're a lot better off than some. How you doing?"

Never a stout man, Morris has grown thin the past year, from a series of afflictions thought to stem from a stomach virus eluding capture. In his late seventies, he looks nearly as aged as Sarah Bakeley; though his skin has not yet returned to softness or attained the translucence of extreme age, his body has seemed to fall in on itself, and stiffened. Where before had been the impression of steady strength, now there is a brittleness that makes others catch a swinging door, gauge the distance to the next chair, reach for his arm.

"Getting' by. How's Sarah?" Morris leans forward to fidget with an overall leg twisted at the ankle.

"She's well," Carrie assures him. "Anxious for summer."

"Ain't it a long wet spring, though?" Morris says. "I figure look out for a late frost, this year."

"Maybe the bloom will be late as well."

"Thaddy, bring us that box there on the cupboard. Let's have us a chocolate."

"How old is this cupboard, Granddad?" Thad gets the candy, standing a moment in front of the handsome hutch. "Walnut, isn't it?"

"Yessir, and not veneer, neither. That was my parents' piece, coming up on a century old now."

Carrie watches more than listens as the two men weave through familiar territory. The history of other old pieces, the rope bed upstairs bought for a quarter, the rockers and dry sink already dispersed to daughters; crops and frosts, terrible winters and blazing summers.

"Never a wind like this," the old man admits. "Not in my lifetime, not like this one."

News of the sons, Thad's uncles. The usual complaints, the inevitable platitudes. Through it all, an engaged, concerned interest from Thad, his eyes watchful, full of love.

"I better get back," Carrie says. "The fire'll be getting low."

"We'll fill your box," Thad says.

"No, now." Morris snaps his chair upright, almost propelling himself out of it. "There's plenty for tonight. I can still manage that."

"It used to be my job, whether you could or not," Thad says.

Morris's face softens, but he does not relent. "You got other jobs, now."

"Dad 'll be here," Carrie says, "as soon as he gets his own drive cut open."

"Tell him there's no hurry, I ain't going no place."

With the winds easing the next day, Carrie counts fallen trees around Sarah's house and on the hillside. The most heartbreaking, the four black walnuts, will also be the most profitable. To get out the oaks and maples up in the woods will mean making an ugly scar, but Mrs. Bakeley needs the money and can be spared the sight. The brush can be cleared for firewood. The woods will heal.

Carrie stands in the yard, her back to the house, face to the sun. This, the only sunny spot on the place, is even more open now, with a tulip poplar, wild cherry, and two walnuts down. When the mess is cleared, enough sun now for a few vegetables; she must get busy and weed the black-eyed Susans and the iris, trim the jungle of forsythia and wild berries, make space for asparagus and rhubarb, maybe some –

Planning, again. Does she really intend to stay here? What would be for her here, ever?

Depression settles over her, familiar and enveloping and undeflectable as the sun on her skin. What is she doing back? Surviving. It's a basic instinct. Why did Sisyphus roll the rock? Maybe next time it would stay put.

After lunch, with Sarah warm and fortified and comfortable on the couch with several issues of the National Geographic at hand, Carrie walks up to her homeplace. Her folks own the house now, and five acres; the brothers sold the Pine Mountain acreage to a newly formed sportsmen's club, and Jem turned most of his share over to the Millers, and with most of the rest gave Emma a new kitchen.

Instead of climbing along the drystone wall through the woods, Carrie walks up the road, which is still blocked to traffic, an eery quiet scene of destruction. Wires loop across broken, uprooted trees and splintered poles. There is only one house between Morris's lane and the farm lane, a new bungalow; its adjoining garage has been damaged by a big oak, a close call.

Jem has worked his way with the chain saw nearly to the road, branches cleared, logs trimmed and winched to the sides of the lane.

"What a job." Carrie sympathizes, with an admiring look around. It's nearly a half-mile lane, with the woods thick on both sides.

"How's the road?" he asks.

"Barely passable on foot."

"Be awhile before Charlie can get through, then. You mind working alone on the peaches?"

"No, I'll be fine."

"I'll come soon as I finish here."

At the barn, Carrie collects her pruning shears from its hook in the old horse stall, and walks along the tractor path, feeling her depression shift to one side. I wouldn't have anything but pruning, Charlie said when she asked him for work. I can learn to prune, she answered, and he rubbed his bald pate and resettled his cap, shrugging and nodding at the same time, and started her on a block of young York apple trees. Jem had raised an eyebrow and looked bewildered, but helped her with the basic moves, and she'd managed very nicely. She enjoyed the work, discovering a knack for it and a new strength. When it was too cold or wet or windy she stayed home with Sarah; still, the little she made nearly doubled the resources of the little log house.

The big beech trees by the spring have escaped with minor damage; she rounds the curve away from the pond and meadow. The track is wet this time of year, with rivulets flowing in the ruts, shining among the stones. At a bend, the peach orchard comes into view, climbing in disciplined rows up the hillside, resplendent in full bloom. The main track circles the base of the hill but she walks up the steep edge along the woods, to the eighth row, where they left off pruning before the storm.

With so much of the cutting at eye level, to flatten and spread the trees, she has to stop often to rub the burning muscles in her neck. But she's also riding a wave, like a runner's high. With blossoms all around her, the sky a new washed blue, the wind now down to a breeze and hinting of warmth, the frost nearly gone from the ground, a cacophony of birdsong assailing her from both woods and orchard, she can put up with a little pain.

She has to strain, like pushing on a little-used gate, to remember the birds beyond the ubiquitous cardinal and dove and robin songs. Concentrating on distinguishing the voices coming from the woods, of flicker, song sparrow, wren, towhee, she misses for some seconds a persistent chip practically at her face. When it finally registers, she notices first a new nest inches from her pruners, and on a twig the two bravest birds in the world. With open beaks they shout at her to be gone or else! They would both fit in the palm of one hand. She lifts the pruners away, which makes one of the pair flit about nervously, scolding around her, but the other steadfastly keeps its perch right at her face. Carrie has plenty of time to memorize its simple grayness, perky tail, white eye-ring; she takes a careful look at the nest, which is extraordinarily tight and tidy, before making a few last necessary cuts and moving on with an apology. She's grinning now, on the crest of the wave, for it's a new bird to her, and the sense of finally passing her sixteen-year-old self is satisfying, no matter how senseless.

"It looked like a tiny titmouse," she tells Sarah. "Without the crest. Or like a gray wren, except there isn't such a thing."

"Start with the titmouse," Sarah suggests.

Carrie checks Peterson's index, turns to the page, and there it is: a blue gray gnatcatcher. "Aren't I a lucky one. Listen to this: 'easily overlooked.' You'd have to be right in their face, like I was."

"It's a new one to me, too," Sarah says. "But that's not saying a whole lot."

"This book is well worn."

"Yes, I did try, by fits and starts. I had the very first Peterson, in 1934. I would never have learned a one, though, without Evvie."

"Evvie?"

"Surely you knew Evvie." Sarah looks at her in surprise. "Oh. No. You wouldn't have, she died soon after Rusty got killed, in the War. That was Thad's father. Thad never knew his father, nor his grandmother either. Evvie, that was."

"Morris's wife?" Carrie looks sadly now at the little gray bird, and replaces the book on its shelf. The room is lined with shelves, all crammed with books. Did every volume speak a memory? She feels her own pressing against her, like leaves piling against a doorstep.

"You ever know Skip? Used to work with Dad?"

"No, not really. I remember the accident."

"He knew the birdsong. He, and my grandmother Mattie. She didn't know all the names, but she was always saying Listen, or Just look at that. Making you pay attention, you know?"

Catching the grief in Carrie's voice, Sarah nods at her, but with no solace to give.

Carrie is running the sweeper upstairs on a Saturday morning when Morris and Thad come by. In the week since the storm has blown itself out, crews have opened the roads, power lines are restrung, a logger has come and looked and agreed to buy all fifteen uprooted trees on Mrs. Bakeley's place, admiring the four walnuts sadly but looking eager nonetheless. The lights turn on again, the refrigerator hums, the pump in the basement pulls the water again to the sinks, the toilet, the bath. Carrie can cook and make tea on the hot plate, without starting a fire.

The weather has done an about-face into summer. A false summer, everyone warns everyone: it can frost in May, remember. But no one wants to remember, with peach and cherry blossoms coloring the landscape, with wild cherry white on the wooded hills as if spotlit, with apple leaves uncurling around the tight pink buds. Already this morning the temperature is edging toward eighty, and the front door stands open into the kitchen.

So of course Carrie doesn't hear the door. And when she registers the voices and turns off the sweeper, she stands for several seconds stunned with déjà vu. Just so, that other April fifteen years ago, she had been cleaning, heard a voice at the door, and run downstairs, and been as surprised as Thad to find a stranger.

And this the same as the past, too: the force-field created when Morris and Sarah occupy the same room, a warmth both bathing and excluding others. Carrie and Thad soon drift out onto the porch, leaving them to catch up, with whatever spin they choose to put on the winter months.

"Come look at the bloodroot."

They admire the carpet of white, and find a patch of bellwort a little further into the woods, and then some Dutchmen's breeches. Looking back over the house, they can see dogwood and redbud in full bloom. "It's spring!" Carrie shouts.

"Yeah. The sound of the sprayer is heard in the land."

"Let's walk."

She catches the surprise in his eyes, and is embarrassed. "They'll be occupied for hours," she says, and turns toward the house. This will be nothing like that, she wants to assure him, nothing at all.

Checking in briefly with Morris and Sarah, they cross the road to follow an old logging trail through the woods, near the creek. After some gentle meandering the pathway dissolves, not so much overgrown as scattered. They sit on a rocky shelf in the sun, where the hill falls away from their feet, looking across a long valley to the east, with the rolling hills diminishing into a haze.

"I always think the Atlantic ought to be there."

"It is," Thad says, "after New Jersey."

She laughs quietly, rolling up the sleeves of her shirt, looking at the landscape as if counting the grain fields, the silos, the orchards. It is nothing like the scene four years ago, it was winter then, this day is not like that. This day is hot, and the spring colors and spring scents hold no reminders of the awkward sudden passion in the December air. There was then the reaching for warmth, for definition, and they agreed on the definition. She went back to Byron, as intended, and Thad married Christine, as intended.

"How's Christine's school going?"

"It looks to be a sound enterprise," Thad says. "Only day care and three grades now, but plenty of interest for a couple more grades. Are you planning to stay?"

"I don't seem to have a plan. But I don't plan to leave Mrs. Bakeley, so that's a plan of sorts, I guess."

He nods. "She's going to outlive him."

"Is he so ill?"

"Haven't you noticed, he's getting a gray look, under the skin."

"But if it's cancer, why can't they find it?"

"I hope they don't."

She understands that, but tears sting. She presses her hands hard against her eyes, but when after a few moments they get up and wander on, she feels comfortable, and somehow more settled than for months. They compete with each other for names – self-heal, wild mustard, mayweed; and in the woods they enter to circle back, spring beauty and anemone, with jacks not yet in their pulpits, May apples not yet blooming. At the creek they step gingerly through a spread of skunk cabbage and find a patch of dogtooth violet that stuns Thad.

"I've never seen these before, how could I miss this? There are hundreds."

She watches him as he kneels to inspect the delicate, half-hidden flowers, stroke the mottled leaves. "Trout leaf lily is another name," she says. "You can see why."

"So this is where . . . . I have a painting of this." He sits back on his heels, holds his hands as if framing a picture, moving them to find the painting. "Got to be here. There, I think that very trunk, that sloping one with all the moss. . . . Could it be, you think, still the same log?"

When she doesn't answer, he gets up and explains. "My father painted water colors when he was a boy. Some of them have survived, my mother gave me a box full just recently. They're all from right around here."

Carrie feels suddenly that her heart is breaking. She hadn't known she brought any part of it back with her intact enough to be damaged. Paintings in boxes, fiddles in closets, abandoned cabins. There is no getting it back, any of it, not really. She moves slowly away, not to rush him but to remove herself from his story.

Carrie has helped Sarah Bakeley settle in one of the bent hickory chairs, swathed in a sweater and afghan, to warm in the slanting Sunday morning sun. Barefoot, in cutoffs and Emma Goldman t-shirt – a resurrected idol that amuses Sarah – she is weeding and clipping grass around the iris in the lower yard, when a car toots lightly twice and pulls into the flat space. Unable to make out who it is through the jungle of forsythia, she moves toward the house, hearing two car doors. The twins, maybe, or one with a beau. Though neither is due this weekend, they bop in and out of home with a cheerful assurance that Carrie can't help but envy and admire. At twenty, the twins both have jobs that are paying their ways through schooling, with future steps carefully planned into nursing and physical therapy.

Carrie gets to the top of the stone steps just as Morris and Thad reach the bottom. "Look at you," she teases Morris, "all duded up."

He pulls his tie loose and unbuttons the collar, grinning at her but with his eyes already searching the porch. "She up and about?"

"Who's that?" Sarah's husky voice sails easily over the railing. "Morris?"

They move up the path to join her on the porch.

"Oughtn't you be in church?" she greets them.

Morris, with a fine sense of the dramatic, pulls his watch from his vest, extending it toward her on its length of chain. "For some of us, church was two hours ago. Me and Thad here have done mass and put away big stacks of pancakes at the Inn. Or Amelia's, it's called now."

"With sausage," Thad adds.

"Like some coffee?" Carrie offers.

"Sure, all right, if Thaddy's got the time."

Thad agrees, and comes inside with her. He's wearing a white shirt, too, but without a tie or vest. She starts the kettle heating on the hot plate, measures coffee into the cone filter, and looks at him curiously.

"Have you gone back to the Valley chapel?"

"No, but when I called Granddad this week he mentioned he'd like to get to Mass."

"You always loved that chapel."

371

His wistful smile is nostalgic. "Sometimes I need to worship the outer light." It is an apt phrase, for the windows of the old stone church break the sunlight into golds and blues worthy of adulation.

Carrie serves the coffee and perches with Thad on the wooden railing. "So what's Amelia's like on a Sunday morning?"

"Pretty quiet, this hour," Morris answers. "They have crowds for dinner, I understand."

"Who is Amelia, anyway?" Carrie asks.

"What?" Morris peers at her in mock outrage. "Don't I recall you doing a history of Potter's Corner in school?"

"Wait. It's coming back. Schultz. They took over the Inn during Prohibition. Amelia and . . . ."

"Warren." Sarah supplies the name. "I'd forgotten about that paper you did. You still have it?"

"In the folks's attic someplace, probably."

"You should dig it out," Thad says. "I bet you could add things now nobody told you for school."

"Like the fact," Sarah says, "that Warren sold liquor out of the kitchen. Or you could get it delivered, by the grocery wagon."

Thad laughs aloud, but Morris looks uncomfortable. Carrie points a finger at him. "And you know something else."

"I know where it come from, is all."

"Where?"

"Nope, that's all over and done, and none of your business."

"I assume the worst, then."

Sarah shakes her head. "No, you're wrong. Not Morris. But it was from up here somewhere, some of it, anyway."

"Just think," Carrie says. "I might be doing that."

"Selling moonshine?" Thad looks at her, surprised.

"No, running the Inn. It might have been my grandmother's, except she didn't want it."

"Not after the way the old man treated her. Mean old cuss, what I heard. Mind, I never really knowed much about it."

"What was it like then?"

"No, now." Morris holds up a hand in protest. "I was only a youngster myself when he died."

Carrie is frowning, working out the dates. "And Gramma was already up here by then. But how come –"

"Whatever she told you, I expect that's all there is to it." Morris is looking troubled.

"She told me just what you said. She married, he died, the Schultzes bought the place. But what happened to the money? How come the Millers had to buy the mortgage on the farm?"

"She tell you that part? Then you might as well know how come. Her granddaddy willed everything to the church in Potter's Corner. I guess that wasn't part of the history anyone told you."

Carrie spreads her fingers in a resigned gesture. "I'm beginning to wonder what I did put in that report. So. Did you drink this liquor you know so much about?"

"Not me. I was raising a family."

Sarah laughs, and tells them it was soft as silk, smooth as satin.

Carrie is surprised to see Sarah awake. Usually she sleeps her soundest at the end of the night, sometimes until mid-morning. "Did the birds wake you? They're raucous, with the windows open."

Sarah considers. "Well, I suppose. I don't remember."

"Want some coffee?"

"It's awfully early, isn't it?"

"Six-thirty."

Carrie waits a moment, then touches the hand so unusually still on the quilt. "Never mind, it's not made yet, anyway."

"What isn't?"

"The coffee."

"Oh. What a luxury coffee was."

"When?"

"In school."

Carrie sits on the bed, trying to be weightless. "Tell me about school."

"Brazen hussy, one professor actually called me. Can you imagine? Me? Agatha thought it hilariously funny, but it frightened me silly."

"Stay in, drop out: it occurs to me that whatever we do, someone will call us bad names for it."

Sarah looks at her, a smile beginning in the faded eyes, large in the thin face. "There's a lesson in that, somewhere."

Carrie smiles back, and goes downstairs. She fills the kettle and stands frozen with sudden dismay. Why has she offered Sarah coffee in bed?

Opening the door to the morning light, Carrie draws some deep breaths. It is nearly June, the air is humid, laden with summer smells now of grass and turned earth, thick with the unmistakable sense of trees and mosses growing. Green. The green feels to her an entity in itself. Like the birdsong coming at her from every direction, it seems disembodied, a part of the whole but not necessarily affixed to anything.

Hearing the bed creak, she hesitates a second, then on a strong impulse hurries upstairs. Sure enough, Sarah is sitting up, clutching the edge of the mattress. She has got her glasses and teeth from the bedside stand, and looks more herself as she tries to give Carrie her usual self-mocking smile, but there is a troubled fear in her gaze.

"Let me help," Carrie says softly, and slips an arm around the bony waist.

"There!" Sarah gains her feet. "That's better. Do you know, I was afraid to stand, what a strange thing."

Afraid too, Carrie holds her the few steps to the bathroom, hoping she is not hurting her. It's like holding a butterfly, there's no place to clamp. She has to help her now, the time has come. And Sarah asks to be settled back in the bed, with a little coffee, yes, that would be nice.

Carrie fixes a tray with juice and toast, the strong coffee with milk that Sarah likes, and brings it up to her. When she sees Sarah in the light, she sees for certain there has been a shift. Sarah's face is alert, her cloud of white hair brushed and normal. But there is no sense of resistance or even of friction against the bed, no marshalling of energy under the covers for making any move through physical space.

"How will I know when to call someone? Like a doctor, for instance."

Carrie runs a finger along a scar on the white painted table in her mother's kitchen with its newly varnished wainscoating and new tile floor. In spite of the new wooden cabinets, new electric stove and refrigerator, it is still a room familiar to her in a way no other room seems likely ever to be.

Emma sits facing her across the table's corner. Her thick light brown hair, kept shorter now and laced with gray, is pushed up into a loose roll. "She doesn't seem sick? A cold or anything?"

"Not that I can tell."

"Listen, I think you'll know. Or probably she'll tell you herself."

"Unless she thought it would make any trouble at all."

"Well. I could come by, see how she strikes me."

Carrie looks up gratefully. "I'd be glad if you could."

"It's been a good while since I been to see her, anyway."

That evening, after the visit, Carrie walks Emma out to her car. The stars are out bright, the night has turned cool. Emma hugs her sweater tighter. "You'll have to just do what she says, I think. About the doctor, I mean."

"She sure hasn't mentioned it yet."

Emma gives a quiet laugh. "No, you'd think lying in bed was the normal way to visit, for all she'll say about it. You could call him and have a talk, maybe."

Her voice is so tender and reluctant that Carrie fights a sudden lump in her throat.

"But who knows?" Emma says. "She might get up tomorrow."

Sarah does get up in the morning, and insists that Carrie go back as usual to work, thinning peaches now. But when Carrie comes in at 5:00, she knows something is wrong. Sarah's not on the porch, nor on the couch.

"Mrs. Bakeley?"

Running as fast as the awkward winding stairs allow, she hears a faint answer from the bathroom. Relief and adrenaline making her trembly, she nearly falls in the door. For a second, she can't see Sarah, then is facing her, lying curiously at ease in the dry tub. A wry smile pulls down the corners of her mouth.

"I had a lovely bath. And now I can't get up."

Carrie doesn't say it, and will ever after wish she had: you're beautiful. The long limbs, nearly fleshless torso, the triangle bare again as a baby's, was like a line drawn across a canvas with a soft brush, white on white. Carrie's breath catches for an instant, but she does not say it.

"How long ago was 'now'?"

"Oh, I don't think very long."

All shyness between them gone now, Carrie slips her arms under Sarah's shoulders and knees. Bracing her legs against the old high-sided tub, she lifts her out without much difficulty.

"Does it hurt?"

"No," Sarah says, but looks immeasurably relieved to be released onto the bed. Carrie helps her into a fresh gown, arranges a light shawl over her shoulders and an extra pillow against her back. "You're looking at me a little as if I were flowers in a vase. And not quite right yet."

"And you look," Carrie responds, "ready to hold court."

After supper, Carrie calls the Millers and talks to Hannah. "Tell Charlie I'll be off for awhile."

Hannah clucks sympathetically. "Lucky you're there. Anything you need?"

"No, I don't think so," Carrie says, but isn't surprised when the next day Hannah appears. "Just passing by," with frozen beef, canned peaches, fresh strawberries and peas.

"Aunt Hannah, you get to heaven, I swear you'll be arranging the pantry before you even take a rest."

"My, you're getting the yard looking nice."

"I've only been weeding some." But Carrie looks around, pleased and surprised to see that the place is looking cared for. "She must have gardened a lot at one time, I keep finding little patches of things."

She writes a note to Thad, she starts some bread rising, she arranges a vase of iris for Sarah's room. And she decides it's time to clean the living room shelves. "If you hear mad thumping downstairs, it's only books being dusted."

Sarah looks for a moment as if she knows nothing about books downstairs. "Oh," she says then. "Those are almost all Ethan's. I've read them, or I suppose I have. For years they felt like mine, but just now, when you said that, I thought, why doesn't Ethan dust them, they're his. Oh, my."

Carrie waits, interested in more, but Sarah comments again on how nice the iris look.

"You want to sit up in the rocker awhile?"

"No. Maybe later."

Carrie goes down with the sweeper, making a mental note to shop for some sheepskin for the bed, and begins pulling books. She thinks of Sarah's words, and her thoughts jump to the shelves of books she and Byron were always leaving behind, traveling light as tumbleweeds. More books would rise in stacks around them; whether they lived in a place four months or two years, the articles, notebooks, newspapers and journals, paperbacks and solemn anthologies would fill their space by an invisible process, like dust filling a spider web. And then they'd sell them, give them away.

Carrie sits back on her heels for a moment, felled by tears stinging hot in her eyes, blocking her throat. Oh, my, indeed. It had all been such heady, crazy *fun*.

It takes some rummaging, but Carrie finds the high school report in the farmhouse attic. She laughs with Sarah over the simple history paper.

"'My great-great-grandfather once ran a tavern,'" she reads aloud, "'which when he died became an Inn, with restaurant and rooms.' No moonshine, anywhere."

"I remember someone saying — forgive the joke — that it was Prohibition that killed him. It's possible, you know, that he only sold the legal stuff."

"He was such a taboo in our house, I never asked her anything about him."

Sarah touches her hand briefly to comfort. "You mustn't blame yourself, though, nor your grandmother either. She left behind a good deal of pain, I think, when she left him." Sarah tells her about the borrowed cane, which Warren had tried to give back to Mattie.

Carrie sighs. "She never complained enough, is the trouble. How are children supposed to pick up any facts of life from people who never complain?"

"You know plenty. You'll just have to dig a little for it."

Carrie looks at her, but Sarah's gaze is on the window which, from her angle on the bed, gives a view of the wooded hill. She insisted that Carrie have the other room, the "main" bedroom, and now Carrie is glad, for this one is six steps nearer the bathroom, and lighter during the day. Sarah sometimes sits in the small rocker by the bed, and goes unassisted to the bathroom, but doesn't attempt the stairs anymore.

Carrie has found sheepskin for the bed, helps her wash, and keeps her rubbed with lotions from the new health food store in town, but otherwise is called upon for little.

"It's like she's just give out," she says gently to Morris, adopting his idiom. "Would you come down?"

His eyes look momentarily lost and frightened as a child's, but clear to an eagerness. Waiting on his porch for him to change into clean shirt and blue work slacks, Carrie resolves to visit him more. "I think you have even more birds here," she says to him on the porch, "than Mrs. Bakeley does."

"It's that time of year, they're all in voice. Evvie she used to could name off a dozen in about a minute's time."

"Mrs. Bakeley was just telling me that."

They climb into the pickup that now seems to be hers on permanent loan, and drive down to Sarah's. Morris pulls the soft-cushioned rocker close to the bed, settling as if they have always visited this way; Carrie brings them a tray with tea and vanilla wafers, and leaves them in peace.

She goes back to her project of rebuilding the pathway through the long bank of daylilies. Pulling at the tuberous roots, eating a few of the buds just as the deer do, she works for twenty minutes or so, then sinks, crosslegged. Why am I doing this? She's never getting up again. There was once a path here but what do you care? What difference does it make to her, now?

She rubs absently at the dirt on her hands, and goes in to wash. Morris and Sarah are laughing at some memory or prediction as she scrubs at the sink, and Carrie thinks suddenly maybe she is coming down again, after all. Do dying people laugh?

She drives Morris home, returning just in time to answer Thad's call. "You don't have to prepare yourself," she assures him. "Just take the same person out of the living room and put her propped up in bed."

"How does she feel?"

"She says fine. She's still completely herself."

"Is she eating?"

"Bites. Swallows of tea. I wouldn't say meals."

"How does Sunday sound?"

"We'll be here."

She is taking bread from the oven when he comes. Mrs. Bakeley is in the rocker upstairs, neatly robed and slippered, with a light triangular shawl over her shoulders in spite of the early heat wave. She greets Thad with satisfaction, with the usual lightly self-mocking air. "You see I'm ready for visiting. Carrie has even shampooed and trimmed my hair."

Carrie shakes her head. "With no grace or skill whatever," she says. "The beauty of it is entirely your own."

Sarah touches the cap of short hair, brushed in gentle waves back from her face. "'Your best asset,' my mother used to say. I at some point realized she meant the rest of me was hopeless."

Carrie fetches a straight chair from her room for Thad, and goes downstairs to cut the bread, make the obligatory tea. When she returns with the tray, Sarah is speaking of Ethan, with an often repeated description of their summer arrivals. "We'd scarcely be unpacked than he'd find a spot of sun and a book. I'd be lucky to see more than the top of his head all summer."

"What a huge leap for you," Carrie says. "From Chicago to this place."

"Some said I'd never stay. I not only stayed, I completely transplanted. Thrived, I would say."

"You could say that," Thad agrees.

"I mean inside, as well as bodily. I made a life here."

It is a rare departure from her reserve about herself, and they wait for more, but she is suddenly tired. Promising to come back his first free afternoon, Thad leaves, and Carrie helps Sarah to the bathroom and to the bed, and wanders downstairs. The living room is still so saturated with Sarah's presence she has often been brought up short to realize there is no one on the couch or by the stove, but this evening the room feels deserted. In spite of the clean bookshelves, the air feels stale to her, the space claustrophobic, as if growing smaller by degrees. And the porch seems lonely, bereft not only of Sarah's presence but Ethan's as well. The little study-hut is crammed with a jumbled past Carrie knows nothing of; she feels at the moment too full of loss and grief to ever consider thinking about any of it. Passing through the living room again, she sees the little messily typed term paper on the desk and nearly rips it up, but slips it instead into a bottom drawer.

Thad comes back late Thursday afternoon. Sarah is noticeably more gaunt, but a visiting nurse has agreed there is no point in moving her. Warning against dehydration, recommending vitamin supplements, she praised the sheepskin and the lotions, and gave Carrie a sympathetic look as she left. Thad sits in the rocker this time, while Carrie perches on the other side of the bed. Sarah asks Thad about the course he has just finished teaching, about summer plans, about his wife and daughter. He answers readily, succinctly. Though both he and Carrie try several times to turn the topic to her, she sidesteps every invitation to reminisce.

"And now I must tell you both something."

They are both disconcerted, but can do nothing but wait out the pause. She seems to be thinking through her decision a final time, and gives a little nod, looking from one to the other.

"I don't have to, of course. You'd find out in good time. My will's in the lock box in the bank, as Carrie already knows. There's a note with it that I'm to be cremated, and a small life insurance policy to cover any costs. No funeral. There's some stock in the canning factory, and there's this place. I've left it all to the two of you."

She lets them take it in. Neither speaks, and Sarah goes on, her voice a little hoarse, a little slow, but with the careful phrasing that has always been her habit.

"I want to tell you, because I want to be sure you understand, this puts absolutely no obligation on either of you, to inhabit it or keep it.

It's in the will, in perfectly legal and unintelligible English, that no restrictions of any sort accompany the inheritance. I made the decision years ago, when you were neither of you even here or likely to return. It is meant as a gift. Not a problem."

Thad clears his throat. "It is a gift. A staggering gift."

"No," Sarah says firmly. "It is a sensible, obvious gift. In one way or another, you'll both put it to good use. And now we'll say no more about it."

Carrie stands in the spot of sun, the grass warm against her feet, and cries out her grief in soft sobs. She makes no effort to stem them. She does not crumble, makes no move to be held or comforted, nor does Thad offer any, though he stands close.

"What will we do?" she says, when she can speak. She wipes at her face, but fresh tears come.

He is looking around, as she is, at the raggedy beloved space, their grief only the flip side of their joy in having known it as Sarah Bakeley's place.

"Look here."

Thad pulls his fist from his trouser pocket, opens it to show a sharp, perfect arrowhead. "My father found this here, when he was a boy and did some work for them summers. My mother gave it to Mrs. Bakeley as a keepsake, and she passed it back to me just a couple years ago. It's not mine, of course, it's some hunter's, dead five hundred years, maybe. But I can use it."

"Use it?"

He waits for her to understand. She takes her time, looking around again at the log house, the study nearly hidden in trumpet vine and wisteria, the quaint guest lodge above, its shingle roof a tangled mass of ivy and vines. "As a connection, you mean."

Thad nods. "I did my first watercolor here. God knows what all you've learned here."

"Thad. Are you embarrassed by what she must have – or at least might have – been thinking?"

He looks at her steadily. "No. And I'm not so sure she was thinking that. She believes in friendship. Deeply."

They walk back toward the house, hugging briefly, warmly, at the pathway. Carrie feels like crying again, but the tears hold off, for now.

"I believe in friendship, too," she says, and just manages a smile.

Sarah does bring up the subject of the will once more, the next afternoon. "I'm afraid I've left you a Herculean Stable, especially out in the study-hut. I meant to get to it myself."

"Anything you'd like me to dig out for you?"

"Oh no, no, a thousand times no. I've finished with all that. Just drag it out and burn it. And then. . . . Carrie, I think you shouldn't stay here."

Carrie's mouth twists. "I can't imagine it, without you in it."

"No, Carrie, you mustn't cry, not one bit, over me. Hear me?"

Carrie nods, with a little laugh, crying steadily now.

"You should go back to school."

"And I think you should get strong again, and put in a couple more years."

"I don't think so. Is Morris coming today?"

"Yes. Yes, he is, for tea."

That evening, after Sarah's usual thimble-full of soup and bite of bread, Carrie settles at the desk, aware that sleep will not come easy. Last night she slept, a sleep of denial and exhaustion. Tonight, there is little point in even trying, not for hours and hours yet.

Opening a notebook, used primarily these past five months for letters, she leafs dully over the couple pages of notes she's made in the last few weeks. Lists, for the most part. Little more than lists, with no intent, scarcely any awareness of what she was doing. Certainly with no purpose in mind.

She turns on the lamp, and the window becomes a solid square of black, reflecting the blank page she has come to.

Listen! he says, and Carrie jumps, startled enough to turn her head before staring again at the blank page.

You know plenty, just dig a little.

What story would that be, child?

You go where life leads you.

It's always hard to talk about love.

Don't you feel it, like if you don't get it, you won't be able to breathe?

I made a life here.

It's always hard to talk about love.

Carrie stirs, stiff in every limb. The voices, the connections: all manner of gift. She pours herself a glass of wine, lights a candle on the desk. She wonders whether the tavern was crowded when David came for Mattie, and who would have been in it.

Breinigsville, PA USA
14 October 2010
247318BV00001B/2/P